Georgiana Darcy's Magical Meddling

A Pride and Prejudice Vagary

Leah Page

Copyright © 2024 Leah Page

The characters and events portrayed in this book are fictitious. Any similarity to real persons, living or dead, is coincidental and not intended by the author.

No part of this book may be reproduced, or stored in a retrieval system, or transmitted in any form or by any means, electronic, mechanical, photocopying, recording, or otherwise, without express written permission of the publisher.

ISBN-13: 9798326287601

Cover design by: Erica Weise

To Mom. I love you.

Contents

Prologue
Chapter One
Chapter two
Chapter three
Chapter Four
Chapter five
Chapter six
Chapter seven
Chapter eight
Chapter nine
Chapter ten
Chapter eleven
Chapter twelve
Chapter thirteen
Chapter fourteen
Chapter fifteen
Chapter sixteen
Chapter seventeen
Chapter eighteen
Chapter nineteen
Chapter twenty
Chapter twenty-one
Chapter twenty-two
Chapter twenty-three

Chapter twenty-four
Chapter twenty-five
Chapter twenty-six
Chapter twenty-seven
Chapter twenty-eight
Chapter twenty-nine
Chapter thirty
Chapter thirty-one
Chapter thirty-two
Chapter thirty-three
Chapter thirty-four
Chapter thirty-five
Chapter thirty-six
Chapter thirty-seven
Chapter thirty-eight
Chapter thirty-nine
Chapter forty
Chapter forty-one
Chapter forty-two
Chapter forty-three
Chapter forty-four
Chapter forty-five
Chapter forty-six
Chapter forty-seven
Epilogue

Prologue

26 November 1828

My Dearest Anne Elizabeth,

My heart is full of emotions, dear girl, for you are now stepping into the bloom of your sixteenth year. It brings me immense joy and a touch of nostalgia as I reflect upon the passage of time. Even before my brother secured your mother, my heart had been wrapped around the thought of you. You were wished for, hoped for, and loved long before you took your first breath in this world.

I have thought many times about the perfect gift for your sixteenth birthday. I had in mind that I would buy you a lovely new necklace, which you will find in the accompanying velvet bag, but your real gift is the diary I kept in my sixteenth year. I have secreted them away for seventeen years, but now it is time to share them.

These pages hold memories, secrets, spells, and evidence of my complete lack of maturity. They also contain the story of your mother and father's romance which you will find enchanting, at times, and disgusting at others. Your father's foibles have been well documented. Be kind and do not let him know that you are aware of how foolish he was seventeen years ago. With your mother's help and a bit of magical intervention, he has come a long way.

I am obliged to impress upon you the importance of discretion, dear niece. The contents of this diary must remain a secret, hidden from all eyes but your own, including your dear sister, Jane Catherine. Until she, too, reaches the maturity of her sixteenth year, you must not share these events with her. This is not a decision I made lightly. In fact, I have wavered on whether to bestow this gift upon you at all. This morning my tea leaves insisted I relinquish this book into your care. And so, I yield to their wisdom.

I ask of you a favor, my dear. Do not judge me too harshly for the words you will find within these pages. When I wrote to them, I was but a young girl of sixteen myself - impish, immature, greatly sheltered, and often bored. I had also just discovered my magical abilities and was alight with a fever to employ them. Just as I asked you to be kind to your brother, I ask that you not alter your feelings for me. I assure you, I have matured a lot since the days when your father courted your mother. Though young and still dancing on the edges of impishness and immaturity, you have been nurtured in the art of magic with a wisdom and understanding far beyond my own at your age. Thus, I trust you will proceed with greater caution and respect where I stumbled.

I do not give you permission to cast any spells written within these pages unless you have proper supervision and your mother's authorization. Except, perhaps, for the two-steps-forward spell. This you may find amusing and of use, particularly with your brother Bennet. I give you permission to wield this spell on rare occasions but do so with utmost secrecy. Never admit to its use, and especially, never reveal that it was I who shared it with you!

As you embark on another year of life, filled with its joys and challenges, know that my love for you is unwavering. I wish for you a birthday as delightful and full of wonder as the magic you carry within.

With all my love,

Aunt G.

Chapter One

Midday, 24 October 1811

Dear Diary,

I am bursting with excitement. Today I learned the most thrilling news! Tonight, my brother will meet his one true love! Mrs. Annesley, my companion, read Fitzwilliam's tea leaves (after he left the table, of course), and that is how I discovered it. He is to attend a ball with his friend, Mr. Bingley. There, he will meet his one true love. Is that not the most romantic thing you have ever heard? It is doubly romantic given Fitzwilliam's aversion to attending balls, as will be the case tonight.

I suppose I should start from the beginning, little niece, as you are likely quite confused by now. Greetings from your Aunt Georgiana, who, as it happens, is also a witch. I have started a fresh diary for your benefit, as you are likely a witch as well. Do not worry about others finding this book. My companion has placed a spell on the pages that allows only witches to read them. After all, it would not be proper for those without magic to peruse the secrets held within this tome.

I learned of my powers when I met my companion, Mrs. Annesley. Before her, I had a terrible companion who took advantage of my youth and inexperience and led me astray. We will not discuss that further. Suffice it to say Fitzwilliam (your father) separated me from that lady posthaste upon discerning her vile nature. He then introduced me to Mrs. Annesley, and I could not have been happier with any other companion.

Mrs. Annesley is the third daughter of a baron. As she

explained it to me, females of rank almost always have magical powers. Their power is, usually, the reason the family gained rank and power in the first place. However, the wealthiest and most powerful homes have long forgotten their powers and stopped practicing. Perhaps, having grown complacent like fatted calves, these families saw no need to pursue their arcane studies further. It is likely that my own mother, the daughter of an influential earl, was a powerful witch. Unfortunately, she died when I was a small child, so I never learned from her. It is possible she was never even aware of her talents.

Yet, this tale concerns both Mrs. Annesley and my own foray into the craft. As I said, Mrs. Annesley is the third daughter of a baron. Though he held a title, he was not particularly wealthy or powerful, and thus, the ladies of that family never stopped practicing their craft. Witchcraft can be a potent boon for a gentleman. A witch who knows what she is about can secure bountiful harvests, avert blights, and influence her husband towards wise investments. Men may fancy themselves powerful and clever, yet it's truly the women steering the course. Remember that, little niece.

At the age of twenty, Mrs. Annesley left home to marry Mr. Annesley. He was the second son of a gentleman farmer, and though he did not inherit the family property, he did receive a very lovely little place along the shore in Kent. Mrs. Annesley has shown it to me in visions, so I can attest to the beauty of the home and setting. Alas, their love was but brief, her husband succumbing to a consumptive disease mere years after their union. I asked once why she did not save him, and she explained that witchcraft does not work like that. She was able to offer him comfort, but even a witch cannot suspend God's will. Currently, a tenant rents the house in Kent, which adds to Mrs. Annesley's small annuity. She opts to serve as a companion until she deems herself ready to wed anew or till work becomes untenable with age.

That is quite a sad story and not at all why you are here,

dearest niece. You are here to learn the story of your father's one true love. And to do that, I must share my background a bit. When Mrs. Annesley became my companion, she began to test me in small ways to understand my powers. Given my father's considerable lands, she suspected our lineage harbored latent talents, but when she learned my mother was the daughter of an Earl, she was convinced I had dormant abilities.

At first, she tried me in little ways that were hardly decipherable to me. For instance, she once offered me tea that was terribly hot, but before it settled on my tongue, I had unwittingly cooled it. Another time, she spelled a young child with messy hands to hug me close. I was left with small handprints of sticky syrup along my skirt. While the child's mother apologized for her son's actions, I took out my handkerchief and dabbed at the stains. They removed themselves with no more effort than a wave of my cloth across the untidiness. I was quite unaware that I had used magic to clean myself, for it happened unconsciously.

Once she was satisfied that I did possess some powers, she tested me further. One day, Fitzwilliam joined us late for breakfast. He greeted each of us and turned to the buffet to make his selections. My reply of, "Good morning, Fitzwilliam," barely had time to echo before the morning's tranquility was shattered —not by the expected clink of China, but by an unexpected maneuver from Mrs. Annesley. Without warning, she sent the sugar bowl hurling through the air toward Fitzwilliam, who stood behind me, gathering his breakfast from the buffet.

A sudden "eep" escaped me, an instinctive reaction to the potential disaster I sensed rather than saw. My hands reached out futilely, as if I could somehow catch the bowl through sheer will. But the expected crash never came. Confused, I turned just in time to see the sugar bowl floating to the ground before landing innocuously behind me on the floor, as if it had chosen to leap from its perch in a bid for freedom and then thought better of it.

"Georgiana, why is the sugar on the floor?" My brother placed his plate near mine and then stalked behind me to pick up the dish.

Stammering, I managed, "I, uh, deemed the sugar too great a temptation and opted to remove it from my sight, especially since my gowns have grown snug around the middle." A lame excuse, but the only shield I could muster on the spur of the moment.

"Nonsense. You look quite well, sister. In any case, if you desire to limit yourself, have a footman remove it from the table. Placing it on the floor is a filthy habit. What would Father have said had he lived to witness this?" His words were stern, yet I sensed his concern was born more of confusion than reprimand.

My eyes darted across the table to my companion. Her expression was one of unperturbed serenity. She sipped her tea as if flying sugar bowls were among the most common breakfast activities. I admit I was a trifle irritated with her at the time. But when we settled in the yellow salon later that morning, she shared the news of my powers with me, and all was forgiven.

That is a bit of a stretch. All was not immediately forgiven because I did not believe her claims. She reminded me of the child's sticky hands, but I dismissed that. "That was not magic," I argued, "it was the result of my own actions." With a scoff, she dotted my skirt with jam! Before I could set myself back to rights, she stilled my hand and suggested that I could clean one stain but leave the other for my abigail, La Roche. The spot I chose disappeared with no more than a wave of a napkin, but La Roche was forced to spend several minutes scrubbing the spot with water and soap before it was put to rights.

Since that day, she has been teaching me to harness my

powers. I have practiced just a few short months, so I have not yet learned much, but I am able to make the roses bloom on command, and I can sweeten my tea as desired without adding so much as a cube of sugar or a drop of cream. That is a more useful spell than one might imagine. Miss Bingley's tea, so bitter it could scandalize, would surely appall you. She allows it to steep for far too long, and the result is an undrinkable brew. With a small tap of my index finger against the porcelain cup, I can take tea with the lady without gagging.

Mrs. Annesley has advised me to keep my powers secret for the time being. Fitzwilliam himself remains oblivious to these powers. He is also, obviously, ignorant of her tea reading skills. Be careful of the lady who always offers to take up the teacups, for I have discovered that is Mrs. Annesley's tactic. Whenever possible, she reads everyone's leaves.

And that, my dear niece, is the abbreviated tale behind this new journal's beginnings. But let us move on to more exciting things. As I mentioned, I have delicious news. Tonight, your father will meet his one true love (as told by his tea leaves this morning) and I have chosen to record their love story for you. If your mother turns out to be as reticent as your father, then you shall never hear the story without my intervention.

My brother and I recently arrived at the estate of Mr. Charles Bingley. Mr. Bingley is Fitzwilliam's good friend. I believe they met during their time at Cambridge, though Mr. Bingley is a few years younger. Mr. Bingley resides at a place known as Netherfield Park. It lies in the county of Hertfordshire just outside a small village called Meryton. I do not believe Fitzwilliam has yet to meet anyone in the community, though perhaps he has met a gentleman or two. He and Mr. Bingley did go shooting yesterday and men do like to do those things in groups. But the point is that Fitzwilliam needs to meet a lady, and I do not believe he's yet had that pleasure. So, unless he plans to accidentally stumble upon a lady this afternoon, the only place he could possibly meet his one true love is at the ball.

My brother is the best of men, but young as I am, I am not blind to his faults. Fitzwilliam might, at best, be described as reticent. He might, at worst, be described as a pompous snob. He hates to be the center of attention and is very uncomfortable among new people. Unfortunately, when he is uncomfortable, he often appears to be rather terrible, at least to those who do not know him. That is why tonight is so special. For a man as reserved as my brother to find his one true love amid a public ball —oh, it will be truly amazing! I cannot help but wonder about the lady who will capture his attention. Will she be shy like Fitzwilliam, or will she possess a natural wit and vivacity that will help to draw him out?

Because I am not yet out, being sixteen, I asked if there was a spell that would allow me to watch the events unfold without attending. Mrs. Annesley believes there are several that might work and is just now checking her books to determine the best options for a young, inexperienced witch. While she is searching her spell books, I shall share some necessary background information for the sake of my future nieces.

I have been studying the art of tea reading myself, but I have not yet mastered it. Yesterday I believed I read that Mr. Bingley would fall off his horse, but it turns out that he was only to fall off the porch, and even that interpretation was not quite right, for he simply tripped down the final step and landed with surprising grace on his feet in the driveway.

Mrs. Annesley's predictions always prove themselves to be correct, however, which is why I was so excited to hear this morning's forecast. My brother (your father) will meet his one true love this evening, and I will finally have a sister! And eventually, little one, I will have you, too.

∞∞∞

Mrs. Annesley returned with a list of possibilities. There are, it appears, three spells suitable for a witch of my novice level to witness another's experiences. The first is a transformation spell. This enchantment might allow me to attend the ball not in person but cloaked in the guise of a small creature. Alas, as a fledgling witch, it is unlikely I could master the art of assuming a form as complex as a bird, to perch unnoticed at the event. Mastering a mouse's form might be within my reach, yet how much could I discern from a vantage so low upon the ground? Inevitably, I would startle at least one lady, and likely a gentleman too, with my mousey presence. Someone might even swat at me with a broom, or perhaps a cane. Attending a ball as a mouse seems like a very good way to lose my life.

The second type is a mirror spell. This would necessitate charming an object already present at the ball. It would then act as a mirror, allowing me to see events happening around the room. Unfortunately, I do not have the ability to place an object at the ball because I will not be attending.

The final option is a riding spell. This is the most complicated of the options, but it is probably the only one that is truly available to me. A riding spell would enable me, the witch, to experience events through another's senses. Obviously, I would need to charm Fitzwilliam for his are the eyes and ears that will matter this evening. Mrs. Annesley has assured me this is physically taxing magic and has urged me to take a long afternoon nap so that I can maintain the connection for the duration of the ball. So that is what I shall do.

I will return this evening to share what I learn. Wish me (and Fitzwilliam, of course) luck!

Chapter Two

Evening

Dear Diary,

I awoke from my nap around five in the afternoon but remained in my room for several more hours. Mrs. Annesley and I used the time to plan our evening. The other members of our party were set to leave for the ball at eight this evening. At half past seven, Mrs. Annesley and I made our way downstairs where we greeted my brother. He sat alone in the parlor savoring a glass of port.

"Georgiana, I am sorry to leave you alone tonight. Were it not for the fact that Miss Bingley would remain as well, I would stay here with you. You know I loathe a ball."

This drew a giggle from me. Fitzwilliam was correct. If he chose to remain at Netherfield Park with me, Miss Bingley would do the same. Without her brother to temper her, her company would prove intolerable.

"I am glad you will attend the dance," I said. "I suspect you will have a fantastic night and, perhaps, you will meet someone special."

My brother scoffed at this. "Hardly. This is a rustic community filled with families of little consequence." Fitzwilliam can act rather high in the instep at times. I know he does not mean it; it is only that he is reticent to meet new people and uses his place in society as a mask. But to others it can be quite off-putting.

"Fitzwilliam, promise me that you will at least try to have a good time and will be polite to the people you meet."

"Of course, of course," said he, waving away my advice. Perhaps a man of eight-and-twenty finds it challenging to heed advice from a mere girl of sixteen.

He stood then and walked to the sideboard to pour another glass of port. Mrs. Annesley gave me a nudge, prompting me to cast my magic. The absence of the Bingley family from the room was a relief, as their presence would have complicated my task. I took the moonstone from my pocket and gripped it tightly between my hands.

Whispers, glances, let me borrow,
See and hear through joy and sorrow.
Through your eyes, a world unfolds,
Through your ears, the tale is told.

I had to whisper this part, otherwise Fitzwilliam would have known I had placed him under my spell. I observed him closely. He did not seem to be impacted by my words at all. He still stood with the decanter in his hand, meticulously pouring a perfect serving into his glass. I, however, felt an instantaneous difference. Normally, casting a spell feels much like scratching an itch. It is delicious and satisfying. This spell did not feel at all like that. My body jumped with new sensations. Electric currents raced along my spine, clouding my mind. It was a bit like the time I had three glasses of wine with dinner. My head lolled to one side, and Mrs. Annesley edged closer to steady me. "I believe you could do with some tea," said she. She wedged me into the settee and then rose to pull the bell cord.

Soon after, the party left Netherfield, and Mrs. Annesley and I retired to my room. Normally, a riding spell would only allow the caster to see what was happening; however, Mrs. Annesley wanted to have her fun, as well. With a bit of her own magic, she cast the visions, so they played like a moving picture on the blank pages of this very diary. It was much like watching a play, but from the comfort of my suite. What a pity that not all possess witchcraft, for watching a story unfold while wearing a nightgown and eating cakes is a lovely way to spend an evening.

There is little to tell of the ride to Meryton. Miss Bingley complained with great vigor that they would be exposed to "the worst sorts of country people." When my brother suggested that the members of Meryton society would likely be very similar to those near our estate in Derbyshire, she exclaimed, "Oh, but surely Mr. Darcy, your presence in Derbyshire elevates the attitudes and comportment of those who live there." Of course, that was a most ridiculous statement, for if it were true and the mere presence of Fitzwilliam could alter the behavior of people, then why would it not work in Meryton?

The party finally arrived at the assembly hall. I knew my brother was nervous by the way he continued to look at his feet and tug at his sleeves. He would not show to his best advantage tonight, but surely his true love would be able to see through the mask of indifference he often wore in company.

The room was very full, with far more bodies than I had anticipated. Pressing my lapis lazuli to my lips, I wished fervently for Fitzwilliam to swiftly encounter his one true love. Lapis lazuli helps a person attain spiritual enlightenment, inner vision, and self-awareness. I cannot speak for my brother's spiritual needs, but a good bit of self-awareness would not go astray.

Soon, an older gentleman greeted the group. Mr. Bingley introduced him as Sir William Lucas. I heard little after that, though, because my brother was occupied by scanning the room. There were many ladies in attendance but far fewer gentlemen. Of a certainty, several ladies would be forced to sit out dances this evening.

Without speaking to anyone, my brother began to walk

away. Though the spell allows me to do nothing more than hear and see through Fitzwilliam's senses, I had enough perception to understand his irritation. There were far too many people there, standing far too close to him. He wove his way through several ladies and a few gentlemen until he found a space along the wall. There he stood sentinel for the majority of the evening.

I must admit, the novelty of watching a scene play out across the pages of the book is very exciting, but the show would have been more interesting had I cast my spell on Mr. Bingley instead. That gentleman danced and laughed all night, twice with a very pretty blonde. For a moment, I pondered whether she was my brother's one true love but pushed the thought away. A woman who could be so charmed by Mr. Bingley would never do for Fitzwilliam.

The night progressed with very little action, until Mr. Bingley approached. "Come, Darcy," said he, "I must have you dance. I hate to see you standing about by yourself in this stupid manner."

"I certainly shall not. You know how I detest it unless I am particularly acquainted with my partner." My brother went on a bit here, but there is little point in relaying for you understand the gist.

Mr. Bingley continued to hound my brother, once pointing out that a "very pretty" young lady sat nearby and was without a partner. That is when Fitzwilliam said the worst and most horrid thing I could have ever imagined. He said, and I swear this is the exact language he used, "She is tolerable, but not handsome enough to tempt me." Then he looked at the poor miss and I could see from the expression of abject mortification on her face that she had heard him!

The worst part, aside from him being terribly rude to a stranger, was that she was a very pretty lady. She had dark curls that framed her face becomingly, and she wore a white gown with dark green trim, a color that complemented her hazel eyes. I briefly thought that she would look very well on Fitzwilliam's arm, but surely, he would not insult his one true love in such a manner upon their first acquaintance. I can imagine no possible way to overcome that sort of introduction. No, she was most certainly not his one true love.

It is rather weary to write "one true love" over and over. I am already forced to write such long names as Fitzwilliam and Mrs. Annesley. Henceforth, I shall refer to this mystery lady as my brother's OTL. My father would have chastised me for being lazy, but as far as I am aware, Father never wrote out the tale of his brother's romance, so he could not understand how my hand cramps, even now. I have heard that every dark cloud has a silver lining. If that is true, then the silver lining of my father's passing is that he is not here to castigate me for writing OTL.

That was terrible of me. Of course, there is no happiness in my father's death. It has been very difficult to be an orphan, for both Fitzwilliam and me. However, Father was a very exacting sort of man. I believe he is largely to blame for Fitzwilliam's rigidity. Nevertheless, I should endeavor to be more circumspect in the words I choose, for my dear future niece should read nothing but the best of things about her long-departed grandfather.

There is little left to tell of the evening. Fitzwilliam made a complete muddle of things. Not only did the pretty lady he insulted overhear his unkind words, but she also went on to share them with others. Horrified, I observed as she conferred with her companion. Her words were hidden by the fan she held near her mouth, but the way the two of them repeatedly looked at Fitzwilliam and giggled, the point was clear. Her intent was to shame him before her friends for his blunder. Though he is my brother, I must side with the mystery lady. Do not censure me for my lack of family loyalty. I understand Fitzwilliam's reasons, but he knows how to behave and chose not to.

Eventually the party dispersed, and my brother climbed back into the Bingley's carriage. The night had little more to teach us, so by agreement, Mrs. Annesley and I closed the diary which served to snuff the connection I held with Fitzwilliam.

"I know tonight did not unfold as I had anticipated, but if Fitzwilliam's OTL was indeed present, surely all will right itself."

Mrs. Annesley said nothing, but she did hold her mouth in that way that indicates she disagrees with whatever I have said. She frequently wears this expression of silent dissent, which I have come to understand all too well.

"You do not think tonight ruined his chances, do you?" Admittedly, Fitzwilliam hardly presented himself as the model suitor tonight, yet I cling to the hope that a truly smitten lady might forgive a single evening's misstep.

"Miss Darcy, the tea leaves said he would meet his OTL. They did not promise a 'happily ever after.'" I had not considered this. OTL and "happily ever after" go so well together that the very idea they would not coincide seemed an anomaly to me.

A rising panic formed in my chest. "Whatever shall we do? I would not like for my brother to live an unhappy life because he did not show to his best advantage. He is far superior when he is in small parties. A ball is an unfortunate place for him to meet new people."

Mrs. Annesley did not respond. I could tell she was running through the possibilities in her mind. She has this thing she does when she is trying to figure out her best options. Her gaze turns inward, eyes fluttering back as her lips whisper secrets that no one understands but herself. It looks a bit like someone trying to add a string of figures without the benefit of pen and paper.

After a minute of this, she placed her hands in her lap

and resolutely stated, "We must have him replay his days, ensnaring him in time until he seizes that which truly brings him joy."

"Replay his days?" I sounded foolish, but I am still very new to these witchy ways and, more often than I should admit, I am dumbfounded by the possibilities.

"Yes. Tomorrow when we arise, it will be the twenty-fourth of October once again."

"Will Fitzwilliam know?"

"Oh, yes, for how is he to ever learn if he does not?" This made sense, for if he did not know the day had been repeated, he would never change. I could imagine him reliving tonight's events, insulting the dark lady, and refusing to dance with anyone over, and over, and over. He would find himself ensnared on the twenty-fourth of October indefinitely.

"Will the others know?"

Mrs. Annesley smiled. "Oh no. Only your brother, you, and I will be aware the day has not progressed. But it is very important that you do not let him know that we are a part of this. We must both attempt to repeat every action, or he will be suspicious."

Mrs. Annesley sent me to my trunk to gather a variety of herbs and crystals for the incantation. Once I had collected everything she required, we opened the doors to my balcony. The spell would work better under the light of a full moon, but the half-moon that shines this evening must suffice.

Mrs. Annesley placed the items on the ground, and we stood on either side, our hands clasped together so that we formed a circle. We raised our faces to the sky and together we chanted:

Round and round the days shall dance,
Until fate grants another chance.
Repeat the steps, correct the night,
Till hearts align in joyous light.

I did not experience a woozy head or any other odd sensations to indicate the words had done as intended. I suppose tomorrow I will know if it worked.

Chapter Three

Evening, 24 October 1811 (a second attempt)

Dear Diary,

Today was far more interesting than I had anticipated. The day began when my abigail, La Roche, woke me. Given La Roche's usual fastidiousness over my attire, her choice to dress me in yesterday's frock came as a surprise. I am always a touch groggy in the morning; therefore, it took me a moment to remember the spell Mrs. Annesley and I had cast last evening. Realization dawned, and with it, a wave of sheer euphoria. It had worked!

I waited as patiently as I could for Mrs. Annesley to arrive so that we could break our fast together. When we arrived at the breakfast room, there were only Mr. Bingley and my brother in attendance, as we had expected. Fitzwilliam's expression was one of profound confusion. I suppose it would be discombobulating to replay a day you are sure you have already completed. Mr. Bingley, however, was unerringly cheerful as always. Bless him.

"Darcy, I must have you attend tonight's assembly with me. I realize it is not how you prefer to spend your evenings, but my acceptance into the Meryton society is important and I could use your assistance." I stifled a giggle. Considering Fitzwilliam's "assistance" from the night before, Mr. Bingley might fare better leaving him behind. But my brother would never win his OTL from the Netherfield parlor.

My brother remained in a state of shocked confusion. He

neither accepted nor declined Mr. Bingley's request. Several times, he consulted the day's paper, scrutinizing the date as if to find it altered. Poor Fitzwilliam. I truly do feel sorry for him. To repeat days would be vastly frustrating, except in a situation when you understand the circumstance. In that case, it is vastly amusing.

When the men excused themselves, Mrs. Annesley stepped to their places at the table. "Just as before. This evening, your brother's fated meeting with his OTL is destined to recur."

I am so glad I chose to shorten that moniker. OTL is much faster to put to paper.

The day progressed as before. Mr. Bingley was kind and friendly, Mr. and Mrs. Hurst were simply there, and Miss Bingley was tiring, though it is easier to stand her when you know what to expect. Only my brother's behavior marked any departure from the day before. Though he is often aloof, today he stood for long periods looking out the window while his hands fidgeted behind his back.

At half past seven, Mrs. Annesley and I replayed our roles of the previous evening. We visited with my brother on the couch while he drank port; however, tonight he drank no less than three glasses and was sufficiently foxed by the time his party left for the assembly.

I shan't bother recounting the evening's events, as they changed little from the previous one. The greatest difference in the two nights was that my brother became as intoxicated as Mr. Hurst after one hour at the party. And, as you might surmise, he was equally rude to the dark mystery lady. This time, however, his words were far more slurred and significantly louder. The dark lady did not appear to be as amused by my brother as she had been the first time they met. I suppose a drunk bore is less entertaining than a sober one. Instead of standing with her friend and giggling at my brother's expense, she stalked away upon hearing his slight.

Interestingly, his eyes followed her the entire evening, even before Mr. Bingley begged him to dance. Could he find her attractive? Though his words deny it, why else would he incessantly watch a lady he deems "tolerable"?

Though often praised for his intellect, Fitzwilliam's social acumen—or lack thereof—starts to paint him as surprisingly obtuse. We may well repeat this day many times over before he gets it correct.

Chapter Four

Evening, 24 October 1811
(The third time is not a charm)

Dear Diary,

Fitzwilliam arose in a state of considerable agitation. He rapped on my door before seven in the morn to inform me that we would return to London post-haste. My normally impeccable brother sported tousled hair and a poorly tied cravat. As I mentioned previously, I am not at my best first thing in the morning, but his pale face and the dark circles beneath his eyes did not escape my notice.

Despite my concern for my brother, I admit to reclining once more, drawing the blanket over my head. In little time, however, my covers were ripped from atop my body, and I was ordered to ready myself with haste. "We will eat on the road," he shouted.

I now find myself in the comfort of my suite at Darcy House, savoring a cup of rich, warm chocolate.

I look forward to seeing my brother's face tomorrow when he wakes up in Hertfordshire as he did this very morning. I should not enjoy his disquiet as much as I am, but really, he is a bit of a dunce about this, and he was ever so rude this morning.

Mrs. Annesley agrees, though she insists we cannot interfere further than we already have. "He must learn for himself, Miss Darcy, as difficult as that may be." I suppose she is correct, though I grow quite tired of this same blue gown. I hope we move to a new day soon, as I would greatly appreciate the opportunity to wear my new rose gown.

Chapter Five

Evening, 24 October 1811 (attempt four)

Dear Diary,

True to my expectations, we found ourselves awakening at Netherfield once more. Fitzwilliam opted for an extended ride, thereby missing breakfast. I set aside some rolls for him, entrusting a footman to convey them to his quarters for when he returned.

During the day, Mrs. Annesley and I honed our skills with the riding spell, using a barn cat as our subject. The spell is quite exhausting for me. Each incantation sends a ripple of fatigue through my limbs, but I am determined to master it. According to Mrs. Annesley, practicing on smaller creatures will help to build my stamina for the larger task of seeing and hearing Fitzwilliam's experiences. Little known perhaps: barn cats lead remarkably thrilling existences. The orange tabby I charmed today killed two birds, a mouse, and fought a calico in the span of one hour! I believe I will practice on a bird tomorrow; cats are very aggressive.

As expected, Mrs. Annesley and I met my brother in the parlor at the correct time. This evening, Fitzwilliam abstained from any libations. After his performance two nights ago, I believed this was for the best.

"Fitzwilliam, promise me that you will at least try to have a good time and will be polite to the people you meet." I have said this each night, but this evening I put special emphasis on the words "promise me" and "be polite." He cast a queer look in my direction but chose not to reply.

When the party left, Mrs. Annesley and I retired to my room where she cast the moving pictures on the blank pages of this book. Just as with every other night, Fitzwilliam stood apart from the rest of the revelers. Unlike past nights, he agreed to dance with the dark mystery lady. "I suppose," he grunted. Though I could not see it, I imagined him moving toward her with a stiff, unbending posture. His attitude was unlikely to win her heart, but at least he had ceased being incredibly rude. Gradually, I am coming to see her as potentially his OTL. Aside from a few glances toward the blonde Mr. Bingley favors, Fitzwilliam's eyes have landed on no one else.

Mr. Bingley had his favored lady, who I now know is Miss Jane Bennet, introduce everyone to her sister. Miss Elizabeth (the mystery lady) raised a quizzical brow when Fitzwilliam requested her hand for a dance, but she did not decline. I must learn how she does that with her brow!

As he escorted her to the dance floor, I harbored hope that this repetition might be our last. But, alas, Fitzwilliam behaved as he is prone to do. He and Miss Elizabeth did not exchange a single word the entirety of their two dances. Her lips parted several times as if to speak, yet reconsideration stilled her words. Her gaze wandered across the dance floor, envying the other couples who were clearly enjoying themselves far more.

"Your brother is slow to warm to his fate," Mrs. Annesley noted dryly.

Each repeat of the day weighs heavier on my spirit, especially seeing Fitzwilliam struggle against his own nature.

Chapter Six

Evening, 24 October 1811 (Five nights!)

Dear Diary,

At last, my brother has figured it out! I shall spare you the day's mundane details. The day largely mirrored the past five, with the notable exception of our brief return to London. Oh, I must also add that today I cast the riding spell on a hawk. I cannot recommend this enough. The liberty to soar must be utterly fantastic! I digress, the most important news of today will follow henceforth.

This evening, after four attempts, my brother acted as one ought at a party. Praise be!

Upon their arrival, Sir William Lucas greeted Mr. Bingley as he entered the door, and for the first time, my brother permitted an introduction.

"Allow me to introduce you to my family," the man offered. Fitzwilliam followed behind the rest of the party to where Sir William's family stood. Initially, Miss Bingley's ostentatious plume obscured my view of the Lucas party. (I really must remember to tell you more about Miss Bingley. You should know more of the lady, as she is our hostess (and a very large pain in my posterior). Eventually, Fitzwilliam shifted to show a mousey looking matron, Sir William's wife, standing next to her two daughters. The first was a girl about the same age as me, and the other was the same lady who had previously shared the joke of my brother's rudeness with Miss Elizabeth. Her name, I discovered, is Miss Charlotte Lucas and she is a dear friend and close confidant of the two eldest Bennet sisters.

Soon after, Sir William introduced my brother's party to the Bennets. Mrs. Bennet, a woman of middling years, oscillated between titters and frets. She pushed one daughter forward, and then the next, proclaiming them the "jewels of the county," "very accomplished," and "excellent dancers." She is exactly the sort of woman Fitzwilliam disdains, but I find her vastly interesting. Never have I witnessed a gentlewoman her age comport herself with such disregard for propriety. It must be freeing to behave as one wishes. As a Darcy, I am aware of my obligations, both to my duties and to my reputation. Yet, the freedom to voice every nascent thought is an alluring prospect. I hope I meet her soon, for I would like to know her.

Next to her stood Miss Jane Bennet, the eldest of what I learned are five sisters. Five! Miss Bennet, as I mentioned in a previous entry, is a beautiful blonde with clear blue eyes. She is also rather tall for a lady. She may even surpass my height, though I am only sixteen and will surely grow a little more. Mr. Bingley was captivated by her. I assume this was true on the previous evenings, but this was the first time I witnessed their introduction. He asked her straightaway for a dance. He was obliged to dance the first with Miss Charlotte Lucas, but I knew from experience he would dance two with Miss Bennet before the night ended.

The next in line for introductions was Miss Elizabeth Bennet. She is the second eldest and second only in looks to her sister, Jane, though I find her infinitely more interesting to look upon. Her sister is rather placid, which is fine for Mr. Bingley, but Miss Elizabeth has an enthusiasm rarely seen in a lady. Also, she has a marvelous way of raising her right eyebrow when vexed. I have practiced it daily in my looking glass but have not yet mastered it. I contemplated spelling my eyebrow into submission, but I was unsure of the proper verse to choose. At best, I would raise my eyebrow in the same quizzical manner as Miss Elizabeth. At worst, it would detach entirely and float above my head like a rogue caterpillar.

Once again, I digress.

The third lady to be introduced was Miss Mary Bennet. Miss Mary is neither as vivacious nor as pretty as her next older sister. She is, however, not unattractive. It is primarily her mode of dress and the looks of irritation she cast toward everyone in her vicinity that make her appear so. Candidly, she strikes me as somewhat tiresome. I wonder if the Bennets hold any magical power because Miss Mary could use a dose of excitement. Perhaps I will ask Mrs. Annesley to test her.

The other two Bennet sisters were across the room and were not introduced to the party. I learned the next eldest is Miss Kitty, aged seventeen. And the last is Miss Lydia, the "liveliest" of the sisters, at least according to their mother, and fifteen years old. Fifteen, indeed! And here I am at sixteen, still barred by my brother from attending even the smallest gatherings. The unfairness of it all chafes, even now, hours later.

"If you are not obligated elsewhere, Miss Elizabeth, may I have the honor of this dance?"

Mrs. Annesley gave a small nod of approval when my brother pronounced his wishes to partner Miss Elizabeth, but I threw my hands in the air and let out a boisterous whoop of excitement. Mrs. Annesley did not chide me for this. She allows me my indiscretions when we are not in company with others. My previous companion would have slapped my hand with a small ruler or switch as punishment for my unladylike comportment.

My immaculate brother, Mr. Fitzwilliam Darcy of Pemberley, grandson to an earl, with a fortune nearing eighteen thousand pounds a year (Miss Bingley believes it is only ten thousand, which gives me great pleasure), has asked a lady to dance the first! And not just any lady. I have come to believe Miss Elizabeth is his OTL. Surely this will be the night that sets our paths to right, and we need not repeat any more days.

Miss Elizabeth bobbed an elegant curtsy and accepted. Soon, Fitzwilliam and his lady stood next to Mr. Bingley and Miss Lucas to begin the dancing. My brother will never be an elegant swain, but he conducted himself admirably tonight… considering.

"Miss Elizabeth, thank you for agreeing to dance with me."

Miss Elizabeth smiled sweetly and even my heart did a little flip. "Thank you for asking, Mr. Darcy. As you can see, men are scarce. My friends and I have an agreement to sit out at least two dances so that all ladies might have a turn on the dance floor. You have saved me from sitting out the first."

Ah, so she had not been sitting out on the prior nights because she was shunned by the gentleman at the party, she was sitting out to give other ladies a chance to dance. I ought to have realized, for Miss Elizabeth was by far the most interesting lady in the room.

"I hope I am a tolerable alternative to sitting alone, Miss Elizabeth." I believe my brother thought this turn of phrase was clever, but I cannot agree. Even Miss Elizabeth looked puzzled.

"Have you had an opportunity to explore the area, sir?" He answered that he had done some riding in the area (no doubt the day he missed breakfast). "If you are fond of lovely views, I suggest you climb Oakum Mount. We cannot boast anything akin to the Peaks of Derbyshire, but I do believe you will enjoy the view nonetheless."

"Do you go often to Oakum Mount?" In writing, it seems innocuous; spoken, it bore the unmistakable tint of flirtation.

"Good man," Mrs. Annesley whispered. We were both very involved in the transactions that played out on the pages of my diary. Never has a staged drama captivated me as the evening's unfolding scenes on the pages of this very book.

"I am very fond of walking, sir. I often rise before dawn and ramble the paths surrounding Longbourn. Technically, Oakum Mount lies within Sir William Lucas' lands, though he does not begrudge anyone from traversing that hill. However, it is usually only me who is there to see the sun rise."

When the dance ended, Fitzwilliam escorted Miss Elizabeth back to her mother and next younger sister before bowing gallantly over her hand. He did not dance another with her, but he did dance most of the remaining with various ladies. He was obliged, of course, to dance at least one with Miss Bingley and Mrs. Hurst. The younger of the two seemed notably vexed by Fitzwilliam's attentions towards Miss Elizabeth. I suppose she anticipated she would be his first partner of the evening. Naturally, he had shared dances with her before. On the first night, he danced first with Mrs. Hurst and then with Miss Bingley. On the second evening he was legless from drink and danced with no one. The third night we were in London. And the fourth evening he repeated the pattern of the first. Not once has she been his first choice, but I suppose hopes do not die easily, especially when one is unaware the night had occurred five times over.

After his obligatory dances with Mr. Bingley's sisters ended, Fitzwilliam made me quite proud by asking Miss Lucas to dance, and then Miss Maria, her younger sister. He did not dance every set, but he did partner two additional local ladies, a Miss Goulding and another whose name I do not recall, though I do remember that she is new to the area and is covered in freckles.

The conversation on the carriage ride home was quite different this evening. Miss Bingley loudly decried every moment of the assembly. According to her, there was no fashion, no sense, and not even a little refinement to be found in the whole of Meryton. Then she said something I cannot remove from my mind. "It is a wonder anyone will associate with the Bennets. With one uncle a solicitor, and another in trade, they are very below the gentlefolk we usually associate with." Fitzwilliam is very rigid at times, and I could tell by the way his hands clenched in his lap that he was bothered to learn this piece of information.

It is unseemly to admit it, but I have ensured that Miss Bingley will awaken tomorrow with an enormous spot on her nose. This assumes tomorrow is truly tomorrow.

As for Miss Bingley's spot, this is a useful little spell I learned while reading *Magical Castings and Curses for New Witches*, a book Mrs. Annesley has deemed frivolous. I quote: "Those verses undermine witchcraft's dignity and grandeur!" Perhaps she is correct; however, should you ever need to thwart your own version of Miss Bingley, I highly suggest these four lines.

> *From laughter's ring and jest's embrace,*
> *A pimple finds its rightful place.*
> *Upon your nose, a spot so bold,*
> *Overnight, it grows threefold.*

Chapter Seven

Afternoon, 25 October 1811

Dear Diary,

At last, we have made it to a new day! I woke up with some trepidation, but when La Roche took my rose gown from the armoire, I knew Fitzwilliam had finally done as he ought to have at last night's assembly.

About the rose gown —I must confess that I was mistaken in my desire to wear it. It is not as comfortable as the blue gown I wore these past five days. I hope Fitzwilliam does not do anything stupid today for I shan't be able to wear this again tomorrow (or rather today).

When Mrs. Annesley and I arrived for breakfast, Fitzwilliam sat alone at the table. Since our arrival to Netherfield, Mr. Bingley has consistently been an early riser, but after a night of dancing and revelry, he chose to sleep in.

"Good morning, Brother." I dipped a careless curtsy. It was only Fitzwilliam, after all.

"Georgie." He took a sip from his cup. Coffee – a choice I knew would vex Mrs. Annesley.

I reviewed the offerings and added various foods to my plate before I sat down across from my brother. "Tell me about the assembly. Did you have fun? Were there any pretty ladies there? Did you dance?"

He put up his hand to stop my barrage of questions. "I had a tolerable time last night," said he. Tolerable! "I danced with several local ladies, and I dare say a few of them were rather pretty."

This response left me wanting. "But was there any one lady who was particularly... captivating?" Mrs. Annesley touched my leg under the table, a silent warning to let things be. While she has been a blessing in my life, I must admit her penchant for sobriety rivals Fitzwilliam's at times.

He dabbed the corners of his mouth with his napkin. "There was no one special."

Hmph. No one special? Only his OTL, though, perhaps, he does not yet understand that. I wish I could tell him so he could hurry this entire situation along. But to share that with him would mean I must also share my secret, and Fitzwilliam is not the type of man to whom one says, "Oh, by the way, Brother, I am a witch." I do not think he would have me thrown in an asylum, but perhaps he would send me to a nunnery for a year or two.

Fear not, dear niece, for that is a jest. Your father would never send me away because he loves me. And because to send me away would create talk among society. Above all, Fitzwilliam detests becoming fodder for the gossip mills.

In the afternoon, the men toured the estate. Fitzwilliam is concerned that the north field is prone to flooding and is determined to educate Mr. Bingley on the dangers of such a thing. Mr. Bingley was happy enough to oblige my brother with a tour, yet I doubt he will ever grasp the full consequences of a flooded field, no matter how much Fitzwilliam explains it to him.

When they left, Mrs. Annesley had me study my book of spells. We did this in my room, as that is the sole way to limit Miss Bingley's interference. We uncovered several incantations addressing the issues of flooded lands and shifting terrains. I painstakingly transcribed four distinct spells thirty times apiece, an act which she believes will better commit the verses to memory. My fingers, cramped from the effort, begged to differ. I have learned many songs simply by singing them over and over. Tomorrow, assuming tomorrow is actually tomorrow and not today, she and I will visit the north field and I will attempt to shift the land so that it properly drains.

According to Mrs. Annesley, the greatest power a witch employs is her ability to assist her husband or family. To date, I have learned small spells. I have mastered incantations to keep the rose garden flourishing through summer and fall. I can pull small amounts of water from the depths of the ground to water a plant or two. Yet, I lack the power to guarantee watering for an entire estate during a drought. And naturally, I can bestow a conspicuous spot upon the nose of anyone who vexes me!

As the clock nears three in the afternoon, Miss Bingley remains conspicuously absent. Delightful!

Chapter Eight

Afternoon, 26 October 1811

Dear Diary,

I cannot be certain, yet I suspect we might live through this day again. This morning, Fitzwilliam arrived late for breakfast. Just as Mrs. Annesley and I finished our meal, he entered, appearing more agitated than I have ever seen.

"Brother, have you been for a ride this morning?"

"Umph." What a grouch he can be! He is perfectly capable of saying "yes." But sixteen years of cohabitation have made me fluent in his grunts.

"Lovely. It appears a very nice day, though a bit cool. I suppose that is to be expected, however, given the season. At least we have not had snow. There have been many years when Pemberley received a few inches, even before the arrival of November."

"Umph," he grunted again. Truly, men are the most ridiculous of creatures. I looked at my brother, really looked at him, I mean. I see him daily, of course, but today I took my time reviewing each of his features. Small lines framed his eyes, and he held his mouth very tight. His hands clenched, knuckles whitening as he vigorously stirred his tea. Every line of Fitzwilliam's face, his entire posture screamed of a frustration only a lady could induce.

I said as much to Mrs. Annesley after our meal. She insisted I am a silly girl of sixteen and far too romantic for my own good, but I believe I was correct, for Fitzwilliam dropped his spoon when I asked, "Have you visited Oakum Mount? I have been told it has the loveliest view in all of Hertfordshire."

So, you see, though I have no real understanding of what happened this morning, I am convinced my brother encountered his OTL at Oakum Mount, and matters went awry.

After breakfast Mrs. Annesley and I rode out to the North Field. When we arrived, we sent our groom to the far side of the pasture claiming we would like some privacy. We sat on a picnic blanket, and I practiced an earth shifting spell. Fear not, it is a subtle spell, and the groom remained blissfully unaware. The next time it rains we will return to see if I was successful. Judging by Mrs. Annesley's pursed lips, I suspect my execution fell short of her expectations.

By the afternoon, we were back at Netherfield, happily taking tea. Well, perhaps not as happily as one might hope. Miss Bingley's nose had healed (Mrs. Annesley was not pleased to learn what I had done) and she sat near me complimenting me on my very great skill on the pianoforte, the excellent painting I had added to a small table, and the graceful way I held my teacup. I was greatly relieved when the gentlemen joined us, for it allowed Miss Bingley to turn her attention to my brother and to leave me alone.

Dear niece, should you read these words, be aware that as a Darcy woman, you will encounter numerous ladies feigning friendship for the sole purpose of gaining access to your brother. Miss Bingley is just such a woman and I find her an absolute trial; however, she had her purpose today.

While she held my brother's attention, I quietly whispered the words of the riding spell I had used each night of the assembly. I leaned close to Mrs. Annesley when I said it so that it would appear as if I were sharing a secret. Whispering secrets amidst company breaches etiquette, yet, arguably, it remains more acceptable than spellcasting.

Should tomorrow unfold as a mirror of today, my aim is to uncover what transpired on Oakum Mount.

Chapter Nine

Evening, 26 October 1811 (I knew it!)

Dear Diary,

My instincts proved correct. Fitzwilliam indeed met with his OTL—Miss Elizabeth Bennet, I am convinced—on Oakum Mount. I do not know what he said yesterday to make such a muck of things, but he acquitted himself quite well this morning. Actually, that is not entirely true. While I might not know his exact words, I grasp the essence of them. But I should not get ahead of myself. Let me start from the beginning.

Last night before bed, I cast a spell on my brother's bedroom door. When he opened it this morning it caused a bell to chime loudly in my ear. Pressing my ear against the door, I listened intently until I was sure he had left the hall. Once assured he had descended the stairs, I grabbed this very diary and ran in my nightgown and robe to Mrs. Annesley's room. Miss Bingley lodged Fitzwilliam and me in the family wing, while relegating Mrs. Annesley to the east wing. I was very put out by this, but Mrs. Annesley said it provides us with another location to hide when we find it absolutely necessary. I believe she only wanted to be as far from Caroline Bingley as possible. I cannot fault her for that, I suppose.

We settled together on the bed, our feet tucked beneath us, and waited as the images cast across the pages.

"Do not mention her uncle in trade. Do not mention her uncle in trade. Do not mention her uncle in trade." My brother repeated this same sentence to himself no less than twenty times as he climbed the hill to Oakum Mount. Thus, my earlier statement was not entirely false. I do not know exactly how his conversation ran afoul on their previous meeting, but I believe he said something denigrating about Miss Elizabeth's family.

While our family boasts no tradesmen, we do have Lady Catherine de Bourgh as my aunt, so you see, we cannot declare our superiority to anyone. I shall have to explain about Lady Catherine at another time, but suffice it to say, she is not a person anyone would be proud to have in their family, despite her title.

When Fitzwilliam crested the hill, Miss Elizabeth stood with her back to him. Clad in a dark green pelisse, her hair neatly tied with a simple ribbon, she looked lovely. I hope my OTL is handsome, as well. It will not do if Fitzwilliam is blessed with a pretty bride, and I end up with a homely fellow. I suppose I will not know if he is unattractive, however, since he will be my OTL. I believe love renders a person beautiful, even if they are only "tolerable." Ha!

"Miss Elizabeth," he called. At the sound of his voice, she turned, her face etched with surprise. She had not been expecting him. I had thought she had encouraged him to visit her on Oakum Mount when she mentioned it during their dance, but I believe now I was mistaken. "May I join you? Someone recently told me this is the best place to watch the sun rise."

Miss Elizabeth offered a becoming smile and dipped a perfect curtsy. "Of course, Mr. Darcy." She turned back to the view. "I believe the sunrise will be especially colorful today. The sky is very clear."

My brother joined her, gazing out over the vista. Oakum Mount offers a lovely view, but it does not compare to the scenic vistas near our home. I will enjoy seeing Miss Elizabeth's face when she sees the sun rise from Pemberley.

"At the dance, you mentioned this view would not compare

to the Peaks near my home. How is that you know so much about the hills of Derbyshire?" My brother looked at his feet instead of Miss Elizabeth or the charming view that had previously shown on the pages of my diary.

"My aunt hails from Lambton. She has assured me there is nowhere in England as lovely as your home county." Fitzwilliam pulled his eyes from his shoes and looked at her then. She had turned her body slightly toward his.

I could not help but whisper, "Kiss her," which drew a disapproving tut from Mrs. Annesley.

"They hardly know one another, Miss Darcy. Life is not one of your books." I suppose she was correct, but a kiss at dawn in a picturesque setting would have been tremendously romantic.

"Lambton lies less than five miles from our estate!" Fitzwilliam exclaimed. I could not see it, of course, but I imagined he was smiling at her, for her own smile grew wider.

"Truly? Perhaps you have met my aunt. Her name was Merideth Barnes before she wed my uncle." I assume my brother shook his head in the negative, for he did not reply to her question, and had he known the former Miss Barnes he would have, surely, announced it.

"Are you close to your aunt, Miss Elizabeth?" I congratulated him for he appeared genuinely interested in getting to know her.

"I am. I had just celebrated my tenth birthday when she entered our family. Before that, I had no female in the family who favored me. My mother is a good woman, but she does not comprehend my need for morning rambles or good books. She mostly left me to my own devices because she could not understand me. I believe I had grown quite wild, so used to setting the activities of my days was I."

The sun began to peak over the horizon, and Miss Elizabeth

turned back to the scene in front of her. My brother followed suit. After a moment, he asked, "Did your aunt help to tame you then?"

Miss Elizabeth laughed. Laughed! Not a timid titter but a true laugh. She faced him again, her eyes glistening with mirth, and said, "I believe she did, Mr. Darcy. She taught my eldest sister and me the rules of propriety, and she often invited us to spend time with her in London where she taught me to play the pianoforte, to maintain conversation over tea, and how to behave as a lady should. I love her dearly."

"Where in London do your aunt and uncle reside?"

Miss Elizabeth's chin tilted up, though I know not if it was in defiance, with pride, or to see my brother's face better for she is quite petite and he is, like all the Darcy men before him, very tall. "They live on Gracechurch Street. It allows my uncle to be near his warehouse."

My brother remained silent for a moment, likely working out how he should respond. "Do not mention her uncle in trade. Do not mention her uncle in trade," Mrs. Annesley and I chanted together.

Finally, he replied, "I believe it would be difficult for a man to attend properly to his family if his place of work was very distant from his home."

Mrs. Annesley and I let out a collective sigh. He had done it! I am sure it was difficult for him. He has been taught that, as a Darcy, we are far superior to most others we meet. He does not allow his social status to thwart his desires to make friends as he pleases, but I believe it will be challenging for him to overcome his learned biases when determining who his mate shall be.

Perhaps I am wrong, and this is the start of a new and improved Fitzwilliam Darcy. Only time will tell.

The remainder of the day went as it had before. Mrs.

Annesley took me back to the northern field to practice my spells. Because the day had reset, I was forced to rework the alterations I had made to the land. I was not surprised by this. Before we cast the replay the days spell, Mrs. Annesley charmed my diary to maintain my words. Otherwise, the things I had written would have disappeared at the beginning of each repeated dawn, and you, dear niece, would be without this lovely retelling of your father and mother's romantic beginnings (Surely, they will become so at some point).

Today, I took greater care studying the land before speaking the magical words. The adjacent field belongs to Mr. Goulding. His land sits higher than Mr. Bingley's, which I suspect is the greatest reason this area is prone to flooding. My focus narrowed to the land just past the hedges delineating Mr. Bingley's.

Soil and stone, now rearrange,
Craft a trench, bring forth the change.
A ditch to carve through field and moor,
No water's wrath, no more to endure.

Much like the riding spell, this verse left me feeling dizzy. I steadied myself by taking hold of Mrs. Annesley's arm. After several tries, I succeeded in elevating the land so that it created what appeared to be a natural ditch between the two. Mrs. Annesley offered no verdict on the correctness of my actions, but she did not hold her mouth as she had the last time.

Chapter Ten

Afternoon, 27 October 1811

Dear Diary,

Today has been exceedingly tedious, as Sundays tend to be. We have not yet spent a full week at Netherfield, which means today marked our first worship attendance. The day began with enthusiasm, at least from Fitzwilliam and Mr. Bingley. We arrived at Meryton church with several minutes to spare. Fitzwilliam, wearing a broad smile, assisted me from the carriage. I must say, he is very handsome when he smiles. Miss Elizabeth will find it difficult to resist him once he is determined to put on his charm. (Or should I say, once he finds his charm?)

Sir William Lucas, followed by his eldest daughter, greeted us with a hearty smile and bow. Mr. Bingley introduced me to the pair, and I can say that Miss Lucas is as amicable in person as she was when she danced across the pages of my diary. After a few moments of conversation, we were joined by Miss Lucas' younger sister, Miss Maria, who I had also seen at the assembly. If possible, Miss Maria Lucas is even shyer than me, so our conversation was rather stilted. Still, it is lovely to talk to someone my own age.

Mr. Bingley's eyes shifted across the church yard. Observing the crowd, he remarked, "This gathering seems smaller than anticipated. Is there another church in the area?"

Sir William seemed to grasp Mr. Bingley's underlying question, for he replied, "This is the only church in the town, however Longbourn Village has another. That is where you will find the Bennets, the Gouldings, and when they are so inclined, the Longs." My brother's face had long since reflected his normal mask of polite indifference, but his eyes lost the sparkle upon hearing this report from Sir William.

It did not take long to understand why the Gouldings and Longs would attend service in Longbourn Village. The Meryton parson appeared to be a kindly and knowledgeable man, but his advanced age and stooped stature made him hard to hear. So difficult was it to discern what the man had said, I was unaware the service had concluded until the pews started to empty. I must have sat with my eyes wide open during the closing prayer! I hope no one noticed.

The remainder of the day has been equally dull. As is our tradition, my brother and I followed the service with an hour in quiet reflection. I had thought of using that time to write my daily entry in this journal, but I am now glad that I chose to delay, for it has got me out of wearisome conversation with Miss Bingley who, as I write, pesters my brother with her own personal brand of relentless determination.

I realize, now, I have shared little about Miss Bingley or the other members of our party. As I have mentioned, my brother and I are currently visiting Netherfield Park, an estate recently leased by my brother's very good friend, Mr. Charles Bingley. In addition to our party, Mr. Bingley also included his sister, Mrs. Louisa Hurst, her husband, Mr. Ralph Hurst, and his youngest sister, Miss Caroline Bingley.

As I mentioned in a previous entry, Fitzwilliam and Mr. Bingley attended Cambridge together. I do not know the story of how they met, but I believe my brother had to rescue him in some way or another. I suspect he has repeated the act many times since. It is not that Mr. Bingley courts danger; it is more that he is drawn to mischief. I must clarify: Mr. Bingley is not one to make mischief; he finds himself in the middle of it.

Because he is a man who wishes to be well pleased, he usually is. Unfortunately, such a man is unlikely to recognize when he is being fleeced. As he was left a vast fortune when his father died, he is an easy target for those who would seek to take advantage of his nature.

Mr. Bingley is not a short man, but he is several inches below my brother's height. He has dark blonde hair that sticks up a bit at the crown of his head, and his face has a rash of freckles across his cheeks and nose, the result of spending many hours out of doors. He is only a few years younger than my brother (I believe he is six and twenty) though he looks to be several years Fitzwilliam's junior, most likely because of his jovial nature. He is also the eldest of his family, though at times he appears to be the youngest for varying reasons.

Three years Mr. Bingley's junior, Mrs. Hurst shares his dark blonde hair and soft brown eyes. She is pretty in a faded sort of way. Last year, she married Mr. Hurst, a corpulent gentleman afflicted with such sloth as I have ever seen, except when food is on the table, drink is in the bottle, or cards are in his hands. He will also occasionally seek pleasure in hunting, though Brother claims he cannot walk too far afield for the best coveys.

Increasingly, I perceive Mrs. Hurst as quite melancholic. She says little, except to agree with her sister or her husband. In the mornings I have spied her knitting baby clothes, but there is no indication she is increasing. In the evenings, she often sits quietly near her sister and plays with her bracelets. She does not read. She does not laugh. She rarely engages in conversation. Now that I have taken time to put my thoughts to paper, I begin to wonder if I should speak to Mrs. Annesley about the lady. Surely there is something magic could do to help her find happiness.

And finally, there is Miss Bingley. As I mentioned, she is the youngest of the Bingley sisters. She is also the handsomest. She is very tall, for a woman, and has an admirable figure which she shows off to good effect with excellently tailored frocks. Regrettably, her penchant for unflattering colors like apricot and ginger does her no favors. These colors clash terribly with her complexion which is much rosier than either her brother's or sister's. She also favors long plumage on her bonnets and in her hair which gives her the appearance of being far taller than she is. When dancing, she looks to be looming above her partner. She stands out like an ostrich among chickens.

As a tall lady myself, I want to applaud her choice. Tall women should do as they please, just as the dainty ladies do. If she cared more for her own happiness and less for the approbation of others (and by others, I mean rich gentlemen), I would be well pleased with her choice. However, Miss Bingley clearly seeks gentlemen's approval (my brother's, in particular) and her height sometimes works against her in this. I do not believe she yet understands how sensitive and silly men can be about these things, but that is likely because she does not notice much beyond her own wishes.

Yet, this does not fully capture the root of my distaste for her. Although she has a great deal of wealth, due to her father's and grandfather's success in trade, her attitude is very poor. She is inclined to dislike any woman she views as competition, but she dotes on me to a sickening extent, always complimenting my choice of gown, my hair style, and my many accomplishments (which I have greatly neglected since learning I am a witch). Her flattery is insincere. She only desires my assistance so that she can capture my brother, but that will never occur as they have nothing in common. (Do not worry, little niece, I will not allow Caroline Bingley to become your mother.)

"Mr. Darcy, have you heard the latest news? Miss Elenor Carter was seen returning from an empty balcony with none other than Mr. Kingston!"

"Generally, I prefer not to engage in gossip about young

ladies," he responded.

"Mr. Darcy, I recently learned that some ladies are now lowering the waistline of their gowns, so that it sits closer to their natural middle. What think you of that?"

"If it is a more comfortable mode of dress, I do not believe it is a problem."

As I said, they have nothing in common! This is just a small sampling of the nonsensical barrage of words she had tossed at Fitzwilliam in the past hour. In addition to the gibberish that gushes from her mouth, she also harbors a mean spirit towards others. Despite her trade background, she behaves as if no one but the wealthiest merits her attention. Not only is she rude to the servants, but she is ill-mannered toward others, as well. You should have seen how haughtily she behaved at the assembly.

"Mr. Darcy, …"

Perhaps I should rescue my brother for a moment. He looks near apoplexy.

∞∞∞

I not only rescued my brother but also secured his promise for us to meet the Bennet sisters!

"Fitzwilliam, I was quite pleased to encounter Miss Lucas and Miss Maria before this morning's church service. Could you introduce me to any other ladies here? It would be pleasant to visit with girls my age."

My brother opened his mouth to speak, but he was not fast enough. Miss Bingley interjected, "Oh, Miss Darcy, I must warn you, there are the lowest of people in this small village. There is no one who will be of interest to you."

I wanted to cry out that I would be happy to know anyone

if it meant I was away from her company, but I did not. Darcys may not cry out, but as my brother often demonstrates, we do occasionally give offense. Happily, I did not do that, either. Instead, I replied, "Thank you for the warning, Miss Bingley, however, my brother stated he danced with several ladies at the assembly. Surely, he would not have engaged with those beneath his notice."

"Darcy, we should introduce your sister to the Bennet ladies. You found Miss Elizabeth agreeable enough to dance with, and Miss Jane is nothing short of an angel." Thank heavens for Mr. Bingley! This was exactly the offer I had hoped for.

My brother nodded, "Yes, I can arrange for you to meet the Bennet sisters. I was introduced to the eldest three, but there are five altogether. I believe the youngest two are near your age."

"Oh, Mr. Darcy," Miss Bingley cried, "You cannot expose your sister to the Bennets." She turned to me then, "I assure you, Miss Darcy, they are not the types of ladies you want to associate with. Miss Bennet is a lovely girl of course," she nodded to her brother, "but the others are barely tolerable." Yes, I promise she used that word!

"The youngest two are practically wild, too young and too silly to be out of the classroom. They behaved very poorly, indeed, during the assembly. The middle sister is quite pedantic, she quoted scriptures and Fordyce all evening to anyone who would listen. And Miss Elizabeth, she is as unrefined a young woman as I have ever seen. Her hair was untidy, her dancing too enthusiastic, and she laughed and laughed the entire evening."

My brother marked his place in the book he was reading and closed the pages with a snap. "Miss Bingley, do you believe me incapable of determining with whom my sister should and should not associate?" Miss Bingley's visage paled, and I rather thought she might swoon.

"Oh, um, no, of course not, Mr. Darcy," she stammered.

Fitzwilliam gave a nod. "Thank you, Miss Bingley." To me he said, "Georgiana, I will take you to visit the Bennets tomorrow afternoon."

There you have it. Tomorrow I will officially meet Fitzwilliam's OTL, unless for some reason this horrible day repeats itself. And if that is the case, I will remove the spell and allow my brother to fend for himself.

Chapter Eleven

Evening, 28 October 1811

Dear Diary,

As it turns out, we did not need to visit the Bennets today, because they visited us! The morning started as it always does. Mrs. Annesley and I attended breakfast where Fitzwilliam joined us. Since the assembly, Mr. Bingley has not broken his fast with us.

While I attempted to eat my eggs and sausages, Fitzwilliam quizzed me on French verb conjugations. He is convinced I should dedicate my time to mastering the passé simple and was quite frustrated that I stumbled a bit differentiating between "er" verbs and "ir" verbs.

"Georgiana, it is, 'je finis, tu finis, il finit!'"

If only he grasped how eagerly I wished him to finis, finis, finit with this tedious discussion. I devote hours each day to commit spells to memory, something I should have started as early as age ten but, for obvious reasons, could not. Thus, I find myself quite behind in my efforts to become a proper witch. There is too little time for French lessons.

Mrs. Annesley interjected with a promise, "Mr. Darcy, rest assured Miss Darcy will dedicate additional time to her French conjugations today." My brother nodded his approval and picked up his paper. I threw a grateful look at my companion.

"Fitzwilliam, when will we attend the Bennets? Do you plan to visit them during morning hours or in the afternoon?"

With the paper still obscuring his face, he replied, "I would prefer to visit during the morning, but we must allow Mrs. Hurst and Miss Bingley to determine when we call on them. Given their aversion to early mornings, I anticipate our visit will occur this afternoon." Setting his paper down, he bid me goodbye and challenged me to practice my French early since my afternoon would likely be occupied with a visit to Longbourn.

But that is not how things unfolded! As suggested, Mrs. Annesley and I did spend our morning in the school room, but instead of French I learned three different spells to use during childbirth. These are important spells for the wife of a landowner, and I advise you to learn each one. You will someday be responsible for many tenants and should prepare yourself to assist them when they are in their greatest need.

Lambing season is on the horizon. Mrs. Annesley has assured me it is best to practice on the animals before attempting my enchantments on human subjects. That seems reasonable, I suppose. Although I do not want anything to go wrong with any creature, I would be devastated to have improperly interfered in a human's birth. I strongly recommend you start your practice with a sheep, or maybe even a barn cat.

The first spell is for the first-time mother. Mrs. Annesley said that many women are very afraid of the unknown aspects of childbirth. One need not be a midwife to know that labor is a dangerous time for a woman, so anxiety over the unknown is reasonable. Unfortunately, fear only exacerbates the pain a woman feels and increases her likelihood of demise. These words, combined with a sip or two of chamomile tea should assist the mother.

Breath of life and touch of grace,
Surround this mother in embrace.
Ease her pain, dispel her fear,

As the moment of birth draws near.

The second spell is to help a woman through the agony of a misaligned birth. I will spare you the details, dear niece, as I am uncertain of your age upon first reading this. In simple terms, there are times when babies are not positioned ideally for birth. Bringing a child backwards into this world is, I am told, the most excruciating pain a person can experience. Should you be with anyone—a tenant, sister, friend, or even an adversary—facing this ordeal, you must recite these words. It will be more potent if you have the mother hold black tourmaline while you chant the verse.

> *Gentle winds and turning tide,*
> *Guide this child to safely glide.*
> *If the path remains unchanged,*
> *Let mother's body rearrange.*

Lastly, there is a spell for mothers-to-be who are vocally expressive during labor. As I mentioned, I have no experience with this, myself, but it seems some women can be rather boisterous during their laboring hours. I do not believe this spell helps the mother, in any way, but it certainly is useful for the women who must attend her.

> *With whispers soft and silence deep,*
> *Calm the voice that will not sleep.*
> *Let not a shout nor squawk be heard,*
> *Just gentle coos, like a sleepy bird.*

After several hours of study, Mrs. Annesley and I prepared ourselves for our visit to Longbourn. Words fall short of describing my eagerness to meet Miss Elizabeth. I am now quite convinced that she is my brother's OTL and your soon-to-be mother. At half-past one in the afternoon, I sat in the parlor along with Mrs. Annesley, Mrs. Hurst, Mr. Bingley, and my brother. Regrettably, Miss Bingley was nowhere to be found. No doubt she believed her late arrival would thwart our plans.

"Brother, might we consider visiting the Bennets today,

leaving the Bingleys to follow suit tomorrow? I daresay, they may even return our visit tomorrow, and will wait upon us here." Fitzwilliam shot me a silencing glance. I do not know if it was my suggestion that annoyed him or the fact that I had made it in front of Mr. Bingley and Mrs. Hurst.

"I am certain Caroline will join us shortly, Miss Darcy. When she does, we can all proceed to the Bennets at Longbourn." Mr. Bingley gave a nervous glance toward the door. Alas, Miss Bingley was no more in attendance than when I had made my suggestion.

Our party sat in silence for several minutes awaiting Miss Bingley's arrival. Fitzwilliam checked his pocket watch no less than three times while we waited, and Mr. Bingley huffed his impatience at least ten times. Still, Miss Bingley did not appear. As I mulled over giving her another spot on her nose, there was a scratch at the door from the butler.

"Sir, Mrs. Bennet, Miss Bennet, Miss Elizabeth Bennet, Miss Mary Bennet, Miss Catherine Bennet, and Miss Lydia Bennet are present and inquire if you are receiving this afternoon."

Mr. Bingley jumped from his seat, "Oh yes, oh yes. Please see them in." I attempted to hide my smile. Mr. Bingley's anxiety was rather charming. After sneaking a glance at my brother, I could see he was little better, though certainly more dignified in his disquiet. He stood, paced to the window, and tugged at each sleeve no less than three times.

Mrs. Annesley, Mrs. Hurst, and I stood to greet our visitors. Mrs. Bennet entered first, followed by her daughters in order of their birth. I had not yet had an opportunity to know Miss Kitty or Miss Lydia, but from the way the last Bennet girl bounced on the ball of her feet, I knew at first glance that she was the "lively" one Mrs. Bennet had mentioned at the assembly.

The ladies took their spaces around the room. Seated on a settee, I extended an offer to share it with Miss Elizabeth.

Regrettably, Mrs. Bennet opted to take the seat beside me. Although I was disappointed to miss out on a private conversation with my soon-to-be sister, I had wished to know the lady better.

"Georgiana, may I have the honor of introducing you to Mrs. Bennet and her daughters? This is Miss Bennet, the eldest, followed by Miss Elizabeth Bennet, Miss Mary Bennet, Miss Catherine Bennet, and Miss Lydia Bennet. Ladies, my sister, Miss Darcy." It was lost on no one how Fitzwilliam's voice lingered on Miss Elizabeth's name... including Mrs. Bennet.

"Mr. Darcy, you are a dear." Mrs. Bennet turned to me. "Now tell me, my girl, why were we not introduced at the ball last week? A girl as pretty as you should have been in attendance, dancing with all the young gentlemen. I daresay you would have been almost as popular as my Lydia." The youngest Bennet preened at these words.

Every eye in the room landed on me. My face warmed and my throat strained at words that could not be voiced. I do hate to be the center of attention.

"That would be quite impossible, madam. My sister is only sixteen and is not yet out."

"Oh, nonsense. Why, Lydia is but fifteen and already making her debut in society. How is a girl to find a husband if she cannot attend events? No one wants an old wife. It is far better to be out when you are young." She turned to me and patted my hand. "Now dear, what are we to do with you this season? If your brother will not allow you to attend the balls, perhaps he will permit you to come to a small house party. The Lucases will host an evening soon. Their home is not so large as Netherfield Park or even Longbourn, but we do always have a fun time!"

"Madam, I —"

Although I did not disagree with Mrs. Bennet, I am certainly old enough to attend small parties, but being the center of attention was causing me great discomfort. I was quite pleased to have Fitzwilliam interrupt the lady's rambling until I happened to witness Miss Elizabeth's pink cheeks. She was clearly embarrassed by her mother's interference. It was my responsibility to set things to right, else this day may be repeated again.

"I thank you, madam. Although I would enjoy attending the party, I must adhere to my brother's wishes. He is, after all, my guardian."

"Your guardian! Where is your mother and father, child? Oh, my poor, poor, Miss Darcy!" At this, she hugged me close to her rather voluptuous bosom and rocked me back and forth.

From across the room, a throat cleared. "Ahem, Mama, have you seen the delicate lace on the arms of these chairs? Perhaps we should do something similar in our parlor?"

Crushed as I was in Mrs. Bennet's embrace, I could only turn large, shocked eyes in Miss Elizabeth's direction. Her face was still awash in dark pink heat. Clearly, she was embarrassed by her mother's actions, and possibly by my own inability to react properly to the lady.

With a final squeeze, Mrs. Bennet released me. "I do say, Lizzy, that is very fine lace, indeed. Mr. Bingley, your sister has lovely taste." She snapped her fingers at her second youngest daughter, "Kitty, take note of this pattern. I need you to sketch it so that your Aunt Gardiner can send us some of the same from London." The girl nodded before breaking into giggles with her younger sister.

Mr. Bingley's request for refreshments drew a soft smile from Miss Bennet and a look of gratitude from Miss Elizabeth. Mrs. Hurst was asked to serve, and unlike her sister, allowed the tea to steep to perfection. Eventually, however, our pleasant party ended. Miss Bingley, having received word of our visitors, glided into the room in a bright yellow gown, a shade more appropriate for someone with Miss Lydia's coloring than her own. "How lovely to have visitors. Mrs. Bennet, it is good to see you again, along with your many daughters." She spat the word 'many' as if it were a curse.

Mrs. Bennet preened, "Of course, Miss Bingley. We could not allow another day to pass without paying our respects. It is so good to have neighbors at Netherfield Park. It has been too many years since this home has been filled."

"Naturally," Miss Bingley responded with a sniff. She squeezed herself on the other side of me, forcing me to sit uncomfortably close to both her and Mrs. Bennet.

"I was just telling the girls to take note of the lace you have placed on the arms of the chairs, Miss Bingley. I believe my brother in town may be able to procure something similar for me."

After tasting her tea, Miss Bingley's lips puckered in apparent distaste. "Is this your brother in trade?" She turned her eyes toward my brother as she said this.

"Oh, yes," Mrs. Bennet happily crowed. "He has the best warehouses in all of London. If he does not have the lace, it cannot be found in the country."

"What a boon, then, it is to have your family stationed as they are, so closely aligned to trade. I am sure it is beneficial to have your brother's connections when it is time to dress your daughters. It must be difficult to clothe five ladies, especially on your husband's modest income."

I was appalled. The gall of Miss Bingley! Not only to mention Mrs. Bennet's connections to trade, but to also imply that her husband could not afford the upkeep of his five daughters! I knew by the tightness of his mouth and the way the muscles in his jaw ticked that Fitzwilliam was also horrorstruck by her lack of manners. I looked around the room at the rest of the group. Mr. Bingley was happily chatting with Miss Bennet and neither appeared to have heard Miss Bingley's conversation. Mrs. Annesley wore a look of distaste upon her mouth. Mrs. Hurst twisted her bracelet in circles around her wrist. The two youngest Bennet daughters held their heads together, giggling. Miss Mary Bennet displayed a sour look, but that is, perhaps, her normal appearance. And Miss Elizabeth, the lady for whom I was most concerned, bore bright red cheeks and flared nostrils.

"Indeed, outfitting five daughters for social events is costly, yet it brings great joy. Though I was not blessed with a son, I have been fortunate to have five pretty daughters. How fine it is for a mother to see her daughters well-attended at a ball." Mrs. Bennet stopped for a drink of tea and a bite of scone. Scarcely before the bits of bread had left her airway, she continued. "The gentlemen always favor my daughters. Why, your brother danced with my eldest two times at the assembly, and who can blame him? She is the prettiest lady in all the county. And even Mr. Darcy danced the first with Lizzy!"

"I am sure that was very exciting for you, Mrs. Bennet, however, it was only a country ball. For your daughters to find husbands they should attend a season in London, but I am sure that is beyond your capacity." Miss Bingley practically hissed this insult before turning a smug look upon Miss Elizabeth.

I cast a pleading look at my brother, but he did not see me because he was too busy watching Miss Elizabeth. Miss Elizabeth, on the other hand, repeatedly clutched and released the fabric of her skirts, no doubt she wished it was Miss Bingley's neck she held in her grip. One additional look at Mr. Bingley, who still chatted amiably with Miss Bennet, told me that I would need to set this teatime to rights. There was no other way.

What I am about to tell you, little niece, must forever remain a secret between the two of us, and, of course, Mrs. Annesley. It is simply impossible to get anything past her. I casually dropped my napkin, and when I bent to retrieve it from near my feet, I placed my left hand gently on Miss Bingley's shoe. Then I softly repeated the words from the quieting spell Mrs. Annesley had taught me for laboring women.

> *With whispers soft and silence deep,*
> *Calm the voice that will not sleep.*
> *Let not a shout nor squawk be heard,*
> *Just gentle coos, like a sleepy bird.*

The familiar feeling of fulfilment told me my words had taken hold. I removed the smug look of satisfaction before I squeezed back into the narrow space between Mrs. Bennet and Miss Bingley.

"My Jane had a season in London when she was sixteen," Mrs. Bennet recounted. "There was a gentleman who I thought was sure to make her an offer. He wrote some verses for her, and very pretty they were."

"Thus, his affection ended," Miss Elizabeth remarked with a hint of impatience.

Miss Bingley raised her nose in the air and then —Why then, to my utter surprise, she cooed! Her eyes widened with shock. "Coo! Coo!" She clapped her hand over her mouth to halt the bird babble. Miss Lydia and Miss Kitty burst into another round of giggles. "Cooooo!" She turned wide eyes to her sister who sat open-mouthed, one hand absently turning a bracelet.

"Caroline, what has gotten into you?" Mr. Bingley asked.

"Possibly a dove, or even a pigeon, sir," Miss Mary solemnly suggested, prompting further peals of laughter from her younger sisters, and I must admit, I struggled to maintain my own composure.

Mrs. Bennet jumped from her seat. "Oh dear, I am sure it is only her nerves. It is a terrible thing to be afflicted with a nervous condition, though I have never once cooed like a bird. However, every woman's body is different. I have also never moved to a new town. It must be difficult on your sister to feel the need to impress her neighbors." Without waiting for directions, the matron then assisted Miss Bingley to her feet and ushered her out of the room. "Let's just get you to bed, deary. I am sure Mrs. Nichols has a draught that will help you to sleep it off. If she does not, I will send to Longbourn for one."

"Coo, coo!" Miss Bingley lamented while Mrs. Bennet dragged her from the room.

"I, er, that is," stammered Mr. Bingley. "I am sorry for the disruption. My sister has never behaved this way before."

"I am certain a nap will set her to rights, sir," Mrs. Annesley said to him, though she looked sternly at me.

"Oh, indeed, a rest, precisely as Mrs. Bennet recommended." He stood nervously and bowed to the ladies. "If you will excuse me, I must check on my sister."

After this, the party turned rather silent, even Miss Kitty and Miss Lydia refrained from their raucous behavior. "Mrs. Hurst, it appears the time has come for us to depart. Would you mind retrieving our mother so that we may leave you to care for your sister?" Miss Elizabeth smiled kindly at Mrs. Hurst.

Mrs. Hurst's eyes widened upon being addressed, absorbed as she was in her sister's birdlike mutterings. "Of course, Miss Elizabeth." She bobbed a wobbly curtsy, looking a bit like a bird herself, and exited the room at a near run.

"Should the weather stay fair tomorrow, my sister and I would be delighted to reciprocate your visit." Fitzwilliam stood behind me now so I could not see his face as he said this, but I was certain he directed his words and eyes only to Miss Elizabeth.

"That would be delightful, sir. We eagerly anticipate your visit tomorrow and the opportunity to become better acquainted with your sister." Miss Bennet responded in dulcet tones. Miss Elizabeth, however, blushed prettily and looked over my head at my brother.

She undeniably is his OTL! Of that, I am convinced. It is sometimes difficult to understand what she sees in him, for he has insulted her multiple times. However, she does not know that. I find, on occasion, that I must remind myself that Fitzwilliam, Mrs. Annesley, and I are the sole people who know the entirety of their acquaintance.

Shortly thereafter, Mrs. Bennet reappeared to escort her daughters to their awaiting carriage. Once we had bid them adieu Mrs. Annesley took me aside and blistered my ears for the "terrible trick" I had played on Miss Bingley, although it was not meant to be a trick. How was I to know the spell would literally make her coo? I thought it was only meant to quiet her.

Lesson learned, little niece. Understand the full repercussions of magic before you practice it in the parlor.

Chapter Twelve

Afternoon, 29 October 1811

Dear Diary,

We have made it through a series of days without repeat, and I begin to believe that Fitzwilliam has finally figured things out regarding his OTL. If you are reading this, sweet niece, be cheered. Your father is not quite the dunce I had believed him to be when all of this began.

Right after breakfast, Mrs. Annesley took me to the green sitting room next to my bedroom for our lessons. Despite her insistence that it wasn't a punishment for yesterday's antics, I was tasked with writing two spells for guiding financial investments. As I have previously noted, Mrs. Annesley is convinced that repetitive writing is key to memorizing a spell, and today she had me write each fifty times over. Fifty times each! Hence, you'll understand if today's journal entry is somewhat brief. Between the lengthy recounting of yesterday's events and today's exhaustive spell writing, my hand is quite sore. In addition, a small callous has begun to form on the first knuckle of my middle finger.

I do believe the financial spells will be useful, though. Fitzwilliam often reviews new investment opportunities, and though he has been largely successful on his own, there have been a few that did not go well for him. It will be good to assist him in this way as it also assists me, Miss Elizabeth Bennet (eventually), and Pemberley's tenant families.

After an extensive amount of time writing, I changed into

my riding habit and joined Fitzwilliam. He had planned for us to take the carriage to Longbourn for our visit, but I convinced him we should ride since the weather is so fine. Riding also allowed us to spend some time alone, which suited me perfectly as I had something to say to him.

Though he appeared quite enamored with Miss Elizabeth, in hindsight I believe my brother was less pleased with the behavior of her family. Eager to see Miss Elizabeth and Fitzwilliam content, and keen to avoid another day burdened with spell writing, I aimed to nudge my brother towards a kinder view of Mrs. Bennet. I believe it would be too difficult for him to properly embrace the ridiculous behavior of Miss Kitty and Miss Lydia.

"Brother, do you like Miss Elizabeth?" I asked as we exited the Netherfield drive. Though it was subtle, the tightening of his hands upon the reigns did not go unnoticed.

"Why do you ask?" Of course, he would not make this easy for me.

"Yesterday, I thought perhaps that you had a preference for her." I pushed slightly ahead and gave him a little time to contemplate my comment. Fitzwilliam is not one to open himself readily before others. He usually needs a small prod and then some time to his thoughts.

After a silent few moments, he admitted, "I do admire Miss Elizabeth for her beauty and intelligence." I sensed a 'however'. "However, she is not of our station in life and her family behaves very badly on occasion."

I had anticipated this response and chose to pretend ignorance to prove my point. "Who do you mean? Miss Bennet seemed to have lovely manners, though I have only met her the one time and cannot say if that is her normal demeanor." I knew it was her normal demeanor, for I had seen her no less than five nights in a row at the assembly, but my brother was not to know that.

"No, Miss Bennet seems to be above reproach. It is Miss Elizabeth's younger sisters, and even her mother, who give me pause."

"The sisters can be easily overlooked because they are still quite young. While I may not giggle through tea, I have made my share of mistakes, too."

"Georgie, that is hardly the same!" Fitzwilliam hates it when I remind him of my imperfections, likely because it reminds him of his own.

"Indeed, our behaviors differ, but none of us can claim perpetual propriety." I slowed my horse and turned to him, "What is it that bothers you about Mrs. Bennet?" I was prepared for this answer, too, but I needed him to say it so that I could properly refute his reasons.

"She is boisterous, lacks manners, and is utterly absurd, promoting her daughters to any unattached man of means. Though they have known one another for less than a week, she has probably begun plans for Miss Bennet and Bingley's nuptials." I giggled. This was probably quite true. "It would be an impossibility to have her as a family member, which is why I must not pursue Miss Elizabeth." This gave me pause. I had not considered that he would not attempt to engage Miss Elizabeth's heart. Luckily, the argument I constructed last night was well-prepared.

"Brother, Lady Catherine is loud, ill-mannered, and utterly ridiculous. If Miss Elizabeth were her daughter, would you find it difficult to accept her?" He pinched his mouth together but did not respond. "Mrs. Bennet may be all the things you said, but she is also kind and thoughtful, and she appeared to love her daughters. Besides she was very pleasant to me. I am sure you noticed her concern when she learned that our mother is dead."

His mouth remained pinched, but he did give a quick nod of his head. "I do not know if you will fall in love with Miss

Elizabeth," I prevaricated, "but if you do, I suggest you do not allow her family to sway you. They may not be like ours, but they seem to be happy and to care for one another. It would be a fine thing to be a part of a boisterous, cheerful family after so many years of only the two of us." Judging by his contemplative expression, I think my argument might have swayed him.

After a while he said, "You might be right, Georgie. Mrs. Bennet was entirely accommodating yesterday when Miss Bingley's unfortunate situation began. She acted with rapidity to aid the lady." An unbidden giggle escaped my mouth. Mrs. Annesley sent a cup of soothing tea to Miss Bingley's room after our guests left, so her bout of cooing did not last long. Still, the lady was in no mood to show her face afterwards. Last evening was blessedly peaceful as a result.

"I had thought perhaps…"

"Thought what, brother?" My heart raced. Did he suspect me?

Fitzwilliam said nothing as we turned into Longbourn's drive. "Nothing. It is nothing." Fearful of where the conversation might take us, I nudged my mare to move ahead and led us toward the house.

The Bennets' home was lovely, though on a much smaller scale than I am used to. Mrs. Bennet has an eye for color which she displays to advantage in her dress and in the accommodations of her parlor. The room was adorned with three harmonious shades of blue. I would not have thought to pair sky, navy, and royal blue in the same palette, but it worked very well. Brother has suggested I should redo my bedroom this spring and I might consider doing the same thing but with shades of pink.

Mrs. Bennet and her daughters offered cheerful greetings to our party. Mr. Bennet, she said, was out visiting a neighbor. "How is Miss Bingley today? Has she recovered from yesterday's malady?"

"She has and I will let her know you inquired of her health. She was not up to attending today, but Mr. Bingley and Mrs. Hurst should join us soon." Mrs. Bennet appeared pleased with my answer, though it was unclear if it was due to Miss Bingley's recovery or the anticipation of Mr. Bingley's imminent visit to her parlor.

Mr. Bingley and Mrs. Hurst arrived before tea was served. Naturally, he positioned himself as close to Miss Bennet as possible. I shared a loveseat with Miss Elizabeth, and my brother sat in a small chair on her other side.

"Miss Darcy, tell me about yourself. Do you have any hobbies?"

I placed my teacup on the saucer before answering. "I take lessons daily with my companion, Mrs. Annesley. I also enjoy music. I play the piano and the harp, though recently, I have not practiced as often as I should. What about you, Miss Elizabeth? What are your favorite activities?"

She gave me a warm smile. "Like you, Miss Darcy, I play the piano, though I have never practiced as often as I should. I suspect your playing will far outshine my own. I often go for long walks before breakfast when the weather allows. And I love to read."

We began a long conversation on books and discovered we have both recently finished Maria Edgeworth's *Tales of a Fashionable Life*. "I enjoyed piecing together the different stories," Miss Elizabeth shared.

"I did, as well. Which of her stories was your favorite?"

Miss Elizabeth must have thought about this question before because she had a ready answer. "I loved each of them for different reasons, but I think my favorite is *Madam de Fleury*. I strongly believe that everyone, regardless of social standing or gender should have access to education." My brother nodded his head in agreement, and I know his opinion is truly in accordance with her own because he funds two schools for young girls, one near Pemberley and another in London.

"What about you, Miss Darcy? Which was your favorite of the stories she included?"

"Like you, I found merit in all of them, yet *Almeria* resonated with me the most. For so many gently bred ladies, there is pressure to marry well. Certainly, I have felt it, and I am not out. I felt a certain sympathy for Miss Turnball's plight."

Miss Elizabeth nodded. "I agree, Miss Darcy. It would be a tragic thing, indeed, to marry for anything less than love." My brother said nothing as we continued our conversation, but I could tell he was listening and thinking.

Soon after, we thanked our hosts for their hospitality and left Longbourn. Fitzwilliam spoke little on our return trip to Netherfield Park. I believe he was contemplating the things he had learned and heard during our excursion.

Overall, aside from the tedium of writing spells over and over, today's outcomes leave me content. I am optimistic that tomorrow will bring a new day.

Chapter Thirteen

Afternoon, 30 October 1811

Dear Diary,

   Today's events have been scarcely noteworthy. We did not visit any of our neighbors, and none joined us for visiting hours, either. Miss Bingley was out of sorts yesterday, though she had long stopped her cooing; however, today she was back wielding her personal style of Darcy torture. She began with me, as she always does, noting how charmingly I embroider. "Your stitches are so remarkably even. It is a marvel how you achieve it!" If this was the first time I heard this compliment I would have been pleased. As I have charmed my needle to make no mistakes, however, it was not the first time. She has complimented me on my sewing and embroidery many times. Unfortunately, before I learned of my skill with magic, I was terrible with a needle. Fitzwilliam endured years of bearing the most unsightly handkerchiefs. I was adept at stitching his initials, but the cluster of oak leaves which were supposed to represent the beauty of Pemberley looked more like a clump of green feathers.

   After a while, she transferred her compliments to my brother. "Mr. Darcy, you have such a quick mind. I have never known another person to read as much as you do. Why, you must be among the most educated men in all of England." Though he did not respond to her, Fitzwilliam did not seem to mind her ramblings. He continued to read, or perhaps pretended to read, while a soft smile played across his face. This prompted me to observe him with greater scrutiny. Miss Bingley continued her one-sided conversation while he held the book and did not turn a single page for more than ten minutes. It was clear my brother had succumbed to daydreams!

I believe I know the source of his reverie. Undoubtedly, it was Miss Elizabeth Bennet occupying his thoughts. As I now recollect the day, I suspect Fitzwilliam met with her early this morning. He attended breakfast later than usual and wore a broad grin upon his face for the majority of his time at the table. This, in and of itself, is an oddity. While I have always considered him agreeable and pleasant, my brother is not one to wander about with an aimless smile. No, that sort of comportment is for the Mr. Bingleys of the world. Later, I overheard him whistling while making his way down the corridor to his quarters. If my brother is not one to walk around with a broad smile upon his face, then he certainly is not a man who gads about whistling tunes!

My spirits lifted when I pieced together the signs, all pointing to his newfound happiness. My brother is happy, perhaps truly happy for the first time in years, and I am so pleased for him. There can be no other reason for it than Miss Elizabeth Bennet.

Apart from that revelation, my day has been rather dull. Today's lessons with Mrs. Annesley centered on Samhain. Of course, I am aware of the general idea of Samhain since many locals in Derbyshire continue to practice the ancient Celtic ritual. I have long heard tales of Samhain as a day when portals open for the dead to communicate with the living, yet I previously paid them little mind. That was before. Now, embracing my identity as a witch, I find myself more receptive to such ideas.

Mrs. Annesley confirmed the tradition has merit and that we might communicate with the dead. "Most people," she explained, "use the evening as a chance to enjoy themselves and drink too much, however for witches the day can bring powerful knowledge from our ancestors."

The celebration begins after midnight on the first of November. Tomorrow night, once the household sleeps, Mrs. Annesley and I plan to venture out and light a modest bonfire. Then we will summon our ancestors and ask for guidance. While I have tried to temper my expectations, the prospect of meeting my mother is undeniably thrilling. She died when I was so young, and I do not know if my memories of her were true or if I have conjured them up somewhere along the way.

Chapter Fourteen

Evening, 31 October 1811

Dear Diary,

The whirlwind of today, coupled with the Samhain rituals, will keep me awake far into the night. I suspect my entry tomorrow will be quite short due to the sheer exhaustion from everything. Nevertheless, I have a duty to my future nieces to properly document the love affair of their father and mother, and I will continue to do my best.

It is currently half past eleven, and Samhain will soon be upon us. Unfortunately, I am still sequestered in my room because Fitzwilliam and Mr. Bingley have not yet gone to bed. If they continue their normal pattern, I should have approximately three-quarters of an hour to write down today's experiences.

I shall begin at the beginning since that is the easiest. Over breakfast, Fitzwilliam proposed a trip into town this afternoon for new music sheets, a bit of sweets, and a look around the bookshop.

"In anticipation of our afternoon itinerary, Mrs. Annesley and I dedicated our morning to setting up a modest bonfire atop a hill about a mile from the house. I trust that the thicket of trees standing between our house and our chosen spot will conceal the fire from any prying eyes peering out of windows. Ideally, the bonfire would be very large, but as it was only Mrs. Annesley and I gathering wood, our version will be rather small. She believes we should still be able to summon our ancestors, but perhaps not as many as we would prefer.

Upon returning to our rooms, I requested a bath. I had become quite sweaty and dirty from carrying downed branches and piling them as directed. Soon after, Fitzwilliam and I left for town. My earlier exertions worked up a fierce hunger in me, so we stopped first at the Thatched Cup, a small business run by a Mr. and Mrs. Stiles, for tea and finger sandwiches. The food's quality rivaled that of the finest London tearooms and surpassed many others I have sampled. The dining room was busier than I had anticipated for such a small town, but Fitzwilliam did not speak to anyone, and thus, I was not introduced to anyone.

Next, we visited the bookshop, where both Fitzwilliam and I purchased a book. He took home a copy of John Roberton's, *On Disease of the Generative System*, a topic I find very distasteful. I, however, am quite excited to read my new book, *The Forest of Montalbano*. Fitzwilliam seemed pleased with the variety found in the small shop, and the owner appeared to be genuinely happy with our patronage. We left the bookshop and turned left to the haberdashery. This is where things went awry.

As we approached the shop, the door opened and all five Bennet sisters stepped out. Fitzwilliam hurried to mask a smile, but the light in his eyes was clue enough, even to those who do not know him as well as I.

"Misses Bennet, well met," I greeted. I briefly thought fate had smiled upon my brother's romance, especially as he began a conversation with Miss Elizabeth. Regrettably, my optimism was misplaced.

"Lieutenant Denny!" Miss Lydia, unbridled as ever, shouted across the street to an officer walking in the opposite direction.

"Lydia! Ladies do not shout at gentlemen, especially from across a street." Miss Bennet's voice, though kinder than most, was laced with a sternness I had not anticipated.

"Oh Jane, it is only Denny. Oh look, Kitty, he is coming this way!" The two girls devolved into a spate of giggles.

"Good day, Misses Bennet, Mr. Darcy," said Lieutenant Denny, bowing gallantly to the ladies before nodding at my brother. I waited for Fitzwilliam to offer an introduction, but none came.

"Denny, you must save the first dance for me at the next ball! It is only fair," Miss Lydia declared with a giggle. She said more, but I am tired and will not share it all here. Suffice it to say, she lavished the poor man with such flamboyant affections that even the ribbons and lace in the shop window paled in comparison.

"Lydia, perhaps we should allow the lieutenant some peace. I am sure he has somewhere he needs to be." Miss Bennet's voice, though still soft, held a subtle note of warning.

Miss Lydia waved her sister's concerns away with a, "La, Jane," but Lieutenant Denny seemed to better understand the situation and hastily said his goodbyes.

"Jane! You ruined a perfectly delightful conversation with a soldier!" Miss Lydia crossed her arms in frustration.

"One must always remember the value of modesty, especially in public," Miss Mary intoned.

Miss Lydia became even more petulant. I glanced at Fitzwilliam, whose discomfort had now solidified into something resembling sheer horror. Accustomed as he was to the more restrained circles of London society, the raw display of sisterly discord and Miss Lydia's unchecked exuberance was evidently more than he could bear. He seemed momentarily paralyzed, a statue amidst the chaos of lively Bennet passions. He looked like he would rather face a French battalion than endure this spectacle a moment longer.

It was then Miss Elizabeth, perhaps sensing the growing tension, made a valiant effort to steer the conversation towards safer shores. "Mr. Darcy, have you noticed how the colors of the season are reflected in the shop's decorations? Quite thoughtful, wouldn't you agree?" Though her voice remained steady, the blush she wore on her face implied she was embarrassed by her family's behavior.

His eyes did not move from the spectacle of Lydia Bennet, his reply, "Yes, quite," was delivered with a stiffness that could rival the starched collars at Netherfield's laundry. Miss Elizabeth took a deep breath but said nothing further.

Miss Lydia's claims of ill-treatment grew louder. With a frustration I did not believe possible, Miss Bennet turned to her sister and said, "Lizzy, I think it is time for us to return to Longbourn."

"Yes, of course," Miss Elizabeth replied. "Good day, Miss Darcy, Mr. Darcy." Miss Elizabeth curtsied. I returned her curtsy and watched her leave.

After the ladies were out of earshot, I turned to my brother. "That was not well done, Fitzwilliam." He said nothing in reply, but the flare of his nostrils told me he heard. Nearly a week has passed without reliving a single day. Tomorrow morning will tell if this day starts anew. I should have Mrs. Annesley enchant the bonfire pile I assembled. I absolutely do not want to repeat that portion of today.

Chapter Fifteen

Afternoon, 1 November 1811

Dear Diary,

    As the clock approached one in the morning, Mrs. Annesley and I ventured out, navigating through the small copse of trees to the hilltop where our bonfire materials awaited. She carried a small torch, which we lit with the flame from the gas light I carried. Once the torch's fire glowed bright, we used it to light the bonfire. Though it was not large, it was still too large for us to encircle it, given that there were only two of us. Joining hands, we began the chant I had been taught.

> *As the portals open on this hallowed night,*
> *Ancestors guide us, give us your sight.*
> *Through this open gate, our two worlds meet,*
> *Offer your guidance, 'til once more you retreat.*

    As the last of the Samhain chants faded into the crisp night air, an eerie silence took hold of the grove. The wind began to blow fiercely, causing our hair to whip and slap against our cheeks with such force that our eyes watered from the sting. In front of us, the bonfire, once a beacon of light and warmth, began to emit thick, choking smoke that twisted and spiraled upwards, merging with the darkness of the night. The small gas lamp, our sole source of light for the return trip, flickered once, twice, then with a soft sigh, extinguished.

    Through the darkness, a voice, soft yet clear, cut through the noise of the wind and crackling fire. "Georgiana." My heart leaped in my chest. The voice, so familiar and yet so distant, filled me with a mix of hope and dread. Could it be? After all these years, had she come back to me? I dared to hope, to believe that my mother had found her way back through the veil to speak to me on this sacred night.

But as the silhouette of the spirit began to take form before me, I realized with a sinking heart it was not my mother. The figure, though feminine, carried herself differently, with an air of authority and grace that was unmistakable. I wracked my brain, trying to place her in the tapestry of my memory. Her features became clearer, and a gasp escaped my lips as recognition dawned.

"Grandmama?" I whispered, my voice trembling with emotion.

The spirit before me, the matriarch of our family long passed, nodded gently, a soft smile playing on her lips as if amused by my initial confusion. It was hardly my fault that I did not recognize her at first. The woman before me appeared to be approximately thirty years of age. The lady I had seen in portraits was more than double that.

The wind seemed to calm at her presence, and the smoke from the bonfire drifted away, bathing us, once again, in its warm light. Here, on this small hill so far from Derbyshire, on Samhain night, my grandmother had come to visit, bringing with her wisdom from the other side.

Upon recognizing my grandmother's spirit, a sense of propriety ingrained from countless lessons on decorum and respect compelled me to dip a curtsy, even in the face of the supernatural. My movement stirred a gentle, amused laughter from her, the sound both warm and eerily ethereal in the cool night air. "No need to be formal with the dead, my girl," she chided softly, her eyes twinkling with the same mirth I have seen many times in the eyes of my uncle.

I straightened, still somewhat in awe. "I am. . . I am just so glad to see you," I managed.

Her gaze shifted, falling on Mrs. Annesley who stood by my side. "I see you've found yourself a teacher," Grandmama noted with approval. "Good. A young witch as yourself needs someone knowledgeable to help her navigate the path of magic."

Swallowing the lump of emotions in my throat, I asked the question that burned within me. "What is it you wish me to know, Grandmama?"

Her expression sobered, and she locked eyes with me, her gaze piercing yet protective. "Be wary of Catherine," she said, her tone carrying a weight of caution and urgency. "My daughter. . . she has a dangerous heart. But do not fear, for she is not as strong as she believes. You can outmaneuver her if you are smart and ready."

Her words sent chills cascading down my spine. Grandmama's warning was clear, and her faith in my abilities and in the guidance of Mrs. Annesley fortified my resolve. With a newfound determination, I nodded. "What should I expect from Lady Catherine?" I asked, but I was too late. My grandmother's form faded and was soon replaced by another.

"Tabitha, there is little time." Mrs. Annesley stepped forward.

"Yes, mother? What is it you wish me to know?"

The spirit looked first to me and then back to her daughter. "Your charge must be taught to protect herself and those she loves. There is little time to waste."

Mrs. Annesley and I shared a confused look. "Why must she be protected, mother? What is the danger?" As with my grandmother, the spirit of Mrs. Annesley's mother faded before we could receive the answer.

Once we were assured no additional ancestors would arrive, Mrs. Annesley relit our lamp with a quick word, and we began our return trek to Netherfield. We parted in the hall; she walked east and I went to the west. "Tomorrow, Miss Darcy, your studies will grow more intense."

I did not know what she meant at the time, but after this morning's lessons, I begin to see the path that her tutelage has taken.

After breakfast, we gathered once more in my sitting room. "Your grandmother said your aunt was not as strong as she believes. I do not know if that means her power is weak or if she is unlearned. Do you have any ideas?"

I pondered this for a moment. "I believe it is most likely that she has power but has not honed it. She often says she would have been a great proficient if she had learned. My instinct tells me this is the source of her weakness."

Mrs. Annesley nodded. "Excellent. A witch's instinct rarely fails her. We will prepare for a powerful, yet untrained witch." She tapped her finger on her lips.

"What is it?" I asked. She was contemplating something important, and I needed to know what it was.

"I wonder why your Lady Catherine poses a danger to you. Have you angered her in some way?"

"I thought about this last night, or rather this morning. I suspect my aunt is less inclined to be a danger to me and more inclined to be a danger to Fitzwilliam and Miss Elizabeth's budding romance." Lady Catherine has long wished for an alliance between our families through the marriage of my brother to her sickly daughter. Fitzwilliam, of course, will have nothing to do with our cousin and Lady Catherine has grown increasingly exasperated by his refusal. But to cause harm to one's own family member just to have one's way makes little sense.

I must have voiced the last part aloud because Mrs. Annesley replied, "A spoiled witch cannot be accounted for." While my knowledge of spoiled witches is limited, I'm well aware of Lady

Catherine's habit of getting her way. I cannot know what she will do, but it will likely be loud and angry.

Mrs. Annesley handed me a heavy tome. "Read this. Inside are seventy-two sigils that can be used to your advantage. Review each and settle on four that you believe will most help protect you and your loved ones. I will assist you in narrowing the list to two. Carrying more than two on your body at any one time can result in weakness."

I flipped through the book, examining the array of symbols sketched within. "What will you do?" I asked.

"I must review my lessons and consult my books. I do not know when we should expect your aunt to show, but we must prepare soon. Please understand, Miss Darcy, this will require all your days and many of your evenings. I nodded my understanding and started reviewing the book.

∞∞∞

After a morning of study, Fitzwilliam and I took a ride. Along the way, my brother spontaneously suggested we visit Longbourn. It is debatable whether his suggestion was genuinely spontaneous. I suspect he had been considering the idea since right after we encountered the Bennets yesterday in Meryton. I was pleased, however, no matter if it was a planned event masquerading as impulsive. It meant Miss Elizabeth could spend more time with my brother, and I could spend less time with Miss Bingley.

Upon our arrival, Mrs. Bennet welcomed us warmly. "Is it just the two of you today?" I said that it was an unplanned visit and we just happened to be riding past their estate. "How delightful it is that we benefit from your exercise," she proclaimed.

"Miss Darcy, please sit here," she indicated a seat nearest

hers. "Mr. Darcy, there should be ample room on the settee next to Lizzy for you." At this, she gave me a sly wink, or rather, what she likely thought was a sly wink since my brother's face blanched and Miss Elizabeth's turned bright pink.

"Oh, Mama, leave Miss Darcy alone. She would much rather help Kitty and me with our task." In the room's corner, Miss Lydia was busily re-fashioning a bonnet. "Come, Miss Darcy, let me teach you how to craft roses from ribbons, if you haven't learned already." As it turns out, I did not yet know how to do such a thing as I have never once remade a bonnet. The prospect was exciting, and I eagerly agreed.

"Mama, might I have your permission to give Mr. Darcy a tour of the garden?"

A self-satisfied smile spread across Mrs. Bennet's face. "Of course, Lizzy, but take Jane or Mary with you to chaperone." Miss Bennet stood upon hearing her name, causing Miss Mary to breathe a sigh of relief. I cannot believe she would have preferred time in the garden over reading her book. My brother also released a sigh. He escorted the Misses Bennet into the hall, and soon after I heard the front door shut.

Mrs. Bennet left her seat and joined us at the table. "Miss Darcy, you must tell me all about your brother's favorite foods. Does he like sweets, or is he a fan of more savory dishes?" My newly found friend giggled at their mother's obvious maneuverings.

"La, Mama, you act as if Lizzy cannot secure him on her own. I declare, every time the man has encountered her, he has been smitten. He is obviously a reserved man, and yet, he danced the first with her at our last assembly." My mind recounted all the moments Fitzwilliam had slighted Miss Elizabeth, yet to the Bennets, his attentiveness must seem unfaltering — precisely my intention.

Movement at the window caught all our attention. Miss Elizabeth's hand rested lightly on Fitzwilliam's arm, as he escorted her along a path. She said something to him, and he laughed. An actual laugh, with teeth and everything! "Oh, how well they look together. They will have the most striking, dark-haired children." My companions erupted into gales of laughter. Perhaps, niece, you will be one of those striking children. I cannot imagine how you would avoid it, as your mother and father are very good-looking people.

"Are you planning to attend tomorrow's party at Lucas Lodge, Miss Darcy?" Miss Kitty held multiple pins in her mouth which caused her words to slur as she said this.

"I was not informed of a party at Lucas Lodge."

Miss Lydia looked up from her ribbon, "You must come. It will be so much fun. Sir William always allows us to dance even though it is supposed to be a dull card party. I will ask your brother!"

I was tempted to allow her to do just that, but I knew her interference, especially in front of others, would only bring out Fitzwilliam's petulance. I decided it was better to wait until we were alone. "I thank you for the offer, Miss Lydia, but I cannot accept. I will broach the topic with my brother later." She did not seem happy with this, but accepted my request and went back to stitching her ribbon.

The couple walked in the garden for the better part of half an hour, while I learned to make two different types of flowers using ribbon. When the others returned from inside, my brother and I said our goodbyes. He wore a happy, if reserved, smile for the rest of the day. As we neared Netherfield, I dared ask, "Brother, Miss Lydia and Miss Kitty will attend the party at Lucas Lodge tomorrow night. I know I am not yet out in society, but could I attend a small house party with you? I promise I will not talk to any gentlemen or ask to dance."

He smiled widely, saying, "Miss Elizabeth also mentioned that you should come. She, along with Miss Bennet, offered to look after you." He has not yet agreed to let me go, but as Miss

Elizabeth has suggested it, I believe my chances are good.

Chapter Sixteen

Evening, 2 November 1811

Dear Diary,

I greatly regret that I did not begin this journal entry earlier today, as I would only have the evenings events to record before retiring. Alas, I was too miffed at my brother to write the first part of the entry when I should have. I shall get to that part in a moment.

The day began earlier than I hoped. I slept little last evening. Every time I closed my eyes, I saw Lady Catherine's face. If you had asked me yesterday my thoughts on the prognostication of her imminent interference, I would have happily told you I was not afraid. However, in the dark of night, my worries grew, and I can no longer keep her from my mind. What is it that she plans to do and when? Will there be time to train for her arrival, and what exactly am I to prepare for?

I said as much to Mrs. Annesley as we were reviewing the sigils I selected. She said that worry solves nothing, and I would be better off spending my time on learning. That is easier said than done, however. She is not the one who will be threatened, after all.

Mrs. Annesley appeared satisfied with the four sigils I chose. With her help, we narrowed it down to two. The first is Andromalius, a strong a powerful spirit who, among other things, discovers wickedness and underhand dealings. He also punishes wicked people. I believe my choice for this sigil is obvious. The second sigil we chose was Bael. This spirit has the ability to grant skill with languages and make a person invisible. Since I am new to the art of witchcraft, I do not yet know a lot of spells, and I know nothing of counteracting another's magic. Becoming invisible, even if only temporarily, may grant me enough time to think about my next steps.

To be of assistance, sigils must be worn on the body. I proposed drawing the symbols on my legs, but daily washing and friction from my undergarments would erase them, necessitating daily redrawing. Mrs. Annesley had a better idea. She procured two bloodstones, one almost completely red, the other a dazzling mix of black and red. We etched each symbol into a stone using a carving spell. Then, using copper we attached the stones to a long string. I will wear the jewelry around my neck. The string is long enough for the stones to be concealed in the bodice of my gown but will allow me easy access should I need to call upon one of the spirits. The bloodstone has other uses, but I am not fully aware how. Mrs. Annesley did not have time to tell me, since we spent every moment until teatime working on the sigils.

During tea, I reminded my brother of the party at Lucas Lodge. "Oh, yes, about that. I am sorry, Georgiana, but I do not believe you are ready to be out, even in a small society. I am sure you understand."

I did not understand, and I told him so! "I cannot believe you have said no! Even Miss Elizabeth believes I'm mature enough to attend." And then, in my petulant, exhausted state I said something truly abhorrent. "I wish only Richard was my guardian and you were far, far removed from me!" Richard is our cousin and he, along with my brother, have shared guardianship of me since my father's death five years ago. Although to say they share guardianship is a stretch. My brother, for all intents and purposes, is the sole provider of my care and oversight. Richard is a colonel in the army and is too often away from home to assist in my raising.

Fitzwilliam flinched at my outburst. Not only had I said something hurtful, but I had also raised my voice to him in front of others. Miss Bingley, Mrs. Hurst, and Mr. Bingley all sat in stupefaction. Mr. Hurst grunted in approval of the ginger cakes before stuffing another into his mouth.

"Georgiana, I believe you have proven my point. You are not old enough to be out. I am not certain you are old enough to even take tea with adults." And then he dismissed me. I did not even have a chance to taste the cake!

Mrs. Annesley followed me to my room and rang my ears for my behavior. "Despite your tiredness and anxiety about the future, your actions were quite inappropriate, Miss Darcy." Her words made me cry harder. I flopped onto my bed and poured out my tears onto the pillow. After a while, Mrs. Annesley sat down beside me and rubbed slow circles on my back.

Between sobs, I asked, "I do not have the energy to perform the riding spell this evening. How will I know what happens at the party? What if Fitzwilliam behaves badly?"

"That is simple, dear. I have spelled his shoes. We will cast the images they see upon the pages of your diary and listen in. There will be little to see, due to the angle, but it was the single item I could procure that I know he will wear. It would be better to spell a necktie or a button upon his coat, but I cannot be certain which one he will select to wear this evening. Still, we should be able to hear everything he does, which is better than nothing."

"You knew I would not be allowed to attend the party?" I sat up from my place on the bed and gave her what I hoped was an incredulous Darcy look.

"No dear," she said as she wiped tears from my eyes. "I spelled his evening shoes and boots with the mirror spell days ago. The riding spell is very exhausting, and I was unsure if you would be able to maintain it. That you have done so, many nights over, tells me just how strong you really are." I preened at the unexpected compliment. None of us are immune to flattery, including myself.

"You are tired. Have a rest, and then find your brother and apologize. He did not deserve to be spoken to as you did, and in front of his friends, at that!" I nodded my agreement and laid back on the bed. However, I did not sleep as well as I should have. Too many things whirled about in my mind. Lady Catherine, my brother's romance, keeping everyone safe. After an hour, I gave up and went out to find Fitzwilliam.

I found him in the library reading a book on barley. "Unless you have come to make your apologies, I do not want to hear it." He turned another page and continued to read.

I wanted desperately to stamp my foot in the face of his casual dismissal, but I stopped myself from doing so. That would only reinforce his belief in my immaturity for social outings. Instead, I said, "I am very sorry for behaving as I did and embarrassing you in front of your friends." And then I waited for him to accept my apology, which he eventually did, but not after making me wait a full minute.

"Thank you," he finally replied. "I hope you understand I do not prevent you from attending because I wish to keep you from having fun. I prevent it because I do not believe you are ready to be out, and I wish to protect you."

"Protect me from what, exactly? I would be with you and Miss Elizabeth the whole time. Unless that is what you fear. Do you wish to keep her all to yourself? If that is the case, I can spend the evening with the younger Bennet sisters. I am certain Miss Lydia and Miss Kitty will be busy flirting with officers, but Miss Mary would sit with me."

Fitzwilliam sighed. "I do not wish to prevent you from spending time with Miss Elizabeth. I simply prefer that you mature a bit more before attending even small country gatherings." I fear, dear niece, that you may not make your debut until you are at least twenty years of age. I pray your mother can sway my brother to more rational thinking.

I longed to argue further with him, but there was no use. I know my brother too well to believe I could say or do anything that would change his mind on this. "I must return to Mrs. Annesley," I lied. Then I dipped a curtsy and quit the room. Staying in his presence would have only reignited my anger.

After, I returned to my room to continue reading *Magical Castings and Curses for New Witches*. I discovered a verse capable of making someone's shoes uncomfortably tight. I considered casting it on my brother but refrained, worried it might disrupt Mrs. Annesley's mirror spell.

∞∞∞

Once the group departed for the party, Mrs. Annesley and I requested refreshments. We settled ourselves on the settee, propped the open diary against a vase, and then waited for something to occur.

The carriage ride to Lucas Lodge was rather interesting to see. While the ride was uneventful, observing it from the perspective of my brother's shoes was quite peculiar. The shoes looked up at five sets of knees. Occasionally, Miss Bingley's ever-present feathers would sway into view as if to say, "I am here, too."

Soon they arrived, and Fitzwilliam's shoes descended the carriage stairs. He was greeted by Sir William and Lady Lucas upon entering the house, soon after which he found Miss Elizabeth.

"I notice Miss Darcy is not with you tonight; I was quite sure you would bring her." Given the angle, I could not see the cut of Miss Elizabeth's gown, but I do know it was white with ivy embroidered along the hem.

"I considered it, but ultimately felt she's still too young." Too young, indeed!

Miss Elizabeth introduced my brother to Colonel Forster. He is leading the militia regiment that is currently stationed in Meryton. Then the two of them held a conversation with Miss Lucas and a gentleman named Jonathan Goulding.

Things were off to a good start. Fitzwilliam was talking to many people and behaving as one should at a gathering. Then, one ill-timed and piercing comment from Mrs. Bennet ruined it all.

"I knew how it would be the first time they met. Mr. Darcy has had eyes for only my Lizzy since the assembly. Mark my words, Harriet, they will be married by Christmas! And he with ten-thousand pounds a year. My Lizzy will have the finest carriages and jewels. I bet he even has a house in town!"

Miss Elizabeth's embarrassment was clear in her voice. "Mr. Darcy, please disregard my mother's words. She…"

"Think nothing of it, Miss Elizabeth. If you will excuse me." And then he left. I do not mean that he quit the conversation; I mean he left. He found Sir William, thanked him for the invitation, then he found Mr. Bingley and explained that he would take the carriage home and send it back for the others.

Today was dreadful and tiring, and now, owing to my frustrating brother and Mrs. Bennet's intemperance, it seems I might have to endure it all once more.

Chapter Seventeen

Afternoon, 2 November 1811
(once more unto the breach)

Dear Diary,

As predicted, today mirrored yesterday, almost exactly. Fortunately, Mrs. Annesley enchanted my sigils to maintain their form, preventing them from reverting. That meant we could spend the morning working on new magic.

I was unaware of how powerful the bloodstone that holds the symbols is. The modest stones on my simple necklace possess significant power. Not only will it help to ensure my protection, but it will also enhance my decision-making abilities. More importantly, it amplifies my magical strength. Using the bloodstone, I am able to cast spells using a single word instead of an entire verse.

Of course, I knew there were small spells I could perform without the benefit of a magical verse. I have mentioned before that I can sweeten Miss Bingley's bitter tea with the tap of my finger against the cup, and I can remove a stain from my gown with the wave of a cloth. However, such minor spells offer no defense against Lady Catherine.

Today I learned: Banish (removes an offending object from my sight), Silence (stops a person from speaking), and Halt (stops a person or object from moving). While holding the bloodstone is not required for these spells to function, their effects are significantly stronger and more enduring when I do.

As thrilling as it was to learn this new form of magic, it was also very tiring and painful. As I have mentioned, simple spells leave a satisfying feeling, much like an itch being scratched or a sore muscle being massaged. Sometimes, a more complicated spell will leave me feeling a little intoxicated. But these spells? They burn. Initially, the fiery sensation was pleasantly warming, but with more practice, it turned into an internal scalding. Mrs. Annesley said my resistance was excellent and that she had never known a new witch to withstand the heat for so long. That comment, alone, stoked my Darcy pride and motivated me to complete another five minutes of practice. Yet, after just an hour of training, I found myself unable to proceed.

Mrs. Annesley gave me orders to rest until teatime, which I have mostly done. I did read a little more from *Magical Castings and Curses for New Witches*. I have been reading the book in the order it was written, but today I skimmed it in search of inspiration. I found a spell that induces someone to tell the truth.

Shadows flee and lies dissolve,
In honesty you now evolve.
Speak words genuine, both good and bad,
Hold no secrets, let the truth be had.

Do you not think this is an odd spell to be found in a book of curses? How can someone be cursed by the truth?

Oh dear, it is time for tea which means it is time for my blasted misbehavior. I do not credit my ability to repeat yesterday's tantrum, but I will give it my best attempt. I will return this evening to share how Fitzwilliam's second attempt at the Lucas Lodge party went.

∞∞∞

Evening

Dear Diary,

I need not have fretted about my teatime tantrum. I had no reason to repeat my performance today. Following yesterday's lead, I brought up the subject of the Lucas' party only to be told, "I have decided to stay home this evening." Can you believe it? This strategy failed him at the assembly and will do so again, yet he persistently plays the fool, thinking he controls the situation.

Predictably, Miss Bingley saw this as an ideal resolution and hastily declared her own absence from the ball. Her brother, however, put his foot down on that subject. Showing uncommon determination, Mr. Bingley asserted, "Caroline, you will attend the party. I cannot force Darcy to behave as he ought toward our neighbors, but I can do so with you."

This sparked a prolonged, boisterous, and tiresome debate from her. "But, Charles, there will be no one worthy of speaking to at the event." Her arguments covered a broad range of topics: no one will have on fashionable gowns, there will be little interesting conversation, the Bennet daughters will behave gauchely, the soldiers will expect her to dance with them, etcetera, and so on. Mr. Bingley remained stalwart in his decision, and several hours later he led his two sisters and Mr. Hurst to their awaiting carriage.

Mrs. Annesley and I joined Fitzwilliam in the parlor. I took up my embroidery while my brother read a book. After an hour of quiet between us, I said, "I wonder if Miss Bingley was correct."

Fitzwilliam lowered his book and asked, "Correct about what?"

"About the dancing. I hope she was. I believe Miss Elizabeth would relish an evening filled with dance. Perhaps Lieutenant Denny will ask her to partner him. I thought him a handsome, agreeable gentleman the day we met in Meryton."

Fitzwilliam's lips thinned. I continued with my conversation, "She is probably dancing with many officers. I have never met another lady with such a sweet and lively disposition. I suspect many gentlemen will ask her for a turn about the room. After all, she is second in beauty only to her elder sister, yet I deem her far more appealing."

My remarks hit their target. Fitzwilliam snapped his book shut, stood and walked to the window. As the saying goes, in for a penny, in for a pound. "Brother, do you think that Miss Elizabeth would agree to write me? She is becoming such a good friend; I would hate to lose touch. I have even considered inviting her to Pemberley come spring. Given her fondness for walking, she would delight in our many paths. We could also visit the Peaks. I believe she would greatly appreciate the view from atop our grand hills."

After several long moments he finally responded. "Miss Elizabeth is a lovely person. I am sure she would have no reservations about corresponding with you."

"And do you believe she would visit me at Pemberley?" He excused himself, claiming fatigue.

I am certain we will experience this day once again; however, before it resets Fitzwilliam should have many things to consider. I am confident that he will not be as quick to forego the Lucas' party the next time.

Chapter Eighteen

Evening, 2 November 1811
(All good things come in threes)

Dear Diary,

I am inclined to believe this will be our last endeavor to attend the Lucas party! As with the previous two attempts, the morning began with additional practice on the new form of magic I am learning. I continued my practice with the Banish, Silence, and Halt spells I learned yesterday. Magic is a lot like exercise; one must build an endurance for the activity. Regrettably, my stamina has not yet improved enough; the inner fire ignited by these spells left me exhausted before an hour of practice was up. I am tempted to be disappointed in my progress, but Mrs. Annesley assures me that I am well beyond what is expected.

"The strongest magic comes from love, Miss Darcy. That is why witches are often stronger near their homes. The people and things they love the most are there. It is why witches often marry close to home. You must focus on the people and things you care most about to increase your magical abilities."

This poses a dilemma, for whom or what else do I love in Hertfordshire besides Fitzwilliam? Of course, I love him dearly, but what else is there here? Perhaps I love Mrs. Annesley. She is the closest thing to a mother I have known in many years, though she is only slightly older than my brother. Indeed, I hold her in high regard and have affection for her, yet I am uncertain if it's love.

I love Richard tremendously as well, but he is currently in London. Perhaps I should write to him and ask him to come to Netherfield with Fitzwilliam and me. That may serve a two-fold purpose. Firstly, it would bring someone I love closer, potentially enhancing my magical prowess. Secondly, Richard could assist me in aiding Fitzwilliam toward his destiny with his OTL, Miss Elizabeth. Perhaps I will write to Richard tomorrow to see if he can spend a few weeks with us.

As with the past two iterations of this day, I attempted to nap after our lessons. Soon after drifting to sleep, I dreamed I was walking on the great Peaks in Derbyshire. It was a warm, sunny day and I lifted my face to the sky to feel the heat upon my cheeks. Without warning, a dark shadow crossed over, blocking the sun from my face. I opened my eyes to see a large dragon with crimson scales flying above.

In fear, I started to run, but the paths on the Peaks are treacherous. I stumbled but managed to right myself. The dragon gave chase. I found my footing and ran harder but I was too slow. The dragon landed in front of my path with a great thud. I backed away. "Please, please," I begged.

The dragon gnashed its teeth and threw back its head in anger. I held my arm in front of my face, prepared for the burning heat of its flames. Instead, it opened its great mouth and said, "I shall know how to act!" It was Lady Catherine's voice.

I begin to wonder, niece, if I shall allow you to read this chronicle of events. What started as fun and exciting has now turned into something far darker. I suppose I will not know until events conclude if I will share this with you. If I do, you must know that Lady Catherine's voice has long put a fear in me. I have always been a rather timid person, though my exploration of magic has improved my self-confidence. In truth, even before I knew Lady Catherine held powers, I found her to be terrifying.

Needless to say, I did not complete my nap. When I awoke, I was sufficiently irritated to convincingly repeat my first day's teatime tantrum. As it turned out, I did not need to replicate my original outburst because, when I brought up the idea, Fitzwilliam said I could attend!

You read that correctly. Fitzwilliam Alexander Darcy, my stringent brother (and your equally strict father, should you read this), gave me permission for my first foray into adult social gatherings! As parties go, Miss Lydia and Miss Kitty assured me that this one was nothing special, but it was special to me. What follows is a faithful recounting of my evening.

On the ride to Lucas Lodge I could not help but notice everyone's knees. The very knees I had observed bouncing along just two nights ago. Of their own accord, my eyes found Miss Bingley's feather as it bobbed left, right, front and back. Had I been observing from home, my view would have been limited to the forward bobs of her feather. Observing in person offered a much richer experience.

Upon our arrival, we were greeted by Sir William and Lady Lucas. My brother ensured I was safely tucked away with Mrs. Bennet and Miss Kitty before he sought out Miss Elizabeth's company.

"Miss Darcy, I am so glad your brother agreed to bring you! Do you like my gown? I added the trim this afternoon." Miss Kitty preened as she awaited my response. I agreed her gown and new pink trim were very becoming. "Come, let us find some punch." She pulled me across the room to the punch bowl where several militia men stood. I looked nervously toward my brother, but he had not yet noticed that I had strayed from Mrs. Bennet's side.

The pungent aroma of the punch did little to warn me of its potency. After a few sips, the world seemed to sparkle just a bit more, and my usual reserve melted away under its influence. Miss Kitty, as it turned out, proved to be the perfect companion for such an evening. Together, we laughed at the smallest jests. I once suggested to Fitzwilliam that I was not one to giggle in parlors, but I proved myself wrong this evening.

Our mirth was momentarily interrupted by the loud declarations of Mrs. Bennet. "I knew how it would be the first time they met. Mr. Darcy has had eyes for none but my Lizzy since the assembly. Mark my words, Harriet – "

To my own surprise, I found myself exclaiming, "Silence!" I truly do not know what overcame me. I do not believe I intended to perform magic; it was instinct. Instantaneously, Mrs. Bennet's voice vanished into thin air. She fanned herself vigorously with her lace handkerchief, mouth moving silently. Mrs. Goulding, likely unused to the quiet, seized her moment to dominate the conversation.

It had worked, and I did not even need my bloodstone! And it had only burned a little, or perhaps that was the punch. Silencing Lady Catherine may pose a greater challenge, yet muting Mrs. Bennet was no small thing. Who knew that all it took to shush Mrs. Bennet's prattle was a single word from me? Perhaps I should bottle my spell and sell it to Mr. Bennet. I would surely earn a small fortune from him alone!

I clapped a hand over my mouth, eyes wide, before the sheer absurdity of the situation set me off into peals of laughter once again. Miss Kitty, ever the embodiment of good spirits, joined in, though she was clearly puzzled by my sudden mirth.

Eventually, we made our way back to Mrs. Bennet's soundless side. Since I was forbidden to speak to gentlemen, Kitty, as I have now been invited to call her, acted the part of good friend. She introduced me to other young ladies in the room, and never left my side, even when Miss Lydia loudly called her over to speak to a new officer.

Later, Miss Lydia flounced past us, decrying the evening's entertainment—or lack thereof. "La, this party is dull! Play a reel, Mary," she demanded. Her slight sway told me she had also partaken of the punch. Fearful that I would be cast in the same light as she, I set my drink, or what remained of it, on the nearest table and vowed to eat something.

Soon after, Mary struck up a lively tune, and the floor was cleared for dancing. Despite my initial reservations about joining in—fueled in no small part by the room's gentle but persistent spinning—I found myself swept up in the excitement. Miss Kitty agreed to partner me for the first dance, given my prohibition from dancing with the officers.

As we danced, I caught a glimpse of Miss Elizabeth and Fitzwilliam. She dipped a curtsy to him, and on his face was something akin to a smile—a rare sight indeed. I realize now that I have little knowledge of what happened between my brother and his OTL this evening. I was far too caught up in my own merriment. I know they danced, as I have just written, and I am confident I saw him escort her to the punch bowl. And —oh heavens —I believe he walked her out to the balcony at some point in the evening! I am positive about it, for now that I think back, I remember them standing near the door, and then they were not.

Goodness! I must remember to decline punch the next time I am allowed out.

With Miss Elizabeth's help, I did, eventually, find my way to the food table. "Kitty, you should have warned Miss Darcy about the punch." Kitty giggled. Miss Elizabeth frowned at her, but it was not a very convincing one. "Young girls," she muttered.

She then placed her hand on my cheek, and I leaned into its warmth. "Dear girl. I should have known better than to let my sister guide you tonight. Sir William's punch is always too strong." Strangely, I felt much better when she removed her hand, but I followed instructions and partook of two small ham sandwiches and a variety of pickled vegetables. By the time my brother joined us, I was returned to my normal state of sobriety, though I will admit I still giggled profusely. I cannot help it; Miss Kitty is very funny.

If we do repeat this day, I sincerely hope Fitzwilliam allows me to attend the party again.

Chapter Nineteen

Early evening, 3 November 1811

Dear Diary,

As predicted, Fitzwilliam finally made it through the Lucas Lodge party. I awoke strangely hoping that we could try at least one more time to get it right. I will not even castigate myself as the most selfish of creatures. Last night's party was immensely entertaining, and I would have enjoyed another opportunity to attend —this time without the punch!

This morning, the Bingleys, Hursts, and our party attended church. Instead of heading to Meryton as we did last week, Mr. Bingley directed our drivers to Longbourn Village. Upon arrival, Fitzwilliam nervously wiped his hands on his trouser legs. I suspect they were a little sweaty. Mrs. Annesley and I endeavored to hide our amusement at his discomfort.

Though it was cold, we remained outside and chatted with our neighbors. The Bennets arrived after we did, a fact that brought visible delight to Mr. Bingley's and Fitzwilliam's faces. Although Kitty was desperate to gain my attention, I did spare a glance at her two eldest sisters. From the becoming smiles on each of their faces, it was clear they were also delighted with our presence at their family church.

"La, Miss Darcy, I did not expect to see you again so soon after last night's party. Though I should have guessed your brother would wish to be in Lizzy's company again, today. It would be a lark if they married. That would make us sisters and I could borrow all your fine clothes. That is what sisters do, you know." I am slowly coming to understand Miss Lydia better, but I was not prepared to explain why I did not wish to share my clothes with her. Besides, we are made completely differently, and I do not think my things would fit her at all. We are of a similar height, but where I am lithe, she is curvy. Let us just say, her cup runneth over, and that is exactly what she would do in the bodice of my gown.

Kitty led me aside, whispering, "Do not mind her. I do hope we become sisters someday, but not because I wish to wear your clothes, though you do dress impeccably. I would much prefer to have your company." My heart rose at this. Naturally, I have had friends, but they have dwindled as I have aged. Most of the girls I grew up with now see me as an opportunity to get closer to Fitzwilliam. But Kitty does not. She admitted last night that she is a little afraid of him. I assured her that there was no reason to fear my brother, but secretly I was delighted. A friend all my own, with no strings attached!

"Did you feel well this morning? I was afraid you might wake up with a megrim after drinking Sir William's punch."

I assured her of my fine health. "Oh, no, I had no complaints when I arose this morning. I did not drink a full glass of punch, though. You drank at least two. Did your head ache?"

She smiled. "I am certain it would have, if not for Lizzy. When we arrived home, she made a cup of tea and insisted I drink it all before going to bed. She has this lovely thing she does when I feel poorly. She cups my face so sweetly and before I know it, I feel much better. She is not as much fun as Lydia, but she is the most caring of all my sisters."

I thought about this comment as we entered the church. Miss Elizabeth had done the same for me last evening before she forced me to eat sandwiches. I felt rather cherished when she held her hand to my cheek. Perhaps Miss Elizabeth has a gift similar to mine? I have wondered before about her family's abilities, but I pushed the idea away. Her mother's origins in trade mean magical talents, usually reserved for the gentry, are unlikely in her lineage. It is possible she could have inherited it through her father's side, but given the state of his estate, I do not believe magic has been practiced by the Bennet family for many generations.

Kitty and I walked to the front of the church. She sat in the first pew along with the rest of her family. I sat directly behind her between Fitzwilliam and Mrs. Annesley. The clergyman at Longbourn church is younger and more spry than the man who led last week's sermon. He was also audible. This week, I could keep up and knew exactly when to bow my head and pray.

After the sermon was complete, our party met once again with the Bennets in the churchyard. "Miss Darcy, it is good to see you again this morning. Your brother informed me that you enjoyed yourself at last night's party." Miss Elizabeth approached alongside my brother. Miss Bingley clung possessively to his other arm.

"I did have a lovely time. Thank you for suggesting that I attend. I begin to suspect my brother takes your advice into consideration."

Eager to assert her presence, Miss Bingley chimed in, "Yes, dear Georgiana is very nearly grown. I, too, recommended Mr. Darcy allow her to attend the party. I am so glad he accepted my guidance."

Miss Elizabeth smiled in her direction. "I am certain your suggestions are highly valued by Mr. Darcy." The scowl Fitzwilliam had worn since Miss Bingley opened her mouth transformed into a half-smile at Miss Elizabeth's obvious jest. Only Miss Bingley would be foolish enough to assume my brother valued her opinions.

Shortly thereafter, our party disbanded. The Bennets, in their boisterous and noisy way, bid us a good day and set off toward their home. We watched until they reached a turn in the path and we could no longer see them. "Charles, as charming as this all is, I must ask that we attend the church in Meryton going forward." Miss Bingley did not explain her reasoning, though I think we all know what it was. The church in Meryton does not have a hazel-eyed Bennet who puts a smile on my brother's face.

∞∞∞

When we returned home, Miss Bingley called for tea. I regret not excusing myself before the maid's arrival, which would have spared me from enduring Miss Bingley's lengthy tirade against the Bennets, their low connections to trade, their lack of decorum, and of course, Miss Elizabeth's poor looks. Jane, she insisted, could not be reproached for her looks for "she is everything lovely." Her next younger sister, however, was maligned for being too dark, too disorderly, and too unmannerly. The more she slandered Miss Elizabeth, the more Fitzwilliam's mouth pinched, and his fingers tightened about his teacup. Fearing he might eventually shatter the delicate porcelain; I did the single thing that came to mind.

Before I go further, I must share that I immediately regretted my decision to use a spell I knew little about. I also regretted (though not immediately) that I used the spell at all. I digress, you will read about it soon enough. As I was saying, to stop Miss Bingley's incessant mockery of Miss Elizabeth, I cast a spell I discovered in *Magical Castings and Curses for New Witches*.

> *With a giggle and a grin, let the breezes begin,*
> *From the depths within, let the thunder spin.*
> *Release and vent, without any lament,*
> *In laughter's accent, an airy event.*

Then I subtly nodded my head in Miss Bingley's direction to

let the magic understand who the recipient of this spell should be. To my surprise it worked within a second, and might I add, a little too well.

"Pppbbbtt." That is my best guess at how to spell the sound that erupted from Miss Bingley's backside.

"Oh, dear," Mrs. Hurst gasped while Miss Bingley's face turned a frightening shade of red.

"Caroline, I believe —" Mr. Bingley began, only to have his words stopped short by the most unpleasant stench I have ever smelled. His hand clapped across his mouth and nose. Fitzwilliam hid his nose toward his left shoulder, no doubt trying to breathe in the spicy scent of his cologne. Mrs. Hurst fanned herself.

To add additional insult, the normally quiet Mr. Hurst chose that moment to speak. "There's more room out than in, I always say." Tears sprang forth in Miss Bingley's eyes.

"I am so sorry." Her voice trembled, and I had to force myself not to cry out my apologies for the embarrassing scene I had caused.

Miss Bingley excused herself and the rest of our party broke up soon after. The expression on Mrs. Annesley's face was grim, so, logically, I expected her to ring my ears over what I had done, but she only said, "I expected better of you. Come, we must check the north field to see how the land fairs. It rained last night, and we should have a better understanding of how your magic faired." Her gentle rebuke caused me to lament far more than I would have had she upbraided me. I vowed to undo my wrong, though I am still not sure how.

After changing into a riding habit, Mrs. Annesley and I quit the house and escaped into the crisp autumn air of Hertfordshire. When we arrived at the field, I could see that my spell had mostly held, and the land was largely well-drained. There was a section, in the northwest corner, however, that sat at least two inches under water. This helped me to better understand where I had gone wrong with my manipulations. Although I had shifted the borders of the field to prevent water from the neighboring estate flooding it, I had failed to level the field. The corner's flooding resulted from water from Mr. Bingley's field accumulating in the lowest area.

I searched my brain to remember the spell I used to shift and alter the land.

> *Soil and stone, now rearrange,*
> *Craft a trench, bring forth the change.*

"No, Miss Darcy. Today I want you to channel your power through your bloodstone to fix the flooding."

I pulled the necklace from the bodice of my gown and held the two small stones in my hand. "Which word do I use?" So far, my practice had included Silence, Halt, and Banish, none of which fit this particular task.

"Try 'Rise.' When you say it, I want you to use your hand to show the land where to move. Hold the image in your mind's eye and do not drop your hand until the earth has submitted to your will. This area is significantly lower than the rest of the field. It may take longer than expected to force it to comply. Resist the urge to quit." With her last words, she patted my shoulder in a show of support, and then walked ten paces away so that I could force my will upon the ground.

In my other sessions, I had practiced on small objects. I silenced a bird (and Mrs. Bennet, by accident), I banished books and foot stools from the room where we sat, and I halted barn cats in their paths and leaves from falling. I had not yet altered the state of anything as large as a field. I worried the pain would be too much. If stopping a cat from chasing a mouse ignited such intense internal fire, how painful would reshaping this field be?

I wiped my sweaty palms upon my gown. "Now, Miss Darcy."

Drat, I could not even go at my own pace. Mrs. Annesley would have me rush headlong into the breach.

After three deep breaths, I commanded, "Rise!" In my right hand, I held the two bloodstones. My left hand lifted, palm up, to chest height, conducting the land to lift as I wished.

The heat in my stomach and chest began before the earth had moved so much as a fraction. My right hand clutched at the stones and my left began to shake. "Hold, Miss Darcy. Remain strong."

I breathed deeply again, willing myself to see this through. A burning sensation surged through me, pulsating painfully like a drumbeat across my organs. Ba-BUM. Ba- BUM. Ba- BUM. In case you are wondering, the Bums are far worse than the Bas.

"Rise," I commanded again. By this point, I am confident I had begun to sweat profusely. I threw my will into the project. If a simple magic spell was going to cause me to require an additional bath, I would very well see it through, thank you very much.

The ground began to tremble, ever so slightly, beneath our feet. "It is working. Hold tight." I did as I was directed, though my hand shook from pain and exhaustion.

I had expected the earth to lift gradually, but that is not at all how it happened. Just as I thought I would pass out from fatigue, the land gave a great groan and – SNAP – all was set to rights. I collapsed to the ground, my shoulders rounded in relief and exhaustion.

"You did it!" Mrs. Annesley was more animated than I had ever seen her. "I should not admit this, but I did not believe you were strong enough to complete this task just yet. I had braced myself to return to this field daily for at least a week."

I offered her a relieved smile. "I am grateful to have this done. I do not want to do this ever again."

"I agree. Tomorrow, we move on to something more

difficult." I fell back upon the ground at this and stared up at the sky. The hawk I spelled only a few days ago flew overhead. I believe I will find a way to sneak away from Mrs. Annesley tomorrow. Surely one day of living vicariously through a hawk will be acceptable after today's difficult work.

Chapter Twenty

Early morning, 4 November 1811

Dear Diary,

   Last night, sleep eluded me entirely. So poor was my slumber that I found myself poring over witchcraft tomes well before the clock struck two. It is my own fault. I had the cheek to smite Miss Bingley with a bout of gas yesterday afternoon. Once my ill-humor with the lady faded, her embarrassment became almost palpable to me. I cannot even begin to imagine my own mortification should such a thing happen to me. After several hours of consideration, I concluded that her forgetting the incident entirely was the only solution. And so, I have spent less than five hours studying the various books Mrs. Annesley has supplied in search of a forgetting spell.

   It was no easy feat to find an appropriate verse. I discovered at least ten capable of erasing a person's memory, yet most would obliterate a full day or even weeks from one's mind. I only need to take approximately ten minutes, perhaps five, from Miss Bingley. I am convinced the following incantation will suffice, though it necessitates physical contact with her, a matter requiring utmost delicacy. Ordinarily, a touch invites one to scrutinize the actions (and words) of the toucher more closely. And the last thing I need is Miss Bingley to scrutinize anything about me, most especially my witchy ways.

By mystic might and silent plea,
Intention clear, let my will be.
Let what's forgotten find its peace,

In silence deep, all recollections cease.

I will return later to share the results. Miss Bingley often makes her way to the breakfast room at least an hour after I have finished, so I will need to remain there for longer than is my desire. The disruption of my morning routine lies squarely at my own feet. As my father always said, I made my bed and now I must lie in it.

∞∞∞

Evening

Much has happened since I last wrote this morning. Awake for the lion's share of the night, I resolved to eat breakfast at an unusually early hour. And because I did not wish to wait several hours for Miss Bingley to make her way downstairs, I did the next best thing and visited her in her room. Employing the thin guise of desiring to borrow her perfume delighted her immensely, albeit at the cost of a burgeoning headache for me. It did allow me to find a clever way to deal with the physical touch the spell required. I sprayed a little perfume on my wrist, and then held up my wrist for her to smell. While she held my wrist, I quietly whispered the incantation under my breath. I believe it was successful, for when I originally asked if she would take breakfast downstairs, she had insisted that she would not leave her room for the entire day. After, however, she indicated that she was rather hungry and planned to break her fast earlier than normal.

I did not see Miss Bingley again until tea this afternoon. She was her normally supercilious self, and for a moment I regretted spelling her with the gift of forgetfulness. But only for a moment. My dear niece, be forewarned, when you gain your powers, you will begin to feel very bold. I would have never considered inducing someone to break wind a year ago, but I have grown drunk with power and have used it ill. Still, if you someday have a brother, I give you permission to use that spell on him.

At tea, Miss Bingley and Mrs. Hurst informed me that the men would dine with the officers tonight. I had not seen Fitzwilliam since breakfast and was unaware of his plans for the evening.

"We should host our own entertainment tonight," Miss Bingley drawled.

Mrs. Hurst's eyes did not light up at the suggestion, but mine did. "Who will you invite? I should like to see the Bennet sisters."

At my proposal, Miss Bingley's nose wrinkled in disdain. "I cannot invite all the Bennets, of course, but I believe Miss Jane Bennet will add a pleasant addition to our evening. I will write her now."

I was appalled, though not enough to cast a spell on the offensive woman. "It would be poor manners to invite only Miss Bennet. You should at least offer an invitation to Miss Elizabeth as well." Miss Bingley opened her mouth to respond but thought better of it. Instead, she gave a curt nod and continued her path toward the writing desk.

I foolishly believed she had taken my advice, until some few hours later, Miss Bennet showed up soaking from the rain, and decidedly alone.

"Miss Bennet! Pray, enter and be swift about it. You are drenched through and through." I ushered the bedraggled lady into the house and asked a footman to hurry to find some toweling and blankets. "Where is Miss Elizabeth? You have not left her in the rain, I hope."

She answered through chattering teeth, "I was invited, but Lizzy was not." I directed a piercing glare at Miss Bingley, who had until that moment stood stupidly alongside us.

After a few moments of awkward silence, Miss Bingley spoke. "I must have forgotten to add her to the invitation. Please know your sister is always invited to attend Netherfield with you." I barely checked the impulse to roll my eyes.

The three of us ladies went into the salon where a large fire was built. Mrs. Hurst stood to greet Miss Bennet from where she sat embroidering a baby gown. I really must ask Mrs. Annesley to help me find a way to cheer the lady.

"Dear me," she cried, "You are as wet as rain, Miss Bennet." I was pleased to see her usher our guest to the fire where she stood for three-quarters an hour to warm herself and dry her clothes.

Mrs. Annesley joined us when the supper gong rang and our group of five made our way into the dining hall. Outside the storm raged. The cold drizzle that had accompanied Miss Bennet's journey to Netherfield Park had intensified into a vehement downpour. "Miss Bennet, I do not believe you will make it home this evening," Mrs. Hurst suggested. "The storm is too intense; even our carriage would scarcely offer safe passage. Caroline, you must have a room made up for Miss Bennet."

Miss Bingley's mouth tightened, but conscious of her role as hostess she agreed. "I will place her near Mrs. Annesley. She will be in no one's way in that part of the house." Such was the lady's audacity! She is as arrogant as Lady Catherine, perhaps more so. At least my aunt has magical powers and her title to rely on.

Though I seethed on behalf of Mrs. Annesley and Miss Bennet, neither of those ladies showed any affront to the cutting remark. In truth, Miss Bennet seemed rather pleased. I suspect she looks forward to seeing Mr. Bingley in the morning. Yet, that arrangement will not suffice, for during supper, a scheme took shape in my mind. If Miss Bennet must remain at Netherfield, then I must have Miss Elizabeth in attendance, as well.

Forgive me, niece, for this next part. It is rather diabolical on my behalf. I gave Miss Bennet a cold. Nothing serious, a mere trifle really. And in truth, it was not even real. It will only feel like a cold to her. Tomorrow she will awaken with what she believes is a stuffy nose, a sore throat, and an achy head. None of that will be true, of course. I will argue that she should not be removed to Longbourn until she feels better, and I will ensure the apothecary agrees with me. If I know Miss Elizabeth at all, I suspect we will see her very early in the day. I do not believe she will be able to resist the urge to check on her sister. This will allow Miss Elizabeth and Fitzwilliam to find many hours in each other's company.

Oh, I almost forgot! I also practiced magic today. The persistent rain and Miss Bennet's unforeseen visit foiled my plans to sneak away and enchant the hawk. I so wished to fly again. Instead, Mrs. Annesley and I continued with the three words I have been working on. My endurance has grown; I sustained my magical exercises for a span nearing an hour and a half. Then I endured a lesson on the tiresome and intricate spell known as "End." If you have not already guessed, this spell will end a day upon command. Unfortunately, I cannot go around ending days. I must wait until Fitzwilliam makes a muck of things again (or until I am invited to another party) to practice it.

Chapter Twenty-one

Evening, 5 November 1811

Dear Diary,

 This has been a very busy day, and since I expect we will live it all again, I will practice my End spell as soon as I finish this entry. Let me explain myself.

 Early this morning, I made my way to check on Miss Bennet. The efficacy of my spell exceeded expectations, rendering Miss Bennet quite miserable with her 'cold'. Mrs. Annesley and I double-checked the words I used, and we cannot explain why Miss Bennet is so wretched. We concluded the only plausible explanation was the lady's apparent lack of fortitude. While I refrain from labeling her a valetudinarian, her resilience has indeed left much to be desired. I do not believe this cold would have kept Miss Elizabeth at Netherfield, but I am happy to report it has worked on Miss Bennet.

 I assisted Miss Bennet in writing to her family to inform them of her illness. I included a note suggesting Mr. Jones, the apothecary, be called upon, though I had no intention of summoning him. Mrs. Annesley charmed everyone in the house to believe he had come, and so they all now believe he has ordered Miss Bennet abed for several days.

 Before breakfast, Mrs. Annesley and I placed a mirror spell on a single object in every public room in the house. Then we added a notification spell. A diminutive mirror within my pocket is enchanted to vibrate, alerting me whenever Fitzwilliam and Miss Elizabeth share a room. If I am able, I will be able to witness their interactions. Mrs. Annesley expressly forbade the enchantment of objects in private quarters, yet I elected to strategically interpret her counsel. I did not spell any objects in private rooms, with one exception. While Miss Bennet was resting, I charmed a shepherdess figurine that stands on her dresser. If Miss Elizabeth discusses my brother, I will know about it. I believe she begins to love him, but I want to hear her say it.

As expected, Miss Elizabeth arrived during breakfast. Unlike most days, we all sat together. I had just finished the last of my tea (I still cannot properly decipher what my leaves foretold), and was rising to leave, when Miss Elizabeth entered. She had walked to Netherfield Park from Longbourn, a full three miles, across wet fields and through mud. Her hems were soggy and dirty, and her hair had escaped her pins. I thought she appeared very pretty with her cheeks flushed from exertion and her nose pinked from the cold.

Fitzwilliam and Mr. Bingley stood to greet her while Mr. Hurst continued with his meal. I waited for my brother to properly greet the lady, but it was Mr. Bingley who spoke. "Miss Elizabeth, how lovely to see you. Are you here to see your sister?"

Miss Elizabeth curtsied to the room. "I am, sir. I received her note this morning and insisted on seeing for myself how she fares." It was just as I expected. Miss Elizabeth, who ensures Kitty never awakens ill after a night of indulgence, would not allow her favorite sister to suffer from a cold. Though I am still not certain of Miss Elizabeth's abilities, I spelled Miss Bennet to continue believing she is ill, even if Miss Elizabeth attempts to cure her.

"I will take you to your sister," I volunteered. My brother, who had previously stood in stony silence, nodded his appreciation to me.

We had no sooner turned the corner from the breakfast

room than Miss Bingley shrilled, "Did you see her hems? They were caked in at least six inches of mud. Her roots in trade are increasingly evident. No gently born lady would arrive at a neighbor's home in such disarray." My hands balled into fists. Had the lady abandoned all semblance of decorum? She could have at least allowed us to exit the hall before she began her diatribe.

"I did not notice her hems, for I was too busy appreciating her care for her sister," Mr. Bingley retorted. I endeavored to hasten Miss Elizabeth's departure, though she dawdled, as any curious person would do.

"You are too easy to please, Charles. What do you think, Mr. Darcy? Surely you would not wish to see Georgiana in such disorder! And I am certain you would not condone her walking three miles across the fields, with no chaperone to protect her."

I held my breath, fearful of what my brother would say. "Certainly not." His deep baritone rang strong through the hall. His agreement with Miss Bingley was unfortunate, yet, mercifully, he offered no further comment, and I was free to hurry Miss Elizabeth along.

Once I settled Miss Elizabeth with Miss Bennet, I found Mrs. Annesley for practice. I had a strong desire to complete all my duties so I would be free to spy upon my brother and Miss Elizabeth.

We continued to practice as we have these past days. My endurance remained strong for approximately ninety minutes before I was forced to quit. Observing my eagerness to conclude the session, Mrs. Annesley graciously released me. "Enjoy the remainder of your day, Miss Darcy. Should you be absent at tea, I shall surmise you are engrossed with the enchanted mirror you now carry." She knows me too well, it seems.

As it turns out, I did not miss tea, but I was late. Miss Bennet had slept the entire morning but awoke just before teatime. I know this because my mirror, which sat upon my nightstand, began to vibrate repeatedly. Bzzzz. Bzzzzz. Bzzzzz. It did not stop until I picked it up and looked into the glass. The view from the figurine was hazy, but I could hear the voices clearly.

"You need not stay with me all day, Lizzy. You should attend tea with the others. I know you are anxious to spend time with Mr. Darcy." Aha! She is anxious to spend time with my brother! It was not the declaration of love I hoped for, but it was confirmation of their growing regard.

"I am perfectly well where I am. I do not wish to leave you while you are so ill. I cannot understand why you have not improved. Your head still aches, you say?"

"Oh, yes," Miss Bennet croaked. "My head pounds, and my throat is very, very sore." She has, I begin to think, a bit of the dramatic about her. I suspect she got it from her mother's side.

"I will call for another cup of willow bark tea." Miss Elizabeth stood and rang the bell.

"Thank you, Lizzy. But after, you must go down and join Mr. and Miss Darcy for tea." When her sister did not respond, Miss Bennet added, "Has something occurred between you and Mr. Darcy? Do you not wish to see him?"

"Jane, I do not know what to think of him." Miss Elizabeth began to pace the room. "When we are alone, I feel as though I am the only person he thinks of. He makes me feel special and beautiful. But there are other times when I suspect he is ashamed of me."

So, you can see why tonight is a perfect time to practice the 'End' spell. It is very likely today will reset anyway. Hopefully tomorrow, Fitzwilliam will refrain from disparaging his OTL, or will at least wait until she has left the hall.

I will not bore you with the rest of the day. Miss Elizabeth partook of supper with us, yet abstained from joining us for cards. Miss Bingley spared no effort in maligning her for an alleged absence of grace, beauty, style, or manners. I regretted taking her memory, but I did not curse her with another bout of gas. I am growing, it seems.

Fitzwilliam spent the evening in a sulk, pointedly refusing to be Miss Bingley's partner at the card table. When we were certain Miss Elizabeth would not return, Mrs. Annesley and I excused ourselves for the evening. I heard Fitzwilliam's footsteps pass my door not long after.

Chapter Twenty-two

Evening, 5 November 1811 (again)

Dear Diary,

Allow me to begin with a triumphant note: It worked! The 'End' spell started a new day as soon as I gave the command. If it was not immediate, then it certainly felt that way. As soon as I said the word it seemed the day had begun again. Abruptly and without any forewarning, I found myself awakening in my bed, while La Roche prepared the same gown I wore yesterday.

Considering the day's repetition, it is clear Fitzwilliam's unfortunate words yesterday morning were the culprit, else we would have started a new day. I confirmed this with Mrs. Annesley since I am still quite unsure of most of the rules of witchery.

This morning, I harbored concerns that Fitzwilliam might not grasp the cause of the replicated day. Unlike his obvious cut at the assembly, yesterday's insult was subtler. And, as far as he knows, unheard by Miss Elizabeth. I sat through breakfast, awaiting Miss Elizabeth's entrance, completely unsure of how to help my brother recognize where he had gone astray. I have been directed to copy my words and actions on previous days when the days duplicate themselves, but I chose to ignore that advice today. How else was I to guide Fitzwilliam?

"I surmise Miss Elizabeth shall visit to inquire after Miss Bennet today," I remarked with studied nonchalance. "They are very close, you know."

"I do not know how she will arrive," said Miss Bingley. "The roads will be too muddy for carriage travel."

"She will walk." At Miss Bingley's widened eyes, my brother continued. "She is fond of walking, and since the roads are currently impassable, that is her only option."

The cards had been played exactly as I had wished. "It is three miles from Netherfield to Longbourn. If she does walk as you suspect, she will arrive muddy and wet." I stopped and looked around the table at the gathered party. "We must not make her feel ashamed if my predictions are true. It is better to have a sister who cares more for the health of her family than for the state of her hems." Fitzwilliam nodded his agreement. I hoped it was enough.

Instead of rising to leave, I waited patiently for Miss Elizabeth to walk in. Curiously, her arrival was somewhat delayed compared to yesterday, but I thought little of it at the time. I requested another cup of tea and had nearly completed it when she finally arrived.

Once again, Fitzwilliam and Mr. Bingley stood to greet her while Mr. Hurst continued his meal. Unlike yesterday, however, it was my brother who greeted her. "Miss Elizabeth." He bowed before continuing. "Would you like to see your sister?"

Miss Elizabeth smiled and curtsied her greeting. "Yes, sir, I was distressed to learn Jane was ill. I could not bear staying at Longbourn while she suffered here without any family to comfort her."

"I will take you to see her." My brother looked at me and asked, "Georgiana, would you like to join us?" I agreed and followed them into the hall. Fitzwilliam offered his left arm to Miss Elizabeth and his right to me.

"Have you ever encountered the sensation of reliving a day?" Miss Elizabeth smiled up at my brother and then at me.

"Of late, that sensation has been frequent," said Fitzwilliam. My heart raced, and I failed to join the conversation.

"It is peculiar, but there's a persistent notion that all this happened before. I would have arrived at least twenty minutes earlier today, but…"

"But what?" I asked.

A slight pursing of Miss Elizabeth's lips preceded her response. "I stepped in a puddle on the way here, and I was struck by the most profound memory of having already done just that thing, in the same location, while on my way to Netherfield. It is ridiculous, I know, but I feel like I could lead us directly to Jane, though I have no way of knowing where her room is." And to my dismay, she did just that. Fitzwilliam suggested she should "test her instincts" or some such nonsense. She did not hesitate at any of the intersections of halls and found Miss Bennet on the first attempt.

After leaving her with her sister, I made my way to Mrs. Annesley to discuss what had happened. "Peculiar," she murmured under her breath. "The spell to end a day must interfere with the repetition of days spell. Did anyone else mention a similar feeling?"

"If they did, no one said as such to me." She nodded.

"It appears Miss Elizabeth possesses a trace of innate talent. There is no other explanation I can think of." I had suspected as much but did not give it much credence given her mother's heritage and the condition of their estate.

"Might you assess her capabilities, as you once did with me?" I asked.

Mrs. Annesley shook her head in the negative. "There is too little time. We must prepare for your aunt's arrival. Such matters must be prioritized." I do not see why Mrs. Annesley cannot do both of those things, but she was adamant. I vowed to test her myself.

∞∞∞

Just before tea, the mirror in my pocket sprang to life with an expected vibration. Once again, Miss Bennet urged her sister to attend tea so she could visit with my brother, and once again, Miss Elizabeth declined.

"Miss Bennet inquired with concern, "Has there been an incident with Mr. Darcy? Is his company no longer desirable to you?" Miss Bennet asked.

Miss Elizabeth's voice softened, "My desire to see him is strong, indeed. Yet, my priority lies in tending to your needs. Besides, I would not want to intrude upon the family. I am, after all, an uninvited guest."

Nonsense, I thought.

"Nonsense," Miss Bennet said. "Miss Bingley and Mrs. Hurst have been everything kind to me. They will act the same toward you. Besides, you must keep Miss Darcy company. I do not believe she cares much for their company. Your presence may offer her a boon."

Miss Elizabeth contemplated the suggestion but, in the end, chose to stay with her sister. "I shall remain steadfast by your side until you have shown at least a semblance of improvement. If Miss Bingley is kind enough to let me stay with you, I will consider taking tea with everyone tomorrow."

I was disappointed in her choice. Acting with haste, I set out to coerce Miss Bingley to invite Miss Elizabeth to stay. I considered spelling her, but decided against it as she has absorbed a lot of magic these past few days. I do not know if magic is bad for non-witches, but just in case I chose to use my persuasive abilities instead. While we took tea, I suggested she invite Miss Elizabeth to remain, but it was Mr. Bingley's insistence that induced her to act.

After tea, Mrs. Annesley and I donned our riding habits and rode to the north field for another look at the flooding. In stark contrast to our previous visit, the land now lay impeccably drained. "Well done!" Mrs. Annesley's praise was met with my gratified smile. "If you promise to read your book on sigils for at least an hour today, I will give you the remainder of the afternoon off from magic practice." I readily agreed. Together we rode back to the house. When we arrived, Mrs. Annesley made her way inside, but I moved to the small garden near the kitchen entrance. I was not able to find a hawk, but I did cast a riding spell on a cardinal and went on a delightful flight across the county.

∞∞∞

My slumber was abruptly interrupted by the persistent buzzing of my mirror against the wooden surface of my bedside table! I anticipated this evening would unfold similarly to the last, but I was wrong. As we did last night, Mrs. Annesley and I excused ourselves from the parlor. I needed to give an hour of reading to the sigils book, and I wanted to record today's events in my diary. I expected Fitzwilliam to follow me to bed, as he had done previously, but I never heard his footsteps.

After completing my entry (or so I thought), I called for La Roche, changed into my nightrail and dressing gown, and slipped under the covers. The day's busyness had me teetering on the brink of sleep until the relentless buzzing of my mirror jerked me awake. I picked up the offending object and looked into the glass. To my astonishment, Miss Elizabeth was in the drawing room with Fitzwilliam! Regrettably, everyone else was there, too.

In her haughty way, Miss Bingley said, "Miss Eliza Bennet despises cards. She is a great reader and has no pleasure in anything else."

"I beg to differ," countered my brother with confidence. "I believe Miss Elizabeth enjoys walking, dancing, and laughing very much. Are there other things you enjoy, ma'am?" From the vantage point of the vase, I could just see him smile across the room at her.

"Mr. Darcy, you have captured many of my favorite activities, though I must admit, I also enjoy games, visiting the theater, and listening to music." Then she walked towards a table and inspected something which I could not see.

"Alas, Miss Elizabeth, my offerings are limited, as I am hardly a voracious reader. My collection is modest at best." Mr. Bingley's words rang clear, but I could not see him in the frame of my mirror.

Miss Elizabeth assured him his collection of books, I learned from context, would suit her fine. She selected one and turned to sit. During this time, Fitzwilliam had moved from the chair he had previously occupied to the settee. A flush crept over Miss Elizabeth's cheeks, but she boldly chose a seat close to him. After this, I know little of what was said. Their words were too quiet to hear through the mirror. I do know, however, that they sat with their heads together for a half-hour before Miss Elizabeth excused herself to return to her sister. Nary one page had been read!

The sound of Fitzwilliam's footsteps just echoed past my chamber signals it is time for me to return to bed.

Chapter Twenty-three

Evening, 6 November 1811

Dear Diary,

Today unfolded in a disappointing manner, both in regard to my magic lessons and my brother's amorous pursuits. I shall start with the magic since that was my greatest dissatisfaction today.

I honored my commitment and devoted a full hour yesterday to the study of sigils. Today, Mrs. Annesley suggested I put my newfound knowledge to use. As you know, my sigils of Andromalius and Bael are meticulously etched onto a piece of bloodstone. I have used the bloodstone quite a lot to increase my power, but I have not yet summoned the deities represented by the symbols on the stones. Today, I was tasked with charging the sigils and gaining the attention of at least one deity. It did not go as planned.

"Take the sigil between your two hands and place it to your mouth." I did as I was instructed. "Now blow gently on the sigil and allow your mind to focus only on the power held within the symbol."

I tried to do as I was instructed, but it was difficult. Once more, I was ensnared by dreams of the crimson dragon. Instead of chasing me it was waging a fierce battle with another of its kind. The second was smaller and more delicate with violet scales upon its back, and a butter yellow belly. Lady Catherine's dragon growled and snapped at the other. She took flight and barreled toward the smaller one until she grew close enough to stick out her legs and rip at the violet one's neck with her long, sharp talons.

The smaller dragon screamed in agony. From my dream state, I silently urged the dragon to fight back, but it did not. It was too afraid, too weak, too tired. The crimson beast slashed again, this time at the smaller dragon's wings. I awoke then, crying.

I have thought of the violet dragon all day. I feel like I was supposed to learn something from the dream, but what? I already knew to be wary of Lady Catherine. Was the dream a message she would try to kill me? I had suspected that days ago. But why would she take my wings?

"Now, summon your deity." Mrs. Annesley's words interrupted my thoughts.

Ceasing my breath upon the symbol, I proceeded as my reading had instructed. "Bael, I ask you to come forward. Hear my plea." Mrs. Annesley and I waited but nothing occurred.

Finally, she asked, "Did you focus your mind only on the power of the sigil?" I shook my head no. She nodded. "As I expected. Try again."

Again, I placed the stone between my hands and breathed onto the sigil. This time I tried my best to focus on the powers Bael held. My mind whirled around his ability to grant invisibility and to speak all languages, but these thoughts did not hold. Once again, the violet dragon swam in and out of my mind's eye. And once again, my summons went unanswered.

Mrs. Annesley sighed. "You are tired, I think." I said nothing. What more could be said? Of late, fatigue is my constant companion. The type of magic I now study is beyond my scope and is very difficult for me. "We will attempt this tomorrow. To prepare, I want you to write a letter to Bael. You will feel like you know him better if you attempt correspondence. Tomorrow you will be successful."

And so that is how I spent my afternoon. Well, it is not entirely how I spent my afternoon, but it was a good portion of it. It is appallingly difficult to write a letter to a deity one has never met. How does one even go about crafting the greeting? I eventually opted for, "Dearest Mr. Bael, though we are strangers, I aspire to become better acquainted with you." My entire attempt was ridiculous, and I doubt Mrs. Annesley's advice will work, but tomorrow will tell the tale.

After I finished corresponding with my sigil god, I wrote a letter to Richard asking him to come to Netherfield Park if he can get away from London. I hope he can. I would like him to get to know Miss Elizabeth. His support will mean a lot to Fitzwilliam, and my uncle.

Have I mentioned my uncle before? In case I have not, Uncle Malcolm Fitzwilliam is the Earl of Matlock. Both Fitzwilliam and I have become very close to Uncle since my father's death. Uncle is not as stodgy as many nobles, but he is still an earl. I suspect he will love Miss Elizabeth once he comes to know her, but he will initially object to her situation. That is where Richard will come in handy. He will convince his father that Miss Elizabeth is perfect for Fitzwilliam. In addition, I could use the extra power that will come from having a loved one close at hand.

Miss Elizabeth made a fleeting appearance to join us for tea. Unfortunately, the gentlemen had ridden to Meryton during that time. My brother's absence encouraged Miss Bingley to behave better than she normally does in Miss Elizabeth's presence. This, however, did not translate to exemplary conduct on her part. She seized no less than two occasions to ridicule Miss Elizabeth's attire and another to denounce her roots in trade. Miss Elizabeth handled it well, though, responding with a hint of sweet humor. The temptation to conjure another gas bubble for the lady was strong, but I chose to follow Miss Elizabeth's lead.

∞∞∞

Thanks to my discreet interventions, Miss Bennet believed herself somewhat improved today, permitting her sister to grace our drawing-room gathering after supper. Fitzwilliam sat at the writing desk penning a letter, exactly the opposite of what he should have done to woo his OTL. Miss Elizabeth took up some needlework. I attempted to look busy, so I spelled my needle to also work at embroidery while I paid close attention to the maneuverings around me.

"You write uncommonly fast," Miss Bingley remarked. My brother rolled his eyes, and I heard Miss Elizabeth quietly snigger. "How many letters you must have occasion to write in the course of a year!" Miss Bingley continued in this manner for a while longer. I hardly noticed her chatter until Lady Catherine's name was mentioned.

"Who do you write to, tonight?" Miss Bingley asked.

"My Aunt Catherine. I received a letter from her today and I am obliged to send my return." A flutter seized my heart.

"Lady Catherine wrote to you, Fitzwilliam?" I desperately hoped he did not hear the dread in my voice.

"It is Aunt Catherine, Georgie. And yes, she did write. She included a page for you." He felt in his breast pocket and pulled out a single sheet of paper. I willed myself to stand and fetch it.

On shaky legs, I crossed the parlor and took the letter from his hands. "Thank you," I said, though I hardly meant it. I opened the paper. It said:

Georgiana,

I bid you come to Rosings Park. It is time you learned of your heritage.

Lady Catherine de Bourgh

That is all. No warm greetings. No inquiries about my health. Only a summons. I harbored a steadfast belief that Fitzwilliam would spare me from attending her, however, and I returned to my seat with more confidence than I had shown when I left it.

"Why do you not call your aunt by her title, Miss Darcy?" Miss Elizabeth had placed her embroidery on her lap and was giving me all her attention.

"She is afraid of our aunt," my brother answered.

"That is not true," I countered. It was a lie. I have grown quite afraid of Lady Catherine this past week. "I choose not to call her aunt as she has never acted as such."

With deliberate care, Fitzwilliam set his pen aside, then turned to chide me. That is the thing with Fitzwilliam, he never does a thing until he has everything prepared to do so. "Georgie, that was eleven years ago. You must let it go."

"I will not, and I cannot believe you ask it of me," I argued.

"What is it she did, Miss Darcy?"

I squinted my eyes at Fitzwilliam before answering Miss Elizabeth's question. "Fitzwilliam gave me a lovely music box for my fifth birthday. I was perhaps too young for such a gift, but I loved it dearly.

"A few months later, Lady Catherine and her daughter visited Pemberley. My cousin, Anne, is five years older than I am. She wanted to play with my music box, but I did not wish her to. She always broke my things, and that was the most precious thing I owned at the time.

"I refused to let her play it. Nurse was on my side, and safeguarded it atop a shelf, beyond our reach. That afternoon, Anne told Lady Catherine that I would not let her see it. I was forbidden from taking tea that day and sent upstairs with my nurse. Later, Lady Catherine escorted Anne upstairs and demanded the nurse let her daughter play the music box.

Nurse handed the box to Anne with a warning to be careful, but it was all for naught. No sooner was the box in Anne's hands, she dropped it, causing it to shatter into a thousand pieces."

"Oh, that must have been a terrible disappointment for you, Miss Darcy. I am sorry your favorite keepsake was ruined." Miss Elizabeth placed a sympathetic hand on mine.

"I am sorry, too," Miss Bingley chimed in, peering over my brother's shoulder. "I am sure your father or brother replaced it for you."

"I did not want a replacement, Miss Bingley. I wanted the one I had been given." I turned back to Miss Elizabeth to finish my story. "I began to cry and became very angry. I shouted, 'You always ruin everything!'. Lady Catherine, unaccustomed as she was to her daughter being chastised, became very angry with me. She grabbed my hair and jerked my head back so that I was forced to look her in the eyes. Then she slapped me hard across the cheek and told me to act like a proper lady and that my mother would be ashamed of me had she lived."

"Oh, dear," Miss Elizabeth gasped. "I think I comprehend your reluctance to call her aunt."

"Georgiana, why is this the first time I have heard of this?" Fitzwilliam's nostrils flared in anger, but I knew I was not its target.

"You were away at school when it happened, and you have never asked for details since." I did not intend to hurt my brother, but I knew I had when his eyes dropped to his lap.

Mr. Bingley, who had previously sat quietly with his oldest sister, chose that moment to comment. "I declare, Miss Darcy, it sounds as if your temper is remarkably like your brother's."

"What do you mean, sir?" Miss Elizabeth asked. "Do you have a temper, Mr. Darcy?"

"I believe Bingley is referring to my unwillingness to forgive when I am badly crossed. My good opinion, once lost, is lost forever."

Miss Elizabeth's eyes widened at this. "Oh, my, that is quite a statement."

I realized to whom Fitzwilliam referred. "Do not be alarmed, Miss Elizabeth. My brother is slow to temper. If someone has lost his regard, they must have done something terrible. Fitzwilliam is not one to anger without cause."

"Exactly, Eliza. Mr. Darcy would never act inappropriately. He is a man to be emulated in all things." Her nose in the air, Miss Bingley then turned toward the pianoforte. "Let us have some music. The conversation has grown too morose for my taste."

So saying, she sat down and began to play. She commenced with Mozart, but upon observing her audience's scant attention, Miss Bingley shifted to a lively reel. Soon after, Fitzwilliam approached the couch we shared and asked Miss Elizabeth for a dance. She smiled prettily up at him and allowed him to help her to her feet.

"Good idea, Darcy," Mr. Bingley cheerily said. "I would be obliged if you would partner me, Miss Darcy." I agreed readily and allowed him to lead me to the make-shift dance floor. The space was too small for our party, and the four of us laughed heartily as we bumped into each other. When the song ended, Miss Bingley played another. Fitzwilliam asked Mrs. Hurst to dance, and she responded with a gentle smile. Mr. Bingley partnered Miss Elizabeth, and I went to stand near the instrument.

When the song ended, Mrs. Hurst dismissed me. "Come back, Miss Darcy. I will take over so Caroline might have a chance at the fun." I did as I was told and was immediately swept up next to my brother's side. A very disappointed Miss Bingley stood across from her own brother, and Mr. Hurst, roused from his sleep, stood up to dance with Miss Elizabeth.

We did not dance another after that, much to Miss Bingley's dismay. After the dancing ended, Miss Elizabeth excused herself to check on her sister. Soon after, Fitzwilliam followed her. Anticipating a secret meeting, I made up an excuse about needing a book and made my way to the library. Unfortunately, my mirror never buzzed. After ten minutes of waiting, I made my way back to the drawing room, thanked my hosts for the fun evening, and made my way to my room.

∞ ∞ ∞

I was nearing sleep when I remembered something important. Mrs. Annesley and I never spelled an object in the halls. My brother likely met with Miss Elizabeth, and I missed it! I will rise early and complete the task as I should have done days ago.

Chapter Twenty-four

Mid-day, 8 November 1811

Dear Diary,

Forgive my absence yesterday. I had planned to write last evening, but the day got away from me and did not go quite as planned. After breakfast, Mrs. Annesley and I secluded ourselves in the sitting room for magic practice.

"Hold the sigil and breathe your life force into it, Miss Darcy, while focusing on the deity." I did as I was told. Today, I chose to summon Andromalius instead of Bael. Despite a restless night, I was resolute in my determination to succeed.

"Great deity Andromalius, heed my call and speak with me." A few moments of silence passed before a fine mist materialized before us.

"You called, Georgiana?" I snapped my head toward the mist. I am unsure what I expected. Perhaps I thought the mist would turn into a person, or a dragon, or even a goldfish. Instead, it remained steadfast to its foggy haze.

"Yes, sir," I replied. "I called for your help. My aunt, Lady Catherine de Bourgh, has threatened me, and I must be prepared. I seek your guidance. Your advice would be much appreciated."

"You should speak to Bael. Bael has the answer you currently seek." The mist floated higher as it spoke.

"But I failed to contact Bael yesterday despite trying."

"Try again, Georgiana. I am not the one you want. I will be here for you later, but now you need Bael." Much to my dismay, the mist began to disappear. I reached out to stop it, but it was no use. I would have better luck forcing a good personality onto Miss Bingley than grabbing mist.

As the mist disappeared, so did all my energy. Without warning, I crumpled to the ground. "Miss Darcy!" Mrs. Annesley cried. "Let me help you." She assisted me to my feet and helped me move to a nearby chair. "Stay here," she commanded. "I will order you tea." I remained where I was as she ordered tea. I must have dozed because before I knew it, the tea was set down in front of me.

"This tea is sweeter than usual. Resist using magic; you need the sugar." I nodded my head and took a cautious sip. It was sickly sweet, far worse than I had imagined, but with each sip I felt my energy returning.

"Thank you," I said. "If you will allow me a few moments to recover, we will try again with Bael."

"Absolutely not, Miss Darcy. No more magic today. What you are doing at present is far beyond the scope of what you are expected to accomplish. This advanced practice is for those with years of study. Contacting a deity on your second attempt is extraordinary. You must allow your energy to return. In a day or two we will try again."

I nodded my head in agreement. "Then what should we do for the remainder of the morning? We studied for less than an hour today. Should I try something small?"

"Indeed, you should not," she rejoined. "No more energy will be spent on magic today. You must get your reserves back up. This has been very depleting for you, and I will not see you harmed further." Once Mrs. Annesley deemed my strength sufficient, she escorted me to my bedroom and helped me onto the bed.

"Rest here until teatime. I will see you then." She placed a motherly hand on my forehead and checked for fever. Satisfied that my temperature was as it should be, she left.

I tried to sleep, really, I did. I had slept very little the days prior and I welcomed the idea of a nice nap. But it would not come. I was bored, frustrated, and desirous of learning what it is that Bael is supposed to tell me. After half an hour in bed, I decided I had enough energy left to contact the deity. To others this may seem like a trifling amount of time, but for those with powers and a fierce desire it is a very long period of time.

Niece, if you are reading this, I very much warn you against such stupid acts as I have done. Against Mrs. Annesley's advice, I called Bael forward. Unlike the day prior, it worked this time.

Like Andromalius, a mist formed before me. Unlike him, a small, wrinkled man emerged from it. He wore an ancient style white gown that flowed to his ankles, and on his feet were roughly made leather sandals. A bright purple aura shone around his person.

"You summoned me, Georgiana?" I had expected a strong voice like that of Andromalius, but Bael spoke in soft tones.

"Yes, sir," I responded. "Andromalius said that I need to speak with you first. He insisted that it is your guidance I most need at present."

Bael smiled gently. "And what is that you need from me, Georgiana?"

I swallowed down my apprehension. Truthfully, I had no idea what I needed. "My aunt, Lady Catherine de Bourgh has threatened me in some way. I was warned by an ancestor." He nodded his permission for me to continue. "I am to prepare for her coming, but I am new to this. I do not understand what it is that I should do."

Bael clasped his hands in front of him. "And you have taken my sigil as your guiding force to help protect you against your aunt?"

"Yes. I studied the book very carefully, and yours was one that most stood out to me. Your powers might be useful in my journey toward whatever is to come. Andromalius insisted that you would guide me —that you would help me understand what it is that I need most from you."

He smiled again. "Yes, I can see that now. Which power is it that you most believe I should grant you." It was on the tip of my tongue to suggest invisibility, but he answered for me. "You require my assistance in speaking and interpreting other languages." I nodded my head, but it was not convincing. "I can see you had not considered this, my dear. It is fine, everyone wants to be invisible, but what you require most is to understand a new language."

I was dreadfully confused by this suggestion. "Which language? Will you grant me the ability to interpret all languages?"

He shook his head this time, "No, you must tell me."

I thought for a moment, but nothing came to me. Then I remembered Fitzwilliam's insistence that I spend more time on my French lessons. But how would a romance language assist me in battling Lady Catherine? Still, I could think of no better option. Even if it was the wrong solution, I could always summon Bael back to me. Until then, I might finally learn how to roll my Rs in the French manner. And it would please Fitzwilliam. "I supposed I should have greater facility with French, sir."

The old man raised his right eyebrow in a manner that was eerily similar to Miss Elizabeth. "French," he repeated.

I nodded. "Yes, French, unless you have a different suggestion."

"My job is not to suggest things to you. It is to grant you the powers you have requested. He reached out and placed a hand upon my shoulder. "So be it. You can now speak and interpret French perfectly. I hope this is the solution you are looking for. If it is not, come back to me when you have a better idea of what it is you need." And with that, the man transformed back into mist before dissolving before my eyes.

As soon as the mist was gone, my muscles went limp. Once again, I fell to the floor in a heap. Unlike the first time, this experience made my head swim. My arms shook as I attempted to crawl back to my bed and a bout of nausea roiled in my gut. I had done too much magic and had made myself quite ill. I sat on the floor and took several deep breaths in an attempt to control my queasiness.

The mirror, which I had previously placed on my bedside table, began to buzz. Fitzwilliam and Miss Elizabeth were together somewhere in the house. Summoning all my energy, I crawled to the side of the bed and took my mirror in my hand. It was approaching teatime and the Bennet ladies had come for a visit.

Mrs. Bennet's shrill voice rang out through the glass, "Yes, I must see my dear sweet Jane, though I am certain she has been very well taken care of."

Mr. Bingley commented from outside my viewpoint. "My sisters and Miss Elizabeth have seen to Miss Bennet's every comfort."

Mrs. Bennet nodded sagely. "Just as I expected. You are too good, Mr. Bingley, to allow my sweet girl to suffer so. I told Mr. Bennet yesterday that Jane was likely receiving better care here at Netherfield than she would have at Longbourn. Not that I am one to ignore my daughters. No, sir, I must tell you, I am quite the slave to their well-being."

"Mama, will you have a seat by me?" Miss Elizabeth sat on the same couch we had shared the previous evening. From the red on her cheeks, I deduced she greatly wished her mother to stop speaking.

"I will sit here, Lizzy, thank you. Mr. Darcy, you should take the seat next to Lizzy. She looks quite pretty today, do you think?" That did it. As I watched my brother's face heat, I knew I must overcome my illness and make my way downstairs. During the best of circumstances, Fitzwilliam is not good at drawing room conversation. This was not the best of circumstances and I could not afford to repeat the day.

Mustering all of my energy, I stood and straightened my gown. It took several minutes, but I was finally able to guide myself down the stairwell, holding very tightly to the banister for fear of falling, and into the parlor with our guests. Mrs. Bennet hastened to stand upon my entrance, and cried, "Miss Darcy, my poor girl. I believe you have caught Jane's cold." Then she rushed to my side.

I do not remember the next part. I was told that I had fallen, and Mrs. Bennet attempted to catch me. She was unsuccessful and we both tumbled to the floor, but she was able to break my fall. I have grown very fond of the lady and her kindness to me has cemented my sentiments.

Fitzwilliam rushed to my side and scooped me into his arms. Mrs. Bennet, undaunted by our fall, followed him closely as he rushed up the stairs toward my room. She and Mrs. Annesley must have competed for who could command the situation.

"Mrs. Nichols, bring cold cloths and broth," Mrs. Bennet directed.

"Mrs. Nichols, we require willow bark tea with an excess of sugar," Mrs. Annesley demanded.

In the end, I drank none of them because I did not wake again until this morning. Although the circumstances are unfortunate, it was the first full night of sleep I have had since Samhain. Unfortunately, I missed an entire afternoon and evening, and I gained the wrath of Mrs. Annesley in the process. Rightly so, I suppose, for she has since informed me that it was not only stupid of me to ignore her directive, it was dangerous, as well. I could have permanently damaged my body and lost my powers altogether.

To her surprise, I made my apologies in perfect French. Though she seemed pleased with my newfound facility with the language, she has not forgiven me. I have been commanded to rest for no less than three days.

"But how will I prepare for Lady Catherine? I cannot waste another day. She could come at any moment" My laments fell on deaf ears.

"You heard me. There will be no more magic, of any sort, for at least three days. You will not even go as far as to temper Miss Bingley's bitter tea."

I reluctantly agreed. "Yes, ma'am."

I do intend to follow her advice this time and have done so thus far. I have now gone more than three hours without magical interference, a waking time record! My single regret is not enchanting the hallways. Who knows how often my brother and Miss Elizabeth have met unnoticed by me?

Chapter Twenty-five

Evening, 8 November 1811

Dear Diary,

Mr. Bingley plans to host a ball!

Tonight, I felt well enough to join everyone for supper. Miss Bennet, who is also feeling better, joined us after supper. Due to my illness, I have not been able to reinstate her spell.

"I say, Miss Bennet, I would like to throw a ball to thank all my neighbors for their solicitous welcome, but I will not set a date until I know you are fully healed from your illness." Miss Bennet blushed and replied softly to Mr. Bingley, her words inaudible from where I sat.

"Oh, Charles, you can't be serious. A ball here? Who from London would come?" Miss Bingley's nose wrinkled at the idea.

"A ball is a fine way to thank your neighbors, Bingley. If your friends in London do not attend, you will still have many good people in attendance." Everyone stared at my brother's declaration. Fitzwilliam never enjoys balls, so his approval stunned us all.

Mr. Bingley was the first to recover his wits. "You see, Caroline, even Darcy agrees that I should hold a ball. You cannot disagree with him, can you?"

"Of course not," she snapped.

Miss Elizabeth turned to my brother. "Mr. Darcy, do you think Miss Darcy might join the ball? I would gladly sit with her, even if it requires me to forego dancing." I held my breath at this unexpected turn of events.

Fitzwilliam glanced at Miss Elizabeth, then at me. "Do you wish to attend, Georgiana?" I swear he had the gall to ask me that!

"Oh yes, I wish it above all things!"

Fitzwilliam nodded. "Then I believe we can arrange it, though I do not think you should stay for the entire evening."

If I had felt better, I would have jumped from my seat and hugged him. However, my energy still flagged so I said, "Thank you, brother. This makes me very happy."

He smiled at me then and reached across Miss Elizabeth to pat my hand. "You must behave, and you cannot dance with anyone who has not yet received my permission. I agreed readily. He sat back and looked again at Miss Elizabeth. "However, I do not think it necessary for you to sit with my sister during the ball. Mrs. Annesley will accompany her."

"Oh, of course. I meant I would be happy to spend time with your sister." Miss Elizabeth looked embarrassed.

"Think nothing of it, Miss Elizabeth. It is that I wish you to dance with me and you cannot do that if you are sitting with my sister."

Fitzwilliam Darcy, you sly boots! I did not know my brother had it in him to be so debonair, like a line from one of my novels! Miss Elizabeth's pleased expression showed she agreed.

"I would be happy to reserve you a dance, sir. Which one would you like?"

His voice dropped, but I could hear. "I would like two dances, please. The first and supper."

If Miss Elizabeth's heart did not take a tumble at my brother's declaration, then it is made of stone. Even my own heart missed a beat, and he is naught but my brother!

"What is it you are speaking of, Miss Eliza?" Miss Bingley sauntered over to us.

"We were discussing the ball. Mr. Darcy has agreed to let Miss Darcy attend, though probably for no more than the first half."

A look of horror crossed Miss Bingley's face. "Miss Darcy, pray do not get the wrong impression of what a ball should be. I shall do everything in my power to ensure quality musicians and decorations, but there is nothing I can do about the quality of our guests."

As you can imagine, the happiness of our trio diminished, even if only slightly, after that comment. Soon, Miss Bennet excused herself for bed and Miss Elizabeth escorted her. I followed suit and said my goodbyes to the room. Mrs. Annesley, who hovered annoyingly for the entirety of the day, hurried to my side, and helped me to stand.

And now, as you have likely guessed, I sit in my room finishing today's entry. Soon I will be off to sleep with pleasant dreams of waltzing with a handsome stranger. Dear niece, I so look forward to sharing stories with you about my first ball, and someday helping you prepare for your own!

Chapter Twenty-six

Afternoon, 9 November 1811

Dear Diary,

Tedious. That is how I would describe my first five hours of the day. I was not made for lying abed, but that is exactly what I was commanded to do. Mrs. Annesley and my brother agreed I should do nothing but write in my journal or read until teatime, at which point I am to be reevaluated. All this despite feeling perfectly well! Well, maybe not perfectly, but better than yesterday. I admit, I am still tired, and there are dark circles under my eyes that were not there before my foray into unsupervised magic.

When Fitzwilliam excused himself from my room, I turned to Mrs. Annesley and begged her to allow me to perform even the slightest spell, but she could not be swayed. I am surprised how hard it is to give up magic, even for a few days. It is much like an opium addiction, I suppose, though with a lot less lethargy and itching.

I feel so alive when casting a spell, and lying here, twiddling my thumbs while reading a dull book, is very disappointing. This is certainly not how I expected my time in Hertfordshire to go, especially after learning my brother would meet his OTL here.

Mrs. Annesley has gone but promised to check on me before tea. If my color is good and I have no fever, she will allow me to attend tea. I had to promise to stay in bed for the rest of the morning. Ahh! How am I to cope with this monotony?

Happily, my mirror buzzed as soon as Mrs. Annesley shut the door. Miss Elizabeth and Fitzwilliam were squirreled away somewhere in the house together, though not in a hallway as I have yet to magic any items thereabouts.

Bored out of my mind, I grabbed the mirror at the first buzz. The screen showed an image of the library. I had spelled a book to provide the best view of the room. My brother stood with his back to me looking at Miss Elizabeth, who remained very near the door.

"Good morning, Miss Elizabeth. Can I help you find something? Bingley's library Is not the best, but there are a few good options here. If nothing suits your fancy, I also have my own personal collection in my room. I am more than happy to share with you."

A lovely smile formed on Miss Elizabeth's face. "Thank you, sir. I have finished the one I borrowed the other day. It is time for something new, preferably short. Jane is on the mend, and I plan to write my mother for permission to use the carriage. I believe my sister can manage the short trip to Longbourn."

"Disappointing," said Fitzwilliam before realizing his gaff. "I mean, it is disappointing that you are leaving so soon. I am pleased your sister is feeling better. I am sad to lose your presence at Netherfield. I have enjoyed having you in the house very much."

Miss Elizabeth smiled brightly. "Thank you, sir." She moved toward the bookshelves, causing me to lose sight of her within my frame, but Fitzwilliam remained. Watching her, he wore an enthralled look on his face.

"Miss Elizabeth, there is something I wish to discuss with you." He tugged nervously at his neck cloth.

"Yes," she responded from across the room.

Fitzwilliam gestured to the chair near him. "If you would?" Miss Elizabeth sat as directed, and my brother chose the seat to her left. "Elizabeth —Miss Elizabeth, I have grown very fond of you. So fond, I am considering you as my future partner." Once again, he pulled his collar and swallowed.

"Do you have something to ask me, Mr. Darcy?" Miss Elizabeth smiled wistfully at my brother.

"Yes, of course. That is —would you consider a courtship with me?"

A courtship? I had been certain he would ask for her hand! "How devastatingly boring of you, Fitzwilliam," I grumbled. I had imagined he asked for a courtship last week at Lucas Lodge. Now I wonder if their venture onto the balcony had another purpose, which I will not consider here. Repugnant!

Miss Elizabeth angled closer to my brother and whispered, "Yes. Yes." Because of their rearranged angles, I could not see all of Miss Elizabeth's face, but I could easily see the blissful smile that adorned my brother's. A full two dimples!

"You have made me very happy, Elizabeth. May I ride to Longbourn and speak with your father?" He held her hand to his lips and kissed it. It was so romantic I nearly swooned. It is a good thing I was already lying down in this awful prison of quilts and goose feathers.

"I beg you, do not," she answered. My worries about my mandatory bedrest evaporated. Surely, she had not changed her mind so already.

She continued. "My mother, you see. Once she learns of our courtship, she will be unbearable."

Fitzwilliam nodded his head with understanding. "I see."

"If it is acceptable to you, I would like a little more time to get to know you. . . privately, without my mother's interference, that is."

My brother cupped his hands on her face and whispered. "That would please me very much, Miss Elizabeth." And then he leaned closer and kissed her. On the lips!

To say I was shocked would be a vast understatement. There have been many times during this courtship that I have wished he would kiss her. And other times when I thought he would, only to be disappointed. But wishing and seeing are two completely different beasts. I could feel my paltry breakfast attempt to leave my stomach and exit upwards. Unless you have not yet inferred, it is not a good thing to see your brother kiss his OTL. It did not matter that I was very happy for him, or that I like her very much. Plainly put, it was disgusting.

I slapped my hand over the glass so that I would not be forced to witness more of this encounter, but I could still hear the smacking noises they made and, once again, I had to fight my stomach from expelling my toast. Out of frustration, I flipped over my mirror and extinguished the connection with the library.

It took me a while to recover, but once I did, I realized how ecstatic I am. A courtship is almost as good as an engagement. Practically no one calls off a courtship. This is most assuredly a sign that Fitzwilliam has secured his OTL and no days need repeat going forward. Huzzah!

When they marry, I will have a sister. No, wait —I will have FIVE sisters! Of course, I will love Miss Elizabeth the most, as she will be Fitzwilliam's wife and the mother to my nieces (greetings again, darling) and nephews. My favorite, however, will undoubtedly be Kitty. We cemented our friendship many days ago at Lucas Lodge, and I look forward to being with her again once I can leave my prison.

I have just looked at the time and see it is a quarter to one. I am quite exhausted from the small amount of activity I have conducted today, if you can call writing in one's diary an activity. I will conclude the rest of the day's events later, that is, if anything noteworthy occurs.

∞∞∞

Evening

I arrived at the sitting room just before teatime. Miss Elizabeth was seated at the writing desk, but all the others, with the exception of Miss Bennet, were gathered around the coffee table.

"Good afternoon, Miss Darcy." Miss Elizabeth greeted me from across the room. "You look lovely today. Much better and more well-rested than last evening. I am pleased to see you on the mend."

I walked over. "I do feel better, though still a little tired." I stood beside her as she wrote, glancing over her head at my brother. When he looked my way, I raised my eyebrow in question, having nearly perfected Miss Elizabeth's expression.

Fitzwilliam's eyes widened. "Is something amiss?"

"Is all well with you?" I dramatically glanced from him to Miss Elizabeth and back. His face held a secret smile, but he said nothing more. Annoying man! There was little point in pestering him, as I lacked the energy, and he would not reveal anything in front of others.

I turned my attention back to Miss Elizabeth. "What are you writing?"

She continued writing as she answered. "I am finishing a request to my mother. Jane is feeling much better, and I believe it is time for us to return to Longbourn. I have asked her to send the carriage this afternoon or tomorrow morning."

She then turned to Miss Bingley. "Your hospitality has been much appreciated, Miss Bingley, but we should not burden you any longer."

Miss Bingley preened at what she interpreted as a

compliment to her hosting skills. "Oh, Eliza, you and Jane are very welcome to stay, though I do suspect you would both be more comfortable in your own home."

Miss Elizabeth shared a secret look with my brother before answering, "Yes, I am sure that is the case."

Miss Bingley may be pleased to see the end of the Bennet residence at Netherfield, but I was not yet willing to let them go. Yes, I have secured my wish, or nearly so. My brother and Miss Elizabeth are now in a secret courtship, but I begrudged Miss Bingley the satisfaction of a Bennet reprieve.

It has been several days since I have upset Miss Bingley, and only seconds since she has last annoyed me. For that reason, alone, Miss Elizabeth needed to stay a few additional days.

I strategically changed the subject. "You have lovely handwriting," I said.

She rolled her eyes playfully at me. "My handwriting is tolerable, I suppose, but I find I must write quickly to keep from losing my train of thought. I do not often blot my papers, but I do often slant my lines."

Mr. Bingley interrupted with comments concerning his own penmanship which allowed me time to take advantage of the distraction. I placed my finger on the paper and whispered:

> *By this script, I cast the lot,*
> *Yes and yea shall be forgot.*
> *Upon this note, through mystic art,*
> *Only nay from thy pen shall part.*

Though it was a simple spell that did not require crystals, bloodstones, or sigils, it drained me severely. I held onto the desk to regain my composure and prevent myself from falling clumsily to the floor.

I had just managed to stand on my own when Mrs. Annesley arrived. "Miss Darcy, here you are. You were to wait for me before coming down to tea."

"I apologize. I was anxious to join the party and failed to remember."

She nodded her head. "As long as you continue to rest and do as I suggest, all will be well." Unfortunately, the look she gave me belied her words and I began to fear that she knew what I had done. I suspect she can see magic, there can be no other possible answer. Nevertheless, she has not yet confronted me.

Before supper, Miss Eilzabeth's note was returned demanding the Bennet sisters stay at least two more evenings. My soon-to-be sister was disappointed, but I was well pleased. My spell had worked, and the outcome had been just as expected. Miss Bingley was visibly dissatisfied with the news. Huzzah! (That is two in one day. Quite good, I think.)

Aside from that, very little else happened this evening. I did attend the sitting room after dinner, but I was so exhausted that I did not stay more than half an hour. Even Miss Bennet, who looked quite frail tonight, stayed longer than me.

Mrs. Annesley confirmed she spelled Miss Bennet to believe she had relapsed to allow Fitzwilliam additional time with his OTL. "Has your brother made any progress with Miss Bennet?"

I only smiled and said, "I think so, but I am not certain." It would not do for Mrs. Annesley to know the truth, for if she did, she would spell Miss Bennet well again and the sisters would leave. And since I very much enjoyed irking Miss Bingley, I do not want that to happen.

Chapter Twenty-seven

Evening, 10 November 1811

Dear Diary,

It is day three of my involuntary imprisonment. If Fitzwilliam and Mrs. Annesley do not let me out of this house soon, I will place a hex on the pair of them! Today is Sunday, but I was not even allowed the pleasure of going to church. Mrs. Annesley stayed back with me, as did Miss Elizabeth with Miss Bennet. The remainder of our household attended service at Longbourn church.

While everyone was away, I used my time to reread my entries. I discovered I had failed to ask Mrs. Annesley about Mrs. Hurst's sadness, so I rectified that mistake as soon as I could.

"I know I cannot perform magic at present, but I would be very obliged if you were to assist Mrs. Hurst with her despondency. I begin to suspect she wishes for a child. Surely there is some magical potion or spell that could assist her?"

Mrs. Annesley shook her head. "I am sorry, Miss Darcy, but it would be improper for me to interfere in such a way. There are, of course, spells and tinctures that would assist her, but she must ask for them herself. For me to act on her behalf would be unethical."

Drat! Mrs. Annesley and her ethics strike again. I was not to be deterred, however. "If you cannot help her to be more fecund, then perhaps you could assist her in being happier. I feel ever so sorry for her. She rarely smiles, you know." Why would she, with such a sister, I secretly added.

Mrs. Annesley looked doubtful. "I do not wish to make her feel happiness when none exists, but there is something I could possibly do. If you will excuse me, Miss Darcy, I need to check one of my books." Mrs. Annesley excused herself and I was left alone in my room, once again. I had vowed earlier to remain abed until teatime and I was obliged to keep my promise, though I truly wished to visit with Miss Elizabeth and her sister. In the privacy of Miss Bennet's room, I am sure I would have successfully convinced Miss Elizabeth to tell me about her courtship. Instead, I willed myself to sleep for a few hours until our party returned.

Soon enough, I found myself downstairs preparing for tea. The Bennet sisters had not yet arrived, so Miss Bingley took the opportunity to disparage their continued presence at Netherfield. "I declare, we will never rid ourselves of these Bennets. They are a blight upon this estate!"

"They will leave tomorrow. Miss Elizabeth has requested the use of my carriage if her father's is not sent first."

Miss Bingley was greatly affronted by my brother's words. "Your carriage! But surely Miss Elizabeth did not have the temerity to request it of you. I tell you, she will stop at nothing to put herself in your way, Mr. Darcy. You must remain wary of her." I smiled at this. I had seen the results of Fitzwilliam's wariness with my own eyes when they met yesterday in the library.

Soon the sisters joined us, and we took refreshments. I would like to say we enjoyed refreshments, but that was hardly the case. Miss Bingley remained, well, Miss Bingley. Mrs. Hurst remained gloomy. Mr. Hurst remained a glutton. My brother remained silent. And Mr. Bingley and Miss Bennet remained oblivious to all of us. The three people with any conversation at all were Miss Elizabeth, Mrs. Annesley, and me.

"Miss Darcy, if it is acceptable to you and Mrs. Annesley, I would like to join you this afternoon. I just read a collection of poems by Mary Russell Mitford that I believe you might find enjoyable." I readily agreed to Miss Elizabeth's suggestion and Mrs. Annesley nodded her head in approval. Anything would be better than lying abed for the remainder of the day —even poetry!

After tea, Mrs. Annesley escorted me to my room and left me to continue her research on reducing Mrs. Hurst's doldrums. I anxiously awaited Miss Elizabeth's arrival, but she did not come. To be fair, we did not arrange a time for her arrival, so she was not at fault. I wished for some company.

I grew bored with waiting and began to concoct ideas in my head about what might have delayed her. It would not have been her sister. The spells upon her had been lifted and any lethargy she still felt was made in her own mind. Perhaps Fitzwilliam was the cause of her prolonged absence. I felt confident this was the case, but as my mirror had not buzzed, I knew they were not concealed in any of the public rooms.

The halls! If they were not in a room with a spelled object, then I would surely find them hiding behind a tapestry or suit of armor. I gathered my energy and made my way into the hallway. They were not on my wing. Likely I would find them in a more public part of the house, or in Miss Bennet's wing. I made my way to that side of the house, careful to make little noise. I did not wish to alert Mrs. Annesley, after all. To my frustration they were not there, either. Nor were they to be found outside the library, near the dining hall, outside the nursery, near the billiards room, or anywhere else that I could manage to go. Dejected, I made my way to the entry hall, and who do you think I saw? That was a rhetorical question, of course. I saw Miss Elizabeth entering with Fitzwilliam. Her cheeks were pink from the cool air and Fitzwilliam's hair was attractively tousled. Both wore large grins. And it did not go unnoticed that Miss Elizabeth's lips were rather swollen. Do you not think it an odd time of year for a bee sting? Ha!

Miss Elizabeth followed me upstairs and excused herself at the intersection of our halls to get her book. In the end, we did not even discuss poetry. She told me stories of her childhood and I reciprocated by sharing stories of Fitzwilliam in his youth. I know they are courting and very near to being engaged, but I must still do my part to keep them together. She especially liked it when I told her about my dog, Crocus, and the merry chase she took Fitzwilliam on, through muddy fields, a stream, and into the pig enclosure.

Chapter Twenty-eight

Afternoon, 11 November 1811

Dear Diary,

Unfortunately, the Misses Bennet left us today. When Miss Elizabeth arrived at breakfast with her sister in tow, I knew we would not host them another night. And since I was banned from using magic for at least one additional day, I could not spell Miss Bennet into thinking she was ill again.

The sisters entered the room just as I was demonstrating my newly perfected French to my brother. "Ah, Mademoiselle Darcy, vous parlez très bien français. Avez-vous suivi des cours depuis de nombreuses années?" My brother turned adoring eyes toward Miss Elizabeth.

"You speak French?" He practically drooled at this new evidence of her perfection. I tried to hide my snigger. She had just spoken with a flawless accent. Of course she speaks French.

Miss Elizabeth hid her amusement at my brother's amazement better than I did, though she did raise her right eyebrow in challenge. "Did I not just speak to your sister in the language, sir?"

Miss Bennet, while filling her plate, addressed my brother. "Lizzy is a polyglot, like our father. They both speak seven languages."

"Seven languages!" Fitzwilliam and I exclaimed together.

"Pray, tell me, which languages do you speak?" I inquired.

"English and French, of course. I also speak and read German, Italian, and Latin. I read Greek, though my pronunciation is terrible, according to my father. And I speak Fae." Mrs. Annesley, who sat next to me, tensed at this admission.

"Fae? As in fairy language? I thought you were not supposed to speak to fairies."

Fitzwilliam scoffed. "Do not be silly, Georgiana. Fairies are imaginary. Miss Elizabeth was only teasing us."

Miss Elizabeth shrugged. "I cannot say if the language is real, but my father and I can speak it to each other, and we each understand one another perfectly."

I waited until she had filled her plate and was seated before I restarted the conversation. "You must tell me more about the Fae language. Is it difficult? Can I learn it? Why does your father know it? Do you use it with anyone else?"

Unfortunately, I bombarded her with questions just as she took a bite of toast, prompting her sister to answer. "All our sisters speak a little. Father's grandmother taught him, and she learned from her own grandmother. When we walk in the woods, we always say, 'Aghch glyl magana, Fae.' It means, 'I come in peace, fairies.' It is a silly thing, but we loved it as girls and have done it ever since. Our father also repeats the phrase and has done so since he was a boy."

"Fascinating," I replied. "Have you ever —" Mrs. Annesley placed a hand on mine which I correctly interpreted as, 'Hush, girl.' I shall tell you why in a moment, but the story started in chronological order, and I shall continue it in that way.

Fitzwilliam, oblivious to everyone else in the room, began speaking with Miss Elizabeth in Italian. Miss Elizabeth may be a polyglot, but I am not, and I had no idea what they were saying. Soon after, our party was joined by Mr. Bingley and a very cranky Miss Bingley. She was not pleased to see Miss

Elizabeth so cozily situated with my brother, and she was even more frustrated to realize they were speaking in Italian, a language with which she also has little facility.

Mrs. Annesley encouraged me to finish my tea, and we soon found ourselves ensconced in my sitting room. "Why were you so anxious to leave the breakfast table?" I asked.

"I sometimes forget that you are new to witchcraft, Miss Darcy. Forgive me." She took a deep breath and explained, "If Miss Elizabeth can speak Fae, she is powerfully protected. Fairies are generally nasty creatures, but they occasionally take a liking to certain families. If generations of Bennets have spoken the language, they have a powerful bond with the fairies." She paced the room, more agitated than I had ever seen her.

"But that is a good thing, is it not? I like the idea of Miss Elizabeth being protected."

"It is a good thing, indeed. I do not know Lady Catherine's plans, but the fairies may be of some use to us in helping to protect Miss Elizabeth. Perhaps, we can convince them to assist in keeping you and your brother safe, as well. Unfortunately, I do not know how to speak to them. And they are known to be so very disagreeable."

I jumped from my seat in excitement. "Bael! He will grant me the ability to speak Fae. I can communicate with them." I took the bloodstone that held his sigil into my hands and placed it in front of my mouth.

"Stop!" Mrs. Annesley grabbed the sigil from me. "You are still too weak, but your idea has merit. You must regain your strength for another day or two. If I deem it safe for you, you may attempt to contact your deity then." I was disappointed with this command, but I agreed. I have no wish to ever be so weakened again.

I sat back down, and Mrs. Annesley continued to pace. After

a few moments of silence, I asked, "Does this mean Miss Elizabeth and the other Bennet sisters have magical abilities?"

"A little," she answered. "Of the ladies I have tested, Miss Elizabeth has the most ability, but it is still very weak compared to mine, and exceptionally weak compared to your own."

"I thought so. I believe she has a talent for healing. She has a marvelous way of cupping a person's face, and then they feel much better. Her sister Kitty mentioned it to me, although I experienced it myself at…" I had said too much. Mrs. Annesley stopped her pacing and looked at me.

"When did she heal you? Was it after your magical episode?"

I shook my head in the negative. "No, it was —ahem — at Lucas Lodge. The evening you stayed home." Mrs. Annesley gave a curt nod of her head but did not ask any further questions. Thank heavens for that. I had no desire to share how little attention I had paid to what I was drinking.

∞∞∞

Mrs. Annesley forbade me from practicing magic, but I was expected to read and learn. Today I started *Connecting with Your Spirit Guide: A Witch's Handbook for Increasing Your Power*. Yawn! Mrs. Annesley is convinced there is something in the book to help me defend against Lady Catherine, so I will give it my full attention. Books of spells are considerably more interesting, though.

After several hours of reading, we attended teatime — our last with the Bennet sisters. Little occurred during our refreshments. Soon after, a carriage arrived to collect the sisters. Fitzwilliam, Mr. Bingley, and I were all a little duller in their absence, but Miss Bingley bloomed as soon as their coachman flicked his reins. They had no sooner made the first turn out of the drive when she began to disparage them.

"Thank heavens. I did not believe they would ever leave!" She took hold of my brother's arm — an arm he did not offer, I must add. "I am so happy their father did his duty and sent his own carriage to retrieve them. I was appalled to learn Miss Elizabeth had requested use of yours. She is a sly one, I must admit." Fitzwilliam's lips tightened, but he did not respond.

Mrs. Hurst surprised me, however. "Caroline, Miss Bennet and Miss Elizabeth were exemplary guests. You should not disparage them so." I turned to look at her and noticed a pleasant look on her face, if not quite a smile. I glanced toward Mrs. Annesley in question. She slyly winked at me. If my exhaustion had not been rescinded from days past, I would have stumbled!

As it turned out, Miss Bingley did stumble. Whether from inattention or surprise at her sister's reprimand, I do not know, but she fell forward up the stairs. I do not like the lady, but I did not wish to see her grievously injured. Without thinking, I put out my hand and said, "Halt!" And she did, just long enough for Fitzwilliam to steady her. Mrs. Annesley widened her eyes at my slip. Magic should not be performed in front of humans, if possible.

"Oh dear, I was so upset at the idea of the Bennets manipulating you, Mr. Darcy, that I lost my footing. Thank you for keeping me safe." Miss Bingley batted her eyes in a sickening manner. I vow to never do such a thing in my life, no matter how rich or handsome the man is.

"It was nothing. I am glad you are unharmed." Fitzwilliam deposited the lady in the entryway and strategically removed her arm from his.

"Believe me, Mr. Darcy, Eliza Bennet is cunning. You must promise to be on the alert in her presence. I would not wish her to compromise you." Too late, I thought.

Fitzwilliam, much to my disappointment, did not defend his lady. He offered nothing more than a slight bow and then excused himself. How very ungallant of him, do you not think? I very nearly cursed him with a spot on his nose, as I had done to Miss Bingley last week. If I had not been so tired from my unexpected use of magic, I would have done so.

Chapter Twenty-nine

Afternoon, 12 November 1811

Dear Diary,

With the Misses Bennet no longer in residence, Netherfield has become very boring. Both Fitzwilliam and Mr. Bingley have been very anxious today, but they resisted the urge to ride to Longbourn to see their respective ladies. Miss Bingley insisted they stay away to "allow poor Miss Bennet a chance to fully recuperate." Both men reluctantly agreed, though I notice my brother had sneaked away early this morning, perhaps to meet Miss Elizabeth. Given his morose attitude, I suspect his efforts were unsuccessful.

Mrs. Annesley continued to deny me the opportunity to practice magic today. She insists I must rest an additional day given my slip yesterday with the Halt spell. She would be very angry to know I have practiced other magic during my recuperation. Despite the lack of magical practice, my education continued. I was forced to continue reading the book about spirit guides. I can confirm it does not get any more interesting.

After struggling for an hour to stay focused, I put away my book and went to the library to find something more interesting. Fitzwilliam sat in the same chair he occupied that day with Miss Elizabeth.

"Oh, good morning," I greeted.

"Good morning, Georgiana. May I help you find a book?"

"No, thank you. I am just looking." I walked to the sparsely filled shelves and began my perusal. It took little time to realize that what I wanted was not available to me. I huffed in frustration, which caught Fitzwilliam's attention.

"Bingley's library is rather paltry. What is it you are looking for?"

Taking the seat next to him, I answered, "Miss Elizabeth's conversation about fairies piqued my curiosity. I hoped to find a book about them. I know little, except that our servants at Pemberley fear them."

My brother smiled. "Yes, the myths around fairies remain strong in Derbyshire. They are said to be fearsome creatures."

I leaned forward, intrigued. "What makes them so terrifying? They are but small creatures made of light."

"Those are fairytale stories, Georgie," he answered. "The stories told at home are more and more chilling." I nodded for him to continue.

"Where to begin?" He placed his finger on his chin. "I suppose I should start with names. It is said you must never share your name with a fairy. If you do, you give them power over yourself."

"What kind of power?" I asked.

"Complete power. If you tell a fairy your name, it will have the ability to make you do anything it wishes."

Fitzwilliam seemed amused by the legend, but I was frightened. He is ignorant of magical ways, but the more I learn, the more I believe is possible. "What if they overhear my name? Will they gain power over me then?" I thought of all the times I had been addressed as Miss Darcy or Georgiana while in the out of doors. Am I now a target?

"No, no, Georgie. You must tell them your name. Never introduce yourself to a fairy." He smiled, again, enjoying what he believed to be the silliness of our conversation.

"What else do you know?"

"Not much, actually. Fairies are said to manipulate objects. They can break, fix, or steal things as they wish. They are also said to move things with their minds. Every time Mrs. Reynolds misplaces something, she insists the fairies moved it." I smiled at Fitzwilliam's story. I, too, had heard Mrs. Reynolds complain about fairies a time or two.

Our conversation soon drifted to other topics. Fitzwilliam was impressed with my newfound proficiency in French and began a discussion about music in that language. I easily maintained my part of the dialogue while my mind churned with thoughts of fairy magic.

"Here you are, Darcy." Mr. Bingley practically floated into the room with excitement. "Oh, and Miss Darcy." He bowed to me.

"What has you so animated, Bingley?"

"What think you of the twenty-sixth of November?" he asked.

Fitzwilliam and I shared a look of confusion before my brother answered. "I think it the day after the twenty-fifth of November."

Mr. Bingley sat across from us. "For the ball, man. Do you think it a fine day for a ball?"

I giggled. "I do not believe Fitzwilliam believes any day a fine day for a ball, but I think it the perfect day, Mr. Bingley. It will allow Miss Bennet sufficient time to recover from her cold." I held back my knowledge that she was already perfectly well since all the magic had been removed from her.

Little else has occurred, thus far, today. And I expect little to happen this evening. I suppose I will be pleased with the lack of activity, since it means that my entry today is rather short. For once, I will not go to bed with aching fingers.

Chapter Thirty

Evening, 13 November 1811

Dear Diary,

The day ended in a very different vein than it began. After breakfast, Mrs. Annesley and I went to my sitting room to practice magic. I was so excited to have regular practice back in my life. You cannot imagine how dull life is without magic! Unfortunately, my excitement was soon quelled when I realized the level of magic I was permitted to perform.

Because I had been so depleted, I had to start with beginner magic. I was not even allowed to perform without a crystal. Mrs. Annesley forced a piece of quartz into my hand and explained how it would be used.

"Quartz has multiple purposes," she began. "It cleans magic and spells from a person, and it also helps with cleaning objects."

"Cleaning objects?" I am certain Mrs. Annesley heard the incredulity in my voice. I could not help it, though. I am a Darcy and as such, I have been raised to have others clean for me.

"Yes, Miss Darcy. I realize you have been blessed to have others see to your homes' needs, but you must learn to do it yourself. There may be a time when you are required to keep your own home. Perhaps you lose a beloved and trusted housekeeper. Or perhaps you wish to assist your maids with their work as a gift to them. In any case, this is what we will do today."

Drat! I honestly thought that we would do something fun today after my long spell of no —I should say, little —magic. Cleaning is not fun, not even when one has magic on their side.

Mrs. Annesley pointed to the mirror in my room. "See that? The mirror is smudged in the corner. While it is not exactly dirty, it could look better. If you had company join you here, I am certain you would be embarrassed by the state of the glass."

I would not be embarrassed, actually. The mirror is hardly worth noting. I nodded my head in agreement anyway. I would not convince her to teach me a different spell no matter what I said, so I might as well go about the lesson cheerfully.

Mrs. Annesley forced me to write the following spell thirty times (her favorite torture), and then allowed me to use the words.

Dirt and grime, now decline.
Mirror bright, let this thing shine.
Leave a sheen, where light can dawn,
Make it gleam, like early morn.

Then, holding the quartz, I pointed my finger at the mirror, and —VOILA! The mirror sparkled. I had never seen a mirror so brilliantly shined, and I vowed to pay closer attention when I visited houses of the landed gentry. Surely such gleaming possessions would indicate a witch's presence.

Later, we continued our practice in the ballroom. She suggested that Miss Bingley would be unbearable in the weeks leading up to the ball. Frankly, I feel rather sorry for Mrs. Nichols and the others. They will be forced to endure Miss Bingley's increased commands and rants during that time. Two maids are already looking for new employment. We shall see if they can weather the event's preparations, or if they will leave us before the twenty-sixth.

"It is your responsibility to use your powers for good, Miss Darcy. Cleaning chandeliers may seem beneath you, but it would mean a lot to the servants—especially those overseen by someone as irrational as Miss Bingley."

She need not have said anything further. My compassion was already engaged. I happily uttered my verse and pointed my quartz toward the large chandelier in the center of the ballroom. In under a minute, the crystals sparkled, and the frame shone. I was just raising my quartz to the second chandelier when Fitzwilliam opened the door and interrupted us.

"Georgiana, what are you doing in here?"

Caught with my hand in the air, I struggled for a response. I have never been good at prevaricating without forethought. Fortunately, Mrs. Annesley does not have the same weakness. "I have been instructing Miss Darcy in dance, sir. She may dance little at the ball, but it is good to remind her of the steps."

"Of course," he said. Turning to me, he added, "I wanted to tell you, Sister, that Bingley and I will be away for a few hours. Bingley wants to visit some shops and then we will stop by Longbourn to check on Miss Bennet's health." Though it was a nice thought, I doubted my brother was truly worried about Miss Bennet's health. I smiled, knowing he was finding an excuse to see Miss Elizabeth.

"Would you like me to come with you, Fitzwilliam?"

"No, no," he said. "The weather has turned very cold. If we were going straight to Longbourn, I would invite you. However, Bingley has several stops planned, including a visit with Colonel Forster. It would not be appropriate for you to join us. Next time, I promise."

Though disappointed, I understood his point. I had no desire to visit the militia camp anyway, though I was disheartened to miss seeing Kitty again. It was on the tip of my tongue to ask him to invite the Bennet ladies for tea when Fitzwilliam abruptly bowed and made his exit. I could not be upset with his haste; he was going to see Miss Elizabeth, after all.

"He is in quite a hurry to get to town," Mrs. Annesley said.

"More likely in a hurry to get to Longbourn," I replied. We both tittered.

"Are you sure they have not come to an agreement? They seemed different by the end of her visit."

"Not to my knowledge." I realize, niece, that this diary portrays me in quite a bad light. I have pranked Miss Bingley on several occasions, manipulated my brother's love affair, and lied to Mrs. Annesley multiple times. However, Fitzwilliam's courtship is a delicate thing. They have chosen to keep it secret for a while, and I cannot dishonor that.

Under Mrs. Annesley's supervision, I continued to clean the ballroom. Each of the room's four chandeliers received a thorough scrubbing, as did the windows. Though we risked the servant's suspicions, I also magically scrubbed the floor until the wood gleamed.

As we left the room, I heard Miss Bingley screech, "I have told you several times now, Meg!" Though I felt sorry for Meg, I was pleased with the good turn I had done for her and the other maids.

I returned to my room to continue reading the spirit guides book, only to have Fitzwilliam join me very soon after. He was fuming and entered abruptly after a quick knock upon my door. I scarcely had time to welcome him. "Come, we are leaving. The servants will pack and follow tomorrow."

"Leaving?" My confusion was immense. "What has happened to warrant our sudden departure? Have you and Miss Elizabeth argued?"

"Of course not," he snapped. "Put on a traveling gown and let us go. I have already notified Mrs. Annesley, and the carriage is waiting.

Though confused and frustrated, I did as he said and hurried to put on a different gown. The look on Mrs. Annesley's face showed she was as confused as I was, but Fitzwilliam's grim expression prevented me from asking him.

By the time we stopped to water the horses and stretch our legs, his expression had softened to one of firm resolve rather than anger. Mrs. Annesley pulled me close and whispered, "You must learn what has happened. We cannot help him solve his problem if we remain unaware." I agreed and set out to do just that.

As soon as the carriage door closed, I began to unrelentingly needle my brother for answers. I probably said, "You must tell me what has occurred, Fitzwilliam," no less than twenty times before he finally snapped, "Wickham!"

"Wickham!" I gasped. "What does he have to do with today's events?"

"He was in Meryton today. I saw him speaking with Miss Elizabeth and her sisters." Fitzwilliam's eyes flared with renewed anger.

"But why? How?"

"Apparently, the cad decided he looks rather handsome in a red coat. He has joined the militia." He turned to look out the window, which signaled the conversation was over, but I would not allow it.

"And what did you do?" I inquired.

"What could I do? I dearly wished to hop off my horse and pummel the man, but I feared he would share your secrets. I cannot allow him to harm you in any way, Georgiana. You are my responsibility."

I ignored his tightly clasped hands and the tick in his jaw. Others might have been frightened of it, but I was not. "You left? To protect me, you left all of Meryton susceptible to his false charms? You left Miss Elizabeth to be his prey? Who knows what nonsense he is, even now, whispering into her ear."

Fitzwilliam's eyes widened. Clearly, he had acted on instinct and failed to think rationally. Therefore, it was as good a time as any to pile on. "Miss Elizabeth is not the only possible victim, and you know it. Miss Lydia will make a fool of herself over the man. Miss Elizabeth might forgive you for a slip with herself, but if you fail to protect her sister, I cannot imagine she will find room in her heart for you."

My brother's Adam's apple bobbed signaling I had said enough. He knew my logic was sound. Though I have a very different personality from Miss Lydia, I, too, was once susceptible to Mr. Wickham's charms. I refuse to share the details, but suffice it to say, little niece, I was gravely taken advantage of by a fortune hunter. Luckily, my brother was there to save me from doing irreparable damage. He must do the same for Miss Lydia, and though I hate to admit it, even Kitty. I adore them both, but they are the types of girls who run toward trouble rather than away from it.

"I will think on it," he finally answered. I knew my job was done. Though we would wake tomorrow in our Netherfield beds, Fitzwilliam's mind was resolved to act differently. I must find time after breakfast in the morning to spell something so I can witness the events.

Our trip to London has not been a complete waste, however. I did find a lovely book on fairies in the Darcy library. Mrs. Annesley has spelled it so that I may keep it with me even after the day reverts. I can now complete that spell, as well, but I am still on a magical diet, so to speak, and I wished to be honest and truthful about as much as I am able.

It is time for supper, so I must wrap up today's entry. I look forward to sharing how today goes tomorrow.

Chapter Thirty-one

Afternoon, 13 November 1811 (sigh)

Dear Diary,

As expected, the day began at Netherfield Park. Fitzwilliam wore a thunderous expression at breakfast, and ate little, but he made no mention of Mr. Wickham or the militia. I, of course, had to pretend ignorance of the entire ordeal, which was a shame because I truly wished to comfort and advise him.

After breakfast, Mrs. Annesley and I returned to the sitting room, and as we had done on the previous iteration of this day, I began to clean. Before we moved on to the ballroom, I asked that we stop by my brother's room and spell his riding boots as we had done before. She readily agreed.

We quietly sneaked down the hall to Fitzwilliam's suite. At Mrs. Annesley's cue, I slowly opened the door. I was tempted to slam it shut upon seeing my brother's valet standing with his back to me, but Mrs. Annesley's hand stopped me. "Sleep," she whispered, and Jones instantly dropped his head. The man was fast asleep while standing up. I have never seen anything like it!

Mrs. Annesley smiled and waved me toward Fitzwilliam's dressing room. We found his boots within seconds. Mrs. Annesley cast the mirror spell on them, and I added the notification enchantment.

"Done," she said with a smile. I followed her to the door, and we made our exit. Just before the door closed, she whispered,

"Wake," and Jones' head lifted, once again in a wakeful pose. I never cease to be fascinated by the power of magic!

As he had before, Fitzwilliam found us in the ballroom practicing the cleaning spell while pretending to dance. Unfortunately, I had to re-clean all the chandeliers and windows due to Fitzwilliam's inability to react appropriately to Mr. Wickham's presence. As he had yesterday, he informed us that he would be leaving for town. Unlike yesterday, when I asked if he wanted my company, he snapped, "Not today, Georgiana!" I would have been offended if I did not understand his discomfort.

I checked my watch and noticed he and Mr. Bingley left a full half-hour earlier than they had before. "He is early," I said to Mrs. Annesley.

"That is understandable," she replied. "He is very nervous today. I would also want to get the confrontation over with." I said a silent prayer that he would find a way to make today a success. At best, Fitzwilliam would respond as he should to stop Mr. Wickham's attempts to discredit him and sway the local populace. At worst, he would behave completely as he should not. In either case, Mrs. Annesley and I would witness it in the mirror, and I would know how to help him on the next repetition of the day. I genuinely wished for him to do as he should. No one has the power to agitate Fitzwilliam as Mr. Wickham does, and I hate that he was forced to do this day twice.

The mirror buzzed sooner than I anticipated. "It is him," I said to Mrs. Annesley. Together we looked into the mirror and found it was Miss Elizabeth standing near him. I knew her from the hem of her coat.

"Mr. Darcy, I did not expect to see you in town today," she said.

"Bingley had business here. We planned to visit you at Longbourn afterward."

"Yes," Mr. Bingley's voice cut in from somewhere outside of my view. "We wished to ensure you remained well, Miss Bennet."

"Mr. Darcy," I heard Kitty say, "did you not bring Georgiana with you?" I was pleased to hear the disappointment in her voice.

From the top of my brother's boots, I could see his subtle bow. "I regret to inform you that Georgiana remained home. She will be very disappointed to know she missed you."

"We would like to see her soon, Mr. Darcy," Miss Lydia said. "I have come to town for new ribbons, and I could use her opinion on the best way to remake my bonnet."

"And I have just purchased new music. She may enjoy playing with me," Miss Mary's quiet but resolute voice added.

"She is my friend," Kitty whined.

On the edge of the mirror, I saw another person — a male figure in dark clothing. I could not make out his face, but it was clear he hovered too close to Miss Elizabeth. If Fitzwilliam had not been so preoccupied with thoughts of Mr. Wickham, he would have been quite angry at the man's actions.

"Oh, there is Denny. Denny! Come here and bring that fellow with you. We have not yet met him." Though I could not see her, I imagined Miss Lydia waving her handkerchief frantically. There was a general admonishment for her loud, improper actions, but I paid little attention to it. This was the moment!

I recognized Lieutenant Denny's voice when he greeted the assembled party. "May I introduce my new friend, George Wickham. Lieutenant Wickham has just joined the militia this morning."

The view from Fitzwilliam's boots showed a man in a red jacket beginning to bow. At the bottom of his movement, I could just make out his face. George Wickham, as handsome as ever, and just as likely to turn my stomach as sour milk.

When he stood, Fitzwilliam's boots took one, two, three small steps forward before BLAT! Or perhaps, THWACK! It is hard to capture the sound in a word. Just imagine the noise of Fitzwilliam's fist connecting solidly with Mr. Wickham's left eye.

"Well, that is one way to deal with the scoundrel," Mrs. Annesley muttered.

I agreed, though I soon realized it was not the appropriate action. Miss Elizabeth came into view when she knelt beside the rogue. "Mr. Darcy, what has got into you?" It was difficult to see clearly, but I watched as she helped him to a seated position.

"Madam, I apologize that you were forced to witness this altercation," Mr. Wickham said. He held a handkerchief to his bleeding nose. "I am afraid Mr. Darcy has never liked me. Even as children, he treated me this way."

Though I willed him to explain himself, Fitzwilliam replied, "If you only knew who he truly is."

"I am sure, whatever he has done, it does not warrant such violence. A gentleman does not assault another man like this, Mr. Darcy. Nor does he deserve the bloody nose and black eye resulting from your attack." My brother said nothing while Miss Elizabeth held a cloth to Mr. Wickham's bleeding eyebrow.

Finally, she stood and turned to Fitzwilliam. "Upon greeting someone, you must use your words, Mr. Darcy. Good day." Then, the angry lady gathered her sisters and the man in dark clothing, and the group walked away.

Use your words. No doubt that is sage advice for my brother. As Miss Elizabeth is Fitzwilliam's OTL I sincerely hope she has the patience to teach him just that. He will require a lifetime of coaching, but I believe she is up for the task.

I have already insisted that Mrs. Annesley and I attend

town tomorrow. She is adamant that it is a poor idea, but I cannot see how Fitzwilliam will solve this dilemma without my interference. We may, very well, repeat the thirteenth of November for eternity if he is left to his own devices.

I waited for him to return to the house, half expecting him to barge into my room again and demand we return to London. Instead, I heard him stomp down the hall. So, there you have it. He has said nothing to Miss Elizabeth of Mr. Wickham's true nature, and he has not warned me the man is in town. I know it, of course, but he is unaware of my cognizance of the true nature of the events. Use your words, indeed!

Because he has been such a buffoon, I decided he needed to pay. When he left his room for dinner, I sneaked in, repeated the sleep spell I learned yesterday from Mrs. Annesley, and magicked his boots a little too tight. He will be able to wear them tomorrow, but he will regret it. And I will enjoy watching him hobble about as I fix this entire situation.

Chapter Thirty-two

Evening, 13 November 1811
(Let us be done with this day!)

Dear Diary,

Today went swimmingly! I am so proud of Fitzwilliam that I can hardly stop myself from jumping right to the end of my entry to shout out his success. I shall endeavor to recount today's events as they occurred, so you are not left wondering what in the world I have written.

The morning began as it had these past two days. Mrs. Annesley and I moved upstairs after breakfast, and I was frustrated to see a dirty mirror once again. I realize it takes very little magic and less than half an hour to clean my mirror and all the items in the ballroom, but it is very frustrating to have to do so for three consecutive days.

I suggested that we wait to complete the cleaning until after the thirteenth has finally concluded, when an agitated Fitzwilliam entered my room. "Georgiana, I will be away for most of the day."

"So early?" I asked. He was leaving at least an hour earlier than his previous departures. It was clear my brother had changed his strategy, but I was not yet confident his approach would be appropriate.

He gave me a grim nod. "I have business to attend to this morning."

I wished to ask what type of business, but Mrs. Annesley's

subtle warning stopped me. Instead, I bid my brother goodbye and anxiously waited until he was down the hall before imploring Mrs. Annesley to hurry to Meryton.

Unfortunately, Mrs. Annesley refusal to cooperate with my plans was as firm today as it had been yesterday. "Miss Darcy, it is imperative that you refrain from interfering with your brother's quest. If his relationship with Miss Elizabeth is to last, he must learn on his own how to secure his happiness."

"I understand the rule, truly, I do; however, I must remind you that Fitzwilliam's relationship with Mr. Wickham is particularly fraught. No one else on earth can anger and hurt my brother the way he does. I cannot continue to allow Fitzwilliam to be harmed by him. I promise this will be my one and only interference." For the sake of full disclosure, I must admit that I crossed my fingers behind my back when I said the last sentence. I cannot ensure I will remain an impartial witness, especially given the looming threat of Lady Catherine.

Mrs. Annesley was appropriately swayed by my plea, and we prepared ourselves for a trip to town. After much conversation, we decided to arrive a little earlier than when Mr. Wickham had previously approached the Bennet sisters. That gave us enough time to request a carriage, change into proper gowns, and establish our plan of attack.

We arrived in Meryton just as the Bennets, along with the man I had noticed yesterday, were exiting the haberdashery. "Georgiana!" Kitty called as I stepped out from the carriage. "I am so pleased to see you." She clasped me close. Her embrace was not proper in company, and certainly not proper given our location on a public street, but it was welcomed anyway. It is so exciting to have a true friend!

"I am pleased to see you, as well," I replied. "And all of you. Have you been shopping?"

Miss Lydia laughingly waved a bundle of purple ribbons. "Yes. Look at this divine color. Do you not think it makes my eyes look even bluer?" She held the trimming to her face, and I had to admit that it did look nice against her complexion and eyes.

"Is Mr. Darcy not with you?" Miss Elizabeth asked. I was pleased by her interest in his whereabouts.

"He is in town, though I know not where. He mentioned he had business to attend to. Mrs. Annesley and I thought we would do a bit of shopping while he was away. Then, if we are lucky, we might find him and take refreshments at The Thatched Cup."

"I love taking tea at The Thatched Cup." Miss Lydia turned to her eldest sisters. "Jane, Lizzy, you must give me some money so I can go with Miss Darcy and her brother. I have spent all of mine on ribbons."

Miss Elizabeth refused her youngest sister's plea, but Miss Bennet nodded her head and pulled a coin from her purse. Miss Lydia happily took the money and then stuck her tongue out at Miss Elizabeth.

"May I join you, as well?" Kitty asked. I smiled my approval and then extended an invitation to Miss Mary who was looking particularly sour at that moment. Her face lifted, and I was reminded, again, that she could be a very pretty girl if she wished to be pleasant.

The man standing between Miss Elizabeth and Miss Mary cleared his throat. "Ahem, my dear cousins, would you be so kind to introduce me to your friends?"

Miss Elizabeth offered me an apologetic look. I nodded in approval of his request. With a thankful smile, she said, "Miss Darcy, I would like to introduce my cousin, Mr. William Collins. Mr. Collins is the rector at Hunsford. Mr. Collins, this is Miss Darcy and her companion, Mrs. Annesley."

Mr. Collins bowed so low that he stumbled forward before righting himself. "I am very pleased to make your acquaintance, Miss Darcy. My noble patroness —"

His words were cut off by Mr. Bingley's approach on his large chestnut-colored stallion. Miss Bennet's face glowed from the happy surprise. "Mr. Bingley, I did not expect to see you in town today," she said.

"Darcy had business here. We planned to visit you at Longbourn when we finished. I wished to ensure you remained well, Miss Bennet." He then noticed Mrs. Annesley and me. "Miss Darcy, Mrs. Annesley, what a surprise to find you here. Did you come with Darcy?"

I dipped a curtsy. "We traveled separately. We hoped to find him for tea once his business is complete."

Mr. Bingley was pleased by this suggestion. "Excellent. If everyone is available, I should like to treat us all to tea once we find Darcy." Miss Bennet's face flushed with pleasure.

Just then, Miss Lydia began to cry out. "Oh, there is Denny. Denny! Come here and bring that fellow with you. We have not yet met him." As I had imagined, Miss Lydia waved frantically at the gentlemen; however, it was her ribbons flapping in the air, not her handkerchief. Like the day before, Miss Bennet and Miss Elizabeth hurried to shush their youngest sister, but I paid little attention, for there, walking toward me, was George Wickham.

"Oh, there is your brother." Miss Elizabeth tugged my sleeve and pointed toward the cobbler's shop. He was grim-faced and walking gingerly toward our group. My shoe-tightening spell had obviously worked.

Lieutenant Denny greeted everyone with a handsome smile. "May I introduce my new friend, George Wickham. Lieutenant Wickham has just joined the militia today."

Mr. Wickham looked pleasantly from one pretty Bennet face to another until his eyes stopped on mine. "Miss Darcy!" I was pleased to have startled him with my presence, though I would have been even more pleased if I had made his shoes too tight. "What are you doing in Meryton?" he asked.

"Mr. Wickham." I nodded and gave my best look of Darcy indifference.

"Is your brother with you?" he inquired.

"I am," Fitzwilliam answered. Mr. Wickham's eyes widened in dismay. I would love to have captured it somehow. It would be fantastic to watch it replay over and over on the pages of my diary, or perhaps in my mirror.

Mr. Wickham's bravado returned with speed. "Darcy, I am surprised to find you in this small village. I have never known you to be comfortable anywhere but London or Pemberley."

"Pemberley!" Mr. Collins exclaimed. "Why, then you are —"

My brother paid little attention to the man. "My friend Bingley has taken an estate nearby. I am here to assist him."

"And that is just as I would have expected. The nephew of my esteemed —" Once again, Mr. Collins' profusions were cut short.

"I learned you were here, and I took care to inform Colonel Forster of your history with gaming, women, lying, and eschewing work. He was pleased to have this intelligence, though he also wrote to Colonel Fitzwilliam for his experiences with you."

"Darcy, you go too far." He cast his eyes in my direction. "It would be unfortunate for you to anger me. You forget, I also know your secrets."

It was on the tip of my tongue to cast the cooing bird spell on the man when my brother responded. "I believe it is you who forgets, Wickham. I have informed every business owner in Meryton that you cannot be trusted to pay your debts. I have sent for evidence from London of the many notes I hold in your name."

"Darcy, I —"

Fitzwilliam held up a quelling hand. "I hope you can make a new life for yourself in the militia that does not include taking advantage of young, gently bred ladies, shopkeepers, or their unsuspecting daughters. If you cannot, I will call in your debts and have you sent to Marshalsea."

Mr. Wickham's nostrils flared in indignation, but he said nothing further to my brother. He turned toward the rest of our group and bowed. "It was lovely to make your acquaintances today. Miss Darcy." He inclined his head toward me before making a sharp turn and exiting. I did not even have time to curse him with a spotty nose!

Wasting little time, Mr. Collins stepped forward and addressed my still-fuming brother. "Mr. Darcy, I am sure you will not be offended if I introduce myself, as I have the great pleasure and honor of being the rector to your aunt, Lady Catherine de Bourgh!"

As if I were not anxious enough, Lady Catherine's name sent shivers down my spine. My brother misinterpreted my reaction and interrupted the foolish parson. "Georgiana, are you well? Why are you here? Should we return home?" Remorse for his tight shoes struck me at once. He is a dear brother, though I sometimes forget.

I offered what I hoped was a reassuring smile. "I am well, Fitzwilliam. Our party was planning to have tea at The Thatched Cup if you would like to join us."

He smiled back and offered me his arm. Then he turned and offered his other arm to Miss Elizabeth. "Tea sounds perfect." Behind us, Mr. Bingley offered one arm to Miss Bennet and the other to Miss Mary.

"Oh, la, Mr. Collins, I do not wish for your escort and neither does Kitty." I presumed Mr. Collins had attempted to be gentlemanly and offered to escort his two youngest cousins.

"Escort Mrs. Annesley," Miss Lydia added before pulling Kitty to the front of the group to walk with me. Kitty pulled me away to whisper and giggle about Fitzwilliam's exchange with Mr. Wickham, leaving a very pleased Fitzwilliam escorting Miss Elizabeth. I pretended to retrieve something from my reticule while I undid the tight boots spell. I did not wish for Fitzwilliam to spend teatime worried about his feet when he should be concerned with his OTL.

Chapter Thirty-three

Evening, 14 November 1811

Dear Diary,

I scarcely know where to begin with today's event. I would like to start with the card party I attended, but I shall save the best for last and begin with my magical practice.

This morning, Mrs. Annesley deemed me sufficiently recovered from my magical exhaustion. After ensuring that I had slept well and my energy levels were high, I was permitted to contact Bael. As I had done before, I took the Bael's sigil into my hands and breathed my essence onto the etching. When I felt ready, I called out, "Oh, great deity, Bael, hear my call. Come forth and talk with me."

Soon, a great lavender mist began to form. It spun in a vortex shape before it evaporated and showed a small, elderly man standing before me. I dipped a curtsy. "Greetings, sir. It is good to see you again."

Bael smiled at me. "You called, Georgiana? Have you more requests for me?"

I nodded. "Oh yes, sir. I believe I have figured out what you wished me to know the last time we spoke."

"Well, go on, child. What is it you want?"

I swallowed, uncertainty washing over me about the correctness of my request. "Um, I would like..."

"Georgiana, you must be assured of your request. Do not ask

it if you are hesitant and unsure it is the correct wish."

I looked toward Mrs. Annesley who's bobbing head entreated me to ask as we had planned. Feeling more confident, I made my request. "I would like to be able to speak Fae."

"Fae? As in the ancient fairy language?"

I nodded. "Yes, exactly. I have reason to believe they live nearby, and I wish to request their help." Bael's wide smile filled me with confidence that I had made the correct decision. I offered him a broad grin in return.

"Very well, Georgiana." He reached out and touched my shoulder. "Now you may speak to the fairies, if," he emphasized, "you are successful in luring them out of their hiding places."

"Oh, thank you, thank you," I gushed. "I suspect I will not require your assistance any further. This is exactly what I need."

Bael's form had already started to dissolve into a lavender mist, but he gave me one last remark. "You should seek my help one more time, Georgiana. Do not come to me until you are sure of what you need." And then he was gone.

"What do you think he means?" I asked Mrs. Annesley.

"It sounds as if you have more to decipher. You will know when the time is right to consult him further." I swear, she is no more help than Bael!

"Are you ready to find the fairies?"

Mrs. Annesley's eyes widened in dismay. "Certainly not," she protested. "Fairies are very unpredictable and intractable creatures. You must spend the day preparing what you will say to them. You cannot approach without knowing exactly what you need or which words you will use."

"That is simple. I will merely request their assistance in keeping Miss Elizabeth safe."

Mrs. Annesley expelled a puff of incredulity. "That is insufficient. You must first know how to approach them. What gift will you bring? What will you say to sway them to your side?"

A gift! I had forgotten all about offering a gift. Perhaps Mrs. Annesley's reluctance to visit today was the most appropriate action. I resolved to read my book further for ideas on how to convince the fairies to speak with me. That is what I did for much of the morning.

At tea, Miss Bingley was not in a fine fettle. In fact, she was a downright grump. Yesterday, our party was invited to attend a card party at the Phillips' home this evening, and the news that Mr. Bingley had accepted on behalf of the entire household did not sit well with his youngest sister. Mrs. Hurst, however, looked very pleased by the opportunity to get out of the house. I do not know what magic Mrs. Annesley performed on her, but her demeanor has radically improved since the Bennet sisters left Netherfield for Longbourn. She still says little, but her face no longer holds the same downcast appearance it previously did.

"Charles, how could you have accepted an invitation to the Phillips? He is a solicitor, and she is even worse than her sister!" I should note that Mrs. Phillips is a sister to Mrs. Bennet. Like Mrs. Bennet, she is loud and prone to saying whatever comes into her head. I met her briefly at Lucas Lodge and liked her very much. Her husband is a local solicitor. I have not met him, but Kitty says he is a very sensible fellow, and I choose to believe her.

"Caroline, it is but a card party. I have not suggested you dine nightly with Mrs. Phillips."

Miss Bingley's disdain remained evident. "It is not myself I am concerned about, but our guests. Mr. Darcy, you must be quite dismayed to have to rub elbows with a solicitor. And poor Georgiana!"

And now the cat is out of the bag. Fitzwilliam agreed that I could attend the party with the rest of the household! He even gave permission for me to wear my hair up, though in a simple style. But more on that in a moment.

"Quite the contrary," my brother retorted. "I have had the pleasure of conversing with Mr. Phillips before, and he is a very knowledgeable man. I look forward to seeing him tonight." I suspect Fitzwilliam had no real interest in talking to anyone but Miss Elizabeth. The argument served its purpose, however. Realizing she had no sway in this decision, Miss Bingley turned her critical eye to something else.

"Who has turned this vase? The pattern should face out so it can be seen upon entering the room. I will have to discuss this oversight with Mrs. Nichols. The maids must be reprimanded." I was the one who had turned the vase in that direction. It allowed me to remotely watch the happenings in the room when Miss Elizabeth and my brother were together, but I was hardly going to admit such a thing to Miss Bingley. Instead, I vowed to make her forget the entire thing using the same spell I had cast upon her days ago. I pretended to admire her bracelet while I whispered the verse. It worked. Her concern for the vase evaporated and soon focused on a curtain that did not hang as it should. Some people!

Before tea concluded, a footman delivered our mail. I was pleased to see a letter from Richard in my pile. I tore it open, hopeful that he had replied positively to my request for him to come to Netherfield.

"Brother, Richard has written. If it is acceptable to Mr. and Miss Bingley, he wishes to visit us here for a few weeks." I turned hopeful eyes to Mr. Bingley. "He would arrive on the twentieth."

Mr. Bingley clapped his hands in delight. "Splendid! The Colonel is an excellent fellow. And he will be here in time for the ball."

My brother seemed pleased as well, but Miss Bingley's ire remained. "This is the youngest of the Earl's sons, is it not?" Her nose curled with distaste. It is true that Richard is the third of three sons, and, as such, quite unlikely to inherit any wealth. But it is not what Miss Bingley said but rather how she said it. You must trust me on this.

"May I write to him and suggest he bring clothes for the ball?" I stood and walked to the writing desk.

"It will not matter. He will prefer to wear his regimentals. He insists the ladies cannot resist a man in uniform." Both Mr. Bingley and I laughed at my brother's quip. It was true. Richard takes full advantage of a lady's love for a red coat. Nevertheless, I suggested he bring formal clothing.

After tea, I attempted to read more about spirit guides. I do not know why Mrs. Annesley insists I finish the book. It is boring, and dry, and did I mention boring? It took me half an hour to pick up the book, so repulsed was I by its dreary pages. Instead, I practiced my cleaning spell and scrubbed my mirror along with the windows in my bedroom, dressing room, and sitting room. I also shined all the furniture. The fact that I cleaned in lieu of reading should speak volumes about my abhorrence for the book. After a while, there was nothing left to dust or shine, and I was forced to crack open the spine of the dreaded tome. I almost finished an entire chapter, before falling fast asleep in my chair.

I napped for at least two hours before being awakened by La Roche. After bathing, I sat down in front of my now sparkling mirror and watched as she deftly managed my hair. In keeping with my brother's insistence that it be styled in a simple fashion, she arranged a low twist at the nape of my neck, softened with a few trailing curls at my temples. She helped me into my gown, a silvery-blue concoction that, combined with my coiffure, made me appear quite grown up.

∞∞∞

We arrived at the Phillips' well after the party had begun. I am certain you can ascertain who was at fault for our late arrival. No sooner had we made our entrance and greeted our hosts, Kitty pulled me aside with a giggle. "You made it! And how well you look. I have never seen you with your hair up." I preened at her compliment.

"You look very pretty, as well, but you always look nice." I looked around the room. It was a crush, if such a thing can be said for a card party in a small market town. "I had not expected so many people, and the officers too. I did not think they would attend."

"Oh, yes," Kitty enthused. "My aunt loves soldiers. She invites them to all her parties." Now on guard, my eyes searched for the one soldier I had no desire to see.

"Have you heard the latest gossip? Oh, why would you have? I should just tell you." I looked back at my friend. "Mr. Wickham, the man your brother confronted yesterday." I nodded my understanding and urged her to continue. "Well, he has run off! He was a soldier for less than a day and has already left."

"Did he have permission? Has he gone to another regiment?"

She shook her head with such rapidity that her curls bounced off her cheeks. "No! Colonel Forster was very upset. He said if he could find him, he would seek retribution!"

My eyes widened. "But the penalty for desertion is death."

"Yes, exactly! It is all so very exciting." I was horrified. Though I have no kind thoughts to share about Mr. Wickham, I do not wish him dead. I considered going straight to Fitzwilliam with the news, but he was happily absorbed in

Miss Elizabeth's presence, and I could not bear to share news of his enemy.

I must emphasize that Fitzwilliam was happily absorbed in Miss Elizabeth's presence. Unfortunately, my aunt's ridiculous little parson ensured their status did not remain undisturbed. "Mr. Darcy, Mr. Darcy. I must have a word with you sir." My brother said something that was inaudible to me as I was quite far away at the time, but being curious about what Mr. Collins would say, I tugged Kitty closer.

"Mr. Collins is very put out with your brother. We must get close enough to hear everything," she said once she realized my agenda.

"I must insist that you give up your marked attentions to my cousin. You will only break her heart. And since you are already spoken for, you are displaying a very displeasing lack of devotion to your intended."

"My intended? I beg your pardon, sir, but I am not engaged to anyone, and I insist you discontinue this conversation." My brother's happy expression was swiftly replaced by a look of Darcy hauteur.

"But sir," the absurd man continued, "Lady Catherine de Bourgh insists that you are to marry her daughter. And no greater beauty is there than Miss Anne de Bourgh. I thoroughly commend you on your choice of brides. She would be heartbroken to learn of the great attention you have paid to Elizabeth, and I must demand —"

"Miss Elizabeth, have you given this man permission to address you so casually?"

Miss Elizabeth's sly smile indicated she appreciated the turn of my brother's mind. "I have not, Mr. Darcy."

He gave her a curt nod. "Then I must insist, Mr. Collins, that you apologize to Miss Elizabeth for your impertinence. You do not have permission to address her so."

"But, but, sh... she is my cousin. I meant nothing by it." Mr. Collins began to make a funny little bowing movement while stepping slightly forward and back. He looked exactly like a chicken searching for worms.

Miss Elizabeth's smile grew larger. "I forgive you Mr. Collins, though it appears you have greatly offended Mr. Darcy. And if Mr. Darcy is offended, logic indicates Lady Catherine would be offended on his behalf. "I suggest you leave us for now." Fully confused, the man bowed three more times to my brother and twice again to Miss Elizabeth before leaving.

"What in the world has got into him?"

Kitty giggled. "He has come to find a wife among my sisters. He first set his sights on Jane, as she is the eldest and the acknowledged beauty among us. But Mama warned him away saying that Jane is being courted by Mr. Bingley and will surely be engaged soon. So then, he turned his eyes to Lizzy. Mama insists Lizzy is also being courted, and that Mr. Collins should pay attention to Mary." I looked across the room where a grim-faced Miss Mary stood with a babbling Mr. Collins. Poor Miss Mary. She would be happy as a preacher's wife, I think, but I cannot imagine anyone would be pleased to wed Mr. Collins.

"If he has been advised to pursue Miss Mary, why was he so upset with my brother and Miss Elizabeth?"

Kitty rolled her eyes and guided me to a table filled with cakes and small sandwiches. "He was not well pleased to pursue Mary. She has not the looks of Jane or the vivacity of Lizzy. But when he learned that Mr. Darcy had been paying special attention to Lizzy, he became very agitated and insisted that she was not being courted and therefore free to receive his attentions. He insisted that your brother is engaged to Miss de Bourgh. At first, Lizzy seemed concerned, but soon her anxieties faded, and she began to laugh at his antics." I was pleased to hear that Miss Elizabeth trusts my brother.

"What about your mother? How did she react?" I could

imagine the histrionics Mrs. Bennet displayed upon hearing of my brother's fictional engagement.

Kitty swallowed a bite of cake before answering. "Oh that. Mama does not hear anything she does not wish to. She is convinced your brother will come to the point with my sister and will not be persuaded otherwise. Unless your brother abandons Netherfield, there is little worry my mother will concern herself with Mr. Collins' rants."

Secure in the knowledge that Mr. Collins would not tear my brother from his OTL, and safe from Mr. Wickham's barbed comments, I took every effort to enjoy the evening with Kitty. Soon, we were joined by Miss Lydia. She was disappointed that Lieutenant Denny chose to partner with Miss King at whist instead of her.

To cheer her, we joined a group playing lottery. I won fifteen fish before losing them all again! Miss Lydia lost her fish within the first few minutes of play, but she enjoyed herself so much she chose to spend the rest of the evening watching Kitty and me. Kitty was very lucky and was the biggest winner at the table. Her aunt let her choose from a variety of prizes. Miss Lydia wished for her to select a green ribbon, but since her sister would have commandeered it, she chose a tin of watercolors, instead.

Chapter Thirty-four

Morning, 15 November 1811

Dear Diary,

The sun has not yet risen, but I am awake. Since the only other thing I have to do is read that terrible book on spirit guides, I have chosen to write in this journal. There is little to share as nothing has yet occurred today, and I already told you all that happened yesterday.

I am awake because I had a bad dream. It has been over a week since the violet dragon invaded my sleep, but he -or perhaps, she —was back to damage my rest last night. How does one determine the gender of a dragon? The first dragon is blood red and looks very angry. I am inclined to believe it a male. But Lady Catherine is a female and is always very angry, so perhaps the dragon is a she.

The violet dragon is smaller and gentler. It has never tried to kill me in my dreams, but it does regularly appear to be rather frustrated with me. I am tempted to give it a name, but as I am too tired to think properly, the best thing I can come up with is 'Violet.' That is not exactly a creative moniker. I shall endeavor to do better once I've had a cup of coffee. Mrs. Annesley will not be pleased with my choice. She likes to read my tea leaves each morning and has been insistent on my drinking tea ever since we learned of Lady Catherine's threat. Perhaps she wishes to see if today is the day I will die. However, today I need coffee, and I will not take no for an answer. She can read my leaves after teatime.

My dream featured the violet dragon. There was no crimson beast there to threaten me or chase the smaller one. I was walking a path at Pemberley when its large body landed before me. Naturally, I screamed, but it held up one talon as if to shush me.

"Gurowul," it hissed in its dragon tongue.

Though I was afraid, I answered it with a shaky voice. "G… good day."

"Gurowul," it hissed, again. I tentatively reached my hand out to touch its snout. "Gurowul," it hissed, once more. Each time, its noises became more insistent.

"Are you angry with me?" I asked. "Am I in danger?" The dragon stomped its back feet, and then beat its wings before taking flight.

I awoke, not with the same panic I had felt after previous dreams, but in confusion. What does the dream mean? Why am I continuously plagued with it?

I believe writing has helped me to relax. There are still three hours until breakfast. I am going to attempt to rest. I will share the remainder of the day's events later.

∞ ∞ ∞

Evening

I am back and feeling much better. After writing my previous entry, I slept for two more hours. At breakfast, I chose tea and, I am happy to report, my leaves did not indicate I would die today or face a great battle. They did imply I would be frustrated today, and I was —on multiple points.

My first frustration was with the fairies. As instructed by my book on fairies, I took an offering with me to the woods. You might ask, 'Who in their right mind can resist a scone with marmalade?' Surprisingly enough, it is resistible as neither Mrs. Annesley nor I saw a single magical creature beyond one another.

Anxious to use my newly acquired Fae language, I said, "Aghch glyl magana, Fae," when I entered the forest. When no one greeted me, I continued. "Aghch dril nymilari nyv Fae chal glynthe" which means, 'I have an offering and would like to speak with you.' The sole response we received was the occasional chirp of a bird.

Mrs. Annesley and I waited for an hour with no luck. She suggested the fairies are testing us and we should return tomorrow with another gift. I read they are drawn to shiny objects. I have an old hair comb that I no longer wear. I will take that.

We returned to Netherfield in just enough time to change for a visit to Longbourn. Mr. Bingley fidgeted the entire ride, which caused Miss Bingley to chide him for his, "nonsensical nervous behavior." Unlike his friend, Fitzwilliam was very calm. I believe his relationship with Miss Elizabeth must be quite secure given that he did not tug at his sleeves a single time.

Upon entering Longbourn, I ran headfirst into my second irritation of the day. Do not mistake that for hyperbole. I had just removed my cloak and was moving forward to greet Kitty when Mr. Collins, eager to greet my brother, walked directly into my path. He made an ineffectual attempt to steady me which had the opposite of its intended effect. I was saved from an unceremonious fall on my backside by Fitzwilliam's quick reflexes.

"I must ask you to pay closer attention, Mr. Collins. You almost caused my sister to fall." Fitzwilliam wore his lord of the manor face, which caused the silly rector to tremble.

"I apologize, Miss Darcy." Then he bowed no fewer than four times. Once to me. Then to my brother. Another to my brother.

And then a final bow to what appeared to be our entire party.

Kitty and Miss Lydia giggled from behind him. "La, Miss Darcy. Come with us, else you will stand here all day waiting for his bows to end." Fitzwilliam took my arm and guided me around the bobbing preacher.

Mrs. Bennet greeted us with her usual effusions. I was directed to sit with Kitty and Miss Lydia. Fitzwilliam was pointed toward a conveniently open seat next to Miss Elizabeth. Mr. Bingley needed no instructions, as he went directly to Miss Bennet's side. Miss Bingley, seeing no way to sit near my brother, reluctantly took a seat to Mrs. Bennet's right leaving Mrs. Hurst to sit to the left of the matron. Mr. Collins was left standing by the door, looking out of place.

"Come in, Mr. Collins. There is a very comfortable chair near Mary." Mrs. Bennet pointed toward her middle daughter. Mr. Collins stepped gracelessly from foot to foot while sending insistent looks at Miss Elizabeth.

"Mrs. Bennet, I believe it would be best if I took Mr. Darcy's seat, and he took the fine chair near Miss Mary."

Fitzwilliam's lips tightened in frustration. "I am perfectly fine where I am," he said.

"But sir, I must advise you —"

"Mr. Collins," my brother snapped. "I do not now, nor have I ever, required your advice. Save that for my aunt." Unused to being spoken to so harshly, the man retreated to the open seat near Miss Mary.

Taking advantage of the lull in conversation, Mr. Bingley happily announced, "We have settled on a day for the ball. Are you available on the twenty-sixth of this month?" He addressed Mrs. Bennet, then turned his eyes to her eldest daughter.

"A ball! How wonderful, how wonderful! The twenty-sixth, you say. That should give us just enough time to obtain new dresses, if we can successfully beat the other ladies of town to the seamstress." Mrs. Bennet's face flushed with excitement.

"We have not finished the invitations yet, madam. If you go tomorrow, the town's seamstress should have time to begin your requests before being overwhelmed by others." Though Miss Bingley's words were not entirely improper, her tone revealed her disgust for anything related to the ball, the Bennets, and Meryton.

Mr. Bingley looked to his sweetheart. "May I request the first dance, Miss Bennet?" She shyly nodded her head in acquiescence. Pleased with her response, he added, "And, if you are amenable, may I also reserve the supper set?" Miss Bennet's face bloomed a becoming shade of pink, but she happily whispered, "Yes."

Not to be outdone, Mr. Collins stood from his seat and plodded across the room to stand in front of Miss Elizabeth. "I dare say, Miss Elizabeth, you would be pleased to offer me your hand during the first and supper sets, as well." If Fitzwilliam's mouth had tightened any further, it would have loosened his teeth.

"I thank you for the request, Mr. Collins, but my first and supper sets are already spoken for. Is there another set I can save for you?"

The man's face turned a dangerous shade of puce. "How can that be? You have only just learned about the ball. Propriety demands you accept my request, or you cannot dance another."

In anger, Fitzwilliam stood, impressing Mr. Collins with his large size. "Sir, you go too far to imply Miss Elizabeth has done any wrong. If you must know, she promised those dances to me when Mr. Bingley first spoke of hosting a ball. I do not plan to relinquish them to you."

Unfortunately, Mr. Collins has not the sense to be

frightened. "Sir, I must remind you of your engagement to Miss de Bourgh. It is unseemly to dance twice with another lady when you are already betrothed to the greatest jewel of Kent."

"La, Mr. Collins. Mr. Darcy told you yesterday that it was a rumor put forth by your patroness. By the look on his face, I suggest you stop pestering the man, and Lizzy, too, else you will be walking around with a black eye to match your jacket." Both Miss Bennet and Miss Elizabeth spoke to shush their youngest sister, but Fitzwilliam seemed pleased.

Showing more intelligence than expected, Mrs. Bennet suggested we all walk in the garden. The day was cold and overcast, but we all readily agreed. Anything was better than being cooped up with a bumbling Mr. Collins and an infuriated Fitzwilliam.

The gentlemen helped us with our coats. Fitzwilliam offered his arm to Miss Elizabeth. Miss Bingley rapidly approached to grasp his other arm, but I whispered "Halt" just in time to prevent it. I did not release her from her path until my brother and his OTL were safely down the lane.

I did not have to halt Mr. Collins as it took him five minutes to put on his coat. However, when he finally made it out of doors, he was intent upon walking with Miss Elizabeth.

"Miss Elizabeth, wait," he called from the door. "I insist you allow me to escort you." Miss Lydia tittered loudly at his actions, but Kitty appeared to be mortified.

"I am so sorry, Georgiana, for my cousin's behavior. He insists your brother is meant for the daughter of his patroness. I fear he will do everything in his power to prevent them from spending time together." I assured her there was no need for apologies and briefly excused myself to say something to my brother.

I did not, however, actually approach my brother. Instead, I stepped closer to Mr. Collins and whispered:

Step twice forth, yet four times flee,
A dance of steps, enforced by thee.
Backward's grasp, four steps you'll take,
Forward's path, is now at stake.

Mr. Collins stopped and turned his face toward me. "What did you say, Miss Darcy."

"I was commenting on what a very fine day it is, sir." He turned dubious eyes upon the grey sky.

"Yes, yes," he answered. Then seeing that Miss Elizabeth and Fitzwilliam had proceeded farther down the path, he rushed to catch up. Or at least he tried. He stepped forward, once, twice. Then on the third step he was pivoted around and took four steps away from them. Confused, he turned himself back around and took another one, two steps before —You guessed it.

"Miss Elizabeth, I must —" TURN "insist that you do not continue to importune —" TURN "Mr. Darcy. My patroness, —" TURN "will be very irritated to learn of your —" TURN. This two-steps-forward and four-steps-back routine kept the absurd man busy for over an hour!

Once I saw that he was properly occupied, I rushed back to join Kitty and her sister. Confused by Mr. Collins' actions, Miss Mary soon joined Kitty and me. Though it was cold, we took full advantage of being together and laughed often, mostly at Mr. Collins' expense. Even Mary took part!

Our party returned to Netherfield after spending over an hour with the Bennets. Nearly everyone was in fine spirits, even Mrs. Hurst who happily relayed her conversation about lace caps with Mrs. Bennet. The only person who did not enjoy the trip was Miss Bingley and she was sure to let us know of her displeasure.

"Charles, you must be more careful in your attentions to Miss Bennet. She will think you are serious about her. It would not do for you to increase her hopes."

"I do not know what you mean, Caroline. Miss Bennet is everything lovely and I hope, someday, to make her more than a friend."

Miss Bingley's dramatic gasp was as good as any stage actress. "Surely you do not mean that! But Charles, they are so far below us. What will our friends say?"

"What do I care what they say? If they are truly my friends, they will be happy for me."

Miss Bingley's nostrils flared, and her eyes squinted. "I grant you," she said through gritted teeth, "Miss Bennet is a very attractive lady. And her manners are gentle. But she has no fashion, no money, and no connections. And her sisters are even worse." She slid her eyes toward my brother. "Why, the way Miss Eliza encouraged that foolish parson to pay his attentions to her. Shameful!"

And this brings me to my third irritation of the day. I had promised to cast no more spells on the lady, but she honestly forces me to act this way! "Miss Bingley, I would urge you to be silent." I calmly said.

"But, Miss Darcy, even you must agree that —"

I held out my hand and said more sternly, "Silence." And that was enough to quiet the lady for the remainder of the day. I have now used that spell on birds, Mrs. Bennet, and Miss Bingley. It is increasingly useful.

Fitzwilliam swiveled his eyes between Miss Bingley and me, but he said nothing. Though he is ignorant of it, I think even he is pleased with my power.

Chapter Thirty-five

Afternoon, 16 November 1811

Dear Diary,

I tried once again to gain the fairies' trust. After breakfast, Mrs. Annesley and I walked out despite the terrible cold that has settled across the region. Mrs. Annesley carried a small bowl of fruit, and I brought my hair comb.

As we did yesterday, we set the offerings at the base of a tree. My scone and marmalade were no longer in sight. Something had eaten it, though I was unsure if it was Fae or a more typical woodland creature. I called out, "Aghch glyl magana, Fae." Before I had a chance to say more, a small glowing creature flitted past my face.

"Did you see?" I whispered near Mrs. Annesley's ear.

"Say something else," she urged.

And so, I did. In the Fae language, I called out, "I request your help, please. A friend of mine may be in danger." The seconds ticked by as we waited for a response. I had almost given up when the small creature flew past my face again only to circle back and hover at eye level.

The fairy, a mere wisp no taller than three inches, was enshrouded in a golden aura of light that shimmered even in the bright sunlight. Aside from its size, it bore an uncanny resemblance to the human shape. A head with delicate features, limbs both graceful and small, a tight waist —all mirrored the human anatomy. There were differences, though.

Most striking were the eyes, large and luminous orbs. And though it wore no clothing, I could not determine if it was male or female. I have concluded its shape was inherently fairy.

"Why should I help you, witchling?"

I was unprepared for this question and looked to Mrs. Annesley for help. I had temporarily forgotten that she does not speak Fae. Resolved, I answered, "I believe my friend is also your friend. She is one of the sisters from Longbourn." The fairy turned toward Longbourn estate and pointed.

"Longbourn? Which one?"

Though my book assured me there was no danger, I was hesitant to share Miss Elizabeth's name. "The dark one. She speaks Fae, as well."

"Lizzy, then." My eyes widened at the use of her name. Recognizing my distress, the fairy continued. "Do not worry. I cannot steal her name unless she tells me it herself. I have heard her mother yell for her many times, and her youngest sister."

"So, you will help me?"

The fairy nodded. "We will assist you. We have protected her from falls and scrapes since she was a child. This will be no different."

"Thank you." I released a relieved breath. "But I must warn you, this may be more difficult than protecting her from falls."

The fairy flitted away, leaving Mrs. Annesley and me in confusion, but only for a few minutes. Soon, it returned with another twenty of its kind. Though they had no wings, the air buzzed with the magic that held them aloft. "Tell my tribe, witchling. What danger does Lizzy face?"

I looked from face to face. Like the first, they all had large eyes and unknown genders. "She…she…" I stuttered, struck by the fear of admitting it was my own family who threatened her. The lead fairy flew to my shoulder and placed one small hand there. Instantly I felt calm and as one with the forest surrounding me. "My aunt poses the threat. She will want my brother to part ways with Miss…, I mean Lizzy. My grandmother warned me the night of Samhain."

The tribe of fairies was abuzz with this news. When they calmed, the leader asked, "When did your ancestor say this threat would occur?"

"She did not, but I believe it will happen soon. My brother and Lizzy are close to an engagement. My aunt will be furious."

The fairy nodded sagely. "We will pay attention to our environment. Leave a window open or a door cracked at Netherfield and at Longbourn if you happen to visit there. We must have a way to enter the house if we are needed."

"Excellent. Thank you so much. May I ask, how will you —" My question was cut off by the abrupt departure of the fairy tribe who left as swiftly as they had come.

"What did they say?" Mrs. Annesley urged.

"They will help. They like Miss Elizabeth." Mrs. Annesley nodded. "We must leave a window or door cracked at Netherfield, and we must find a way to do the same at Longbourn whenever we go there. They must have a way to enter."

"Leave that to me, Miss Darcy. I will ensure the fairies always have access to our homes."

∞∞∞

We were very chilled when we arrived home. Mrs. Nichols shooed us toward the large fire in the parlor and ordered a maid to bring hot tea. We held our hands to the fire and let the flames warm our bodies. That is how Lady Lucas and her two daughters found us. Shivering in front of the fire.

"Oh, how delightful," I said when they were announced. "You are just in time for tea. Mrs. Nichols ordered a pot when we returned half frozen from our walk."

"Are you an intrepid walker, Miss Darcy? I doubt even Eliza would have walked out today."

I urged the ladies to sit before responding. "Not so daring, though I do like to be out of doors when the weather allows."

Miss Lucas laughed. "And you think the weather allowed it today?" I laughed as well. I certainly could not tell her the truth, so I chose to turn my conversation to other things.

"I believe Mr. Bingley and my brother are making their way to our neighbor's today to invite them to the ball. Mr. Bingley has set a date."

"Oh yes," sighed Miss Maria. "My first true ball! Mr. Bingley and your brother brought our invitation just before we left to visit you."

"It will be my first ball, as well." I was pleased to find a commonality with the young lady. While I do not like to be the center of attention, Miss Maria is truly very shy. We have been in company several times, though I have scarcely said five words to her.

"It will be divine," she sighed again. "I hope a soldier asks me to dance."

"I am sure they will, my dear. You will be the belle of the ball." Lady Lucas lovingly patted her daughter's hand.

"Mother, you know very well it will be the Bennet sisters who will be the belles of the ball." At her sister's fallen face, Miss Lucas added, "But I will help you prepare, Maria, and you will look very lovely, indeed. I am sure you will dance with many soldiers."

"I wonder who else will attend," Maria pondered. "Do you think Mr. Collins will remain until then? I am sure he will wish to dance with Miss Elizabeth, though I doubt your brother will appreciate that," she added.

I dared not confess that he had asked for and had been denied Miss Elizabeth's first and supper sets. "We visited Longbourn yesterday. I believe Mr. Collins plans to stay until the night of the ball."

Lady Lucas tipped her head toward her eldest daughter. "You must assist your friend, Charlotte. I doubt she wishes to be saddled with Mr. Collins' attention when she could spend her time with Mr. Darcy, instead. You must interfere on her behalf."

Miss Lucas' face heated at her mother's words. "Mama, are you suggesting that I attempt to turn Mr. Collins' attentions toward me?"

"I have only suggested that you put yourself in his way, Charlotte, not that you do anything underhanded. If Miss Elizabeth will not have him, and I am certain she will not, then you have every right to try for yourself."

"What about Mary?" Miss Maria asked. "Mrs. Bennet will wish Mr. Collins to marry one of her daughters."

"I do not believe Miss Mary cares for Mr. Collins, either," I shared. This piece of intelligence seemed to please both Miss Lucas and her mother.

Our party finished our tea, and soon the Lucas ladies were on their way to visit another family. Mrs. Annesley and I braved the cold as we waved to their carriage.

"Miss Lucas would be a good partner for Mr. Collins. She would temper his… enthusiasm."

"Do you think she would want him? He is a buffoon, and she is so sensible."

Mrs. Annesley turned to me. "Not everyone has your advantages, Miss Darcy. Remember that."

I greatly dislike it when people say these things to me. I am aware of my circumstances. But even someone with far less wealth than I possess must think twice before pledging themselves to someone like Mr. Collins.

Mrs. Annesley moved up the stairs and I rushed to catch up with her. "Will you assist Miss Lucas in gaining Mr. Collins' attention?" Mrs. Annesley smiled, which meant she will interfere in some way with their paths. "You must give Miss Lucas the right to refuse. Do not spell her to accept him," I urged.

She rolled her eyes, the second time this week! "I would never force anyone to marry against their will. I simply plan to encourage him to dance with her at the ball."

And so you see, dear niece, this diary may now detail two love stories. My brother's to his OTL (your mother), and now the potential for love between Miss Lucas and Mr. Collins. I do not suspect that will be as interesting a story, however. Certainly, I have no desire to perform a riding spell on that gentleman. I have already spent more time in his presence than I would ever wish.

Chapter Thirty-six

Evening, 17 November 1811

Dear Diary,

Richard arrives tomorrow! I am excited to see him and have him here, especially as my time with Lady Catherine draws near. I can feel it. I dreamed last night that she arrived at the ball and made a terrible scene. She used her magic to explode the punch bowl, pull down all the chandeliers, and wreak havoc on the entire event. All along the two dragons fought just outside the ballroom windows. They were very easy to see as I have done such an impeccable job cleaning the glass.

As you can imagine, I awoke early again. Lately, my dreams have made it impossible to sleep in. On the positive side, I have never been so alert upon waking each morning. I suppose there is an upside to nightmares.

Since I was already up, I got dressed and went to find Mrs. Nichols. I wanted to discover the plans for Richard's arrival. As I expected, Miss Bingley put Richard in the east wing next to Mrs. Annesley. Of course, I could not override Miss Bingley's wishes, but I longed, too. Richard is very intelligent and will recognize the slight when he learns that Fitzwilliam and I have been included in the family wing. Fitzwilliam will be furious at the perceived injustice. Ah well, that is for Miss Bingley to deal with.

I offered a list of suggested dishes to Mrs. Nichols. Richard loves a full breakfast with heaps of eggs and sausages, but he has a weakness for sweets and always ends his morning meal with toast and jam. I suggested she pull out a jar of the delicious strawberry jam she served when we arrived. I also suggested trout, if she can find it, pheasant, of course, and a dessert made of late season apples or pears. She seemed very pleased to add these items to her list of offerings.

As today is Sunday, our party arranged ourselves in the front hall at exactly half past nine to attend services. Miss Bingley was irritated to learn we would, once again, attend services in Longbourn Village rather than at the Meryton church. Mr. Bingley successfully ignored her diatribe on the 'rustic' environment the Longbourn church provided.

Though the weather had warmed, it was still quite cold. There were few people standing in the churchyard when we arrived, but that did not stop Mr. Bingley, Fitzwilliam, or me from waiting for the Bennets. Despite the cold, the family had chosen to walk to the church, and we soon saw them emerge from the forest onto the lane.

"There they are," Mr. Bingley pointed to the family though they had already caught all of our attention. "Is not Miss Bennet the loveliest lady you have ever seen?" Fitzwilliam did not acknowledge this comment, his eyes firmly locked on the Bennet sister who had captured his attention.

"Georgiana!" Kitty exclaimed when she entered the yard. "Are you waiting on me? It is so cold!" I laughed and greeted her warmly.

"Oh dear, we must get you inside. Your cheeks and nose are as red as a berry. I will not have you getting sick on my watch, Miss Darcy." Mrs. Bennet ran her gloved hands over my frozen cheeks before patting them warmly and leading the rest of us inside.

As before, Fitzwilliam escorted Miss Elizabeth to her seat and sat behind her. Mr. Collins was irritated to see this, but a remnant of his two steps forward spell must remain because he rushed forward to interrupt the two but was swung around on his heels and forced to walk back four spaces. It took him five minutes to find his seat!

During service I noticed my brother would stop and tilt his ear toward his OTL while she sang. I will grant, Miss Elizabeth has a fine voice, but only a fool in love would make such a scene to listen. And, mind you, according to Darcy standards, it was truly a scene. But Fitzwilliam is a man in love. That much is obvious to all of us. Miss Bingley has grown ever more irritated and disenchanted with the Bennets' presence and I lay that solely at the feet of my brother's budding romance.

When the service ended, our party once again assembled on the lawn to chat. "Mr. Bingley," Mrs. Bennet called, then cleared her throat to pull the man's attention away from her eldest daughter. "If you are not already engaged, I would like to invite your party to supper this evening."

"I have already spoken to Mrs. Nichols about tonight's supper. Perhaps another night." Miss Bingley's mouth pursed, and her eyes dared her brother to contradict her.

But contradict her, he did. "Nonsense. There is plenty of time yet for Mrs. Nichols to rearrange her plans. We can have tonight's meal tomorrow." Then he clapped as if remembering something great. "That will be perfect, actually, since Fitzwilliam arrives tomorrow. It will give Mrs. Nichols more time to arrange for his visit if she is not so worried about tomorrow's menu."

Miss Bingley opened her mouth to correct her brother's assumptions, but Mrs. Bennet was too quick for her. "Excellent news! I look forward to seeing you all tonight. Perhaps you can stay late for games?"

Mr. Bingley practically emoted, but I was more interested in the pleased smile on my brother's face. Fitzwilliam Darcy was actually pleased to be invited to a family dinner with the Bennets. Richard will be dumbfounded when I share this with him.

"Miss Darcy, you should come home with us today. Jane has given me her ball gown and I would love your help making it over. Because Kitty is so small she will wear one of Lizzy's, though it will not look so well on her because she does not have Lizzy's dark eyes."

Kitty's eyes shot daggers at Miss Lydia, but I ignored the dig. Miss Kitty is very pretty, and, after seeing the gown, I think she will look very fetching on the night of the ball. Instead, I looked to my brother for permission. "You can spend the day with your friends, if that suits you." I assured him it did.

"Miss Darcy, you surprise me." Mr. Bennet, who has previously been speaking with a local farmer, made his way to our circle. "I did not expect you to be the kind of girl who would enjoy sitting in corners talking of soldiers and trim and giggling profusely. Tell me you do not also importune your brother for more pin money when you overspend your portion the first week of the quarter." His eyes twinkled allowing me to notice for the first time his resemblance to Miss Elizabeth.

I wanted to say that I recently discovered that I am exactly the kind of girl who giggles and talks of soldiers, but I never ask for more pin money as my current allowance is very generous. I did not say any of this to the teasing man, however. Every eye was upon me, and I found myself quite tongue-tied.

Mrs. Bennet playfully swatted her husband's arm. "Oh, Mr. Bennet, how you do go on. You must remember, not everyone has your penchant for silliness. Miss Darcy hardly knows what to think of you."

Mr. Bennet smirked. "Yes, I have ever been known for my silliness, dear." The comment might have been taken as condescending if it were not for the fact that Mr. Bennet clasped his wife's waving hand and kissed it. A pretty flush overtook the matron's face, and in that moment, she looked as young and pretty as her eldest daughter.

Releasing his bride's eyes from his own, Mr. Bennet looked at each daughter and then, looking to me, asked if we were ready to escape the cold. Kitty squealed her delight that I was coming with them. Mrs. Annesley caught my attention, so I excused myself for a moment to speak with her.

"If you can do it surreptitiously, share this gift with the fairies." She pulled a small pear from her pocket. I quickly hid the fruit in my own skirt pocket and thanked her for remembering. Then I made my way back to Kitty and Miss Lydia who were waiting for me. Miss Mary looked back at us longingly from her place next to Mr. Collins. Poor Miss Mary, to be saddled with such a walking partner.

As we approached the place where I had met the fairies, Mr. Bennet called out, "Aghch glyl magana, Fae." Soon each daughter repeated his greeting to the fairies, and I shared my own greeting which caused Kitty to laugh.

"Do you even know what you said, Georgiana?"

I smiled. "Yes, your sister told me about greeting the fairies when she walks past their home."

"Oh, yes. Lizzy and Papa take the fairy legends very seriously. They even practice the language when they are alone in his library. Lizzy swears she has met the fairies, but she is very good at telling stories. None of us believe her, of course." This was interesting news to store away. It seems I am not the only person who has had the privilege of a fairy introduction.

Miss Elizabeth pulled away and stooped next to the very tree where I had stood yesterday. She pulled a biscuit from her pocket and laid it at the base of the tree. "Dril," she quietly whispered. When she left, I placed my own offering next to hers. "Dril," I repeated, telling the fairies I also had an offering.

"You are as fanciful as my sister," Kitty teased. I rushed ahead with her but paused long enough to look back. The same fairy I met yesterday stood next to the small pear. The stem stood a little taller than the fairy's head. At its temple, the fairy wore my hair pin. It had used its magic to shrink it down to an appropriate size. Next time I will take a variety of ribbons as an offering. Perhaps fairies, like ladies, enjoy looking pretty.

∞∞∞

The day passed with rapidity. I helped Miss Lydia embroider flowers on her ball gown and assisted Kitty in choosing the best ribbon trim for her gown. As expected, Miss Lydia was incorrect in her judgement of Kitty's gown. Changing the ribbon color from the deep green Miss Elizabeth chose to a soft blue that better suits Kitty's coloring will make her dress very attractive. Though her mother would disagree, I think Kitty is far prettier than Miss Lydia, anyway, and a becoming gown will emphasize that.

Soon, it was time to dress for dinner. Mrs. Annesley sent a gown for me, so I had a change of clothes and was not forced to wear my church gown for the evening meal. I hurried to finish dressing and left the room to avoid the sisters' squabbling. In the hall I ran into Miss Elizabeth. It seems neither she nor I require much time to change for supper.

"Miss Darcy, I am so happy you spent the afternoon with us. I think your friendship has been very good for Kitty. She greatly values your budding relationship. I hope you can maintain it when you return to London."

"I hope so, too," I said with honesty. "Kitty is a very good friend to me. I hope we can remain so for the rest of our lives." When she did not respond, I ventured on. "Perhaps we will be closer than friends, someday. Perhaps… sisters?"

Miss Elizabeth blushed, but finally replied. "I hope you are always in one another's company."

I pushed past my normal reserve. What was the harm, I thought. I can always spell her memory away if I make a muck of things. "I hope we might be sisters someday, Miss Elizabeth. I believe you have captured my brother's heart. Has he, perhaps, captured yours as well?"

I did not think it possible, but Miss Elizabeth's blush grew even more intense. Her mouth worked, looking for words. Finally, she said, "I do not think it is my place to say, Miss Darcy. But do know, I would treasure being your sister if such a thing were to come to fruition."

In that moment, I could feel my love for Miss Elizabeth grow. Not only because she would welcome and cherish me as a sister but because I could see her love for my brother. It was written all over her face.

"There you are Lizzy." We looked up from our conversation to see Mrs. Bennet hurrying toward us. "Is that what you are wearing? What will Mr. Darcy think? You must change right away. Put on the green gown, you look very fine in it." She gently pushed her daughter back toward her room then turned to me. "I am quite confident your brother has eyes for my Lizzy. I will not have her lose his interest over a poor choice of dinner gowns." Then she wrapped her arm in mine, and we walked down the stairs together.

Fitzwilliam and the rest of the Netherfield party arrived soon after Mrs. Bennet and I reached the parlor. The small smile he wore on his lips fell when he saw Miss Elizabeth was not yet with us, but it was unnoticeable to the average person. Mr. Bingley's audible sigh at Miss Bennet's absence was far more conspicuous. Mrs. Bennet and I both had to stifle a giggle.

"Georgie, did you have a good afternoon?"

"Oh, yes," I answered. "I helped Miss Lydia embroider her ball gown and assisted Kitty in finding a better color to trim her own. They will both be very lovely."

"Speaking of the ball," he ventured. "You are not yet out, but I would dislike it if you do not also have an appropriate gown to wear. Would you like to visit the local modiste and have a new gown of your own?"

Oh my goodness, absolutely, yes! I exclaimed in my head. "Of course!" I exclaimed out loud. Fitzwilliam seemed pleased with my enthusiasm, but his eyes soon shifted from mine to the door. If you guessed that Miss Elizabeth had arrived, you were correct. She wore the green gown her mother suggested, and she looked lovely. I looked toward Mrs. Bennet who nodded her head and offered me a sly wink. The lady is brilliant in her own way.

Miss Elizabeth made her way to our side, but seeing that I was a third wheel, I excused myself and made my way toward Kitty and Miss Mary who were also now in attendance. "Is Miss Lydia still getting dressed?" Kitty rolled her eyes.

"She has the distinct impression that she owns everything that her sisters possess. She attempted to take Kitty's light blue ribbons and wear them tonight."

"The ones that you plan to wear to the ball?" Kitty's eyes were wide as she gravely nodded her head.

"Yes, but they are safe now. Kitty brought them to me, and I locked them in my box. Lydia would have to steal the entire box to get them, and then she would have to destroy it to retrieve them. Even Mama would find that appalling, though she usually allows Lydia to have her way."

Just then a pouting Lydia stomped into the parlor. Seeing Kitty and Miss Mary, she wrinkled her nose in disgust and found a seat near her mother. Miss Bennet entered directly behind her, much to Mr. Bingley's great relief. And soon, Mr. Bennet found his way into the room.

"Ah, so we have all assembled. Gentlemen, may I offer you a drink?" Mr. Hurst was the first to assent. Mr. Bingley and Fitzwilliam agreed with less enthusiasm but no less thanks.

Aside from Miss Bingley, who openly disdained everything

about the Bennets and Longbourn, and Mr. Collins, whose witlessness prevented him from making proper conversation, the party was happy and talkative. Soon, the bell rang for dinner. Mr. Bennet escorted Mrs. Hurst to dinner, and Mr. Hurst escorted Mrs. Bennet. Fitzwilliam, of course, escorted Miss Elizabeth, and Mr. Collins trod behind going two steps forward and four steps back. Mr. Bingley offered Miss Bennet and Miss Bingley his arms. Kitty, Miss Mary, Miss Lydia, and I walked in last.

Dinner was a lively affair. Mrs. Bennet served partridge, trout, and ham along with turnips, greens, and a delicious potato soup I had never had before. I must ask for the receipt since I noticed Fitzwilliam also enjoyed it. Perhaps Miss Elizabeth will bring it with her when they wed.

Mr. Collins also enjoyed the soup, though he continued to say, "I have never enjoyed such exemplary boiled potatoes."

"They are not simply boiled, Mr. Collins. It is a soup." Mrs. Bennet reminded him each time, but it did not stick for he repeated himself at least four times.

When the meal ended, the ladies followed Mrs. Bennet to the parlor where we prepared the room for card games. The men joined us soon after. Mr. Bennet and Fitzwilliam were suspiciously delayed. If Mrs. Bennet noticed, she was unexpectedly discrete about it. But when the two men finally found their way into the room, she, once again, nodded her head in my direction and placed her index finger on her nose as if to signal, "I told you so." Once again, I had to stifle a giggle. I am going to enjoy having her in my family very much.

Miss Bingley made a valiant attempt to clasp Fitzwilliam's arm as he walked past, but he employed a technique I have seen him use many times before. In a swift move, he clasped his hands behind his back and held his arms tightly to his body. In this way, he was able to bypass her grasping hands and made his way to a smiling Miss Elizabeth. I suspect I will have the right to soon address her as Elizabeth. Elizabeth Darcy! How well that sounds.

It is growing very late, so I will conclude this entry. I must add that we played cards well into the evening. The younger girls played lottery, even Miss Mary! Mr. Collins joined us, and between Miss Mary and me, we were able to take all his fish!

Fitzwilliam turned pages for Miss Elizabeth as she sang and played. When Miss Bingley took her turn at the piano, my brother was conveniently called to take Mr. Bennet's place at the card table. Clever, clever Mrs. Bennet.

Chapter Thirty-seven

Evening, 18 November 1811

Dear Diary,

In anticipation of Richard's arrival, I awoke early. After checking in with Mrs. Nichols on his room arrangements, I made my way downstairs for an early breakfast. Unsurprisingly, Fitzwilliam had just sat down for his first cup of coffee.

"Good morning." I dipped a curtsy and gave him my sweetest smile. Perhaps if I show constant sweetness, he will confess his relationship with Miss Elizabeth.

He offered a return smile from over his coffee cup. "Good morning, Georgie. Are you excited to see your cousin today?"

"I am very happy he is coming. I think our party will be much better with his presence."

Fitzwilliam swallowed his coffee before answering. "Yes, Richard does tend to carry excitement with him, no matter where he goes."

A bit of excitement was precisely why I wished Richard to be nearer. Though I have grown more confident in my magical skills and abilities, I am apprehensive about Lady Catherine's looming threat. Whatever excitement she chooses to cause, it would be better to have Richard nearby. Between him and my brother, I am guaranteed to be as well protected as two non-magical beings can provide. I could, of course, not say any of this to Fitzwilliam. Instead, we ate in a companionable silence until we were joined by Mrs. Annesley and Mr. Bingley.

Fitzwilliam and Mr. Bingley excused themselves from the breakfast table first. Fitzwilliam stopped to kiss my cheek before he left. No sooner had he turned to leave than Mrs. Annesley grabbed Mr. Bingley's cup. She sighed. "Such a boring man."

I giggled. "What does it say?" She handed me the cup, wordlessly urging me to read the leaves for myself. I screwed up my nose as I attempted to read the leaves. My improvement in this part of magic has been negligible. "He will walk with his lady?"

She sighed again. "Yes, as he has done practically every day for weeks. I don't need to read your brother's leaves to know that he has progressed much further in his pursuit of Miss Elizabeth.

"Well, that is good since Fitzwilliam rarely drinks tea for breakfast." Mrs. Annesley pinched my nose in a playful manner that has been missing these past few weeks. Then she pointed to my own teacup and wordlessly insisted I finish my own tea. When I did, I took a hesitant look at my own leaves. "I think... I think I will find success today."

Mrs. Annesley took the cup from my hand. "Exactly. You are getting better at this." She stood. "Come with me. I believe I know exactly what success you will achieve today."

I followed her into the hall and toward the front door. Before I knew it, I was bundled in a warm coat and bonnet. We walked down the lane, and across a small path until we reached a field where a dozen cattle grazed. "Today, you will practice the Banish spell on something large." Before my face had a chance to show my disappointment with this announcement she added, "Without using your bloodstone."

That statement changed my perspective quite a bit. It is one thing to banish something small without a bloodstone, but to banish a cow, that is quite another. Banishing something small like a cat or a napkin is rather simple, especially now that I have practiced it many times. But to do such a thing to a grazing heifer? Needless to say, I was skeptical this would work. "Why must I try this without a bloodstone? I always keep them around my neck. If I am forced to use the spell on Lady Catherine, they will be available."

"In theory, you are correct. However, when magic is involved, anything can happen. Though your grandmother warned that Lady Catherine is not as strong as she believes she is, it does not mean she is without any strengths. You may be so busy defending against her powers that you have little time to use your stones. In any case, it is good for us to know the extent of your innate powers."

Though I was still unsure of my abilities, I nodded my head. "Let's begin with something simple. Take out your bloodstone, hold it in your hands, and banish that cow to the adjacent field." She pointed to a white female currently licking at an itchy spot on its rump.

I removed the bloodstone necklace from where it lay against my skin and held it out toward the cow. The day was warmer than the past two, and I took a moment to enjoy the sun on my face before gathering my magic and releasing it with a single command. "Banish," I commanded. Before my eyes, the enormous creature disappeared only to reappear one-hundred feet away in the adjoining pasture. I chuckled when I saw the confused look on her face. With the power of the bloodstones, and the sigils engraved upon them, it took very little of my energy to do as I was asked.

"Excellent," Mrs. Annesley praised. "Now use the spell to bring her back to exactly where she stood before." This request proved more difficult. Given that the heifer was now much further from me, I had to concentrate more on pulling her back. Still, with the help of the bloodstones and sigils, I was able to move her back on my first attempt. Unfortunately, the activity did impact my energy levels and I was forced to rest against a tree for a few minutes before continuing my practice.

"Are you ready to try again?" I agreed that I was and moved back to stand with her nearer to the cattle.

"See the calf standing there? The one with the black on its nose?" I followed her pointing finger and identified it.

"Yes. Is that the one you want me to move?"

"Yes. I think you should start with a smaller target since you will be without the use of magical tools." Smaller was a relative term. The calf was smaller than the adults but having been born in the spring, it had grown rather large.

"Without using your bloodstones, move that calf to the next field." A weight settled in my stomach, telling me I was not ready for this, but I did not share that with her.

Trying my best to look confident, I stepped a few feet away and concentrated on the calf. After three deep breaths, I lifted my hand, glanced at the next field to confirm where I wanted the cow to land, and called out, "Banish!"

Nothing happened.

"You must concentrate, Miss Darcy. Let your power gather in your chest before pushing it out."

"I will," I promised.

My mouth was dry, and I forced my tongue between my teeth and lips to release them from the tight hold they had on one another. I inhaled again and willed my magic to gather. Normally, I allow my magic to flow, but to force it to collect creates a new sensation —somewhere between a tickle and an itch. I tolerated the sensation for as long as I could before I commanded, "Banish!"

It worked! In the blink of an eye, the calf disappeared from the field where I stood and reappeared in the next.

"You did it!" Mrs. Annesley's smile rivaled my own. "Very, very good, Miss Darcy. I knew you could!" We celebrated for a short period before she sobered. "Now, you must return it to its herd.

My sense of accomplishment evaporated. If moving the cow back while using a bloodstone proved tiring, I knew this would exhaust me. I did not wallow in self-doubt, however. I steeled myself for the task; I am a Darcy, after all.

With unyielding determination I walked a few feet away from Mrs. Annesley and forced my full attention on the calf. I took four deep breaths and willed my heart rate to slow. I allowed the magic to pool in my chest. Its tingling sensation filled my ribcage and up into my throat before I finally gasped out, "Banish!"

To my surprise, the calf disappeared from the pasture where he stood grazing and reappeared thirty feet in front of me. It was not exactly where I had planned to put him, but it was close. The simple fact that I had accomplished my task on the first try elated me. I was not going to let a matter of twenty feet discourage me.

It did not discourage Mrs. Annesley, either. "That happened so fast! If I had not known you were using a spell, I would not have even paid attention to the cow's transition. How did you manage it?" Her sentences ran together in her excitement, and she gave me a surprisingly strong hug.

She stepped back and placed her hands on my shoulders. "I have another challenge for you, but only if you think you can manage it."

My high was so great, I would have agreed to anything at that moment. "Of course! What else shall I move."

Mrs. Annesley turned to face the tree behind us. "I would like for you to try to move this tree."

And just like that, my euphoria fell. "A tree! Why, it is

massive!"

"Not so massive," she argued. "It is the smallest tree here." This was true. Standing only fifteen feet tall, it was not so large as the tree I had rested against. Still, it was a tree.

"The difficulty will be the roots. Though the tree is small, its roots will be strong." My face must have shown my hesitance because she then changed the course of her conversation. "Perhaps today is not the time to try. You should rest. We will come back tomorrow."

I straightened my shoulders. She may not have intended to challenge me, but in my mind a gauntlet had just been thrown at my feet. "I will do it."

She patted my shoulders. "You can do this. I believe in you." I attempted a smile, but I feared it was not very convincing.

Once again, I stepped away and concentrated. This time I took at least seven deep breaths before I calmed myself enough to allow my magic to pool. When the sensations reached the top of my throat and threatened to choke me, I ordered, "Banish!" The tree disappeared from in front of my eyes.

With excitement, I turned to face the field behind me. And there, standing tall in the middle of an expanse of grass was the tree. It was beautifully positioned to grow large and offer shade in every direction to anyone who might need it.

"Perfect!" Mrs. Annesley exclaimed. "I am so impressed. I have known for a long time that your power is immense, but to accomplish such a feat without the assistance of any magical tools is practically unheard of."

"Truly?" Mrs. Annesley has hinted several times that I have the potential for power, but it is difficult to think of myself as being someone special.

"Oh, yes. Your magic has grown tremendously in the past few weeks. You can do things with less fatigue. And you have more innate abilities than any witch I have ever known. I do not know what Lady Catherine threatens, but I am confident you will be ready." Seeing my eyes widen, she rushed to assure me. "Do not fret. I will be right beside you every step of the way. You will not face her alone."

Having decided that I had practiced enough for the day, Mrs. Annesley and I began our short walk back to the house. By the time we arrived, the buzz from my success had worn off and I had grown very tired.

We handed our coats to the waiting footman and walked up the stairs toward our rooms. Before we turned toward our respective wings, Mrs. Annesley offered some advice. "Get some rest before your cousin arrives. And remember, if you can move a rooted tree from one field to another, you can remove an elderly lady from the space where you stand."

I am hopeful my grandmother's prediction was incorrect. Perhaps Lady Catherine poses no threat to any of us. But since Fitzwilliam and Miss Elizabeth appear to be moving rapidly toward the altar, I must be prepared. That news will infuriate Lady Catherine as nothing has ever done before. Yes, I am hopeful that there will be no need for magic and that my ancestor was incorrect, but just in case I need to be better every day. And today, I proved that I have the strength to do something very difficult.

∞∞∞

Richard arrived just before tea was served. He was dusty and tired, but in good spirits. Despite her wishes, Miss Bingley held our refreshments until he was able to cleanse some of the road grime from his body and clothes.

"It is so good to see you, Gopher." He hugged me close and kissed the top of my head. I laughed despite my absolute hatred for the pet name he has called me since I was a babe.

"I am not Gopher, Richard. I will be out next year, so I must insist that you call me by my name."

He put his hand over his heart. "I would never wish to cause my little cousin embarrassment. I will endeavor to call you Gopher only in front of family, close friends, and casual acquaintances." I swatted his arm.

"Richard, I am pleased to see you." Fitzwilliam clasped our cousin's hand and gave him a hearty slap on the back.

"No more than I am, Darcy. I was overjoyed to receive Georgiana's invitation." He emphasized my name in his typical dramatic fashion.

Fitzwilliam turned to me. "You invited Richard? I thought he requested to visit us."

Though I could feel my face heat, I refused to ignore his comment. "I thought you might need some assistance."

My brother's eyes widened. "Assistance? With what?"

Richard gave a hearty laugh. "It seems our little Gopher was worried you would make a muddle of your romance with— What was it? Oh, yes. Miss Elizabeth Bennet." Richard had not forgotten the lady's name any more than Fitzwilliam had. He simply loves to play. He really should have taken to the stage instead of the military. If it were not for the fact that he is the son of an earl, I suspect he would have.

Fitzwilliam narrowed his eyes at both of us, but we ignored him. Richard escorted me into the parlor for tea where the Bingleys and Hursts sat waiting.

"Colonel, it is good to see you," Bingley greeted. I know your cousins have anticipated your arrival. And I am very pleased to have you here in time for my ball."

"Do not go on any more about the ball," Miss Bingley whined. "It has consumed my entire day already. I have not an ounce of energy left to give it."

The corner of my cousin's mouth quirked, but he refrained from laughing outright at her. Richard greeted the rest of the party, bending gallantly over Miss Bingley's, Mrs. Hurst's, and Mrs. Annesley's hands. Then, sitting, he rubbed his hands together and declared, "This is the finest-looking tea I have seen in ages. I do not know if my eyes are happier with the variety of food on the table or the lovely visages around it." Miss Bingley rolled her eyes at his declaration, but Mrs. Hurst's face turned a vivid shade of pink.

Our small meal proceeded in much the same fashion. Mr. Bingley boasted of his warm welcome to the neighborhood and his desire to give back by hosting a ball. Miss Bingley lamented every compliment given to the people of the area, and openly disdained the idea of the ball. Mrs. Hurst tittered at every flirtatious comment Richard parried her way, while Mr. Hurst, as ever, remained quiet and focused on his cakes. Mrs. Annesley also remained quiet, though out of politeness rather than gluttony. And Fitzwilliam and I basked in our combined joy at our cousin's arrival.

"You have said much about the goodness of your neighbors, Bingley, but what about their looks. Are there any beautiful daughters to be found in Meryton?"

"To be sure, Colonel. The Misses Bennet are among the most beautiful ladies I have ever encountered. Miss Bennet, in particular… though I, er, I would not wish…"

Richard nodded his head. "Understood Bingley. But what about Miss Bennet's younger sisters. Are they as pretty as she is?"

Mr. Bingley's face flushed so that I could hardly see his freckles any longer. "Well, yes, they are all quite lovely. Miss Elizabeth is very pretty, as well, though she has dark eyes and dark hair, unlike the rest of her family. But you must not flirt with her either, for she is meant for —"

"She is meant for no one," Miss Bingley shrilled. "Miss Eliza

Bennet is a complete hoyden, and why anyone would think she is lovely, much less second only to dear Jane, I cannot comprehend."

I do not know how it is possible, as my brother's posture is always erect, but Fitzwilliam managed to sit even taller at that moment. His hand tightened on the handle of his tea, and I silently directed magic toward the cup to prevent him from breaking it and cutting his hand.

"Be that as it may, Miss Bingley, I would like to judge for myself the loveliness of the Bennet sisters." He turned to Mr. Bingley. "Do you think it is too late to visit them today? Certainly, visiting hours are over, but I have often found that a house full of ladies will forgive a man in uniform the occasional breach in manners."

Mr. Bingley clapped his hands together. "That is a perfect solution. Mrs. Bennet is a gracious hostess, and she loves a man in uniform. Why, I believe she might even be put out with me if I did not bring you to meet them this afternoon."

"Oh, Charles," Miss Bingley moaned.

"I think you are correct, Bingley. Mrs. Bennet will be irked with you if she is not the first in the neighborhood to meet your guest." Fitzwilliam smiled as he said it. I could tell he cared not a whit for Mrs. Bennet's feelings; he wished to see his OTL.

Soon after, our party was traveling to Longbourn. Mr. Hurst declined the trip, no doubt to continue his love affair with the remaining cakes. Though Miss Bingley lamented the idea of visiting "those loud Bennets," she joined us. Unfortunately for her, Mrs. Annesley also attended, which required two carriages, necessitating one for the Bingleys and another for our family. Try as she might, Miss Bingley could not inveigle her way into our equipage.

We had just introduced Richard to the Bennets when Miss

Lydia and Mr. Collins began to vie for his attention. "Colonel Fitzwilliam, I am very pleased that you will come to Mr. Bingley's ball. I love to dance with a man in a red coat. Have you asked a lady for the first set yet? Mine is still available." I do not know how he managed it, but Richard's face remained free of both humor and disgust. Instead, he bowed over her hand and thanked her for the warm welcome.

"Colonel Fitzwilliam, sir, I must take this opportunity to welcome you to my future home." Mr. Collins greeted him with several ostentatious bows while simultaneously shaking his hand in a vigorous manner.

"And I should like to welcome you to my current home," Mr. Bennet drawled.

"Oh, yes. Oh, yes. I did not mean. It is just that you are here along with Mr. Darcy. My dear patroness, Lady Catherine de Bourgh has spoken of the two of you so many times. I did not believe I would ever have the satisfaction of greeting you both. The only thing that is better is if you were joined by your father, the earl. And to think, here in my own home!"

Richard did smirk at this, for it is difficult to overlook the foolishness of Mr. Collins. "I believe it is your future home, Mr. Collins."

It was not long before Mrs. Bennet arranged for the young people to walk in the garden to enjoy the warm day. Fitzwilliam attended to Miss Elizabeth, but it was Richard who walked out with her. Fitzwilliam's face tightened with how neatly Richard arranged it.

"You have had the great pleasure of Miss Elizabeth's company for weeks, Darcy. Allow a poor soldier a little time in a pretty lady's presence." Miss Elizabeth laughed at my cousin's antics, and though she did not know I was paying close attention, I saw her wink at my brother. This appeased him somewhat. He offered his arm to Mrs. Annesley and, though not offered, found Miss Bingley perched upon the other.

Kitty and I walked together, while Miss Mary was saddled with Mr. Collins. Mr. Bingley, as predicted by the tea leaves, escorted Miss Bennet. Miss Lydia, irritated by the attention her sister received from my cousin, rushed forward and, as smooth as Miss Bingley, clutched her hand on his free arm. Richard smiled down at her but did not stop his conversation with Miss Elizabeth.

I was not privy to their words, but I did overhear Miss Bingley's caustic remarks. "See there, Mr. Darcy, Eliza Bennet has no manners at all. She has paid you the utmost attention, grasping with desperation to claim your notice. And now that a new man has come into her home, she has thrown you over. And for your own cousin. It is a good thing you are immune to her meager charms."

"The nerve! I would like to slap Miss Bingley," Kitty whispered in outrage. "To think that Lizzy would have eyes for anyone but your brother. I am sure she is only being nice to your cousin for Mr. Darcy's sake. You must believe me, Georgiana, Lizzy is quite enamored with your brother.

"I am aware," I answered. "And I suspect my brother's feelings are even deeper. We may end up being sisters after all!" At this pronouncement the two of us erupted into a fit of giggles.

Given the lateness of our visit, we did not stay at Longbourn for long. Soon, I was handed back into my carriage with a promise to see Kitty again later in the week. Fitzwilliam stood with Miss Elizabeth for as long as possible, allowing Kitty and I to continue our conversation.

When we finally finished, Richard climbed into the carriage. "Well, Gopher, it seems you have made a friend of Miss Kitty, and your brother has made more than a friend of Miss Elizabeth." He dipped his head in the couple's direction and then laughed when Fitzwilliam drew her hand to his mouth for a kiss.

"She will be my sister soon, I think."

"I hope so," he said. "I like her a lot. She will be good for him." We both hid our smiles when Fitzwilliam entered and sat across from me.

Chapter Thirty-eight

Noon, 19 November 1811

Dear Diary,

I had another dream about the violet dragon. This time it was very upset with me, though I could not understand why. "Gurowul, mwah, bwahhh," it ranted over and over, but I could not understand it. The beast stomped his feet and flew away, only to come right back and repeat the same growling message over and over. I had the distinct impression it was trying to tell me something, though I had no idea what.

I was finally startled awake near five of the clock. Though I was still tired, I knew I would be unable to sleep, so I took out the mind-numbing book about spirit guides. However, this morning's content was not boring at all. I read a passage that put everything into perspective. The book said:

> *There is no single way a spirit guide will present itself. For humans, the connection to a spirit guide is difficult to maintain. Through the discipline of meditation, humans can link to their guide, though likely only on occasion. The connection between magical beings and their spirit guide is easier. Creatures such as fairies, pixies, and the like customarily commune with their guides daily. These beings are lucky to see their guides whenever they desire their assistance. For witches, the practice of communicating with a spirit guide occurs during the dream state...*

The book continued with more information, but I was too excited to read it. I understood why Bael suggested I would return for another request, and I knew why the violet dragon continued to plague my dreams. It had a message for me!

With excitement, I jumped from the bed and pulled Bael's sigil into my hand. Then, remembering propriety, I donned my most serviceable gown. I missed several buttons in the back, but it was better than what I had on before. There was no need for Bael to see me in my nightgown! Once I ensured my appearance was as proper as possible for a five o'clock rendezvous with a mystic guide, I took the bloodstone into my hand and began the process of breathing my essence into the rock.

Soon, a lavender mist formed in front of me, and as expected, Bael stepped out from the haze. "You have called me, Georgiana?" His eyes held a special light that I had not seen previously. I did not understand it at the moment, but I soon apprehended his pleasure.

"Yes, I have discovered what I need to know. With your permission, I wish to speak the language of dragons."

A broad grin spread across the old man's face. "Excellent, though it took you longer than I imagined." Still smiling, he touched my shoulder and said, "Georgiana Darcy, you can now speak to dragons. Use it wisely and take their counsel. Dragons are well-known for their wisdom."

I curtsied once, and then in my excitement, twice. I must have looked as foolish as Mr. Collins, but it did not matter. I can speak to dragons! Perhaps now I will understand why the violet beast continues to visit me and what it wishes me to know.

When Bael left, I readied myself for bed once more, so eager was I to speak to my spirit guide. Unfortunately, my excitement was too great, and I could not return to sleep. Instead, I continued to read my book on spirit guides (it is still incredibly boring, by the way). Afterwards, I practiced the Banish spell. The bed in my room is truly hideous, but the one in the room adjacent to Mrs. Annesley's is lovely. It proved difficult to move the bed to a space I could not see, but after visualizing the location for some time, I managed it.

To make it work, I had to first banish my bed to the hallway outside of Mrs. Annesley's room. Then I banished the bed I wished for into my own room. Then I moved my original bed into the space that was now vacant. Though my new bed is very beautiful, the mattress is abysmal. I will rearrange the mattresses once everyone is asleep this evening. The Banish spell is proving increasingly useful, perhaps more so than the Silence spell.

At this point, I was beginning to grow tired and thought I might find rest again. However, just as I laid down, the mirror buzzed on my bedside table. Fitzwilliam and Miss Elizabeth were together! It had been days since I had received a notification, and I was humming with anticipation of what their rendezvous meant.

"Fitzwilliam," Miss Elizabeth whispered into the cool November air.

"Elizabeth." His shoes moved toward her and, when they drew closer, I could just make out the clasp of their hands. "I feared I would never spend time alone with you, again. That beetle-headed Collins is determined to keep us apart."

Miss Elizabeth laughed, a high, tinkling sound that delighted my ears. "He may intend to do so, but he has proven inadequate to the task. Why, did you see the man in the garden the last two times you have visited? He could not decide if he was coming or going, though that did not quell his diatribe against my unsuitable designs upon your person."

Fitzwilliam chuckled. "I like your designs upon my person, madam." The view from his shoes prevented me from seeing, but I could still hear the telltale sounds of their kisses. Repulsed by their display of affection, but thrilled by their growing regard for one another, I put the mirror down and rang for La Roche.

∞∞∞

Evening

Though I most wished to see Kitty and for Fitzwilliam to visit Miss Elizabeth, we visited no one today, and no one visited us. I contemplated inviting the Lucas ladies for tea but felt it best to leave Miss Bingley undisturbed. Though she loves the attention she gets from hosting, she abhors anyone from "trade" in her home. And since Mrs. Bennet's brothers are in trade and Sir William Lucas once owned a shop in Meryton, she deems them all as tradesmen. After my early morning magical endeavors, I chose to avoid the barrage of complaints she would deliver after our guests' departure. I now wish that I had not given in to my desire for peace, for I did not find it.

After tea, I took advantage of the light and chose to sketch. I have always enjoyed drawing, but I have been so busy with magic these past months that I have not practiced. I had it in my mind that I would sketch a picture of the fairy standing next to the small pear as a gift the next time I entered the woods. Fitzwilliam sat at the desk writing to his steward, while Richard sat in the middle of the room reading a book. He has few opportunities to be idle, and he has chosen to take advantage while he is on leave.

I must give Miss Bingley credit —she remained strangely quiet for longer than I expected. However, too soon for my comfort, she wandered over to my spot near the window to admire my work. "What an exceptional drawing, Miss Darcy. But whyever would you sketch a pixie?"

"Pixies have wings; this is a fairy."

"Whatever it is, why would you draw something so whimsical? I suggest you spend your time sketching faces or landscapes. I would be a willing model if you require one. Your brother would enjoy a portrait done by your own hand, I believe."

"Thank you for the offer, but I would like to finish this drawing. I have only a little left before I use my pencils to color it in."

This did not suit the lady at all. "If you change your mind, I will be happy to sit for you. Or perhaps you will prefer my help another day."

Richard, having heard our conversation, placed his book down and strolled over to look at my rendering. "I like it, Gopher. Perhaps you can draw a dragon next. I would enjoy a dragon sketch." I beamed up at him. I had already begun a drawing of my spirit guide. Perhaps I will finish it and gift it to my cousin.

"Oh, to be sure, Miss Darcy's talent is exceptional. I just question the subject." Richard held her captive with his blue stare causing her face to heat. "I mean, of course, Miss Darcy's choice is perfectly acceptable and appropriate for a young girl of her station. But as she will be out soon, she must begin to focus on talents that will gain her the notice of a gentleman. I think she would be better served to work on capturing faces."

"I believe the fairy she has drawn has a face." Richard's words were clipped. I felt vindicated by his attitude toward the lady.

"Of course," she hastily replied. "And such a lovely face it is. With —" she walked closer to reinspect my drawing. "With such large, expressive eyes. I declare, is there nothing a Darcy cannot do? Mr. Darcy is an excellent dancer, reader, card player, fencer, and rider. And, of course, he is the best landlord in all of England. And Miss Darcy can play, sing, sew, and draw."

"You are correct, Miss Bingley. My cousins are both excellent at many things; however, I know of at least one area of deficiency for each." He winked down at me.

Fitzwilliam's attention had been caught. "Do tell, Richard. Where do Georgiana and I fall short of the mark?"

Miss Bingley's eyes widened. "Mr. Darcy, your cousin is only teasing. There is no deficiency to be had by you or your sister."

Richard ignored the lady and answered my brother. "I believe, Darcy, that you perform poorly in crowds, particularly when you do not know many people. Your sister is the same. You are both reserved and shy around strangers."

Fitzwilliam laughed. "You have outed us to Miss Bingley, Richard. Poorly done." I laughed too.

Miss Bingley, thwarted in her attempt to praise my brother and me, lifted her nose and walked away. "If you will excuse me, I must speak with Mrs. Nichols about tonight's supper."

Chapter Thirty-nine

Evening, 20 November 1811

Dear Diary,

My dragon visited last night. Her name is Berwyn, and she is perfect! I must tell you everything exactly as it was said, since I do not wish to forget a moment of our conversation.

"Georgiana, I must speak with you. Tell me you have finally understood who I am and can now understand me." Her violet scales shimmered in the sunlight.

"I can. I am sorry it took me so long to grasp our connection. I thought you were a dream."

She placed her large front paw on my shoulder. I was surprised by how tenderly she rested it there, allowing hardly any weight to press upon me. "It is fine. You can understand me now and it is not too late. Come, let us walk for a moment."

We walked down a brightly lit path that was reminiscent of Pemberley, yet unfamiliar. The trail was bordered by hundreds of wildflowers sprouting in vibrant spring colors. I bent down and plucked a spotted orchid and handed it to my guide. "For you. The purple veining reminds me of your beautiful scales."

She offered me a smile, or at least what I think might pass for a smile from a dragon. "You, dear child, remind me so much of your mother."

This stopped me in my tracks. "You knew my mother?" Tears pricked my eyes. I forced myself to blink them away.

"I did. I was her spirit guide before you. I am Berwyn. I have long served the women of your family. Before your mother, I was your great-grandmother's spirit guide. Now that was a fearsome lady. No greater witch have I ever known. Your mother and aunt did not match her magic, but you—I believe you may be the strongest of your line."

"But is it enough? My grandmother warned me to be wary of Lady Catherine. I am mostly untrained. I did not even learn of my powers until August. Even with my innate abilities, will it be enough?"

Berwyn stopped and looked at me, her front paws rested on her generous waist. "Do you not trust me? I am your spirit guide. I have sworn to protect and advise you to the best of my ability. I never led your mother astray and I will not do so to you, either."

Fearful that I had offended the great creature, I stepped forward and cautiously rubbed my hand on what I could only describe as her forearm. "No, no. I do trust you. It is for myself that I hold misgivings."

Her face softened. "Do not fret, little one. I am here to tell you how to survive her." Then she began a long story of her history with Lady Catherine.

"Your aunt has always been too assured in her powers and too indolent to hone them. She often threatened your mother with ill magic, and on occasion, attempted to use it. But your mother was an excellent student and practiced her magic daily. Your aunt's threats were largely just words."

"She —she didn't kill my mother, did she?" I had never considered the thought before but knowing that Lady Catherine had threatened her with magic made me wonder.

"No, dear heart. Your mother was not killed by any magical circumstances. She simply never recovered from her last delivery. She was not physically strong enough to hold on."

The tears that had been threatening to fall since we began our conversation about my mother, finally spilled. "So, I killed my mother?"

Berwyn clasped me to her large, warm body. "No, my sweet. You did not. Your mother gave birth to another son when you were two years old. He was early. Neither survived." My anger rose. Why had I not been informed of this? Sensing the tendency of my thoughts, Berwyn said, "Do not blame your brother. He was away at school and did not know of it either." My heart broke anew, not only for the loss of my mother but for my brother's loss.

When I had regained my composure, we began our walk again. "What advice do you have for me? How might I prepare myself for Lady Catherine?"

Berwyn turned her serious eyes on me. "Your aunt should never have been granted powers by her ancestors. You must stop her. When the time is right, you must take her powers. It is not an easy spell, and you will require assistance from a mystic."

"How am I to do such a thing? I did not even realize it was possible!"

"It requires multiple sources of power to complete, but you have access to ancestors, magical creatures, and mystics who can help you. Lady Catherine's spirit guide has indicated the time is growing near. You must prepare yourself."

I wanted to ask if Lady Catherine's guide was the fearsome crimson dragon, but I was too late. Berwyn flew away and I was wrenched awake by her absence.

I sent word to Mrs. Annesley that I needed to see her before breakfast. When she arrived, I told her everything I had experienced and the advice I had received. "What do you think it means? How am I to steal her power?"

"Do not fret, I am here to guide you. I must consult my

books, but I believe I know the solution. Do not contact your mystics until I have more information for you. Until then, take a day off from magic to enjoy yourself. After breakfast, we will visit town and order your ball gown."

"Take a day off from magic! How could you suggest such a thing? Berwyn says the time is drawing near. I cannot relent in my efforts now, not when there is so much at stake."

"Be easy, Miss Darcy. I will not lead you astray. I simply need to review my books. Our rest will only be for one day."

∞∞∞

After breakfast, Mrs. Annesley and Richard escorted me to town to commission a new gown. Though busy with other orders, Mrs. Plotts was pleased with our commission and promised to have my gown prepared for the first fitting no later than the twenty-third of the month.

While Mrs. Annesley spoke with the seamstress about her own order, Richard and I walked toward the front of the shop. "What is wrong with you today? I thought you would be overjoyed to order your first ball gown." Richard clasped his large hand around my shoulder and pulled me to his side for a quick embrace. "Are you upset because your brother is seeing Miss Elizabeth? Have you decided you do not like her?"

"What? Oh, no, of course I adore Miss Elizabeth. She is perfect for him. They will be happy together, I think."

"Then what is it? Why are you so distracted today?"

I could not tell Richard everything, but I ventured to tell him as much as possible. "I am concerned over Lady Catherine's reaction when she learns that my brother is in love with someone who is not her daughter."

Richard laughed. "I doubt she will care if he is in love. She is not the type to give credence to such a thing. She will be incredibly angry, however, when she learns he plans to marry the lady."

"Has he told you that?" I asked, bouncing on my toes in excitement.

"Ha! As if your brother would tell me anything. You know better." I tilted my head, waiting for further explanation. "I can see it in the way he speaks to her and about her. He is in love. If they are not courting yet, they soon will be."

I bit the inside of my cheek to prevent myself from sharing Fitzwilliam's secret. When the urge had passed, I said, "I think they will announce an engagement, not a courtship."

"Is that a bet, little Gopher?" He chuckled.

Pleased to have a distraction from Lady Catherine's imminent threat, and happy to have inside knowledge not yet shared by my cousin, I confidently replied, "Yes. I bet five pounds they will announce an engagement before they announce a courtship."

Richard barked a laugh. "You have quite grown up on me, but I will be pleased to take your five pounds, cousin."

∞∞∞

Later in the day, the Bennets, along with Mr. Collins, visited our party, much to Miss Bingley's horror. "We have come to offer our help with planning the ball, Miss Bingley. We would not wish for you to grow ill with the stress of it all." Mrs. Bennet fingered the lace at her collar while she spoke.

Miss Bingley rolled her eyes. "Whatever would make you believe I would become ill by planning a simple country ball? I am hardly as delicate as your own daughter, who could not leave our house for many days due to a trifling cold." Miss

Bennet's face pinked at the reminder of her convalescence.

"Oh, to be sure, you are quite hardy," Mrs. Bennet replied. "I remembered your bird episode and worried you would relapse. But if there is nothing we can do to assist you, we can just sit and have a nice conversation. It is the neighborly thing to do, after all."

"Bird incident?" Richard questioned, earning him an angry look from Miss Bingley.

Though everyone else remained tight-lipped about the event, Miss Lydia had no qualms relaying the episode. "Colonel, you would have died of laughter if you had been here to witness it. Miss Bingley was overcome with a fit of some sort and could not stop chirping like a bird. 'Chirp, chirp, chirp,' she would say whenever someone spoke to her."

Miss Mary, unable to overcome her desire to always be right, corrected her sister. "She did not chirp, Lydia. She cooed like a dove or a pigeon."

"Ahem," Miss Elizabeth cut in. "Miss Bingley, tell us about your plans for the ball. Have you hired local musicians, or did you send to London for them?"

Miss Bingley looked grateful for the change in conversation. Unfortunately, her natural hauteur was not absent for long. "Local musicians? At a ball hosted by my brother? Hardly! I sent to London for the best quartet available. I doubt any of the residents of Meryton will have heard music so well performed."

Fitzwilliam cleared his throat. "I have had the unfortunate luck to be stuck inside all day writing letters of business. If you are all amenable, I suggest we take a turn in the garden. Georgiana assures me the weather is fine for so late a day in November." Miss Elizabeth looked at my brother with great affection while he spoke.

"Fantastic idea, sir! My daughters do love a turn about the

garden on a pretty day. I, of course, will remain inside. Perhaps we could continue our conversation on the newest bonnet styles?" Mrs. Bennet dipped her head in Mrs. Hurst's direction. The two had grown rather close in the past few weeks of visits.

We made our way to the front hall to gather our coats from the waiting footman. Miss Bingley eyed my brother, who stood helping Miss Elizabeth with her outerwear. I could tell from the look in her eye that she intended to interrupt their time together, so I did the only thing I could to prevent it. Just as I had done with Mr. Collins, I spelled her with the two-steps-forward, four-steps-back verse. Between her and the rector, the two barely made it out the front door. When one was moving forward, the other was moving back. I watched them bump into one another no less than five times before being whisked away by Kitty.

Miss Mary, Kitty, and I happily walked and talked for thirty minutes before returning to the house. Miss Lydia, of course, was perched upon Richard's arm. He remained a good sport about it, though I am certain it was exasperating to have such a young girl upon his arm. (She is even younger than I am!)

Mr. Bingley, as boring as Mrs. Annesley accused him of being, escorted Miss Bennet to and from the house. Not once did I see their heads or bodies move improperly close, nor did I see him whisper in her ear, though the lady did blush often enough to make me wonder if I had missed something.

My brother's walk with Miss Elizabeth, however, was filled with delightful improprieties. Never fear, little niece, your father and mother did not flaunt their relationship in front of others. I am talking about small things that are allowable to a committed couple, which Fitzwilliam and Miss Elizabeth are (though only I know it).

When he thought no one was looking, Fitzwilliam often kissed the back of her hand. They walked too close. He whispered in her ear. It was hardly anything scandalous, but it was enough to cause Richard to look back at me and roll his eyes. I will enjoy winning his five pounds.

Mrs. Bennet met us at the door when we returned. "Girls, leave your coats on. We must be going. I need to stop by Lady Lucas's before we return home." Richard assisted Mrs. Bennet with her coat.

"Oh!" she exclaimed as she fastened her button. "I nearly forgot. I am hosting a small dinner party in two days. I would be pleased if you would all join us. Colonel, you must tell me some of your favorites. I have already learned the preferences of your cousin and Mr. Bingley, but I must be assured that there will be something you favor on the table." I promised Mrs. Bennet I would write down some of Richard's preferred dishes and send them to her.

"Excellent," she said before bussing my cheek as if I were one of her very own daughters. Kitty giggled at her mother's impropriety, but my heart swelled.

Chapter Forty

Afternoon, 21 November 1811

Dear Diary,

As I was dressing for breakfast, my mirror buzzed. It is the second day in a row that Fitzwilliam has met Miss Elizabeth which must mean they are moving even closer to an official engagement! I sent la Roche on a fool's errand to retrieve me some tea (so parched was I!) and picked up the mirror. Richard and Fitzwilliam had ridden out and, it appears, had quite unexpectedly stumbled upon Miss Elizabeth and Miss Mary. If it was not unexpected, Fitzwilliam is a far better actor than I had given him credit for.

"Miss Elizabeth, Miss Mary, what a pleasure to find you walking this morning. But you must be cold!" Though I could not see from the vantage point of Fitzwilliam's boots, I heard Richard dismount from his horse and walk toward the ladies. Soon, Fitzwilliam followed.

"You must be freezing, ladies. It is a very cold morning for a walk," Richard continued.

"No colder, I suspect, than it is for a ride, sir," Miss Elizabeth replied. Though I could not see it, I imagined a pert smile and a lifted brow upon her face.

Richard laughed. "It is cold no matter what the exercise, but you forget there is great warmth to be had when sitting atop a beast as large as my battle horse."

"Ah, if the only way to gain warmth is to gain it from atop a horse, I fear I would rather be cold."

"You do not care for horses, Miss Elizabeth?" Richard sounded horrified.

Miss Mary answered for her sister. "Lizzy loves horses; she just does not care for riding them."

"It matters not, Richard. If Miss Elizabeth prefers to walk, then I am happy to escort her. Assuming we are not interrupting, that is." Nicely done, Fitzwilliam. I must say, his romantic qualities have improved these past weeks.

The foursome broke into two couples. My brother, of course, escorted his OTL. Behind them, Richard and Miss Mary walked together. Obviously, I could not hear the latter couple's conversation, but I was pleased with what I heard from Fitzwilliam and Miss Elizabeth.

"Fitzwilliam, please remind your sister to send a list of the Colonel's favorite dishes. My mother is quite concerned she will have nothing to serve him."

Fitzwilliam laughed. "I hardly think she will have nothing to serve the man. I have eaten at her table if you recall. She is an excellent host, and her table is always well-set."

"You are being purposefully obtuse," she laughed. "But seriously, my mother wishes to find at least one dish your cousin will enjoy."

"Richard is easy to please, but I will ensure Georgiana does as she promised. Never worry, my dear." It is difficult to see properly from the tips of Fitzwilliam's boots, but I think he pulled her a little closer and patted her hand.

Soon, their conversation shifted. "Are you excited about the ball?"

My brother chuckled. "Until this one, I have never before wished for a ball. It is a new experience for me to look forward to a night of dancing."

"And why is that, sir? Might it be that you enjoy the pleasure of Meryton society?"

"I think it more likely that I enjoy the pleasure of a beautiful lady who has stolen my heart." I blushed at my brother's words. Perhaps I should stop eavesdropping on their meetings.

"And what, exactly, do you plan to do with the beautiful lady who has stolen your heart?" Miss Elizabeth said in a breathy whisper.

Fitzwilliam's voice pitched lower. "I plan to be by her side the entire evening and dance every dance with her. I have it on good authority that Bingley will call for a waltz. I plan to hold my lady too close and enjoy every moment with her in my arms." I flipped my mirror back over. Indeed, I must refrain from spying on their conversations in this way going forward! My actions were timely. La Roche returned soon after, carrying a tea tray. Though I was not thirsty, I drank it in large gulps. My tea leaves said I will not receive the answer I seek. . . I think.

∞∞∞

After breakfast, Mrs. Annesley and I consulted, once again, about my conversation with Berwyn. "It is time for you to call Andromalius. His mystic power is required to assist you with your spirit guide's suggestion." She stood next to me as I pulled the appropriate sigil from my gown and held it between my hands. Soon, a gray mist swirled before us.

When I last spoke to Andromalius, he remained in a foggy form, but to my surprise, today, he emerged from the haze as a small, black gargoyle. Standing, his head came just to my waist's height. Mrs. Annesley and I attempted to hide our shock. A real live gargoyle!

"Have you a proper request for me, Georgiana?" His vivid green eyes glowed in his dark face.

I wetted my dry lips. "Y-yes sir. I believe I now know the best way to apply for your assistance."

He gestured to the couch. "Then let us have a seat and discuss it." Mrs. Annesley and I followed him as he hobbled clumsily toward the seat. With a small jump, he landed on the couch and circled around multiple times until he found a comfortable spot to sit.

"My aunt," I reminded him.

"Ah, yes. Lady Catherine de Bourgh. What has the great dame done now?"

Mrs. Annesley dipped her head, a silent urge for me to continue. "It is not what she has done, rather what we fear she will do. Two nights past, my spirit guide warned me about her."

"You have finally spoken to Berwyn, you say? Good, good."

I nodded. "Yes, and she has indicated that when the time comes, I must steal Lady Catherine's powers. I did not know such a thing was possible until she mentioned it. She said I must apply to you for assistance."

Andromalius stood and paced the length of the couch. One, two, three, four, five small steps. Turn. And back. "It is no small thing to steal a witch's power, Georgiana. You ask very much of me."

A ball of fear welled in my throat. Was he planning on refusing my request? How would I defeat whatever the lady threw at me without his assistance? "I realize this is an appeal you would rather not consider, but my guide insists it is necessary. I do not know when to expect her, but I suspect it will be soon. She will be very upset when she learns my brother plans to marry. She is convinced he is intended for her own daughter."

He stopped his pacing and turned his glowing eyes on me. "I am aware of Lady Catherine's irrationality. But to take her power, that is a concern. I must only do what is right and good."

"So, you will not help me?" I forced my voice to sound stronger than I felt.

"I did not say that. It is only that I must better understand the situation before I cast my judgment. I will return when I know more." Then, he hopped off the couch, shuffled toward the window, and held out one finger. "Open." The window lifted and a cold gust of air blew in. "I will see you when the time is right, Georgiana." He flew out and away.

"Do you think he will help us?"

Mrs. Annesley closed the window. "I do not know. He is known for his hatred of wickedness and underhanded dealings. If he discovers something about Lady Catherine, I think he will not be able to resist action. Until then, we must continue to prepare. Put on something warmer; we will visit the fairies again."

We did visit the fairies today, but they did not answer my call. I left my finished drawing at the base of the tree and promised to return soon.

Chapter Forty-one

Evening, 22 November 1811

Dear Diary,

Today has been unexpected. So unexpected, in fact, that I cannot bring myself to jump ahead and tell you the craziest parts until after I share the other details of this day.

This morning, I awoke later than is my usual habit. It had rained last night, which left behind a cold dampness in my rooms. My eyes had fluttered open early, but when I realized how chilly the air was, I snuggled back into my thick blankets and went back to sleep. When I finally arrived at breakfast, Fitzwilliam was taking his last sip of coffee.

"Good morning, sleepyhead," he greeted as I sat down. "I did not think I would have the opportunity to greet you before Richard and I left for Meryton."

"What is pulling you two to Meryton so early this morning?" I took a sip of steamy tea, allowing its heat to warm me from the inside. The breakfast parlor was colder than usual, but not as cold as my bedroom.

"We are off to visit my old friend, Colonel Forster. I have just learned that our mutual acquaintance, Wickham, has deserted, and I wish to know more of what has been done to apprehend him." Richard's voice was light, but there was an unmistakable glint of steel in his eyes. If it is within Richard's power to find and punish Mr. Wickham, it will be done. The two excused themselves, and soon it was only Mrs. Annesley and me remaining at the table.

Fighting the chill in the air, I hurried to finish my tea. Out of habit, I looked at my leaves. "Prepare for tomorrow," it warned. I slid the cup to Mrs. Annesley for her interpretation—I still do not trust my ability to read leaves.

"Eat a hearty breakfast," she suggested. "It appears that we have much to prepare for before tomorrow."

After breakfast, Mrs. Annesley and I braved the cold and walked to greet the fairies. The picture I had drawn no longer sat at the base of the tree. I hope the fairies took it, as opposed to a gust of wind during last night's storm. As before, I called out my greeting, but no one came. Sensing that I was being watched, I ventured a message in their native tongue. "The tea leaves have indicated Lady Catherine will arrive tomorrow. Please be ready in case she threatens Miss Elizabeth. I know you wish her to remain safe, just as I do. I will ensure you have access to the house." When no one came to ask questions about my warning, Mrs. Annesley and I left.

Upon our return to the house, she instructed me to practice the Banish spell. I had not yet taken the time to change mattresses, so that is where we began. Mrs. Annesley was impressed with how easy it proved for me to pull my original mattress to me from across the house. My regular practice has improved my facility with this spell, and my endurance has grown.

With that chore complete, I went on to practice the Halt and Silence spells, all while waiting on pins and needles for Andromalius to rejoin us. But his gargoyle form never showed itself.

Mrs. Annesley and I practiced until teatime, and then for a little while longer. Soon I was required to prepare myself for supper with the Bennets. I have always enjoyed spending time at Longbourn, especially in Kitty's company, but tonight I wished to remain home and plan for Lady Catherine's impending arrival. I am very glad that I did not give in to my desires, for the following is a faithful account of how our meal at Longbourn unraveled.

The evening began, as they often do, with Mrs. Bennet's effusions. "Come in, come in!" She waved her ever-present lace handkerchief as the door opened to us. "Oh, it is so cold. Miss Darcy, your cheeks are bright pink." She cupped her warm hands on my cheeks to warm them.

"I am quite well, Mrs. Bennet."

"Nonsense. I will not let my daughters suffer so from the cold, and I will do no less for you." Then, to my surprise, she bussed my cheek. If possible, my heart opened even wider to the lady than it had been already. Though Fitzwilliam would have melted into a puddle of shame had Mrs. Bennet done the same to him, I could tell from the slight upturn of his lips that he was pleased by her warm welcome to me.

Richard's appreciation of the lady was more transparent. "Mrs. Bennet, we thank you for the warm welcome and the invitation. Mr. Bingley and my cousin have assured me that tonight's meal will be exemplary. I have been told you set a fine table, madam."

Mrs. Bennet blushed at the praise. "Colonel Fitzwilliam! My Lydia has told me you are a charmer. I see she was correct." Miss Bingley let out a huff of irritation, but no one paid her any attention. She is always huffing, you know.

Once we had left our outerwear with the butler and footman, Mr. and Mrs. Bennet ushered us into the sitting room where we were happy to greet the Bennet sisters, along with the Lucas family. Mr. Collins was a less pleasant companion, but our party did our part to make him feel appreciated—at least until he attempted to impose upon Fitzwilliam and Miss Elizabeth.

Fitzwilliam, no doubt drawn by his OTL's sparkling eyes,

made his way to her side. Mr. Collins, ever vigilant in his desire to keep the two apart, sprang forward. "Mr. Darcy, you should —" TURN "take my seat. It is the better option and closer to the" TURN "fire." This went on without end until Mrs. Hill arrived to announce dinner. Fitzwilliam stood and offered his arm to Miss Elizabeth. Turning, he offered the other arm to me, but Miss Bingley, ever vigilant, was too quick—or she would have been if not for remnants of my spell. Though she has the social intelligence to not babble incessantly while she does it, she still found herself treading the same path as Mr. Collins. One, two, TURN. One, two, three, four, TURN. It was the exact comedy I needed given my fears for tomorrow. Oh, how foolish and unprepared I was then. Allow me to jump ahead a bit, I am sure you are on the edge of your seat. If not, I have not done my job in preparing you for my foolishness.

Let me begin by saying my tea leaves were wrong. Let me rephrase, I do not yet know if my tea leaves were wrong, but I do know they did not tell the entire truth. Why? Lady Catherine came tonight. TONIGHT! I had spent the entirety of the day preparing for tomorrow only to have my harridan of an aunt show up this evening. Mrs. Annesley and I were both floored! Now that I have that out of my system, I shall proceed to tell you the story.

Just as the footman placed a plate of trout on the table, our attention was drawn to a disruption in the hall. "I will have my way! Do you know who I am?" I knew who she was. Lady Catherine's voice is an unmistakable mix of shrill displeasure and unparalleled hauteur. Mr. Collins also recognized her voice, for he stood, forcing his chair to tumble behind him.

"Mr. Collins, as this is not yet your home, I beg you to take more care of my possessions. I would like to enjoy them before I shuffle off this mortal coil."

"It is my patroness. Lady Catherine de Bourgh. I must—" I suppose he planned to escort her in, but his words and plans were cut short by the lady's presence in the dining hall. "Lady Catherine, you grace us with your benevolent and esteemed presence." He then, as you might have predicted, began a series of bows and, once, a curtsy that baffled my mind.

Lady Catherine paid the bobbing chaw bacon no mind; she was far too interested in Miss Elizabeth. "Fitzwilliam Darcy, I demand you remove yourself from the presence of these low, grasping people immediately. Do not think I have no knowledge of your near compromise. Do not fear, nephew, I am here to save you from these Bennets."

"Madam, I must insist that you cease your insults. The Bennets have been very kind to my sister and me. I cannot fathom why you have come all this way to insult them in this vile manner."

"Can you not?" Her voice edged higher. "I have it on good authority that you have been bamboozled by nothing more than a piece of muslin. Are you Miss Elizabeth Bennet?" She turned her steely eyes on the lady. "You are not even pretty, though I can see how your haymarket wares might gain my nephew's attention, but you shall not keep it. I will not allow it."

"Not pretty," Mrs. Bennet exclaimed. "I will have you know, my daughters are known as the jewels of the county. Even Sir William says it to be true."

"They are, indeed," Sir William confirmed.

"Aunt Catherine, you must desist!" I had never heard Fitzwilliam raise his voice before. I have, of course, heard him speak rashly or with emphasis, but to yell... at a lady... in public! It was unthinkable and I had never been prouder.

"Fitzwilliam Darcy, you will not speak to me as if I am some commoner. I am Lady Catherine de Bourgh, and I will be heard."

"You will not continue to be heard here, madam. You are

free to go back to Rosings Park and lament the Bennets at your leisure, but we will not listen to your vile insults." Mr. Bennet, silent until this moment, stood at the head of the table. Never before had I witnessed the man look as menacing.

Lady Catherine's face turned a terrifying shade of purple. I gripped the bloodstones tightly between my hands anticipating her attempt to harm my brother or Miss Elizabeth in some way. But I was mistaken. After all the planning and care I had taken to prepare for Lady Catherine's wrath, she did not employ even one second of magical interference. Have we been mistaken all this time? Is she so out of practice she has rendered herself incapable of casting a spell?

"I shall know how to act!" she bellowed to the room. Then later we heard, "Get your dirty hands off me. I will put on my own coat!"

Needless to say, Fitzwilliam and I were mortified by Lady Catherine's behavior. Richard was as well, though he possesses the talent to hide it far better than we do. "If you will excuse me, Mrs. Bennet, I will ensure that my aunt is placed back in her carriage. On behalf of our family and the Earl of Matlock, I apologize for her behavior today and the disruption." Then, with a gallant bow, he left the room.

As you might imagine, our time at Longbourn did not end on as happy a note as it began. Fitzwilliam, embarrassed and angry, retreated into himself. He did not partake of any additional food and stood at the window, looking out in the inky yard, when we finally made our way into the sitting room. I suggested we spell the group so they would forget the entire event, but Mrs. Annesley suggested I not waste my energy on such a thing. "It is better that everyone understands Lady Catherine's temperament, especially since she did not employ her magical abilities." Though reluctant to do nothing, I must agree with her prudence in this. Lady Catherine is a termagant and the more people that know of it, the more people who can save themselves from being in her presence.

Of course, Mr. Collins does not agree with my conclusion. That man is still very much in the corner of his "esteemed patroness." Though everyone else ate quietly for the remainder of dinner, Mr. Collins had no qualms about speaking his mind, or lack thereof.

"None of this would have occurred, Cousin Elizabeth, if you had listened to me. I have warned you that you are far too low for Mr. Darcy. And since he is already promised to his cousin, Miss Anne de Bourgh, your actions have not only been imprudent, but they have also been wanton." Fitzwilliam's grip tightened menacingly on his cutlery, but it was Richard who stopped the numskull from speaking.

Standing, my cousin pulled his sword from its sheath and extended it across the table so that the very tip edged the parson's chin up, forcing his beady eyes to meet Richard's. "Sir, for your own safety, I implore you to quiet your never-ending prattle. If you, once more, imply my cousin is unfaithful to his promises, or that Miss Elizabeth is, in any way, at fault, I will meet you outside. Do I make myself clear?"

"Ye-ye-yes, Colonel. Of course, Colonel." Richard tipped the sword's edge a little higher so that it poked uncomfortably into the man's wattle.

"Enough. I grant you permission to finish your meal in silence. If you cannot do that, then you are dismissed." When I tell you that Fitzwilliam was the lone person who failed to startle at the threat, I mean it. My brother was far too ensconced in the workings of his mind, and far too used to Richard's brashness, to pay attention to the threat. The Bennets and Lucases, however, sat wide-eyed and frozen.

"Had I only known that a simple sword would have stopped the man's babble, I would have borrowed one days ago." Mr. Bennet smirked at his youngest daughter's quip.

As we donned our outerwear, Fitzwilliam stood to the side with Miss Elizabeth. Though she did not look angry, there was a melancholy about her that was unmistakable. Fitzwilliam whispered something near her ear, and she nodded her head. Probably, they plan to meet tomorrow to discuss things. Hopefully, I can wake early enough to watch from my mirror. Today's entry has already taken a very long time to record, and I have not even told the most exciting part yet.

∞ ∞ ∞

When we returned to Netherfield Park, Lady Catherine's carriage sat in the drive. "Ballocks!" Richard muttered though he did not think I heard it, or perhaps he did not care.

The door to the house was opened and a frantic looking Mr. Nichols greeted our party. "Sir, your guests have a visitor," he informed Mr. Bingley.

"Ah, yes, I imagined as much when I saw the carriage. Darcy, would you like to attend her alone, or should we all go in to greet her?"

"Really, Charles, you act as if she is someone to be feared. I found her presence tonight quite refreshing myself." Miss Bingley swept past and opened the door to the parlor. "Welcome, Lady Catherine. We are pleased to have you here at Netherfield." Richard rolled his eyes, while Fitzwilliam's mouth, if possible, pinched even tighter and a tic rippled the skin near his left eye.

"Darcy, I am ashamed of you. I have been here for over an hour with no one to attend me. To think, my own nephew, my nearest relation, has allowed me to sit alone while he enjoyed the company of that tart, Eliza Bennet."

Fitzwilliam's head cocked at what I believe was the insult to his OTL, but I was mistaken. "What did you call her?"

"A tart, Fitzwilliam. She will be fine enough for you once you are married to Anne, but you must first do your duty to my daughter. You have been engaged since you were children!"

"I will remind you, madam, that I have never asked your daughter for her hand, nor have any contracts been signed. I am not now, nor will I ever be, engaged to my cousin. But that is not what I meant when I asked you to repeat yourself. What name did you use when you referred to Miss Elizabeth?"

Lady Catherine stood tall and tilted her nose to the sky. "You are aware of her name, Fitzwilliam. My sister did not raise a fool."

"She did not," he growled. "Say her name."

Her eyes locked with his before she said, "Eliza Bennet. Such a shabby name."

My brother's nostrils flared. "And how did you come to know about Miss Elizabeth?"

Lady Catherine waved her hand in dismissal. "That is none of your concern." Miss Bingley's spine grew stiff as every eye in the room, sans Lady Catherine's, of course, turned to her.

"I know enough," Fitzwilliam spat.

"You know nothing," Lady Catherine snapped. "You know not what I can do. I can force you to marry my daughter. I can rule you if I choose!" Mrs. Annesley gripped my arm, prompting me to retrieve my bloodstones.

"And how will you do it? You are an old woman, and I am a gentleman of considerable means. I will do as I wish and with whom I wish. You have no control over me!"

Lady Catherine pulled a piece of obsidian from her reticule and held it out toward my brother's face.

By will of mine, command and bind
Thy actions now to my desires.
No will to resist, nor dare to oppose –

I had read this spell before and instantly recognized it. Lady Catherine would bind my brother to her will and force him to do as she commanded. I did not think; I acted as I had been taught to do. "Banish!" I yelled. I did not even allow my power to build in my chest, but it did not matter. I could feel her presence far from me, back at her home in Kent.

Everyone in the room, aside from Mrs. Annesley, stood in dumbfounded confusion. After several seconds of stunned silence, Richard dared to speak. "What the?"

Fitzwilliam took my arm and pulled me from the room. "We must speak." He escorted me up the stairs to my room, though to say he dragged me there would be more apt. "What did I just witness?" I said nothing. "Georgiana, I demand you tell me what is going on. Did you just cast our aunt out of this home? Tell me I am not losing my mind." He dragged his fingers through his already tousled hair. "You must tell me, do you have our mother's gift?"

While he ranted, I attempted to remember the forgotten memory verse so I could remove his understanding of what he had just seen, but his last question stole my attention. "Our mother?"

He took my hands in his much larger ones. "She had a talent for…"

"For magic?" He nodded his head. "She showed you her abilities?"

Fitzwilliam sat down upon the small chair nearest the fire. "When I was a boy, she would use her power to entertain me. She would grow flowers in the winter so I could present them to Mrs. Reynolds, or she would summon a lizard from the ground for me to play with during the summer. Once, when Father insisted I eat all the turnips on my plate and refused to allow me from the table until I did, she spelled them so they tasted like strawberries. We never discussed her power; it was always just there. There have been times I have wondered if you…"

I pulled a chair close so I could sit near him. "Then yes, I am like our mother. I did not learn of it until this summer. Mrs. Annesley has been helping me discover my talents.
At first, it was small things like…" I stopped myself from confessing too much.

Fitzwilliam took my hands in his again. "Does that mean you have practiced more serious magic lately?" When I indicated I had, he asked, "Why?"

I explained about the night of Samhain and our grandmother's warning. "You have known of Lady Catherine's threat all this time and told me nothing!" My brother's emotions shifted from nostalgia to anger. "How can I protect you, Georgiana, if you do not tell me things?"

"Because, Fitzwilliam, a mere man cannot contain Lady Catherine. She requires magical interference and that is my domain not yours."

"I do not like it," he grumbled. "It is my responsibility."

"I do not like it either," I rejoined. "I would very much have preferred to spend my days casting spots on Miss Bingley's nose, but I could not. It is my responsibility as a Darcy to protect you and those you love from threats. Lady Catherine will not stop. She will know that I am a witch now, and she will return with increased ire. We must plan to protect you and Miss Elizabeth from her wrath."

"And who will protect you, my dear sister?" He cupped his hand to my cheek. "You are my only family, Georgiana. I will not see you injured." Sensing the strength of his fear, I sat with him for a long time and shared everything that had happened these past weeks in Hertfordshire, including the repetition of the days spell (he was not well-pleased by that one). I also shared about the mystics attached to the two sigils I wear and the fairies' presence nearby.

"I have alliances," I promised. "I also have Mrs. Annesley. Together we will defeat Lady Catherine, though I am not certain what that entails yet. But your knowledge of this will make it easier to keep you safe. You protect Miss Elizabeth, and I will do my best to protect you."

It was several hours later when we concluded our conversation. "What am I to say to Bingley? He will not share knowledge of your powers with anyone, but Miss Bingley cannot be trusted."

"Never fear. Mrs. Annesley has spelled everyone to forget by now. I suspect they are all abed and resting, unconscious of what occurred here tonight."

"Is that how you made everyone forget when the days repeated?" I did not answer. He need not know all the secrets of magic.

It is now well into the morning, and time for me to rest. I must start my day very early to plan for what will come next and I cannot do that if I continue to write.

Chapter Forty-two

Morning, 22 November 1811
(Day three —I will explain later)

Dear Diary,

My day began when Fitzwilliam stumbled into my room and bellowed for me to wake up. With reluctance, I opened my eyes and sat up. "It cannot yet be morning," I grumbled.

"It is morning," he snapped. "In fact, it is the very same morning as the last time you woke up."

"How can that be?" I asked.

"I do not know, Georgiana. You are the one who set this dratted spell in motion. You tell me!"

I rubbed the sleep from my eyes. "If the day has repeated, it means you behaved in a way that interferes with your goal of obtaining your OTL."

"OTL?"

I rolled my eyes. "Your One True Love. I explained that to you last night." He ran his hands through his already messy hair and began to pace. I ignored him. I have long grown accustomed to his pacing.

While he marched from one corner of my room to the other, I replayed the previous night's events in my head. "Aha! I know where you failed."

He stilled and looked at me with irritation. "Go ahead, then. Tell me how I have so badly failed, once again."

I attempted to reign in my feelings of smugness. "You did not speak to your lady when she most needed it."

"What? I spoke to Elizabeth the entire evening. I hardly said a word to anyone else."

I only just refrained from rolling my eyes, again. "You did not speak when it mattered most. When Lady Catherine chastised and offended Miss Elizabeth, you remained quiet. When Mr. Collins implied she had behaved badly, you remained quiet. And then, when you had a chance to comfort her after, you admirably performed the role of statue as you looked out the window."

He began to pace, once more. "I will grant you that I allowed Richard to handle Mr. Collins, and I remained silent while we were in the parlor because I was so angry I could not find words befitting a gentleman. However, I must argue that I did confront Lady Catherine."

"You did, but it was Mr. Bennet who finally put an end to her words, not you. In any case, the day has been repeated, and you have another opportunity to prove yourself to your OTL. And, lucky for you, she will never know that you behaved badly yesterday."

Fitzwilliam looked as though he wished to further justify his actions of the previous evening, but I stopped him. "Our greatest worry now is what to do with Lady Catherine. Because she is a witch with considerable power, I cannot guarantee that she will be unaware of what happened last night. I must consult Mrs. Annesley on how to prepare."

"How should I proceed?" Fitzwilliam is a man of action; therefore, it must have greatly chaffed him to be forced to sit and wait.

"I know you wish to help me, but the greatest gift you can provide is to ensure Miss Elizabeth's safety. Mrs. Annesley and I will take care of the rest."

My grim-faced brother nodded his agreement. "I do not like it, but I must bow to your knowledge. I am sorry that I cannot offer you more assistance or protection. It shames me to be so weak." His head hanging low, he exited my room, and my heart broke into a thousand pieces.

I allowed myself a quarter-hour of sorrow before I climbed out of the bed and rang for La Roche. There was much to accomplish and little time to do it. That said, I shall not bore you with the details of the day, as I know you are anxious to learn what happened at dinner. I will say that I was, once again, unsuccessful in contacting the fairies. In addition, much to my great irritation, Andromalius never showed his short, winged self. He is probably, even now, perched on the side of church ignoring me completely.

Before we left for Longbourn, Fitzwilliam suggested that he ride out to meet Lady Catherine to prevent her from approaching Miss Elizabeth and me. With Mrs. Annesley's assistance, I was able to convince him that he must attend supper as planned. A mere mortal has no defense against a witch, even one as supposedly untrained as Lady Catherine. He would provide no protection for Miss Elizabeth while he was away from her, and I could provide no protection for him.

Better prepared than we were the day before, Mrs. Annesley and I ensured that a window remained cracked so that fairies could easily enter the house in case they were needed. Then, with no little trepidation, we sat down for our meal.

As with the night before, the footman had just placed a plate of fish on the table when a loud commotion was heard in the hall. "Unhand me, you fool. I will not be gainsaid!" A crash and a masculine grunt followed the command. Battle-hardened, Richard stood with his hand upon the hilt of his sword. Across from him, Fitzwilliam also stood, angling his body so that Miss Elizabeth's was shielded.

"Georgiana," she screeched as she entered the room. Her

eyes were wild, and her hair had come loose from its pins. "Do not think me unaware of what you are or what you have done! You are but a girl, untrained and ignorant. I am Lady Catherine de Bourgh, and I will have my way in this. What say you to that?"

Though my knees wobbled, I dipped a curtsy. "Lady Catherine, I wish I could say it is a pleasure to see you again this evening. What is it you want tonight?"

From down the table I could hear the incessant ramblings of Mr. Collins, though I had no time to grasp his words. Likely he was jawing further about how thrilled he was to see the great lady. Well, he can have her, I say!

She turned her incensed gaze on my brother. "And you! I have not forgotten how you treated me last night. You will do as I say!"

"Aunt, I believe you have finally gone off your rocker," Richard attempted humor. "I spent the entire of last evening with Darcy and you were nowhere near us."

"Imbecile," she bellowed. "Fitzwilliam, what say you to my command. Will you make this easy or difficult on yourself?"

My brother's hands were clasped in tight fists. "Madam, I regret to inform you that your wishes must remain unfulfilled. I must act in accordance with my own wishes and my own heart."

"With this, this trollop!" She pointed an accusatory finger at Miss Elizabeth. "Try as you might, you little upstart, but you will never be Mrs. Darcy as long as I live." Miss Elizabeth, having no memory of the previous evening, sat in stupefaction. "Have you nothing to say for yourself? Are you as ignorant as you are lowly born?"

Miss Elizabeth's wit surfaced at this insult. "I assume you expect me to say I am pleased to make your acquaintance, but I must refrain from telling untruths. I am, in fact, quite displeased by the vitriol you have spewed. What have I done to deserve such venom?"

"What have you done, indeed!" Spittle flew from Lady Catherine's mouth. "You have attempted to steal my nephew from my daughter. They have been engaged since birth. What have you to say to that?"

Miss Elizabeth's eyebrow quirked. "Mr. Darcy is the most upright gentleman of my acquaintance. If he were engaged to your daughter, there is nothing I could have done to steal him from her."

Lady Catherine drew back her shoulders. "Their engagement is of a peculiar nature."

Undaunted, Miss Elizabeth responded. "If what you say is true, then you have nothing to worry about. But since you are worried, then I must conclude your accusations are untrue."

Lady Catherine's eyes blazed. I was so focused on them, I almost missed the spell she hissed.

Shadows flee and lies dissolve,
In honesty you now evolve.
Speak words genuine, both good and bad,
Hold no secrets, let the truth be had.

It took me a moment to remember, but I recognized it as the truth spell I had read in *Magical Castings and Curses for Young Witches*.

"Go ahead girl, tell my nephew what you feel for him." Without hesitation, Miss Elizabeth began to speak her true emotions for my brother.

"Fitzwilliam, you must allow me to tell you how much I admire you. You are the kindest and most intelligent man I know. And I love, I lo…, I loo…"

So wrapped up was I in Miss Elizabeth's confession of love that I must have missed another spell, for soon her mouth began to foam and her tongue began to swell. She was quite literally choking on her own words. Her face turned purple as she gurgled out unintelligible noises. Fitzwilliam held his fingers to her mouth in an attempt to unblock her throat, but there was nothing he could do. She was not choking on anything tangible. It was pure magic that blocked her breath.

"Elizabeth," Fitzwilliam cried as he pulled her to him. "Make it stop, Aunt. Please I will do —"

Thinking quicker than I, Mrs. Annesley stood and commanded, "Breathe!" Life flowed back into Miss Elizabeth as she bent over the table taking great gulps of air."

Finding my nerves I shouted. "You have gone too far, Lady Catherine. Too far, I say!"

Unaffected, she directed her fury at me. "You dare to interfere with me, Georgiana? You are but a girl. What can you possibly do? You will not banish me again. I have made sure such an event cannot occur tonight."

"I suspect you are not quite as fast and smart as you believe yourself to be," I challenged.

Outraged, she bellowed, "How dare you?" Then she lifted her hands and commanded, "Rise!" Without warning, the table lurched from the floor and smashed into the ceiling, causing it to break into hundreds of pieces. Once again, she commanded, "Rise!" and each shard of wood lifted from the ground and floated in front of our faces. Then with the sudden command of her hands, the pieces flew at each person. Richard used his sword to battle as many sharp pieces as he could, while Fitzwilliam pushed Miss Elizabeth to the ground.

Sensing no other way to put an end to the madness, I held my bloodstone firmly and demanded, "End!"

Chapter Forty-three

Afternoon, 22 November 1811
(Day three, the real one this time)

Dear Diary,

Since my last entry, I have had a busy yet unproductive day. Mrs. Annesley and I mentally rehearsed every spell I've ever learned. We refrained from practicing any actual magic for fear of exhausting our reserves. As mentioned previously, my tea leaves indicate today is the final day of this madness. I'm unsure of its meaning, but I anticipate things may worsen before they improve.

Aside from remaining ignorant of Andromalius' whereabouts and unable to communicate with the fairies, another concern has troubled me today. Why did the day repeat? Fitzwilliam's behavior last night was exemplary. Although he couldn't rescue Miss Elizabeth, no blame can be placed on him; he is, after all, only a man. He did his utmost to shield her from our aunt. After discussing it with Mrs. Annesley, we believe that, on this occasion, it is not Fitzwilliam who must correct his actions to move forward. Since we cannot rely on Miss Bingley or Mr. Collins to resolve this predicament, the responsibility to advance us to the twenty-third of November falls to me.

Fitzwilliam has been a jumble of nerves today. He threatened at least four times to ride out and intercept Lady Catherine. It required considerable persuasion on my part to convince him that it was a dreadful idea. One would think, after witnessing her capabilities, that he would be more prudent. However, as mentioned before, he is just a man.

While Fitzwilliam, Mrs. Annesley, and I strategize on how to thwart Lady Catherine, Miss Bingley remains oblivious to our awareness of her involvement in this debacle. Fitzwilliam has not forgotten that she informed the great lady about Miss Elizabeth. He has vowed never to welcome her into any of our homes once this matter is resolved. Good riddance, indeed. I proposed making her coo like a bird throughout the entire ball, but he insists on a punishment that will be more poignant.

It is nearing time to dress for our evening at Longbourn. Wish me success; I will surely need it.

∞∞∞

Evening

Before I go any further, I will say that I am alive, Fitzwilliam is alive, Miss Elizabeth is alive, and (in case you cared even a little) Lady Catherine is alive. Now, with that out of the way, I can tell you everything that happened after I last wrote. Prepare yourself for quite a tale. I have spelled my pen to write while I dictate. Why I did not think of this before, I cannot say, but I have already determined it is a brilliant solution. I could have spared my fingers so many cramps!

After writing my last entry, Mrs. Annesley joined me in my rooms to go over our plans for the evening one last time. The lady has impeccable timing, for no sooner had we sat down to rehash our strategies than we heard a pecking upon the window. In case you have not yet guessed, it was Andromalius, still in his gargoyle form, flapping his wings furiously and gesturing to be let in. He is one of the most powerful mystics in the world, yet he required our assistance to open the window.

I rushed forward and pushed open the sash. "About time,"

he griped, as he flew past, landing heavily upon the Turkish carpet Miss Bingley had brought with her from London. I assume she placed it in my room to ingratiate herself with me. It is a finely made piece, I grant her that much, but the garish oranges and yellows are not to my taste. The brightness of the colors was even more enhanced against the faded black of Andromalius' gargoyle skin. However, that is neither here nor there. I am supposed to be writing about Lady Catherine's last stand. Oh fiddle. I stray from my task. Back to the story at hand.

Andromalius landed upon the rug, as I said, and began to pace, his short legs and awkward proportions making his movements resemble the toddle of a young child. "Where have you been? We have awaited your arrival these past two days. I could have used your assistance with Lady Catherine."

He dismissed my rebuke with a flip of his hand and continued to pace. "I can assure you, Georgiana, I am not inept. I have been fully aware of what Catherine was up to the past two days. I was confident you could handle her, and I see I was correct."

"Then why are you here now?" Andromalius turned to face Mrs. Annesley. Until now, she had never spoken to the mystic.

"Because today you and Georgiana require my assistance. I have come to warn you that she will arrive within the hour. You must hasten to Longbourn and wait for her there. Take your brother."

"An hour! For the past two nights, she has arrived during dinner."

Andromalius shrugged. "That was then, and this is now. She is as angry as I have ever seen her. And an angry woman is a dangerous woman."

"I cannot imagine her being angrier today than she was last night." Unconsciously, my mind replayed the scenes from last night and her attempt to shred us all with pieces of broken table.

He shrugged again. "It took me some time to grasp the full depth of her depravity, but I must now concede that your spirit guide was correct. Something must be done to quell Lady Catherine's ambitions."

"Does that mean you will help me steal her magic, as Berwyn suggested?"

Andromalius stopped pacing and climbed awkwardly onto the settee next to Mrs. Annesley. "I do not yet know if that is the proper solution. We must see how she responds today. But know that I will be with you to help, if necessary. Hold onto your bloodstone and call out your command. If I agree, I will grant my assistance."

"And if you do not?"

"If I do not, you must use that Darcy intellect to find another solution." Then, without warning, he took flight and exited through the still open window.

"Fetch your brother. I will call for the horses to be saddled. There is too little time to prepare the carriage." I nodded my head to Mrs. Annesley's command and rushed out the door to find Fitzwilliam.

In short order, the horses were saddled, and the three of us were galloping toward Longbourn. Lady Catherine is a dangerous woman in our presence; she would be deadly to Miss Elizabeth without our help. There was little time to waste, but I needed to make one stop before we approached the Bennets.

"I know it is a bit longer, but I want to take the path through the woods. I must speak to the fairies." Fitzwilliam's eyes widened at my proclamation, but he did not say anything. His reintroduction to the world of magic was, no doubt, surprising. Given his predictable nature, I cannot but commend him for how he has handled everything thus far. I anticipated an entirely different reaction.

We entered the woods, slowing our pace to accommodate the narrowness of the path and the unevenness of the terrain. From atop my mount, I called out in fairy tongue, "Greetings. We come in peace, fairies." There was no response, but I continued. "I have news. Lady Catherine arrives today. Andromalius, the mystic, has warned me of her arrival and the grave danger she presents to Miss Elizabeth. If you are listening, I beg your assistance." No one showed themselves, possibly due to my brother's presence in our group, but I could feel they were near and listening. Mrs. Annesley sensed it as well, given the silent nod she directed toward me. Soon, we were on our way to Miss Elizabeth.

∞∞∞

Upon our arrival at Longbourn, the butler announced our presence. Mrs. Bennet was seated at a small table with Mrs. Hill, the Bennets' housekeeper. Both looked up as we entered.

"Come in, come in. We did not expect to see you so early given that you will attend us tonight for supper."

Mrs. Hill closed the ledger they had been studying and excused herself. "We will continue our conversation tomorrow, Hill. Please have a maid bring tea."

In as serious a tone as I have ever heard of him, Fitzwilliam said, "Thank you, Mrs. Bennet, but we must decline. If it is acceptable to you, my sister and I would like to speak to Miss Elizabeth."

Mrs. Bennet looked at him in confusion. I am certain she has been expecting my brother to ask for a conversation with her second daughter, but she could not have anticipated I would be present for the conversation. "Certainly, certainly. Hill, please have someone fetch Lizzy." Mrs. Hill curtsied and left.

True to form, Fitzwilliam paced to the window and gazed out. He appeared the picture of a bored gentleman, except for the constant clasping and unclasping of his hands. Mrs. Bennet, hardly the fool some believe her to be, noticed. "Mr. Darcy, please be seated. Lizzy will be right down, I assure you. She has been looking forward to visiting with you this evening. Your presence, and yours as well, Miss Darcy, will be a pleasant surprise for her." Reluctantly, Fitzwilliam sat down to wait.

His torture was short-lived. Miss Elizabeth presented herself within minutes of our arrival. Despite the chill in the air, she agreed to a short walk in the garden with Fitzwilliam and me. Mrs. Annesley chose to keep Mrs. Bennet company, but not before giving me a look indicating she would be close at hand if needed.

Fitzwilliam led us to the nearest bench. After wiping away some debris, he indicated that we should sit. "Though I do not object to your presence at Longbourn, I am quite concerned about the nature of your visit. You seem rather agitated, sir."

"If I seem out of sorts, Miss Elizabeth, it is because of something I have recently learned. My Aunt Catherine is on her way to Longbourn, and I am fearful of what she might do."

"Lady Catherine de Bourgh?" No doubt she had heard more of the great lady than anyone could wish given the blabbering of her imbecilic cousin.

"The very one. I am certain Mr. Collins has told you much about her, although he could not have told you anything of her true nature. Our aunt has a vindictive, ugly temper that I cannot vouch for. I have recently learned, however, that she is also in possession of other... *attributes* that make her a danger to you, and possible, to your family."

"Surely you jest, Mr. Darcy. Your aunt may be upset by the nature of our relationship, but a danger? Surely not."

Frustrated, Fitzwilliam bid me to speak. Taking her hand in mine, I began. "Miss Elizabeth, I have something to share with you, but it is a secret and you must promise me that you will not share it with anyone else."

Sensing the gravity of our conversation, she promised, "Certainly, Miss Darcy. I would never share a confidence."

"I know. My brother would not be so enamored with you if you were the kind of lady who would give up another's secrets." She squeezed my hand, encouraging me to begin my story. "Miss Elizabeth, although it may be difficult to believe, I am a witch."

Laughter bubbled from her mouth. It was not the response I expected, though looking back, it was a logical reaction, especially for someone as jolly as Miss Elizabeth. "Show her," Fitzwilliam demanded. His strident words sobered her, but only slightly. It was not until I banished him twenty paces down the path that she fully regained her composure.

"But? How?" she asked in confusion.

"Most women of the gentry are witches. Even you have a little power, though Mrs. Annesley tells me it is weak."

"Me?" Her voice was weak with the shock of this news.

"Tell her the rest." Fitzwilliam had walked back from where I had moved him.

I turned back to his OTL. "Lady Catherine is also a witch, and likely not the good kind. There is no time to tell you everything, but this is the third time we have lived this day. For the past two nights, she has joined our party at dinner and wreaked havoc. Last night she attempted to kill us all by smashing the table and stabbing us with the shards of wood." Elizabeth face wavered between confusion and disbelief. Not wishing to tell her everything just yet, I continued. "I have it on good authority that she is even angrier today."

"How could someone go beyond the anger that induces them to kill an entire dinner party?"

Fitzwilliam scoffed. "If you knew my aunt, you would better understand."

"There you are!" In synch, our heads swiveled to the front of the garden at the sound of Richard's booming voice. "How dare you sneak away and leave me to wither at Netherfield under the sharp eyes of a sulking Miss Bingley." Seeing the serious miens we all wore, Richard's jovial barbs dissolved on his lips. "Here now! The three of you look positively ill. What is the matter?"

"We have word that Lady Catherine is on her way to Longbourn."

Richard laughed. "Is that all? I grant you, Aunt Catherine is a termagant, but that is no reason to look so grim. She can do no more than hurl angry words."

To everyone's shock, Lady Catherine's voice boomed from the front of the house. "Let me in, you blundering fool. Do you know who I am? Bring me Eliza Bennet this instant." From the corner of my eye, I saw Fitzwilliam take Miss Elizabeth's hand in his.

"We must hurry," I commanded. "She cannot be left alone with the Bennets. There is no telling what she will do."

"Now really, Gopher. Aunt Catherine is not that bad."

The sound of a window opening drew our attention. Mrs. Annesley had created a path for the fairies! I uttered a silent thanks before taking off at a run to the front entrance. Just as our party reached the steps, Lady Catherine came storming out onto the portico.

"There you are, Fitzwilliam. I insist you stop this charade today and end your relationship with this, this lightskirt! You have defied me for too long. I will not play nice any longer!" Her face grew redder with every word, and spittle clung to the corners of her mouth.

As she continued her rant, the entire Bennet family rushed

out to join us. First Mrs. Bennet and Mrs. Annesley arrived, followed soon after by a bending and scraping Mr. Collins. It was not long before each of Miss Elizabeth's sisters, and even her father, stood on the front stairs. "What say you, Fitzwilliam? Will you give up this harlot, or shall I do it for you?"

"I will not, and you will do no harm to my lady," my brother bellowed.

Lady Catherine made a high, shrill, maniacal sound that might have passed for a laugh in another circumstance. "Fine, then I will do it for you. Let her death be on your hands, boy. Then you will know not to defy me again!" Before the lady could move, Mrs. Bennet, never one to think before acting, let out a loud screech and rushed forward, pushing the lady with all her might. Lady Catherine stumbled, wobbling on the top step, but soon regained her balance.

"You fool. How dare you lay hands on me!" Holding out one hand she commanded, "Banish!" In the blink of an eye, Mrs. Bennet was no longer before us.

I panicked, wondering where she had gone, but then I heard her loud squawking from the roof. "Oh, my nerves! No one ever believes me when I say how much I suffer!"

I looked back at Lady Catherine. Her hand was clasped tightly, and I could just see the tip of a white stone peeking out from her grasp. It would give her power, but it was no match for bloodstone. "Do you believe me now, Fitzwilliam? I am not one to be thwarted."

"Here now —" Mr. Bennet began, but his words were drowned out by Mr. Collins.

"I tried to warn them, your ladyship. I did. I told them that Cousin Elizabeth is too far below Mr. Darcy's station. I also insisted that Mr. Darcy is already engaged to your lovely daughter. But they would not listen. Never mind. You are here now, and I will assist you. Come with me, Elizabeth." He pushed forward, gracelessly bounding down the stairs only to have an unseen force turn his body back around and force him back up the stairs. I appreciate the longevity of the spell I cast, but I really must investigate why it does not wear off.

Unfortunately, on Mr. Collins' trek back toward the house, he collided with Lady Catherine on what I believe was his third step. "Idiot! Be gone from my sight. Banish!" Soon Mr. Collins was also on the roof with Mrs. Bennet. The poor lady! As if her nerves have not suffered enough. "If we are lucky, he will fall off the edge," the witch before me grumbled.

"If he can ever make his way to it," Miss Lydia cackled.

"Be quiet, girl!" Mr. Bennet's voice was harsh and Miss Lydia's jollity instantly ceased. "Get in the house, all of you. You too, Lizzy. Come in now. This is between Lady Catherine and her nephew."

Miss Elizabeth's eyes showed her desire to stay near my brother, but Fitzwilliam urged her to follow her father's command. "Go now. I will not be able to concentrate if you are here." A reluctant Miss Elizabeth moved forward but was stopped when Lady Catherine bellowed, "Halt!"

Miss Elizabeth froze mid-stride. "What have you done to her?" Mr. Bennet yelled. He rushed forward to rescue his daughter but was also halted by Lady Catherine's command.

"You asked for this, Fitzwilliam. This is all your doing. If you had only married Anne like I suggested, none of this would have happened." Like Mr. Bennet, Fitzwilliam dashed forward to rescue his OTL, but he was too late. "You are as much an imbecile as that foolish rector of mine. You are but a man, nephew. You cannot stop me!" With that, Lady Catherine mumbled words I could not make out, and she began to lift from the ground taking Elizabeth with her. A green light circled as they floated ten feet above us. Still frozen, Miss Elizabeth did not move as a bolt of green lightning flashed from the swirling light. The first bolt jolted her shoulder, but the second charged her directly in the chest.

"Halt!" I yelled, holding the bloodstone between my fingers. My magic bounced off the churning green light.

"Your cheap magic will not harm me, niece. You are no match for my power and years of experience!"

"Halt!" I started to yell again, but a bolt of green lightning struck at my feet. I jumped backward, never finishing my command.

"It is moonstone," Mrs. Annesley called above the din. A buzzing noise that I had not yet noticed worked to drown out her words.

"What? Moonstone?" I yelled back. "But that is not more powerful than bloodstone!"

"It is in the wrong hands," she cried.

My mind raced through every spell I had ever learned, but before I had time to use one, the buzzing noise grew too deafening to ignore.

"What in the world?" I looked up to see what had caught Richard's attention. Thousands of fairies had converged upon us.

"Stop now, or there will be consequences!" The lead fairy still wore my hair comb to hold its hair back from its small face. Paired with the fierce expression it wore, the hair adornment looked less like a pretty accessory and more like the headpiece of a warrior. Lady Catherine could not understand the Fae language, though it was unlikely she would have paid it any mind, even if she had comprehended the command. She is, without a doubt, the most immoderate, obstinate, bull-headed person I have ever met. No, she would not have stopped for a fairy's request.

The fairies began to swarm around Miss Elizabeth's and my evil aunt's floating bodies. As they grew closer, she swatted them away as if they were swarming bees. "Get away from me you dreaded creatures. Get away!" She slapped her hands violently until one collided with a small Fae body, sending it flying backward." The loud buzzing grew until it was a deafening roar.

I do not know if I have adequately explained the full extent of a fairy's magical power. Aside from dragons, fairies are the most powerful of the Earthbound creatures. The fact that they can fly without wings should give some indication of the strength they hold. But in case you are still not convinced, I will attempt to fully explain events as they unfolded.

I soon realized the sound I heard was not a buzz, but a tonal resonance that emitted from their mouths. Akin to a tribal chant, it grew and grew until my ears ached. Just when I thought I could stand it no longer, a vivid white light erupted from the circle they had formed, tossing Lady Catherine out of the green light that encircled her. Down, down, down she fell until she landed with a sickening crunch, half in and half out of Mrs. Bennets' boxwood hedge. Miss Elizabeth also fell, but with the fairies' assistance and Fitzwilliam's quick thinking, she was safely set down in the driveway. My brother cradled her shaking form to his chest. "There, there. You are safe now," he murmured.

"What have you done?" Lady Catherine attempted to climb out from the shrub, only to be forced backward by the fairies' power. "Get me out of here!" she screeched. But the fairies would not relent. Around and around, they circled her until her hands and legs were bound by invisible bindings.

"Damn you!" (I promise she said this. Niece, if I do let you read this, you must promise never to use such a vile word.) She writhed against her bonds, but it was no use.

The head fairy hovered above her purple face. "You have offended me, and now you shall pay." Lady Catherine's eyes widened in fear. The fairy spoke in heavily accented English, but its message was clear.

Gathering my voice, I held out my bloodstone. "Lady Catherine, today you have gone too far. I demand your magic." The rhythmic flapping of heavy wings drew her eyes to the sky where Andromalius hovered.

"This is the wildest dream I have ever had," Richard mumbled from beside me. I giggle now as I record today's events, but at the time, I was far too concerned with the fiasco in front of me to laugh.

"Catherine, I cannot believe what I have witnessed." Andromalius landed his heavy body next to the bush where she continued to fight against her constraints. "Today, alone, you have attempted to harm Miss Elizabeth and your niece, and you have threatened your nephew. You have put two humans in harm's way on the roof of this house, and you have gravely offended the fairies. I should allow the Fae to have their way with you, but I will intervene on your behalf and in honor of your excellent mother." Lady Catherine spat in his direction, but he moved deftly to the side. "I promise, your fate is better in my hands than in the fairies. You will thank me later."

Turning he bid me to hold my hands out toward Lady Catherine. "This will hurt," he warned. Then, he turned his stocky body back to her and commanded, "From this day forward, Catherine, you will be a witch no longer. I transmit your power to another!"

"No!" Lady Catherine screamed as I was flung backward by the power of her magic. It flowed in painful streams through my fingertips, up past my elbows and into my shoulders. There it joined with my blood and began to circle my body in great, pulsing loops, surging left and right, circling my torso, my hips, my legs, and then my feet. The pain was so intense I could not even scream.

When I could no longer stand it, I fell to the ground. Richard was closest to me, and he gathered me in his arms. "Gopher, talk to me."

"I, I," I stuttered, but could not speak further for the power of Lady Catherine's magic continued to surge and pulse throughout my limbs and torso.

"You are killing her," I heard my brother yell.

The pain continued to rush through every cell of my body while Lady Catherine's unrelenting barrage of insults and complaints spewed from behind the mystic. "Stop it! Do you know who I am? I am Lady Ca—"

"Ah, ah, ah," Andromalius warned. "You have already lost your magic today. Do you really wish to share your name with the fairies?" Lady Catherine's eyes widened in fright, but it was not long-lived.

"How dare you! I am a Fitzwilliam witch. We have been bound to this earth through our magical powers for a thousand years. How dare you take them from me!"

Andromalius shrugged. "I attempted not to. When your niece came to me and suggested it, I was appalled. In my thousand years in this realm, I have known two other witches who have lost their power. You are the third, and hopefully, the last. I take no pleasure in this, Catherine, but you did it to yourself. Not only did you attempt to harm your nephew, but you attempted to kill Elizabeth and Georgiana, two witches. The penalty for harming a fellow witch is stiff. You knew this."

"That harlot is not a witch."

"She is weak, I grant you, but she has power." Though I was still writhing in pain, I could make out the small gasp from Miss Elizabeth's lips. I suppose it took a gargoyle to convince her she has talent.

Lady Catherine's power continued to surge through me. Though she was in apparent discomfort, I can assure you that I was in great pain. Much of which I share with you has been confirmed by Mrs. Annesley as I was too intently focused on my own condition and little of what happened around me was understood.

According to Mrs. Annesley, my body writhed and jerked of its own accord. My back arched in such a way that only my head and hips maintained contact with the ground. At one point, I opened my eyes to see both Richard and Fitzwilliam standing above me, each with their hands on my shoulders attempting to keep me on the ground. "Be well, Georgie. Stay with us, stay with us," Fitzwilliam whispered.

I was close to death. There is no way the body can survive such torture except for sheer will. I opened my eyes and saw the people I love surrounding me. Fitzwilliam and Richard were kneeling beside me. Miss Elizabeth had lifted her body from the ground and was attempting to crawl toward me. Mrs. Annesley had laid a hand on my shoulder to lessen my pain. And somewhere, on the roof, Mrs. Bennet stood. It was at that moment that I understood what Mrs. Annesley meant when she said the people you love bring you power. It is not magical power I gained from them, but the power to survive the horrible agony of the transfer.

I willed myself to live. "I am — I am well," I responded in whispered gasps. The pain crescendoed until, suddenly, there was nothing.

"The transfer is complete. You did well, Georgiana. Turning to the fairies, he commanded. "Do not harm her." Then, his short legs ran a few steps, flapping his black wings until he launched himself in the air.

Miss Elizabeth, still stunned from her altercation with Lady Catherine, crawled over to where I now sat with the help of Richard's strong arms. "Please tell me you are unhurt."

"I am tired, but well. Were you injured in your fall?"

She offered a small smile. "Perhaps a slight turning of my ankle, but nothing I have not suffered a dozen times in the past."

"Hussy!" Lady Catherine spat in our direction but was promptly knocked back to the ground from her seated position by a powerful burst of fairy magic.

"Thank you," Elizabeth said in the Fae tongue. "You helped save me. I will never forget the kindness you have shown me."

"What did you say to them?" Fitzwilliam sat as close as he could to his OTL, her hand held snugly in his.

She and I shared a smile. "Before I tell you, I need you to admit you were wrong when you judged me as a silly miss for speaking Fae."

"But I never said —"

"You did not need to," she laughed.

∞∞∞

Richard helped me to my feet. A wave of nausea overtook me, and I fell to my knees and retched. "It is the excess of power," Mrs. Annesley explained. To my cousin and brother, she commanded, "Take her back to Netherfield. I will spell the Bennets to forget this occurred and to believe the party has been completed. Miss Darcy will be in no shape to attend a dinner tonight, and I doubt Miss Elizabeth will, either."

"Thank you," I replied.

"But my mother, she is still on the roof." Miss Elizabeth's eyes looked up to where Mrs. Bennet kneeled, peering over the edge.

"Lizzy Bennet, if you do not get me down right this minute, I shall force you to marry in a potato sack!" Miss Elizabeth attempted to suppress a guffaw, but she was unsuccessful.

"And me as well. My patroness would have you arrested, Miss Elizabeth, for placing me up here."

Miss Elizabeth laughed heartily at this reprimand. "It was

not I who summoned you to the gables, sir. I must remind you, it was your own dear patroness who did so."

Summoning my strength, I lifted my hand and ordered, "Banish!" Mrs. Bennet and Mr. Collins stood before us, once again.

"You should have left him on the roof," Richard whispered.

Mrs. Bennet fanned herself wildly with a piece of lace. "Miss Darcy, thank you, thank you so much for your help today!" She got down on her knees, where I still knelt on the drive, and kissed first my left cheek and then my right. "You are as good a daughter as I have ever had. May I call you Georgiana?"

I smiled. "I would like that, Mrs. Bennet."

"Oh, none of that. You must call me Mama, as the others do. You will soon be my girls' sister if I am correct in my assumptions. You must also be my daughter, then, and I will be your mother." Mrs. Annesley assured me she would not allow Mrs. Bennet to forget this exchange, though she must forget all the magical events that preceded.

My teacher was gone for many hours. It was necessary to attend Lucas Lodge to spell them into believing the dinner had already occurred, as well. I stayed awake waiting for her return, though it was a great difficulty to do so. When she arrived, she filled in gaps in my memory. Much had been excluded due to the intense pain I suffered.

Tomorrow, our party will check on Miss Elizabeth, who was not spelled to forget the events. Together, Mrs. Annesley and I have concocted a plan, but it relies on Miss Elizabeth's cooperation.

Chapter Forty-four

Evening, 23 November 1811

Dear Diary,

It is a new day at last, and what a day it has been! Last night, Berwyn visited me in my dream. "Congratulations, Georgiana. You were able to gather your allies and defeat your aunt. I know it was difficult, but it was necessary."

"Thank you for everything. I could not have done any of this without your advice. I know it took too long for me to understand what was required of me. I am grateful you did not give up and continued to visit me in my dreams." She blushed, if such a thing is possible for a dragon.

When she left me, I woke up with— you will not believe this— my nose touching the ceiling! I had so much magic in my body, I literally floated in my dream. It took a good deal of magical energy to make my way back into my bed. By the time I was under the covers I was sweating from the effort.

"Mrs. Annesley, we must do something about this excess magic." I had caught my companion in the hall on her way to the breakfast room. I struggled to maintain eye contact, so intent was I on keeping my feet on the floor.

"What do you mean? You do not wish to have your aunt's power? It will make you the most powerful witch in the world."

With my eyes still on my feet (daring them to lift even a quarter inch off the ground), I replied, "Absolutely not. I have no desire to be the most powerful witch. Not only would that be too much pressure, but it would also make me the center of attention, at least for those in the magical world. I was thinking that I could give my powers away."

Mrs. Annesley nodded her head in understanding. "Excellent. I will help you with this after breakfast." So saying, we made our way to the breakfast room where a feast of food was laid out before us.

Fitzwilliam sat at the table, drinking a cup of coffee. "I asked the housekeeper to add a little extra to the menu this morning. I suspected you would be tired and hungry after yesterday's events." My brother can be a complete nincompoop at times, but he is a lovely brother. As thoughtless as he sometimes is with his words, he has never been thoughtless in his actions toward me. I hope, niece, that you are as lucky with your brother as I have been with my own.

After breakfast, Fitzwilliam, Richard, Mr. Bingley, Mrs. Annesley, and I made our way to Longbourn. Miss Bingley and Mrs. Hurst were busy with plans for the approaching ball and could not attend, though I could tell Mrs. Hurst dearly wished to join us. Given the timing of the day, it was unlikely that Mrs. Bennet would serve tea for our party, so Mr. Hurst also elected to remain at Netherfield.

"Georgiana, my sweet girl. How are you this morning? I have asked Cook to save some of the remaining rum cake from last night. You were so fond of it, I wished you to have an additional piece." There was no need to tell the good lady that we did not have cake last night as she remembered. Clearly, Mrs. Annesley's spell worked just as it was designed.

"Thank you, Mama." On hearing the affectionate title, Mrs. Bennet leaned in and kissed my cheek.

"Where has Mr. Collins gone?" Richard scanned the room looking for the annoying parson.

"Him," Mrs. Bennet huffed. "It is the strangest thing. He insisted his patroness required his presence and left right away. I told him to wait until morning, but he was too intent on having his way. There is absolutely no reason to travel at night, I said, but that man is ever the fool."

Richard laughed. "I have thought the same thing, Mrs. Bennet." I must remember to thank Mrs. Annesley for her role in relieving us of the good parson's presence. If she could only do the same for Miss Bingley.

After some conversation, Miss Elizabeth suggested a walk in the midday sun. Everyone donned their coats and gloves and headed out into the garden. It took some doing to extricate myself from Kitty and Miss Mary, but I was finally able to join Fitzwilliam and Elizabeth alone.

"How are you feeling, Miss Darcy? Have you experienced any negative side effects from taking on your aunt's magic?"

"It is funny you should ask that, Miss Elizabeth. I have had some side effects, and I was hoping you could help me."

"Me? But I am a very weak witch, according to the gargoyle, though I still cannot fathom that to be true."

"It is true. You have an innate ability to heal a person. I experienced it myself after, er —"

"After?" Fitzwilliam was overly concerned to hear the rest of my recollection. I could feel my face flame.

"It does not matter how I know, only that I do know." I continued. "To be frank, I am now carrying too much magic for one person. I need to share some of it with someone."

"Your brother?"

"No, no. I cannot give my magic to a man. It must reside in a female." Turning to my brother, I asked, "Fitzwilliam, will you give us a moment alone?" He reluctantly moved back to walk with Mrs. Annesley. "As I was saying, I need to share my powers with another female. But first, I must ask: do you plan to marry my brother?"

Miss Elizabeth blushed, but she did not shy away from the

answer. "If he asks me, I will say yes."

"Because you love him?"

I did not believe it possible, but the pink in her cheeks deepened to crimson. "Yes. I love him dearly. I cannot imagine my life without him in it."

"You are destined for one another." Confusion was written across her face. "I will tell you all about it someday. But today, I must ask: Will you allow me to share my magic with you?" I put up a hand to stall her objections. "Before you say no, I must tell you how most witches use their powers. As Fitzwilliam's wife, you would use the magic to help the crops grow, keep the tenants healthy, and guide your family's investments. Though it has not been my experience of late, there will be very little fighting other witches or visiting gargoyles."

"That is a shame, I would love to invite the gargoyle to tea."

I laughed. "His name is Andromalius, and though he is of another realm, I suspect he would enjoy tea with you."

After a moment of levity, Miss Elizabeth sobered. "Do you really believe that it will help Fitzwilliam if I take some of your powers? I worry you will regret your decision to part with them, but I do want to be a helpmate to my husband, assuming he asks me." She blushed anew.

I placed my hand on hers. "It would allow you to be a great helpmate, not only to my brother, but to everyone who relies on the Darcys for their income."

"Then I will do it. I do not wish to sound chicken-hearted, but will it be as painful for me as it was for you? I will do anything to help Fitzwilliam, mind you. I only wish to be prepared for the pain."

"I will relieve your worry. I spoke about this with Mrs. Annesley this morning, and she assured me it will not hurt either of us. When magic is freely given, it requires no discomfort."

I turned back to Fitzwilliam and my companion. "She has agreed. Will you assist us?"

"She has agreed to what?" Fitzwilliam stepped forward.

"To receive my excess powers. It is too much for one person to carry. Miss Elizabeth will be an excellent vessel for the Fitzwilliam witch magic.

Fitzwilliam had the same concerns as Miss Elizabeth but was soon on board when he learned that neither of us would suffer any pain. Mrs. Annesley led us to a more secluded area of the garden. "This will not take long, but we must be quick lest someone stumble upon our hiding spot." Miss Elizabeth and I joined hands, and together we chanted:

> *By the mystic ties that bind,*
> *Let this power shift be kind.*
> *Through the ritual we decree,*
> *Share the gift, set magic free.*

The familiar tingle of vibration began in my toes until it worked its way up my body, swirled around my torso, and finally released itself through my fingertips. I knew when the magic entered her body by the widening of her eyes and the soft "Oh" that escaped her lips. Within a matter of seconds, the deed was done. Though I felt amazing, having rid myself of the superfluous magic, Miss Elizabeth swooned. Luckily, Fitzwilliam was there to catch her.

"I thought you said this would not harm her!"

"It did not. I am not hurt; I am only unused to the feeling. It is rather overwhelming." Miss Elizabeth's voice was weak.

Mrs. Annesley placed her hand on Miss Elizabeth's cheek. "You are a little warm. It is expected. You must rest for the remainder of the day. Tomorrow, you will feel much better. I suspect well enough, even, that I can hold a short lesson."

"Oh, it will be so fun to have lessons with you, Miss Elizabeth!"

Though frail, she managed a faint smile. "You must call me Elizabeth. You have shared too valuable a gift with me for there to be such formality between us."

"And you will call me Georgiana!" My brother's pleasure in this exchange was obvious to everyone.

Fitzwilliam helped Miss Elizabeth into the house and asked the butler to call for a maid. "Please help Miss Elizabeth to her room. She is not feeling well. And please, have someone contact me if she begins to feel worse." The maid assured him she would see to Miss Elizabeth's health personally and assisted the lady up the stairs.

"I feel we have hardly visited at all today, Georgiana. You must visit again tomorrow."

"I am scheduled to try on my gown for the ball this afternoon. Would you like to come with me? I am sure Mrs. Annesley would not mind." Kitty squealed her delight and Mrs. Annesley agreed that it was no trouble to bring her with us.

We had a delightful afternoon together. Kitty has a fine eye for fashion, and her advice to the modiste was excellent. My gown will benefit from it, that is for certain. I shall wait until the day of the ball to describe it fully. I wish to see it completed before I share with you just how beautiful it is. I think even Miss Bingley will agree that a "nobody from nowhere" did an excellent job making my gown.

Chapter Forty-five

Afternoon, 24 November 1811

Dear Diary,

Today we attended church in Longbourn Village. "Charles, I must insist that you desist from this quest to woo Miss Bennet. Not only is she too far beneath our notice, but the dilapidated church she attends is beyond the pale!" I will allow you to guess who said that.

Mr. Bingley's retort, however, was nothing short of genius. "I suppose you are correct, Caroline. Not, mind you, about Miss Bennet—she is nothing short of perfection—but about her church. If our mortal souls are in danger, then we must attend service in Meryton." A smug smile overtook the sour look Miss Bingley had worn moments before, that is until her brother opened his mouth to continue. "I must warn you, sister, that I cannot vouch for Darcy's soul. He may choose the perilous path to perdition and attend with the Bennets."

Richard attempted to suffocate his laughter, and even Fitzwilliam struggled to hide his smile. "You are correct, Bingley. I believe I will chance perdition, as you put it, for a chance to listen to the better preacher. Enjoy your time in Meryton, Miss Bingley."

Realizing she had been duped, Miss Bingley backtracked. "I did not mean to imply that the preacher at Longbourn is not superior to the one in Meryton, but that the church itself is less pristine. However, you make a good point, Mr. Darcy. We should see to nourishing our souls over our comfort. Charles,

I believe we should attend church with the Darcys and Colonel Fitzwilliam."

Our party soon stood in the churchyard awaiting the Bennet family. They emerged from the path leading from their home. "There she is, dear, your sixth daughter. I wonder, where will she stand in your ranking of favorites. Will she replace one who bears the Bennet name? Perhaps our Lizzy will move from fifth to sixth place."

Mrs. Bennet swatted her husband's arm. "Oh, hush, Mr. Bennet. You do go on and on sometimes." Then she stepped forward and kissed my cheeks. "You look as lovely as ever, Georgiana." I thanked her kindly, making sure to address her as Mama, which pleased us both.

Kitty greeted me with a warm hug and a smile. "Mama is so pleased to have you call her that. She always wanted more children, you know. A son would have been preferred, of course, but really, she would have been pleased with any child. She was told she could not conceive after Lydia, probably because she was the biggest and fattest baby anyone has ever seen."

"Hush, Kitty. You are only upset because I am the youngest and already the tallest of all, while you are short and slight like Lizzy." The two sisters continued to bicker, which allowed me an opportunity to step away and greet Elizabeth.

"How do you feel today? Have you recovered from your fatigue?"

Her bright eyes, previously glued to my brother's smiling face, turned to me. "I am quite well, thank you. I look forward to my first lesson!"

"Mrs. Annesley has said that if we walk slowly enough, we might be able to practice briefly on our walk back to Netherfield." It had already been arranged that the Bennet sisters would spend time with me this afternoon.

"I wish you had not told me. I will not be able to pay one whit of attention to today's sermon. All I shall think about is magic!"

"Perhaps you may think about one or two additional things," my brother suggested in a low tone, causing Elizabeth to color.

Soon we were called into the church for services. Being now an honorary Bennet sister, I was invited to sit in their row between Kitty and Miss Lydia. Fitzwilliam, Richard, and the rest of the Netherfield party sat directly behind us.

The sermon was taken from the twelfth chapter of Romans. *Be careful to do what is right in the eyes of everyone. If it is possible, as far as it depends on you, live at peace with everyone.* Elizabeth leaned forward and whispered, "Mr. Collins should have mentioned this to Lady Catherine weeks ago." Kitty could not hide her confusion, while I struggled to hide my mirth. No doubt, even without her magic, Lady Catherine will never be one who lives at peace.

Soon enough, the sermon ended and Mr. and Mrs. Bennet led us back into the church yard. "It is so cold," Kitty complained. "Please tell me you have informed Mrs. Nichols of our attendance today and that she will have her famous chocolate waiting for us?"

I laughed. "I informed her you were coming, and I reminded her just this morning of your preference for chocolate. She promised to serve it with raspberry cakes."

Kitty bobbed up and down on her toes. "Excellent! Let us find your carriage and be off."

I locked eyes with Elizabeth. "I had thought to walk back if that is acceptable to you. If you are too cold, you can take the carriage, but I would like to stretch my legs."

Miss Bennet preferred to ride in the carriage where she would be near Mr. Bingley. Miss Lydia also chose the carriage after learning that Richard preferred to be out of the wind. "I have too few opportunities to choose my form of transportation. While I am on leave, I will ride in a carriage as often as possible." As expected, Kitty and Miss Mary followed suit, which left Fitzwilliam, Elizabeth, Mrs. Annesley, and me remaining for the walk.

"I begin to believe that you are well-skilled in the art of subterfuge, sister. In addition to the spell you cast to repeat the days, I wonder what other meddling you have instigated."

"Speaking of that, I would like to know more about the repetition of days. You mentioned it before Lady Catherine arrived, but I do not understand." By silent agreement, Mrs. Annesley and I opted to change the conversation. I will tell Elizabeth about the spell one day, but I prefer to wait until she bears the Darcy name before I do.

"There will be time for conversation later. For now, let us take advantage of our relative privacy and practice a spell or two. Are you ready, Miss Elizabeth?"

Elizabeth's eyes sparkled. "Lead the way, Mrs. Annesley. I am your willing and enthusiastic pupil."

Mrs. Annesley suggested we take a lesser-used path toward Netherfield. "Miss Darcy's lessons began by learning a spell to extend the blooms on a rose. There are no flowers at this time of year, but the spell should work just as well on a dried leaf. Mr. Darcy, please find us three leaves. They should be dried but still intact." Fitzwilliam did as he was told and returned with three oak leaves.

While he was searching, Mrs. Annesley shared the spell with Elizabeth. "When you first begin to cast spells, you must imagine the thing happening in front of you. Later, when you become more proficient, you will be able to simply speak the words. Are you ready?"

Elizabeth nodded her understanding. "I have never been more ready in my life!"

Fitzwilliam handed each of us a leaf. Mrs. Annesley nodded.

"Then let us begin." We each placed our leaf on an open palm and spoke:

> *The breath of life, as soft as a kiss,*
> *Grant this plant eternal bliss.*
> *Turn the wilt, reverse the gray,*
> *Let freshness rule the light of day.*

Mrs. Annesley's and my leaves changed rapidly. It was Elizabeth's first attempt at intentional magic; therefore, her leaf's transformation was more gradual. Fitzwilliam and Elizabeth gasped when the withered brown leaf began to slowly morph into a fleshy green one.

"I have done it, Fitzwilliam!" She held the leaf in front of his face and stood on tiptoes so that their eyes were more closely aligned.

"So you have, my love." He took the leaf from her hand, then kissed her open palm with reverence. Immediately after, he remembered that he was in company. I should like to paint a picture of my brother's face as he was at that moment. I would require three colors: black for his hair, deep blue for his eyes, and a vivid shade of crimson for his face.

When the two lovers (it pains me to write that) collected themselves, Miss Elizabeth asked, "What else shall we do today?"

"Oh no, you must work your way up to it. Magical endurance requires time. Just one spell today."

"But surely, there is one small thing I can try, ma'am. I am so anxious to learn."

Mrs. Annesley turned to me. "Miss Darcy, what is your favorite small spell that requires the tiniest bit of magic?"

I slid my eyes to Fitzwilliam and then to Miss Elizabeth. "I can teach you how to tighten someone's shoes."

"You are caught out, sister!" Fitzwilliam's voice was stern, but he wore a broad grin on his face. "I knew my shoes could not have shrunk on their own."

A light, tinkling laugh fell easily from Elizabeth's mouth. "You must teach it to me, Georgiana. I would like to use it when Lydia attempts to steal my bonnets and ribbons." I taught her the spell as we walked the remainder of the way to Netherfield, and together we concocted a plan to employ it on Miss Bingley. I know, I know. I promised to turn a new leaf with that lady, but surely, I can be forgiven this one instance.

Chapter Forty-six

Evening, 25 November 1811

Dear Diary,

Today, Mrs. Annesley and I spent most of our time assisting Miss Bingley and Mrs. Hurst with preparations for the ball. Mrs. Hurst has maintained her pleasant attitude, but Miss Bingley's has deteriorated to the point that I am tempted to magic her into the attics. I was put on flower arrangement duty, which suited me perfectly since I could easily employ my magic to ensure the flowers looked their best, and I could work without Miss Bingley's interference.

"Charles, have you seen Mr. Darcy? I wanted his opinion on the menu before I finalize it with Mrs. Nichols." Mr. Bingley and Richard exchanged sly glances before answering.

"I have not seen him since our ride after breakfast. He is probably holed up in his room writing letters and doing other boring things." Richard's eyes sparkled at Mr. Bingley's obvious lie. It was clear they knew where Fitzwilliam could be found, and it was not in his room, as they claimed.

I also knew where my brother was. Actually, I did not know where he was, but I was positive I knew who he was with. My mirror, secretly stored in the pocket of the apron I wore, had buzzed several times an hour prior. Fitzwilliam was with Miss Elizabeth. Unfortunately, the constant company I kept prevented me from looking into the glass and seeing what they were up to. I really must find a spell that allows me to check the mirror at a later time!

"Miss Darcy, are you ready to visit the seamstress? We need to pick up your gown and ensure that it fits." Mrs. Annesley added a final sprig of greenery to the arrangement she had designed.

I wiped my hands on my apron, carefully removing the mirror and placing it in my pocket. "Richard, would you like to go to town with us?" He and Mr. Bingley agreed they would be pleased to get out of the house for a few hours, and soon the four of us were on our way to Meryton. In town, the gentlemen headed toward the bookshop, while Mrs. Annesley and I made our way to the dress shop.

"Miss Darcy, we have just put the last touch on your gown. I think you will be quite pleased with how it turned out." We were led to a dressing room while a young girl was asked to bring my gown. We did not have to wait long before she returned, her slight form carrying the gown across outstretched arms so that it did not drag on the ground.

"Here you are, miss." The seamstress ordered another girl to help me undress, and soon I stepped into the gown and slipped it up and over my shoulders. I should probably wait to reveal it when I write about the ball, but I am too excited and can wait no longer. The gown is made of ivory muslin that was so finely milled it appears to glow. The waist is trimmed in rose pink, and along the band, peonies in both darker and lighter shades of pink have been embroidered. The embroidery continues down the front right of the skirt. The peonies grow larger the lower they go on the skirt, until they reach approximately five inches in width at the hem. When I move it gives the appearance that I am stepping out of a shower of flowers.

"It is beautiful! I cannot believe you and your staff have completed such intricate work in time for the ball."

"T'was nothing, miss. My daughter, Laurel, worked on it. She is a deft hand at embroidery."

"Indeed, she is. She could earn a pretty penny in London

with such skills." The seamstress beamed at the recognition, though it was nothing short of the truth.

Mrs. Annesley had me turn around so that she could inspect the fit of my gown. "It fits you perfectly. I do not see anything that requires additional alterations." I was helped out of the gown and back into my clothes. "Box it up, please. Jeffries will take it to the carriage for us." Mrs. Annesley directed a footman to wait for our parcel. Then we went in search of Richard and Mr. Bingley.

We found them in the bookshop speaking with Mr. Bennet. "Is your gown everything you wished for, Gopher?"

I chucked him lightly on the shoulder for his continued use of the silly nickname. "It is absolutely divine, Richard. You will not recognize me when you see me in it."

"I beg you, Miss Darcy, do not regale us with details of your gown. I hear enough talk of lace and shoe roses from my wife and daughters."

Feeling more comfortable in Mr. Bennet's presence, I answered in a saucy tone. "Then you will be disappointed to learn, sir, that the gown has not a single inch of lace to be found."

His eyes shone. "Your new mother will be very upset to learn that, Miss Darcy, but Lizzy will approve."

Soon, Mr. Bennet excused himself to speak with the proprietor of the shop, and our party headed next door where Richard purchased Mrs. Annesley and me each two pieces of chocolate. When we returned to Netherfield, Fitzwilliam was in the parlor. Miss Bingley had trapped him in a conversation about women's headwear and he looked ever so grateful for our entrance.

"Fascinating, Miss Bingley. Truly, I did not know there were so many things to consider before choosing a feather for one's hair. Unfortunately, I must cut this conversation short. I have something I need to discuss with my sister." Then he stood, held his arm for me to take, and guided us from the room.

When the door to the library closed, I laughed. "Fitzwilliam, I am sorry that we left you so long with Miss Bingley. I thought you would remain with Elizabeth for longer."

"How did you know where I—" Understanding dawned on his face before he muttered, "Magic."

"Did you really wish to speak to me, or was it only a ruse to get away from your captor?"

He laughed and escorted me to a chair, then took the one across from me. Carefully, he smoothed the fabric on his pants and jacket before he began. "I have something I wish to tell you."

I leaned forward. I suspected what he planned to say, but that did not dampen my anticipation. "As you know, I have spent a lot of time with Elizabeth these last months."

"As you should. She is your OTL, after all."

A dreamy look overcame his face. "She is, indeed. Given that you have played such a vital role in our romance, what I am about to say should come as no surprise to you. Today I asked Elizabeth to be my bride. You will soon have a sister."

I leaped from my chair and hugged him tightly. "Oh, I am so happy! I cannot imagine a better woman to fill the role of Mrs. Darcy."

He squeezed me to his chest. "You will finally have the loud, boisterous family you have always wished for."

"Pemberley will never be quiet again! I will invite Kitty to visit, and I suspect Mrs. Bennet will want to come often." Fitzwilliam groaned. "Do not be that way! She is to be your mother soon. And though you may not appreciate her antics, you must admit she loves her family very much, and she has been so very good to me."

He kissed my forehead. "You are correct. Though I wish her

behavior was different at times, I cannot fault her love for her daughters —all six of them."

"When will you announce your engagement?"

"Mr. Bennet plans to share the news during supper tomorrow night."

"Miss Bingley may faint away—right into her white soup!"

Fitzwilliam laughed. "Surely, she has seen the writing on the wall by now. My interest in Elizabeth was hardly subtle."

"Miss Bingley has the pleasure of being willfully obtuse when it comes to you. I will ensure she behaves herself."

"Do not cast anymore of your magic on the poor lady. Do not think I have not figured out it was you who caused her to sing like a bird."

I giggled. "She did not sing, she cooed."

He rolled his eyes. "In any case, leave the poor woman alone. She is annoying but she does not deserve your curses."

"Even the one that prevented her from coming near when you and Elizabeth are together."

Fitzwilliam pretended to think for a moment. "I suppose you may continue that one."

So you see, tomorrow Fitzwilliam and Elizabeth's engagement will be announced to the whole of Meryton, and it will all unfold while I am wearing the world's most gorgeous gown. And my purse will be five pounds heavier, thanks to my bet with Richard. The Netherfield Ball will go down in history as one of my all-time favorite nights!

Chapter Forty-seven

Morning, 27 November 1811

Dear Diary,

Please forgive me for missing a day's entry. I had every intention of completing this yesterday, but between helping Miss Bingley with last-minute ball arrangements and my own preparations, there was not time to write before the event. Though he insisted I leave after supper, Fitzwilliam allowed me to stay for the entire event, which meant I was occupied for the remainder of the evening. So you see, there has been no opportunity to capture yesterday's events until now.

I have already shared the details of my gown, so I will not bore you with them again. Heaven forfend my niece does not wish to know about fashion, but she may take after her grandfather, so I will refrain. I must say, however, that I have never looked lovelier. Everyone said as much. Fitzwilliam's eyes got watery when he spied me on the stairs. "You look so much like our mother." He hugged me tightly to his chest.

"Gopher, you look quite the grown-up lady. I truly may be forced to stop calling you by your childhood nickname," Richard added.

"Miss Darcy, you are quite stunning, indeed. Why do you not stand near my brother? He has always been one to admire great beauty," Miss Bingley crooned. I believe she has begun to see the writing on the wall regarding Fitzwilliam and has turned her sights on me. She would be very disappointed to learn that I have no interest in Mr. Bingley.

The Lucas party arrived first, followed soon after by the Gouldings, Kings, and Phillips. Fitzwilliam drummed his fingers against his thigh until Mr. and Mrs. Bennet finally crossed the threshold. He started toward Elizabeth, but I placed a hand on his forearm as a reminder to stay in his place. To the world, they were not yet engaged.

Mrs. Bennet greeted everyone in her usual fulsome manner. "My, my, Miss Bingley. What a wonderful job you have done decorating for tonight's event. I was unsure if your health would allow you to do it, but I was mistaken. Everything is perfection. Just perfection, I say." Then she made her way down the line. "Mr. Darcy, so good to see you this evening. You look well." Fitzwilliam made a polite reply, stating that Mrs. Bennet also looked lovely. "And my Lizzy? Does not she look exceedingly well, sir?"

His eyes roamed up and down the form of the lady in question. "She does, indeed, madam." Satisfied that Fitzwilliam's interest lay exactly where she wished it, Mrs. Bennet moved on to me.

After being kissed soundly on each cheek and made to turn around twice so she could see the beauty of my gown, Kitty joined us. "It is stunning," she gushed.

"Yours is, too. Lydia was wrong, that color is incredible on you." We stood together for several minutes until Elizabeth and Fitzwilliam joined us.

"Georgiana, your gown is divine. It looks as if Laurel worked her magic on your embroidery. She always stitches the most amazing designs."

"I told her she should come to London. She could make a fortune embellishing ball gowns for the ton."

"Shall we go into the ballroom, ladies?" Fitzwilliam was eager to have Elizabeth to himself and likely pleased to forego additional conversations about ball gowns. Kitty and I followed the couple into the room, but there we broke apart. Kitty and I made our way closer to a group of soldiers, where Miss Lydia already stood, while Fitzwilliam escorted Elizabeth to Miss Lucas. Poor Miss Lucas, Mrs. Annesley had planned to throw her together with Mr. Collins at the ball, but Lady Catherine put an end to that. Though, as I think about it, perhaps that is not such a bad thing for Miss Lucas, after all.

Miss Lydia gesticulated for us to hurry to her side. "There you are. Come stand by me! I was just telling Denny that he must dance with me for the first dance since I am the best dancer of all the Bennet sisters and the liveliest too!"

Lieutenant Denny's ears turned red. "Miss Lydia, I would love to dance with you, but it cannot be the first. I have already promised to escort another to the floor for that set."

"Oh, la, Denny, you play at being a gentleman, but it is no concern. Dance with me and say that you have forgotten the other lady. It happens all the time. Why at the last assembly, Samual Keene danced the first with me even though he had promised the set to Mary King."

Though he answered Miss Lydia, his eyes turned shyly toward Kitty. "I am sorry to disappoint you, Miss Lydia, but I wish to dance with my intended partner."

"Fine then, but do not be sorry when my dance card fills up and I have none left for you! I will see if Colonel Fitzwilliam wishes to dance." Miss Lydia turned on her heel and flounced away.

"Thank you for remembering our dance, Lieutenant." Kitty's eyes remained on her shoes and her face heated to a very becoming shade of pink.

"How could I forget? I have anticipated it every moment since I first requested it." Kitty's face heated to an even brighter (and less becoming) shade of pink. We stood together until Mr. Bingley gathered everyone's attention and indicated that it was time for the first dance. The crowd clapped politely, and gentlemen moved to and fro to gather their partners.

"Shall we?" To my left, Richard held out his arm. Apparently, Miss Lydia's attempts to woo him away from his designated partner did not work, either. Kitty and Lieutenant Denny followed us. Richard's rank as the son of an earl required us to stand at the top of the formation; Fitzwilliam and Elizabeth stood to my right, while Sir William Lucas and Mrs. Goulding stood to my left. The music began signaling that I should curtsy to my partner. Soon, I took my first steps to the left, and then turned right. I was nervous and forced myself to count "One, two, three, four, five, six," fearing I might miss a step during the minuet. But Richard is an excellent partner, and I was soon too enraptured by his wry comments about other couples to pay attention to the rhythm. I am not certain how it was possible, but my dancing improved as a result.

I danced the second with Fitzwilliam, the third with Mr. Bingley, and much to Miss Lydia's frustration, the fourth with Lieutenant Denny. By that time, I was quite winded and thirsty, so instead of dancing, Mr. Lucas escorted me to the punch table and kept me company by an open door. Of course, we did not dare to move further out onto the balcony to take advantage of the cool temperatures. Given his preoccupation with Elizabeth, Fitzwilliam paid little attention to me last night, but he would have wrung both my and Mr. Lucas' necks if he had caught us outside together.

The supper set was next and since Mr. Lucas did not already have a partner, he asked me to dance with him. He is an agreeable sort, but a poor dancer. Our time chatting about local folklore was more enjoyable than the dance. I was quite relieved when he escorted me into the dining room and helped me into a seat near my brother.

The footman poured me a glass of wine, and I took a deep drink. "Careful, sister. Though we are among friends, it would not do to overindulge."

"I am only thirsty, Fitzwilliam. Besides, if I drink too much, Elizabeth can set me to rights."

"What do you mean?" Elizabeth leaned forward to look at me from Fitzwilliam's other side.

"You do not know?" Her look of confusion told me that she did not. "It is why I suspect you were a witch in the first place. With a single touch, you can cure drunkenness. I do not know the extent of your abilities, though."

"That would explain why I am the designated sickroom attendant at Longbourn, then."

"Not for much longer, my love." Fitzwilliam slid his hand under the table, where I suspect their fingers intertwined.

"Not for much longer at Longbourn, but Elizabeth will be responsible for all the tenants and servants at Pemberley," I added.

"I will not have my wife expose herself to disease, even at Pemberley. We will hire a doctor to do that work."

I turned so that I could look at him in the face. "That is impossible. As the resident witch, it will be Elizabeth's duty to care for the ill. It is, in large part, the purpose of our power."

"I will not have my wife getting ill." Elizabeth's eyes widened, perhaps because she was first witnessing Fitzwilliam's unbending side.

"Do not be silly. Witches do not die from diseases. Elizabeth will likely outlive you by twenty years."

"How comforting," he harumphed.

I rolled my eyes at his petulance. "Do not fear, sister. He is rarely so rigid. You will need to learn to ignore him as I do when he acts this way." Elizabeth laughed, and the corners of Fitzwilliam's mouth lifted ever so slightly.

Servants surrounded the table placing plates of cold meats, pickled fish, aspic jellies, and salads on the table. I took my fill of a cold lobster salad but refrained from partaking of the aspic and pickled fish. "I see I must refrain from ordering aspic for our suppers at Pemberley. It appears you share your brother's aversion to it."

I wrinkled my nose. "I abhor it, and should I never see it again it would be too soon."

Elizabeth's laughter tinkled. "Noted."

Soon, the second course was served. Miss Bingley had outdone herself, ordering roasted duck, venison stew, and a multitude of vegetables be served. Miss Elizabeth leaned forward and whispered to me. "I am glad to see Miss Bingley overcame her trouble with her tight shoes to order an excellent meal. Roasted duck is my favorite."

"Mine, too," I confessed.

"Then it appears I know at least one dish to serve often for supper." Fitzwilliam said nothing, only sat back and looked well pleased that the two ladies in his life were happily engaged in conversation.

Soon the plates were cleared, and Miss Bingley signaled for the desserts to be served. After the last dishes were placed upon the table, Mr. Bennet tapped his spoon against his crystal wine glass. The clear sound alerted everyone around the table to stop talking. "If you will allow me to interrupt your conversation and enjoyment of this excellent meal for a moment, I have an announcement to make." Standing, he held his wine glass aloft. "I would like to propose a toast to Mr. Darcy and my own precious daughter, Elizabeth Rose. Yesterday, I granted my permission for the two of them to wed. I hope you will join us in a few weeks' time to celebrate their nuptials."

The room was instantly awash in the sounds of "How could he?" and "I knew how it would be the night they first met!" But it was Mrs. Bennet's cry of "A few weeks? I will need at least three months to plan a proper wedding!" that caused

Fitzwilliam to flinch.

"My mother would be so enamored with the procurement of a special license that she would not lament the additional time needed to plan a wedding."

"I shall go tomorrow and speak with the archbishop." Elizabeth winked at me before accepting the well wishes of Mrs. Goulding.

The rest of the night was a blur of activity. Fitzwilliam, against the dictates of society, danced two more with his intended, for a total of four dances! Miss Lydia finally danced with Lieutenant Denny, and Mrs. Bennet called me over to pronounce that we would now truly be mother and daughter when the wedding is completed. By that time, she had one too many celebratory glasses of punch. I summoned Elizabeth and asked her to use her magic to sober up her mother. Then I sat with the sweet lady and listened to her plans for the wedding. I did not share that Fitzwilliam plans to apply for a special license. I will allow Elizabeth to break that news to her.

"We will finally be sisters," Kitty said, taking my hands in her own. The musicians had long been gone and only the Bennets remained.

"You must promise to come to Pemberley after Fitzwilliam and Elizabeth's honeymoon is complete. Fitzwilliam has already promised that you can stay with me as long as you wish!"

"Lydia will be so jealous!" Her face beamed with happiness, and she hugged me tightly before responding to her father's suggestion that it was time to go.

Fitzwilliam put his arm around my shoulder as we watched the Bennets leave. "Are you happy, sister?"

"I am quite happy. You have not only given me one sister, you have provided five, and a mother, as well! Who knew that your OTL could bring so much to the marriage."

"Who, indeed." We waited until the Bennets' carriage turned the bend before we reentered Netherfield.

"Bingley, I must return to town for a few days. I plan to leave early tomorrow morning. Would you like to join me?"

Mr. Bingley took one last longing look down the drive before the butler shut the door. "I appreciate the offer, but I believe I have business here. I will see you when you return." If that remark means what I believe it to, Mrs. Bennet will need to call for her salts!

It is now eleven of the clock, and Fitzwilliam should be close to Darcy House in London. I do not expect his return for at least three days. Until then, I have many plans to keep me busy, starting with today. Kitty informed me that the Bennets and Lucases always gather to discuss the events of a ball on the following day. And this time I have been invited! Mrs. Annesley is waiting for me now, so I must draw this entry to a close.

Epilogue

Afternoon, 11 December 1811

Dear Diary,

Today I gained not one, but FIVE sisters! When Mrs. Annesley predicted Fitzwilliam would meet his OTL, I only thought of his happiness. It was not until much later that I realized how well this marriage would turn out for me as well. Kitty, of course, is my best friend, but I have also gained true friendship with each of her sisters. And, of course, I am especially close to Elizabeth.

As predicted, Mrs. Bennet was suitably impressed by Fitzwilliam's ability to procure a special license. Unfortunately for him, she was not so impressed as to allow a wedding in a week's time as he had hoped. After much negotiation, she relented from her three-week minimum stance and allowed them to wed today, after a mere two weeks of engagement.

Despite the short period of planning, Mrs. Bennet managed to arrange a beautiful wedding ceremony and an even more scrumptious breakfast. At Elizabeth's insistence, the wedding was small. Family members and the Lucases attended from Meryton. The Bingleys, Richard, my aunt and uncle, and of course, I, sat on Fitzwilliam's side of the church. Mama, as I have truly come to think of her, was stunned to learn that an earl would be in attendance. She ran Mrs. Hill ragged preparing for his arrival, but her efforts were worth it. The house looked lovely, Elizabeth looked beautiful, and I have yet to partake in a finer wedding breakfast.

"Are you sure you are fine with staying here? Aunt would be pleased to take you to London with her." Fitzwilliam has been concerned since he learned of my plans to stay at Longbourn while he and Elizabeth honeymoon.

"I am certain. Mrs. Bennet has plans to host several dinners while you are gone, and we will attend the December assembly."

"That is exactly what I am afraid of," he grumbled.

"Do not fret for me. I know how to behave, and I know how to act should any man misbehave in my presence. Besides, I will have Mrs. Annesley with me."

"Fitzwilliam, you must stop distressing yourself over your sister. Mama will treat her well. I promise she will have all her limbs when we return for Christmas." Elizabeth sidled up to my brother, their bodies just short of touching.

He smiled at his new bride. "I know I am being ridiculous. But the last time I allowed her out of my sight, things did not go well. You will learn, Elizabeth, that it is difficult for me to stop worrying."

She wrapped her hand around his. "The care you show your sister is one reason I love you so, but in this, you must relent. Georgiana will be happy and safe here."

"And we will be happy and safe in Darcy house." He raised her hand to his lips. I have seen this exact same action no less than fifty times now, and it still makes me both happy and a little ill.

"Before you leave, I wanted to ask if I could invite both Kitty and Mary to stay with us when we return to Pemberley."

"Of course," he agreed. "You do not wish to also invite Miss Lydia?"

"I like Miss Lydia, of course, but I think it would be good for her not to be the center of attention for once. And it will be good for Kitty and Mary if they were."

"Brava, Georgiana. You may like my youngest sister, but I love her. Still, I agree. She will be well-served not to get her way this once. I must suggest that you keep these arrangements from her until we arrive for Christmas. Otherwise, she will be relentless in her efforts to sway you."

"Excellent advice, sister. It is enough that I must also rebuff Miss Bingley's requests to visit Pemberley. I do not wish to add Miss Lydia's laments, as well."

"Miss Bingley has asked to come to Pemberley? Does she wish to visit with you, Kitty, and Mary?" Elizabeth's face was awash with confusion.

"Hardly," I laughed. "Fitzwilliam has banned her from his properties, and she thinks that if I invite her she will still be allowed entry to our homes."

Turning to her new husband, Elizabeth asked, "I believe you have some explaining to do."

Fitzwilliam lifted her hand to his lips. "You are my wife, and I will harbor no insults against you in my presence. She has not treated you as she should have, but my greatest complaint is that she chose to write to Lady Catherine about you. You could have lost your life because of her jealousy!"

Elizabeth placed a hand on his cheek. "Lady Catherine would have made an attempt on our relationship, no matter how she discovered it. But I am perfectly content to only see Miss Bingley in social settings. So refusing her an invitation to our homes is acceptable to me."

Soon, our conversation was broken up by a group of well-wishers. Elizabeth hugged and chatted with her friends and family, but after a while she relented to my brother's anxious desires to be alone with his wife. Though the day was unseasonably cold, everyone escorted the newly married couple out and bade them adieu.

"Oh, my sweet, sweet Lizzy. I always knew she was too clever to remain a spinster as she claimed." Mrs. Bennet waved her ever-present handkerchief as the carriage trundled away. "And soon I must say goodbye to my Jane, though she, at least, will not go so far away as Derbyshire."

I suppose that is something I should elaborate on. Miss Bennet, or Jane, as I have come to know her, has agreed to marry Mr. Bingley. Three days after the ball, Mr. Bingley finally came to the point. Mrs. Annesley and I were not surprised, as she had read his tea leaves the morning he proposed. Neither party wished to disappoint Mrs. Bennet, which means they must endure a much longer engagement than Elizabeth and Fitzwilliam did. In January, we will travel to Pemberley. We will return in May for Jane's wedding. By then, Mrs. Hurst should be nearing her confinement.

Yes, you read that correctly! When I discovered her happy news, I immediately sought out Mrs. Annesley for answers. She insisted she did nothing to interfere with Mrs. Hurst's ability to conceive. In truth, I do not care. I am only pleased for the lady. She has shown herself to be a dear sister to Mr. Bingley, and a lovely friend to Mrs. Bennet. She will be an excellent mother.

Miss Lucas has also become engaged since last I wrote. Mr. Collins sent a letter to Sir William asking for her hand. There was nothing romantic about their engagement—it was all done via letters—but, as Mrs. Annesley assures me, it will ensure Miss Lucas has a comfortable life. I am dubious that comfort is sufficient, but the lady seems pleased. They will marry in January.

After the ball, Richard returned to his station in London. While on a covert mission in one of the seedier parts of town, he happened upon none other than Mr. Wickham! The gentleman (if one can call him such) was drunk and losing badly at cards. Richard completed his duties that night, but the next day he sent four soldiers to arrest the cad. Mr. Wickham is now in a holding cell in London awaiting his fate. Richard has adamantly argued he should be hanged for desertion, but Fitzwilliam has suggested transport. I do not know what the outcome will be, but I am confident he will no longer harangue our family.

A maid has just informed me that Mrs. Bennet wishes to take us to town, most likely to gossip about the wedding. So, I must end this entry soon. Before I go, I must add a hearty "God bless you" to my sweet niece who will, perhaps in seventeen or eighteen years, read this journal. I hope the story of your parents' romance was of interest to you. It certainly did not unfold as I had anticipated, but with the help of magic, a good dose of patience, and a bit of intellect (my own, of course), everything turned out as it should.

I would be remiss if I did not also add:

1. You are loved.
2. You are a Fitzwilliam witch and, as such, are very powerful.
3. Ask your Aunt Georgie for advice when you are confused. I have clearly proven myself to be quite bright.
4. Learn to read tea leaves early; they tell you so many interesting things!

~The End~

Thank You

Thank you for reading Georgiana Darcy's Magical Meddling. I hope you enjoyed reading it as much as I enjoyed writing it. If you liked this book, please leave review on Amazon and/or Goodreads. Comments from readers mean so much to fledgling authors, and they help other readers to make decisions about their next book.

Books By This Author

Trust And Honesty

Where trust is woven in words and proven in actions, there lies the path to true love.

Inspired by his friend's unconventional romance, Darcy is determined to win back the only woman who's ever captured his heart. Yet, finding the right words proves challenging for him. Will he manage to push past his reticence and prove that he is her perfect match?

In an act of courage that defies the strictures of decorum, Elizabeth Bennet pens a letter to Mr. Darcy, hoping to heal the wounds of a proposal gone awry and her own hasty rejection. But will her nerve falter in the face of her family's disgrace?

"Trust and Honesty" weaves a captivating retelling of the timeless romance between Elizabeth Bennet and Mr. Darcy, proving that sometimes, love's truest expression is found in the words we dare to share. This novella-length book spans 54,000 words, delivering a heartfelt journey of love and redemption.

Follow Me

Facebook

Instagram

About The Author

Leah Page

Leah Page loves books, hiking, and the Bengals (Who Dey!). She has a passion for travel, is doing her best to learn Spanish, and has plans to live "a little bit of everywhere" when her husband retires. For now, you can find her sitting at her writing desk in Kentucky while her sidekick pup sleeps in her lap.

Find Leah online at www.leahpageauthor.com.

Printed in Great Britain
by Amazon